SEEKER

The Narvan · Book Four

Jean Davis

SEEKER: Book Four of The Narvan

www.jeandavisauthor.com

ISBN-13:   979-8-9850814-4-2 (print)
             979-8-9850814-5-9 (ebook)

First Edition: May 2022

Published by StreamlineDesign LLC

Also by Jean Davis

The Last God
Sahmara
A Broken Race
Destiny Pills and Space Wizards
Dreams of Stars and Lies
Everyone Dies
Not Another Bard's Tale
Spindelkin
Frayed
19

The Narvan

One Shot at the Sphinx
Trust
The Minor Years
Chain of Gray
Bound in Blue
Seeker
Tears of the Tyrant

ONE

Since coming home from Veria Prime two weeks ago with her bald head covered in tattoos, my daughter had been avoiding me. The boys enjoyed having their very own Seeker at our Artorian estate and Ikeri didn't seem to mind using her relaxation gifts on them, or Stassia, Neko, or even Fa'yet when he'd visited. Everyone but me. Our once close relationship had been strained since I'd shown her what kind of man I really was.

After several failed attempts at starting a conversation that gained me no more than a glare or a mental brain jab, I'd taken to being busy elsewhere. There was plenty to do.

Consulting with Nan, who had done the Arpex alteration on me, ate up most of my time. We'd been over all sides of the possibility of sharing the procedure with non-Artorians. On top of that, I juggled Kess and Jey's demands to do the alteration regardless of its seeming impossibility of success. Stassia and I shared the task of advising our half of the Narvan, but we'd both been working from home, dividing our efforts so we could provide as personal attention as possible. It had only been a couple weeks since Jey and Kess had laid out their barely veiled demands for the alteration, and now all our efforts in our half of the Narvan had Jey, who controlled the other half, convinced we were up to something. Kess was even more sure of it. Stassia and I needed to keep our position in the Narvan strong in case the inner-system war Jey claimed he also didn't want, became a reality.

It felt like a war was brewing at home too. Not only was Ikeri driving me out of my mind, the strain of it all was starting to boil over to Stassia and my sons due to me missing every family meal, and generally not being present any other time. I needed to fix things with Ikeri before everyone else in the house started to hate me too.

Geva must have been laughing hysterically over the fact that a ten-year-old girl could make me so damned miserable.

In light of any god possibly laughing at me, I slipped on my moderately-loaded, armored coat before leaving the bedroom. It felt good. Normal. A few days ago, I'd started wearing it during vid meetings to give the illusion that I wasn't only working from home.

If Ikeri would just talk to me, home would be a more pleasant place. I snarled at the hallway walls as I left the safety of the bedroom. I'd been working there through my link all morning but I couldn't ignore the rumbling in my stomach any longer. How was I supposed to fix anything between us if we couldn't even be in the same room?

When I passed the dining room table, Ikeri's lit datapad caught my eye. Any insight as to what was going on with her would be a gift from Geva herself. It was likely a conversation between her and Seeker Tomias regarding a safe place for her to employ her Seeker skills or maybe she'd been venting to one of the acolytes she'd trained with. Hells, I'd take anything that would give me a hint at a legitimate conversation starter beyond 'I'm sorry'. That wasn't getting me anywhere.

I glanced into the common room and the kitchen to see if Ikeri was lurking. No one was in sight. Unless she was sitting at the security station, I was clear to invade her privacy. The light on the screen dimmed. Only a minute left before it shut off, and I didn't have her log in. Not that I couldn't have cracked it, but my conscience informed me that was going a step too far.

To be safe, I checked in with Neko, who informed me that he was the one at the security station and all was well. A touch on the screen brought the backlight up to full brightness. I allowed myself a glimpse at what was definitely a message. My breath caught when I saw it was addressed to me.

Nothing Ikeri did was haphazard. Maybe she'd heard me leaving the bedroom and baited her trap. That had to be what it was. Did she want me to read it or was this a test to see if I would respect her privacy as any decent person would?

After the memories I'd shared to show the dangers of people like me who might now be after her, Ikeri knew without a doubt that I wasn't a decent person. And there were plenty of us in the known universe. A young girl, so obviously marked as a healer, a novelty being non-Verian, and the daughter of parents with many enemies, made a tempting target. Even on peaceful Veria Prime, she'd brought out resentment in the calm and loving acolytes and other Seekers due to attaining her rank at such a young age. Any one of them could talk to the wrong person about what she'd done to earn her new rank, igniting the ambition of any credit-hungry fool. I might be known as a heartless bastard, but they'd bank on me paying any sum to prevent my daughter from being harmed. Assuming they didn't already have a buyer lined up. A Seeker who could bring back the dead was price-less. My hands formed fists at my sides.

I closed my eyes, blocking out the tempting message. Was I sup-posed to avoid reading it to prove that I could be the father she'd known before she'd begun her healing sessions with her mother and seen us for who we really were?

Our lives had been different prior to our return to the Narvan, quiet, peaceful—allowing her an idyllic first few years of her early childhood. Now that we were back, Ikeri had learned what the regen tank was, how grievous the injuries were that repeatedly put me in it, and seen enough of my memories to understand why so many people wanted me dead.

At only ten, she was as revered as any elder Seeker, powerful and able to see the truth and pain hidden in a mind with the deftest touch. She was far too perceptive to be considered a child. And I was the advisor of multiple planets, a scarred man with far too much blood on his hands, who had exterminated the powerful and manipulative High Council and purged the Narvan of the terrifying memory-eating Arpex. As special as all of that made both of us, our accomplishments had also torn us apart.

Maybe something in her message would help put us back together. Resolved to my choice, I began to read.

It is too hard to speak to you, to look at you, after what you showed me and what I've seen. It was one thing to know, and I had for years, but I could ignore it so you could be the father I loved. You weren't like that anymore.

But then you made me feel you doing those things. No mat-ter how hard I try, I can't make that go away. And you are that person again.

Maybe someday I will be able to accept what you are. Maybe not. I miss you and I don't want to be near you all at once. I tried to bring you calm, to fix you, to help you be the father I knew. He was a good man.

I thought I was doing the right thing by saving you, something amazing. Tomias says it was. He gave me robes and praise. The other Seekers and acolytes say it was a miracle.

They're all wrong.

Mother has arranged for me to stay with Uncle Isnar to help the memory menders there. I'll be leaving for Karin in the morning. Please don't see me off. I have seen your wrath, but I can't bear to do my hug of penance.

It was selfish of me to bring you back and now everything you do is my fault. You were right, we would have survived without you. I see that now.

I'm sorry I didn't let you die.

I found I'd been holding my breath and let it out all at once along with the will to stand. There could have been a whole crowd in the room and I wouldn't have noticed. My eyes were locked on the last line and I couldn't stop reading it over and over.

If I'd only been wise enough to ignore her trap, I could have gone about my day, oblivious. Knowing she hated me on some level, but like her, able to pretend despite it. I could have convinced myself that Ikeri was only annoyed and we'd return to what we had been someday soon. Now I couldn't unsee the truth of it. There would be no someday.

She'd locked me out of her mind that day on Veria Prime when she'd become a Seeker, severed our connections. I thought it had been a tirade over my tirade and could accept that as fair, knowing we'd make up eventually. But she had no interest in making up, only in getting away from me.

All I could do for her was to not be there when she left, not touch her, not see her, not speak to her.

"Vayen," Stassia's voice cut through my swirling thoughts. She stood between me and any route of escape.

I slowly pushed the button to turn off the screen, making Ikeri's words flash to black and vanish though they were now branded in my mind. Tearing my gaze from the dark screen, I sought out something other than Stassia's face to look at. The rust-brown painted walls and simple wooden table and chairs offered little to rest on. The still frame on the wall of my pink-cheeked, laughing little girl only drove home the words of the same girl now only a little older. Ten years old and I'd already screwed things up beyond the point of no return.

"Finish up in there already," Stassia said, mistakenly assuming I'd been working through my link implant. The only words flying through my mind were the ones I'd just read.

The steaming white cup of tea in her hand provided a safe focus. I clamped down on our bonded connection, making sure none of what was on my mind seeped through.

"What," I said, forcing the single word past the lump in my throat.

"Are you all right? You look a bit off." She took a sip and swallowed. "I know you want to dive back into everything, but you have to give your body time to finish healing."

I was plenty healed from my last stay at the University where they replaced my heart, reduced the worst of my scars, and normalized my artificial hand and eye. I'd been working out with her or Neko every damned day since I'd come home. Both my stamina and strength were back on track. I needed something to do with them before I exploded.

I handed her the datapad. "Ikeri left this in here."

Stassia set her cup down and took the pad from me. "I've been meaning to talk to you about her." She pulled out the chair across the table and sat. "Ikeri is going to stay with Isnar for a while. Maybe some space will help both of you get back to normal. I miss seeing the two of you together like you were."

"Me too."

She reached out and rubbed her fingers over the back of my hand. "Your temper is fierce, but it burns out quickly. I'm afraid she's got mine."

"I've noticed."

She was her mother's daughter in so many ways. I'd needed Ikeri badly when Stassia had fallen victim to the Arpex and forgotten me, our bond, and far too many other things that kept me sane.

Now I had Stassia back, for the most part. Though there were still so many holes in both our memories, we were reluctant to ask for Ikeri's assistance with all the tension running through the house. Even here on Artor, the largest house we'd ever owned, there didn't seem to be enough space to fully avoid one another.

Maybe once Ikeri was gone, I could borrow one of Tomias's new acolytes for a few days. As if I'd ever have a few days of leisure to enjoy exchanging memories with Stassia. I snorted.

She gave me the eye, the one that said I better explain my short-answered self before she started prying.

"Just going over the reports from the Arpex hunters and Nan's thoughts on attempting the process on Jalvians." I had been...a couple hours ago.

"Can we focus on Ikeri for a few minutes?" Her hand retreated to the warmth of the cup. "I'd like to do a nice going away dinner for her tonight. Neko can take Daniel out to get what he needs for the meal so you can keep doing what you're doing. Here. Where I know you're safe."

It was my turn to glare. "You know I'm not working from home forever, right?"

As much as I enjoyed the quiet and safety of our Artorian estate, I hadn't been outside in too long. Meetings happened in the room she'd set up off the foyer, by vid, or through my link. Apparently, I was cleared to overexert myself there all I wanted.

"Neko is getting bored," I said.

"He only got back from his vacation six days ago." She shook her head. "He's looking much better, don't you think? A couple more weeks of only having to shadow Daniel and Markus will help him get back into top form."

Time off had done wonders for my overworked bodyguard, I had to admit. However. "A couple more weeks?" I stood. "You've had your way for long enough. I have work to do, and I can't do everything from here."

With the High Council obliterated, Jey, Kess, Stassia, and I had opted to keep the advisory business running as usual for the Narvan and the Nebula. The public didn't know the Council had ever existed. Other than choosing to be more public figureheads than before and the complete lack of financing that the Council had offered, no one outside our meetings knew anything had changed. Inside, the meetings were a completely different story.

Since our return from Pentares, Stassia and I held half the Narvan, while Jey advised the other. Kess, who had been ordered by the Council to cooperate with his hold the Nebula, seemed to see the wisdom in doing so and had continued in their absence. Having the Narvan and Nebula united was to everyone's benefit. Unfortunately, there were some matters, like the Geva-forsaken Arpex modification debate, that had us at each other's throats.

"How about I go pay Jey a visit so we can make some headway in this stalemate he and Kess have going?"

She leaned forward, both hands gripping her cup. "You can meet with them here."

"I'm hobbled here. Both he and Kess are feeling secure in their stomping around and having a fit all over the Narvan and Nebula because they know you're keeping me at home."

"Jey knows damn well why I want you to stay here. And Kess can go—" She huffed, waving one hand in the air.

The Stassia with all her memories would have finished that sentence with a string of colorful profanities. As it was, she often struggled with what place Kess had in our recent past. Too many of those events were tied to bits of me that she hadn't yet recovered.

There was too damn much of what Stassia and I had been to one another to recover. She was here and beside me, trying her best to be the mate I missed in the limited time we had between managing Ikeri's ire, the usual overwhelming load of Narvan advisory duties, and the situation with Jey and Kess. I knew that. I appreciated all she was doing and the unStassia-like level of patience she exhibited while doing it. Yet, I couldn't help feeling that I'd never get her back completely, no matter how many memories I shared. They were mine, colored by my thoughts and feelings, not hers.

I took her still raised hand in mine and squeezed it. She smiled.

"Okay then, how about if I go make sure Fa'yet has Ikeri's rooms up to our specifications?" I suggested.

"Now?" Her smile vanished. "What about dinner?"

"I'll be back by then." Not if I could help it.

"Before you go anywhere, you better get to the ship and make a new baseline tank profile."

I couldn't argue with that decree, even if I didn't appreciate the chiding tone in which it was delivered. "I will."

"I don't understand why you need to do this now. Isnar has everything under control. You trusted him with all of us before. Surely, he can watch over Ikeri alone."

"Because I need to know she'll be taken care of." That sounded like a logical reason. Stassia appreciated logic.

She shoved her half-full cup away, sloshing the contents onto the wooden surface and knocking the datapad halfway off the table with her elbow. "I don't want you to go."

Stassia pursed her lips and jumped up from the chair to grab a cloth from the kitchen counter. She tossed it on top of the spill, then turned to me. "This is an important night. She needs you here. *I* need you to be here."

Our bonded connection filled with her twisting emotions. While we'd only briefly had close to the full clarity an Artorian couple would have shared once when we'd lived on Veria Minor, her conflicted thoughts were clear enough now. Frustration rose above everything else. She wanted me here but knew how hard it was for me and Ikeri to be in the same room. She wanted us fixed and knew what had caused the fracture, but despite her own Seeker training, hadn't been able to make headway with our daughter. Beyond that was the utter aggravation of missing so many memories where I was concerned and having to rely on me for what few of those she did have. She hated having to depend on anyone for her own sanity.

I got up and placed my hands on her bare arms. Her irritation made her skin warmer than usual. "I said, I'll be back."

"Don't lie to me. I remember enough of you to know that mollifying tone."

On one hand, she didn't remember the fights, the bad times, or all the shit we put each other through. She also didn't remember much of the good years either. It was like we'd started over, but on an accelerated level. Except I carried all of our baggage.

The fact that I could shape her view of me with what memories I chose to share made me uncomfortable. I didn't want that responsibility. I wanted her to know everything she had before the Arpex had feasted on her mind, even the super shitty stuff. All of it made her who she was—until that day we'd crossed the Arpex.

Now she was too much like me, faking her way through the gaps of memories yet to be replaced. There were times I wondered if she wanted me around because she loved me, or if it was merely convenient because I held the parts of her life that were missing.

The second-guessing and the uncertainty often made me shorter with her than I meant to be. I missed the woman I'd known so well, the good parts and the ones I shuddered to recall. She had still surprised me from time to time, but within familiar boundaries. This Stassia was an unknown. Like now. Was she going to berate me for leaving and lying in a tone that would make me reconsider, or go for the guilt? My credits were on guilt. She'd been doing a lot of that the past few days, and I'd had enough. I wanted the woman back who wasn't afraid to stand up to me, the one who had a razor tongue and the steel spine to back it up.

Daniel burst into the kitchen with Markus on his heels. Neko followed close behind. I let go of Stassia so she could meet this intrusion head-on. Meanwhile, I took the opportunity to escape and Jumped.

I caught the first syllable of what I guessed to be "Dammit" as I stepped out of the void and into the foyer of Jey's home on Jal.

His wife, Dayana, met me with surprise, her pale face devoid of its usual cosmetics. "Vayen, we weren't expecting you." She said loudly as she stepped back, glancing down the hall to Jey's office. "Were we?"

Heavy footsteps hurried down that same hall and brought Jey to me in seconds. "We were not."

His brusque tone made me thankful for my Arpex enhanced skin under my armored coat. Nan may have dialed my alterations back a few degrees, but Jey didn't know I was no longer quite as impervious as his prior pulse testing had illustrated.

Without his uniform or armored coat, I'd hoped his large Jalvian form would be a bit less broad, but there wasn't a layer of padding or extra armor in there. He really was big and not in a growing fat and relaxed sort of way.

It had been a good number of years since I'd seen him casually dressed, not since we'd both worked for Stassia. Wearing only a light-weight pair of pants and a thin undershirt, Jey raised a blonde eyebrow. "She let you out?"

"You make it sound like I was a prisoner." I belatedly checked the time and realized it was near midnight on Jal. "Sorry, I didn't realize it was so late."

"You always know the time," Jey grumbled. "I was headed out soon for a meeting anyway. What's the emergency?"

I took a breath and tried to expel the slimy feeling from my mind. But it wouldn't go away, not since Nan had suggested we might be ready to accept volunteers for the Arpex alteration. Jey and Kess had been fighting hard for the chance of creating their own bullet-resistant soldiers. They didn't seem to understand or care that it was a very unpleasant procedure. I knew. I'd endured it. Twice. And neither by choice.

While I did enjoy the benefits of the alteration, I had only asked for a select few Artorian men to undergo the conversion to create other Arpex hunters. They'd been created, not with the intention of being semi-invincible soldiers, but to help track down and kill Arpex in the Narvan.

Knowing non-Artorian volunteers would likely not survive the alteration weighed heavy on my conscience. However, giving in was the only way I was going to get Jey and Kess off my back about the Arpex modifications that they so adamantly demanded for their people. Nan's studies had shown the odds of success were minuscule but possible. I'd shared those studies, but it sure seemed like the only part either of them had read was the fact that success was a possibility.

"We'll take one volunteer from each of you for the procedure. Your choice as long as it isn't you or Kess. This is an experiment. We can't guarantee favorable results."

"I'm quite familiar with how experiments work. You're a walking one, remember?"

I nodded, letting him enjoy his little barb so we could get on with this futile gesture. The only upside I saw was that granting Jey's request would prevent further strain on the delicate amity between Jal and Artor. Two lives for the betterment of billions.

I'd killed people for years at Stassia's side, for the Council, for contract hire. Why the hells did it eat at me so badly now?

It occurred to me that I'd grown a conscience between now and then. Her name was Ikeri, and the wound she'd dealt was something the tank couldn't fix.

Jey studied me with his calculating blue eyes before his lips curled a fraction. "Our chances of success are higher with a larger selection of volunteers."

"I said one."

"And I'm negotiating. Or have we lost that option between us?"

Laying down the friend card in a game that already didn't set well with me pissed me off. I hadn't stood my ground from the beginning of the conversation. He'd sensed a weakness and was drilling his way in. Damned Ikeri. Advising the Narvan didn't allow for a conscience, not to the degree she expected of me. Was I willing to trade my half of the Narvan for my daughter's acceptance?

Maybe I could strike some level of balance. Jey was a safe person to try that with. Safer than my other options, anyway.

"I'm not opposed to negotiating," I said calmly. "But do you want to risk more than one man at this point? The odds are slim. This is our first live trial."

He shrugged. "The possible benefits far outweigh the risk. What are a few volunteers compared to the chance to have bulletproof soldiers?"

Clearly, he wasn't operating under the same conscience yoke that I was. He wasn't wrong either. With the possible benefits to the lives of half of the Narvan in his hands, the chance of losing a few made sense.

No. My muscles tightened further. Losing lives wasn't supposed to make sense. I was supposed to be adamantly against this.

According to a ten-year-old girl, who didn't have an inkling of the bigger picture.

"You have volunteers already?" I asked.

"Of course. I knew you'd see logic evenutally."

"Logic?" Like concluding that my test of balance had gone to shit in a matter of minutes and would never work? The realization did nothing to improve my mood.

As aggravated as I'd been with Jey and Kess at our first meeting when their demands were laid down, I'd been able to keep my temper under control. But Stassia and the calm our bond provided wasn't next to me now. Adrenaline, began to course through my system, enticing me into a rush I'd missed while stuck in recovery at the University and then at home, shackled in Stassia's care.

"For when I gave in, you mean."

Jey's casual stance tightened. "Kess and I will each provide six volunteers."

"Out of the question. Three."

"Six," he said firmly.

My hands twitched, begging to hit something other than a sand-filled bag. I reminded myself that Jey and I were partners working hard to remain on good terms.

"Four."

His gaze darted to my hands before drawing himself up to stare me down. "I'll have my six at the University in the morning. I've let Kess know about your offer as well."

"That wasn't my offer," I managed to say through clenched teeth.

"Sure it was." He grinned as though the tension between us had vanished. "We negotiated, remember?"

"I do not."

Jey chuckled. "Must be an Arpex made you forget." He gestured toward his common room. "Drink to celebrate our agreement?"

I most certainly didn't appreciate his humor. My blood demanded a fix, knuckles nearly popping with the force of my clenched fists.

"You're throwing those six men away," I said. "Their lives are on you and your drive for the impossible."

I Jumped to the ship before I ruined our tenuous goodwill.

Negotiation, my ass. He'd known I was off my game from the moment I'd arrived. If I was going to see Kess, I had to get my shit together. That included being willing to indulge my temper, which meant I needed to create a new tank profile.

To appease Stassia, I let her know where I was. She smiled in my head, melting away my urge to pound on something.

Feeling calmer, but annoyed for again being appeased when I'd had a glimpse of what I'd been missing, I forced my hands to remove my clothes. After initiating a new profile update, I got onto the platform and was soon in the embrace of the gel.

When I woke twenty minutes later, I got up and checked my new baseline, comparing it to the last one. The baseline after our return from Pentares had been drastically different than the one I'd used in the years before I'd been incarcerated by the High Council. That update had had to account for my scars, the artificial hand and eye, and countless other injuries I'd had to heal naturally from in the meantime. Now, my newest profile included an artificial heart and being fused with an Arpex. Was there enough of the original me left to be considered Artorian anymore?

I brushed the fine sheen of gel flakes from my arm, trying to remember what my skin had felt like before the alteration. Skin was skin and I'd never paid much attention to it other than if it was against someone else's or covered in blood. Now it was hard, like a callous, and though I could feel my fingers and their warmth on my arm, there was a distance to it, not what memory told me I should feel. My new Arpex skin looked normal, and made me more bullet-proof, damage-resistant, even able to withstand most of the effects of a pulse pistol, but it was like being trapped inside a thin layer of armor I could never remove.

At least I was no longer hearing Arpex speak in my head since we destroyed the ones that had plagued the Narvan. If only I could be so fortunate as to not have to talk to Kess anymore either. Sadly, he was far more embedded in our lives than the Arpex had been.

I took a quick shower to wash away the gel flakes. When I walked back into the tank room to get my clothes, I found Jey there with blood dripping from his face and holding his arm to his chest. In the half an hour since I'd last seen him, his night had certainly gone to shit.

"I take it your midnight meeting didn't go well?" I asked, heading to the controls to load up his profile.

He let out a disgusted growl. "Do you mind? I did not need to see your naked ass to make this night any better."

I ignored his grumbling about my nakedness and instead got his profile up. Once that was taken care of, I dressed while he undressed and got on the platform.

"Anything I need to know about?" I asked as I surveyed his wounds.

"Only a disgruntled general." He winced as he shifted his broken arm. "And a good deal of his staff."

"I take it they've all been dealt with then?"

"I have people on it." The tank took him away before I could question him further.

The fact that he had a general openly acting against him was troubling. The mess the Arpex had caused when they erased the Prime's memory of Jey had been fairly contained. At least I had thought so. Was this only one general with a personal gripe or something larger? I'd have to ask Jey after we got the alteration experiment taken care of. I half-hoped the procedure would work on his volunteers just so we'd be on better terms. Though, that would mean I'd also have to deal with an army of bulletproof Jalvians in short order.

There was already one Jalvian that seemed to be bulletproof. Knowing I was going to see Kess, I stopped by the armory on the ship to set myself up properly.

TWO

Just before I stepped into the void to see Kess, it occurred to me that I'd told Stassia I was going to check on Ikeri's room security. If I wanted to keep her off my back, I was going to have to do that first, even if it offered no opportunity for excitement. I Jumped to Karin.

Fa'yet's estate was similar to my own, large, sprawling, and filled with security measures. Not only did he employ the tech he'd used at his previous home, he now employed guards. Perhaps living with us for a few years had shown him the benefits of having other living beings around. Or maybe seeing the threats we'd faced together had made him more paranoid than he'd been before.

I stood still in the foyer while his system acknowledged that I was not a stranger in immediate need of termination. One of his three new staff members, Merona, a slender woman with thick hair that hung past her waist, hurried toward me, her heeled boots striking the tiles with a steady rhythmic pace.

"Advisor Ta'set." She bowed her head, her hair falling around her in a dark veil. "We weren't expecting you." Her deep red dress clung to her like a second skin, leaving little to the imagination. "How may I be of assistance?" she asked.

"I wanted to do a check of everything before my daughter arrives."

"Of course." She offered me a gracious smile. It was hard to tell if she was just doing her duty or if it was genuine. I guessed that meant she was good at her job. "Where would you like to begin?"

I'd previously met his two security people. They were both fully capable, as they would have to be to gain Fa'yet's approval. He'd been the one to round off Neko's training, and I could find no fault with him.

Having encountered the security systems in his previous home, I had no doubt these were at least as thorough as those had been. All

I could do here was deliver an ominous threat to his staff to keep Ikeri safe. Fa'yet had likely already done that too, but I needed to do something. Ikeri might hate me, but she was still my daughter.

"Let's start with the systems."

Merona bowed her head again. I wondered if her neck got tired from doing that all day. Fa'yet seemed to like his staff traditionally trained. The fact that he allowed a staff in his house at all had surprised me the first time I visited his new estate. He'd always been a solitary man. Then again, all of his staff were women. Maybe he'd taken my suggestion to be with whomever he wanted and to lock himself away and let others be in the public eye to the extreme. But as long as he had Karin in order and the populace was generally happy, I wasn't going to complain. If his delegating allowed him more time to personally shadow Ikeri, I was all for it. Despite Fa'yet's dislike of children, the two of them had grown close. If Ikeri didn't want me around, he or Neko were my next choice.

Merona stood over my shoulder while I spent the next hour accessing the security system. Not that I suspected anything was neglected, but I went over it closely anyway. Flipping through camera views and sensor readings reminded me of my first few months of working for Stassia. Back then I'd prayed for anything to happen to break the monotony, but now, knowing Ikeri would be living here, I was glad nothing did.

When I sat back, satisfied that everything was in order, Buria, one of Fa'yet's two bodyguards, detached herself from the shadows of the hallway. Her dark skin was well suited to hiding in dimly lit places. Her teeth caught the light before anything else. Unlike Merona, she wore black from the sculpted collar that began at the base of her skull, to the armored suit that hugged her impressively fit frame, all the way down to the flat-footed boots that rose over her knees. She wore her hair in two black knots on either side of her head. The strands between them were slicked to her scalp in perfect order. Each silent step brought her to me with power and purpose.

Her partner, Nena, must have been off duty or I would have expected both to be in audience. Fa'yet had shown me the two of them when they'd first been hired. He'd arranged a demonstration of their skills under the guise of enticing me to take a guard from the same company to fill the spot in my service that he'd vacated. Despite his pitch, I was fairly sure he was just showing them off. And he had a right to do so. They were impressive. Neko was talented, loyal, and I knew his every move, but these two women were very easy to sit back and watch. A fact that I'd noticed even after their demonstration had ended.

Fa'yet did have a point. Hiring a second guard was on my endless list of things to do.

"Merona asked me to assist you," Buria's velvety voice informed me.

"It seems my daughter will be staying here with you for a time."

Buria bowed her head, yet her eyes never left me. "You are concerned for her safety. The Premier informed us you would likely be paying a visit."

"I'm sure he did. I'd like to see Ikeri's room."

"Of course. This way." Buria walked beside me, matching me step for step in an easy stride. She led me away from the public rooms.

Fa'yet's estate bore a good deal of opulence. With his open position in the government, having a public residence befitting a Premier wasn't an issue. He was no longer a quiet and secretive Kryon operative that had to hide his penchant for the finer things in his ordinary little house. As we walked through the halls lined with weavings, carvings in wood, metal, various plas creations, and several plants I knew from Artor, I realized I didn't recognize anything from his previous home. Perhaps he'd kept everything there on hold in case this whole venture went awry.

"Did the Premier have a hand in the decor?" I asked, wondering at the lack of his old things.

"Oh yes," Buria bowed her head. "He chose everything himself. Some items are from the storeroom of the previous Premier, and others from artists or design houses on both Karin and Artor. He has very good taste."

"That he does."

All three of the women he'd chosen illustrated that fact. Like Neko and most of the occupants of Pentares, they appeared to be of no specific race, nothing distinctive other than their shades of brown skin and dark hair color to tie them together. Merona was slender, while Nena and Buria had a thicker build more similar to a Jalvian or Artorians. If they had anything internal to set them apart, Fa'yet hadn't mentioned it.

We passed a closed door, which was an oddity in the open floor plan that mostly featured high, arched openings between rooms. The few rooms with doors had been standing open. "What's in there?"

"We're not allowed in that room. That's his private space."

"Out here? That's not like him."

"Oh, not his sleeping space. His private office."

"Ah, that makes more sense." A solitary oasis in all the openness.

We continued into the middle of the house. As with Fa'yet's previous home on Karin, he kept his personal rooms walled off from the rest. This time he'd chosen the middle of the estate, a space with no outside walls or windows. He'd given Ikeri a large room right next to his own. Buria opened the door and stood outside while I went in.

It was a room far larger than Ikeri had ever enjoyed, and it had been fully furnished, I dared guess just for her. Flowering vibrant green plants spilled from giant pots under ceiling-mounted grow lights. A massive bed covered in a thick white cloud of a comforter stood at the center, surrounded by soft blue walls and a plush carpet underfoot. Everything was perfect. A bedroom garden for a girl otherwise at home on Veria Prime. I wondered what she'd make of the opulence compared to her little cove in the acolyte dorm.

I examined the ceiling and walls, making sure there were no hidden passages, obvious jump points, or possible structural weaknesses. The multiple locks on the door eased my mind a fraction more. Fa'yet had done everything I could have asked for. He and Stassia must have been planning this for a while and had felt springing it on me at the last minute to be the best course of action.

They were probably right.

The only things missing were some personal touches, perhaps something to let her know I'd been there and made sure she would be safe, but yet respected her request to be left alone.

I Jumped to our abandoned home on Veria Minor and went up the simple stairs to her room. The same room where she'd held me in an illusion while Seeker Etara had worked her magic to turn the terror of the Arpex hatching from my body into sterile whispers. Years before, Ikeri and I had played there for hours on end. I picked up a handful of lightweight wooden blocks, the bright paint chipped on the corners and the sides dented from the destruction of our towering creations.

The pillow that had been graced with the touch of her soft curls night after night fit under my arm. As did the still frame of the four of us from her wall. Dressed as Verian as we could get, my hair short and face unscarred, Stassia's hair long and loose. Ikeri, all of two, balanced snuggly on Stassia's hip. Daniel at four, looking annoyed at having to stand still as he held my hand. That was the father she wanted and loved.

I returned to Karin, to the foyer which was my only jump point in Fa'yet's home, and waited again for the all-clear from the sensors. Merona again greeted me, masking her confusion with a quickly-placed professional smile. She escorted me to Buria, who was still standing outside the door to Ikeri's room. Her smile wasn't as professionally tolerant. It let me know I should have said something and she had better things to do than stand outside a door to an empty room.

Merona left us when Buria again opened the door. She followed me in this time, examining each item I'd brought with me both visually and with her hands. Finally, she nodded and stepped back, but she didn't leave me alone.

I placed the pillow on the bed and activated the fastener on the back of the still frame to adhere it to the wall beside the bed. If Ikeri didn't like it, she could look the other way. Or move it. Or maybe toss it into a drawer in the cabinet that sat below it and ignore it completely.

The blocks, I stacked on the table beside her bed, one by one, turning them slightly so they seemed to spiral upward in a rainbow of color just as she'd begged me to do every day before she'd had the coordination to do so herself. A peace offering.

There was nothing more I could do here. Buria and Nena were every bit as capable as Neko, and Fa'yet wouldn't let anything happen to Ikeri.

Unlike when we'd first brought her to Tomias for training, or even when we'd allowed her to live on Prime because we were too busy holding the Narvan together to Jump her home every day, this was letting her go. I'd thought I'd have several more years before she'd be off living on her own, maybe doing some sort of internship or advanced training. But here she was at ten, politely telling me to stay the fuck out of her life.

Since the day I'd first held her in my arms, I'd feared we'd come to this. But I wasn't ready. Not yet.

Unfortunately, I'd brought this on myself and as much as I didn't like it, I couldn't blame her. Isnar Ka'turok, the man in the still frame, was gone. He'd never been truly happy or satisfied, but Ikeri was too young to know that. She'd thought Isnar was who I'd evolved into, that I'd left the violence, threats, and darkness behind, but he was only a mask, an alias, and as enjoyable as those few years had been with Stassia and the kids, I didn't think I could ever pare myself down to fit into that man again.

Stassia's agitation at my sudden and lengthening absence began to seep through our bonded connection. Telling her why I was missing Ikeri's going away dinner would only cause an ugly fight between mother and daughter. Better Stassia be mad at me for blowing off yet another family event. I'd figure out some way to appease her once Ikeri was safely moved out of the house.

I also still needed to visit Kess to see if I could make him see the futility of throwing lives away. The mere thought of Kess made me run my hands over my coat, verifying that I was properly prepared. We might currently be allies, but that could change at any time. If it did, I did not want to endure chiding from my mate who, thanks to my recent health crisis, was in top form on that task.

"Buria, how much longer are you on duty?"

Her thin brows rose. "May I ask why you are inquiring?"

"I'd like to borrow you for a couple hours. Or Nena, if you're needed here."

"We can switch out early, I suppose. Might I know what you would borrow me for?"

"I need to pay a visit to Twelve and everyone in my household is otherwise occupied."

"I've never been there. Is that a problem?"

"As long as you can do your job while taking in the sights, no."

She bowed her head. "Give me a few moments to relay this information to the Premier and prepare. I will meet you in the foyer."

I made my way back to the foyer unguided. Merona's split second of a scowl informed me this was against protocol. For all I knew, my breach would mean Nena had to sweep the whole house in case I'd done anything untoward in my free-roaming time.

"Buria will be joining me shortly," I said.

She bowed her head politely enough, but her tone was definitely edgy. "Has the Premier authorized this?"

"Who does the Premier work for?"

"Of course, Advisor Ta'set, it's just that her absence will leave us shorthanded."

"You'll have all the hands you need tomorrow when my daughter arrives. The Premier can watch his own back for a few hours. He's had plenty of practice."

Buria arrived, wearing a waist-length jacket that added considerable bulk to her already impressive form. "I have notified the Premier of my excursion. He has given his approval."

Merona bowed her head again. It was a marvel that her hair remained straight and free-flowing with all the submissive nodding.

"Will you be sharing a jump point?" Buria asked.

In answer, I placed my hand on her arm and looked her up and down slowly, taking her into memory in order to Jump us both. She didn't need to know my points. If she wanted to visit Twelve in the future, she could make her own.

We arrived in a shop Kess had set up for us as a jump point. He kept guards posted there and paid them to keep out anyone uninvited. Jey and I were on the invited list. Thankfully, because the guards were well-armed and diligent. Buria took them in with a cautious nod, not quite the bow she used at Fa'yet's home. That was fine by me. The whole subservient thing had always irked me. Respectful, I appreciated. She wasn't mine to train though, so I let it go.

I contacted Kess to let him know we were nearby. He flashed me an address without saying a word. The building wasn't one I recognized, but that also wasn't a surprise. I didn't get around on Twelve a whole lot these days. Not like when Stassia and I had taken contract work there.

We walked to the bar in question. A crowd stood outside in a long line. Not a bar then, one of his clubs. I groaned, apparently out loud, because Beria gave me a strange look.

"Too damn many people, all sweaty and crammed together, and the music gives me a headache. It's just noise."

"Guess that means you're too old." She grinned, looking far more excited now that our destination was confirmed.

"I'll have you know that's not true." Granted, the silver strands in my hair thanks to the Council's years of hospitality and the facial scarring, even if only half as noticeable as it had been, did make me appear a good twenty years older than I was.

She shook her head, dark eyes twinkling. "Good to know." She held her hand out, offering me to the head of security at the front of the line. The waiting patrons grumbled and scowled.

Many of the women wore short dresses with lots of exposed skin despite the perpetually chilled breeze of Twelve's air circulators. The men wore tight clothing too, though they made more of an effort to not appear like they were uncomfortably cold. The filtration system always seemed to be working overtime here, yet the air still held a lingering stink, like there were too many bodies for the system to keep up with.

A few men and women in line wore attire closer to ours. From the look of the crowd, everyone waiting to get inside was either shopping for or selling their body or services.

"Well?" Buria urged.

"Been a while since anyone took you to a club?"

"I would have dressed differently if I'd have known where we were going."

"This isn't a date."

She grinned again, white teeth shining against her midnight skin. "Then I guess I'm good as I am. Will we be going inside?" she prodded.

I gave the security guard a look. He pressed the black dot on his sleeve and spoke into it. A few seconds later, we were ushered inside.

"Impressive." Buria did her best not to gape at the near-naked male dancers on the pillars along the walls. The blue uplighting gave their bodies an otherworldly glow as they gyrated to the thumping music.

She leaned in close to be heard over the noise. "Are they all like this?"

"The clubs?"

Buria nodded.

"The ones Kess owns, yes." He'd found a successful formula. Some of the clubs had dancers on a ledge and others in cages. Some had more men and others featured more women, plain furniture or plush, and the lighting varied from flashing to dim. The music differed, though it was all too damned loud. The drinks were all the same: Expensive, small, and with too much ice and not near enough liquor.

Buria gave the bar a longing glance.

"You don't get out much, do you?"

"We work a lot and train the rest of the time. I'm sure you know how it is."

She had a point. "I do, but we also drink a lot. The Premier keeps a tight fist on his liquor collection, I take it?"

Buria gaped. "We're not allowed to even look at it. Those were his exact words."

I laughed. "He used to be a bit more generous. Then again, I never worked for him."

"He's not so bad."

I held up a hand. "I don't need to know about what happens in the privacy of his own house." I'm sure he enjoyed himself plenty. I would have, given his freedom and the available company.

As it was, my lovely mate was near screaming in my head and the music did little to drown that out. Daniel was right along with her, though not screaming, thankfully, but annoyed at having his mother upset and wondering where the hells I was. Neko was playing mediator, attempting to get a solid answer out of me.

I finally opened myself to Stassia. *"Enjoy the dinner. I'm sure it's more enjoyable without me there. Let Ikeri be happy on her last night at home."*

"You couldn't just...I don't know, play a good father for one night so we could all enjoy this together?"

"I've tried, Stassia. She doesn't want me around." The words of Ikeri's note flooded my mind, making my steps unsteady. Buria's hand was on my sleeve in a second, putting me back on course.

"You're planning to stay gone until she leaves," she accused.

"Take care of her, all right?"

Her tone softened a degree. *"I will."*

A tug on my arm alerted me that Buria required my attention.

"Who are you with?" Stassia asked, her threatening tone right back on full.

"One of Fa'yet's guards. I didn't want to pull Neko away from Ikeri's dinner."

"It better not be that one who makes eyes at you."

"What are you talking about?"

"Nena, and you know exactly what I'm talking about."

I hadn't noticed Nena's eyes. However, Buria had one of her hands wrapped around my arm and was deftly weaving us through the pressing crowd while my attention was locked on Stassia.

"He's in the back, up there," she said in my ear, nodding to one of Kess's men who was gesturing us over to a stairway.

"Not Nena," I said.

"Good. Or we'd be having a whole different conversation right now."

We seemed to be having that conversation anyway, but it didn't seem wise to point that out. *"You do realize how this bond works, right?"*

"I know what you've told me. I've also read about more than a few of your people violating their vows despite it, and I've seen first-hand how women look at you."

"Even Nena, with whatever her eyes do, isn't Artorian."

"Neither am I," she said sharply.

"You know what I mean."

Her tone grew sharper. *"That's your defense? Really? She can't get into your head? The rest of you works just fine."*

Dammit, standing in the middle of a busy club wasn't the place to be distracted by angry and jealous Stassia. *"I promise, you have nothing to worry about."*

"You better hope not."

"I'll check in with you later. Go enjoy your time with Ikeri."

She gave me one more annoyed stab in the head before dialing back our connection.

"Everything all right?" Buria asked.

"Annoyed wife," I said using the term Jalvians and Stassia's people used. I'd never quite gotten used to it on Pentares even though we'd lived there together for two very long years.

Buria pulled her hand away. "Ah. I wouldn't want to be on her bad side."

"No, you definitely don't."

This current Stassia seemed to have quite a jealous streak and it was very vocally aimed at women who dared look at me for a second too long. Some days I found it funny. Others, her insecurities got on my nerves. This was one of those days. The muscles in my neck and shoulders tightened to an aggravating degree.

We reached the stairs, having been knocked into repeatedly all the way across the room. I ran my hands over my coat to make sure everything was still where it should be, a habit before walking into a possibly dangerous situation.

"Anything I need to know before we get up there?" she asked.

"I don't like Kess, and I don't trust him. But we work together. Keep your eyes open and be on alert, but covertly. Kess would enjoy knowing I was concerned for my safety, and I try to avoid doing anything he likes at all cost."

Buria chuckled. "I see why the Premier is fond of you."

"Fond?" What that hells had the two of them been talking about that any level of fondness or otherwise had come up?

Her jaw clamped shut and she visibly swallowed. She hurried up the stairs in front of me without another word.

Kess greeted us from a bright yellow couch at the rear of the room. A gaudy metal sculpture covered the entire wall behind him, depicting Geva knew what with giant metal jutting columns that might have been legs with bloody ends where the feet should be. Or hair with red tips? I had no idea. What was more important was the fact that he had three men, all the size of Jey, positioned around us. Buria stayed close, but not so close as to interfere with any movement on my part.

"And who is this?" Kess rose from his couch and started toward Buria.

I met him halfway across the room before he got close to her. "I'm here to discuss your volunteer for the Arpex alteration experiment."

His gaze darted to Buria before meeting mine. "Ah yes, that. Jey informed me of your arrangement. Six volunteers, was the deal, yes?"

"I'd prefer one. No need to waste lives in what is likely going to be an unsuccessful endeavor. Unless you have six Artorian volunteers?"

"You make it sound like you already know the outcome."

"What I'm saying is that I know the procedure works on Artorians." I had a lot more to say on the matter, but we'd been over it fifty times already and he and Jey had been deaf to any detail that wasn't in their favor.

"I'll stick with six volunteers," he said confidently. "I have a wide array of stock to choose from. We need to know what works best."

I glanced at his guards. "You refer to your people as stock?" If they took any offense, they didn't show it.

"My, aren't we sensitive today? Been a while since Anastassia allowed you the freedom to roam. The big universe too much for you?"

I closed the distance between us in three strides. His guards tensed, one drew a weapon, the other two had hands on them.

"Anastassia didn't allow or restrict my freedom at any point. I'm here as a courtesy, but I could leave if you have better things to do."

Kess shed one of his particularly slimy smiles. "Come on now, Anastassia rules over you. It's painfully clear to anyone who sees the two of you in the same room."

"We're not in the same room at the moment. Would you like to push your luck with me alone?"

Kess gave a subtle head shake to his anxious guards, but his smile remained in place. One of Buria's boots scraped on the floor behind me, likely to let me know exactly where she was.

He got one more syllable out before I cut him off.

"Consider whether you'd like to throw our truce away over whatever comes out of your mouth next."

His smile slumped into a scowl. "You may have never had luck killing me, but you can sure kill the humor in a room." He slid one step back and waved his guards to stand down. "If Jey gets six, so do I. I'll have my *volunteers* at the University in the morning."

"Their lives are on you."

He nodded. "I'd say it's good to see you out and about, fully recovered, but life was easier when you were down."

"I'm sure. Get used to life being hard again."

He snorted and settled back onto his couch. "Would you care to stay for a drink or do you have better things to do?"

"Better things, elsewhere."

Kess jutted his chin toward Buria. "I'd say that's true. Does Anastassia know about this? I mean, I know she's fairly open-minded, but she was never excited about sharing."

"She doesn't have to. I'm just borrowing Buria for the night."

"You may want to leave before you give him more ammunition," Buria muttered.

Kess laughed. "I like her. Here." He held out one hand and plunged the other into a pocket to come out with four round, red plas tokens. "Have a couple on me. They're valid at any of my clubs if you'd rather go…elsewhere."

"Thanks," I said without meaning it in the least. However, I would take his free tokens. A couple drinks was the barest tip of what he owed me for being an asshole I had to tolerate.

He tossed them my way and I managed to catch them all in one hand. I was surprised he hadn't made a messy toss of it just to see if I'd go for them on the floor, but maybe he knew he was already on my nerves.

Business concluded, I took Buria's advice and headed for the stairs.

"Couldn't you have done that from the Premier's home or your own?" she asked once we were back on the main level.

"Kess gets all prickly if I don't give him equal treatment with Jey. Mostly though, I wanted to make sure he understood that I was fully recovered and back in business."

She nodded. "Where to next?"

I rolled the tokens in the palm of my hand. The thought of a drink made my mouth water. If only there were a table out of the press of bodies and Kess's view. Then I spotted the open drapes on one of the cushioned nooks along the wall. I led Buria through the crowd and inside. The room was just big enough for four chairs and a tall, round table. Out of the cavernous main dance floor, the dark little room provided a welcome haven.

Though the music was still loud, I could hear Buria without leaning in when she asked, "What are we doing in here? I thought you said you didn't..."

My eye that had been replaced after the explosive end to the High Council saw her clearly in the dim room, her curious gaze searching my face and a tempting smile on her lips. A shiver passed over me with the realization that she wasn't opposed to the idea.

Stassia had been worried about the wrong woman. Or perhaps, right about me. Despite the bond being in place, I was fully aware of Buria's not exactly flirting, her body next to mine, and my attraction to it.

"Nothing that Kess implied, no," I said easily, wondering if I meant it. "But I'll drink for free. You want one?"

The alcove muted the frantic flashing lights outside, but still cast alternating red and blue shadows over Buria's face where she stood so close that her arm brushed against me.

"While I'm on duty?" she asked.

"It's just a drink. Have a seat."

She sucked on her bottom lip. "You won't tell the Premier?"

"Drinking is against his rules?"

She nodded.

"You're off duty, right?"

"With him, but not you."

"I won't tell if you won't."

Buria grinned. "I think you'd make a much more enjoyable boss."

Images of what I would enjoy flooded my head. Damn, the bond was supposed to prevent any of this. Not that I minded, exactly, but Stassia definitely would. I cleared my throat and attempted to get my wandering thoughts back in control.

"Trust me, there's very little to enjoy. Just ask Neko sometime."

To ground myself, I opened our bonded connection, not interrupting Stassia, but getting a feel for what she was doing. If nothing else, letting her know that I was relaxed and unwounded would maybe put her at ease. Her prickly end of the connection let me know she wasn't happy with my absence, but she also shared a glimpse of Neko, Markus, Daniel, and Ikeri sitting around her as they shared an animated conversation and some confection that Daniel had made. For a split second, I considered ditching Buria to Jump home, to be part of that moment, but then reality hit me. If I showed up, the conversation would abruptly become strained and Ikeri would excuse herself. Maybe giving into her wishes would eventually gain me some favor. I hoped it would.

I left Stassia's mind, slid into a wobbly chair, and set the four drink tokens on the sticky table. Buria sat beside me, both of us facing out into the gyrating crowd. It only took a few moments before one of the attentive wait staff ducked her head in to ask if we needed drinks. Buria cast me a questioning glance.

"Yes, two. Strong. Make it expensive since Kess is paying." I dropped two of the tokens into her hand.

The woman eyed the tokens and stammered. "But what do you want?"

"Whatever your boss drinks. I'm guessing it's not behind the bar. Find it and pour two."

"I don't know as I'm allowed to do that. Not with these, for sure."

Did I feel like causing a scene? Fuck it. This was Kess's club and I had a bodyguard with me so why the hells not? "Maybe this will help clarify my order." I pulled my actual ID card from my pocket and held it up for her to see. Since we'd gone public, I made a point to carry it. My face might not have been plastered everywhere as much as Kess, who advised the non-Fragian worlds of the Rakon Nebula, but even this waitress in a club on Twelve knew the name of the Advisor of the Narvan.

She took a moment to really look at me, which likely wasn't easy in the dimness of the nook, and then at Buria, whose skin being several shades darker than mine, truly blended into the shadows.

"You can even check with your boss if you want. He gave those tokens to me all of five minutes ago."

She nodded quickly. "I'll get those right out, sir."

True to her word, our drinks appeared in short order, though delivered by another woman. Other members of the curious staff glanced our way every time they had an excuse to walk by. I considered closing the curtain but didn't need rumors of what I might be doing in a closed nook in one of Kess's clubs with Buria getting back to Stassia. I let the staff have their ogling entertainment and sipped my drink.

Buria took one sip and let out a gasp before setting the glass back on the table.

I laughed. "It's the good stuff."

She grimaced. "That's good?"

"It is. Maybe you need something a little lighter?"

"A lot lighter." She slid her glass over to me.

After waving down one of our observers and handing over

another token, I got Buria situated with one of the club's standard ice-filled, low-alcohol, fruity concoctions. She sipped at it far more appreciatively as she watched two male dancers on the pillars outside our nook.

"They're all slaves, you know."

She gave me a sideways glance. "I did not know."

"The Nebula has no laws against it."

She watched them a bit longer while I did some network digging to see what I could find on Jey's Jalvian situation. Political ranting covered many of the primary news vid feeds. The Prime had made some unpopular decisions of late and Jey's name was publicly attached to several of them. I'd have to talk with him once this experiment at the University was over.

When I came out of the network, I realized I'd sucked down both of my drinks. Buria had also finished hers. Kess's quality liquor lent me a warmth in my stomach and a level of liquor-induced relaxation I hadn't enjoyed while under Stassia's watchful eye.

Seeming to notice she had my full attention, Buria asked, "You don't support the slavery laws?'

"No, but I don't control anything out here, so no one asks my opinion."

"But if you could, you would change the laws?"

Even when I did have a small amount of say in the matter, when Stassia and I had held Merchess within the Nebula, we'd kept the slavery laws in place. The slave trade held the economy together. It kept the Merchessian families paying their tithes which had helped finance all the good we were doing in the Narvan.

"I'd have to look into it." There were so many things to take into account. While I wanted to simply say yes, I couldn't do that, not even in front of a guard who wasn't mine in a club where the question didn't really matter. The answer mattered to me, either direction it went.

"Did you know we were slaves?" Buria said with the same semi-annoyed matter-of-factness I'd dropped on her ogling of the dancers.

That snapped me out of my thoughts in an instant. "We who, the whole company?"

She nodded. "Many of us have been training since our early teens, those of us who met the requirements. Others were trained in paths they were better suited for."

"Where did you come from? How did they acquire you?"

"I don't remember where other than I was hungry and scared. I was with someone, an older person, I think, a relative maybe. She traded me for credits so she could eat. I do remember her telling me that she was sorry."

"Are you still thirsty?"

Her eyes widened, the whites stark in the shadows. "Yes, but—"

"It's against the rules, I get it. Let me rephrase then. I'm still thirsty, and I'm attempting to be polite."

She tilted her head as if contemplating her answer while watching me with deeper calculation than before. "Yes, I will have another."

I waved one of the eager staff over and ordered for both of us.

"This company the Premier hired you from, he didn't tell me much about it other than it was highly regarded."

"We are the best," she said easily.

"Where is it located?"

"Outside the Narvan."

"I gathered that. Could you be more specific?"

"Not unless you're sincere in your interest to acquire one of my sisters."

"All women?"

Stassia wasn't going to like that, but it sure beat training someone from scratch. Not that Neko hadn't had any experience, but it had taken a good deal of Stassia's and then Fa'yet's effort to get him up to my standards. With Markus and Daniel continuing their education on Veria Prime and Stassia and I working, Neko was going to be worn thin again in no time.

Beyond that, Stassia and I couldn't always work together. I'd gotten rather used to taking care of some things on my own, like personal meetings with certain people. She tended to say or do things that aggravated me in those meetings, like when she occasionally forgot she wasn't running the Narvan solo anymore. Not that I didn't want to be near her, but some time apart would be good for both of us.

My nerves needed a break and some freedom. *Freedom.* That word grated on me now that Kess had used it.

If Neko was tied up with the boys, that left me with Stassia. All. The. Time. I groaned. Having enjoyed even these few hours on my own, the thought of going home to work by link or vid made my nerves itch.

I couldn't very well borrow Nena or Buria regularly. Fa'yet would need them once Ikeri moved in. Going out solo was just plain reckless given the ongoing system-wide recovery from the Arpex mess and simmering tensions between the Jalvian and Artorian worlds. Even with all Jey and I had accomplished since my return from retirement and imprisonment, I doubted we'd see an end to that anytime soon, if even in my lifetime.

Buria kept a watchful eye on everyone from our tiny oasis in the chaos. I pondered her profile where the flashing lights touched her high cheekbones and slender nose, wondering what it would be like to have her around. The thought of working beside Buria made me smile.

I couldn't work beside Buria, I reminded myself. Not an option. But maybe I could talk Stassia into taking some shifts with Ikeri. The two of them would want to spend time together. That would also mean they could get along somewhere that I didn't have to have that wound reopened every time I saw them together talking and laughing without me.

Ikeri and I had been so close. We'd had a perpetually open natural connection between us, much like the bonded one I'd foraged with Stassia. She'd never had that kind of relationship with her mother. Maybe that was the difference. Stassia had enjoyed a middle ground and that was still acceptable, but me, who'd once had everything, was shunned.

Daniel could take on some shifts of watching over Ikeri eventually. He was certainly motivated and enthusiastic, but he needed a lot of training and to grow up first. Being responsible for another person's life was a big weight to put on someone's shoulders, and as much as I appreciated his efforts to help, I wasn't ready to burden him with that just yet. Especially not after seeing him warm up to Markus. Daniel deserved a few years to enjoy the relative lack of stress and responsibilities. That should have been his whole childhood. I'd managed to botch that for him too. At least he was still speaking to me.

While my children got along, they saw the universe differently. Ikeri wanted to fix it. Daniel wanted to explore and experience it all. He'd taken Markus under his wing and brought a smile to the young Jalvian boy's generally confused and worried face. I'd been working with Daniel, showing him how to stay in Markus's mind, to make him feel safe. Partly to expand his skills and stamina and also to free up my time.

I still found Markus curled up beside me at night more often than not, but he did start each night sleeping in Daniel's room. That gave me and Stassia some time alone in bed. I always slept better when he was nearby. However, Stassia had never been fond of kids in our bed, even the ones she'd given birth to.

Kids and guard shortages, smothering mates, infuriating partners, and three worlds worth of problems, it was enough to make me wish for the simpler times when all I had to do was work my shift next to Stassia and then hand the responsibility off to Merkief or Jey. Even the most stressful contracts we'd taken in that first year were nothing compared to the overwhelming and never-ending load of stress bearing down on me now.

Hells, maybe I should have stayed bored out of my mind on Pentares.

I glanced at Buria. No, there were benefits of being one of the advisors of the Narvan. Sadly, they were few and far between and encumbered by far too many strings. I sighed.

When our drinks came, I handed over my last token, paid for Buria's, and then I sipped at mine. A practice Stassia had imposed on me. Buria played with the condensation dripping down her tall narrow glass, making patterns with her long fingers.

"Would you consider it? Taking on a few of my sisters?"

"A few? I was toying with one. How many of you are there?"

"Near fifty ready for sale when I left. Many are trained as guards like Nena and me."

"I'm assuming they're not actually your sisters or your mother was a very busy woman. Were you close to them that you wish to see them employed?"

Buria smiled, laughing softly. "Close, yes. Most of us lived together in the same room." She raised her glass and drank, clearly savoring the flavor of the prohibited liquor. "Most of us didn't have a real family or didn't want to remember them if we did."

"And this new family, were they all sold to this company like you?"

She nodded. "Those who could remember their prices would often tease or taunt one another over them."

Outside our nook, the two male dancers slid down the side of their pillars to be given a filled cup by another slave, along with a wrapped packet. They cautiously unwrapped them at a corner and ate the contents quickly, getting jostled all the while by passing patrons. A wayward elbow knocked into the cup in one of their hands, spilling the contents onto the floor. The other poured some of his into the near-empty cup.

Buria shot up from her seat beside me and over to the two men.

Without saying a word, she took up a post in front of them, backing them against the pillars. She stood there, arms crossed over her chest, looking annoyed at the universe. I wouldn't have approached her and neither did anyone else. The dancers enjoyed the calm pocket of space in which to consume their meal.

When they'd finished, one of them whispered something in her ear. Then they scrambled back up the pillars and resumed their dancing. Buria made her way back over to me. She sat there with her hands in her lap, staring at her drink.

"Something wrong?"

She shook her head.

"We do need to get going. Are you going to finish that?"

Buria glanced at my empty glass and then picked hers up woodenly and drained it. She stood, staring at the table, head down, her smile gone.

I let her be while we made our way out of the club and down the street in search of a quiet spot to set up a jump point. If she ever wanted to take a well-deserved break outside of Fa'yet's estate, I wanted her to have a point of her own. Taking it in carefully now that the excitement had worn off would be the best way to establish a point for her.

Her silence continued. Once I'd located a suitable place, I finally gave in to curiosity.

"What did he say to you?"

"Did you know they are for sale? For sex, I mean? With anyone who will pay?"

"Not surprising."

Her raging glare informed me I'd spoken unwisely. "And you're all right with that? Just not surprising? That's all you have to say about your friend whoring out his slaves? That he has slaves at all, let alone a whole planet full of them?"

"As I said, the Rakon Nebula isn't under my control. I think I also made it pretty clear that Kess isn't my friend. He's a business partner. That's a very different relationship. Somewhere between strained and tolerated, sums it up fairly well."

Her anger fizzled as quickly as it had struck. She bowed her head. "I'm sorry. I shouldn't have spoken to you that way."

I shrugged. "You have a right to your opinions and to make them known."

"Opinions are best kept to oneself."

"That sounds like some pretty restrictive training. Were you allowed to do anything?" Her demeanor triggered an uncomfortable twinge in my gut and flashes of my time in grey.

Her gaze slowly lifted from the ground to meet mine. The corner of her lips wavered into a tentative smile.

"I take it smiling is not against the rules then."

"Smiling is encouraged. It makes our masters more pleased with us."

I stopped walking. "Masters?"

"Our trainers or those that hold ownership of our contracts."

"Are you saying the Premier bought you?"

She stood beside me, smile gone, and gaze back on the cracked plascrete walk. "Well, yes, that's how our contracts work."

I'd been too busy enjoying her company and the thought of getting out of Stassia's veritable house arrest that the full implications of *slave* hadn't hit me.

I'd been one of those for a time, and I was still dealing with the physical and mental repercussions.

"I am fortunate to have been purchased by one such as he," Buria said.

"No, you should have been hired. That's what decent people do." I couldn't fathom Fa'yet purchasing slaves. He was above that, wasn't he? Surely he'd have made things right with his new employees, especially since he lived in the Narvan where I did have a say about slavery. It was fucking prohibited.

"The Premier does pay you, right?"

"Our contracts say that compensation of any sort is not allowed. We may accept gifts, but only from our masters."

"He better be gifting you with a damn good salary."

Buria took two steps back. "I've angered you."

"Your contract angers me and the Premier angers me. You do not."

I ran my hands over my coat, taking inventory of the contents. Finding them satisfactory, I let my aggravation with Jey, Kess, and now Fa'yet and the universe in general, flow through my body.

"Buria, I think it's time you brought me to meet your sisters."

THREE

Buria initiated a link connection with me. I eagerly accepted, excited by the prospect of being able to talk to her anytime.

That couldn't get me into any trouble. I had countless link contacts. This was nothing special. I repeated that to myself a few times, but the thrill made me smile regardless.

She looked me over in a long and lingering way I didn't often encounter. Or, according to Stassia's recent jealous seething, maybe I just didn't normally pay attention to it.

One thing I couldn't avoid noticing in that instant was that Stassia was entirely correct, the rest of my body worked just fine. That was disconcerting, because with the bond in place, it wasn't supposed to. And it was still in place, I verified that before panic had a chance to sink in. Physical attraction with anyone other than Stassia had never happened before.

"Is everything all right, Advisor?"

I cleared my throat. "Yes. Quite fine, actually. Have you ever done a double Jump?"

She nodded. Even in the breeze of the air filtration, her hair didn't move, remaining tight against her scalp and neatly in the two knots on either side of her head. I wondered how long it was and if she ever wore it down.

"The Premier made us practice after the link augmentation, but we'd known him a while by then. I'm not as familiar with you."

"I would hope not. Anastassia would have words about that and loaded weapons would probably be aimed at both of us."

"She is fortunate to have you."

"You'd have to confirm that with her." Right at the moment, I was pretty sure the only fortunate thing in the universe was that Stassia wasn't nearby or in my head.

Buria ran her hands over all the bumps and curves under her form-fitting jacket. Her long lashes hid her gaze as she verified her weapons.

"How about you show me the location, and I'll take care of the Jump?" I offered.

"I'm not sure I can do that correctly. I'm not like you."

"The Premier hasn't shown you how to flash jump points?"

She shook her head. "He tells us what we need to know. I have nothing of value to share."

"I highly doubt that."

Her head jerked up, attention glued to me again.

What the hells was I doing? A little voice in my head explained that I was trying to be friendly. Stassia had told me I wasn't good at it. I was practicing, with one of the women who would be watching over my daughter. We should be on friendly terms, shouldn't we?

"Do you know how to establish your own jump point?"

She shook her head. "The Premier provides all the points we need."

"You might want a couple of your own. For your off time."

"That's not allow—"

"He can't dictate what you do when you're off duty, for Geva's sake. He doesn't own you."

She raised her thin, arched eyebrows.

"Well, he won't when I'm done talking to him. Here, I'll show you how to make a reliable pattern to use."

I held out the short, sturdy blade I used for carving point patterns. Keeping her gaze glued to my face, her warm fingers lingered over my hand before she finally took the blade. It took a moment for my brain to remind me I was supposed to be explaining about patterns and how to make them unobtrusively.

When she started in on the wall with the blade, I didn't have it in me to step back and give her room to work. I was shielding her while she was distracted. Just being considerate.

Maybe I shouldn't have had that last drink. Or maybe my sudden onset of lust was some odd side effect from Nan's last alteration adjustment. I took a deep breath and tried to keep my focus on the pitted surface of the grey wall.

But my gaze kept drifting back to Buria.

Her coat shifted over her shoulders and across her back with every movement. The muscles in her legs flexed under the tight fabric of her pants while she carved.

It wasn't like I was basking in the pleasant distance the liquor had put between me and all the obligations of my life. Not as if I could vividly imagine what Buria's lips felt like or that her hand was gripping something other than my knife. Not one bit.

When she finished carving, she turned around to find me right there and almost dropped the knife. She chuckled as she recovered, handing the blade to me. I made quick work of putting it away. Dammit, we both needed a distraction before Anastassia caught wind of my illicit thoughts.

"Do you mind if I take the location from you?" I asked. "We've been standing in the open longer than I'm comfortable with. It won't hurt."

Buria nodded. I slipped gently into her mind. There were a lot of images there, flashes of faces, a crying girl, a haggard woman vehemently apologizing, darkness and terror in the blackness. Pain, shame, sobbing, more faces. It was all a disorganized mess of memories lurking just below her calm and collected exterior.

What I witnessed there sobered me quickly. I hoped that during her stay, Ikeri would get close enough to Buria to help her.

"Can you focus on where we need to go?" I asked, my voice distant to my own ears.

An image solidified, sweeping over the rest, cold and without feeling. A room with a tall door. No, two doors that split open down the middle. They were pale green with bronze-colored trim along the bottom third. A warm grey tiled floor set on the diagonal. Long deep purple drapes hung aside two narrow windows twice my height. Birds flitted outside against a dome-covered too blue sky. A colony somewhere.

"Can you focus on the details, something specific to that room?"

A print lined the upper half of the room, crisscrossing the beige walls with soft earthy rust-colored lines. It would have to do. The probe, even light as it was, would give her a headache if I kept it up much longer.

Pulling all the details she shared into a three-dimensional image of the space took a moment. I took in the sounds, the running water of what her memory told me was a fountain in the corner, and the hum of an air circulation system. Once I was sure I had everything she had to offer, I dropped the probe and formed the Jump. With my hand on her arm, the void overtook us.

We stepped out into the room she'd given me.

"They will make us wait," she said, nodding toward a scattering of plush chairs amongst greenery growing under a giant round skylight in the middle of the room. Despite what I knew this place to be, the atrium-like lobby was appealing. The air was fresh, the furniture and floor clean, and the plants well-tended.

"While we wait, why don't you tell me how angry I should be?"

Buria sat beside me, leaning close. "What do you mean?"

"If you hadn't been sold to these people, what would your life be like, or that of your sisters?"

She paused, looking up at the projected bright blue sky outside the round window above. "I would have been sold somewhere else. We would be on the streets, dead, any number of things. Well-fed, clothed, and trained, definitely not."

"What you're saying is that this form of slavery is likely better than what would have befallen you had you not been sold to them."

Her gaze fell to her hands on her lap. She rubbed her fingertips with her thumbs. "Even if it wasn't the best or worst thing, I had no choice. I was only a child."

"I understand that. Were they kind to you here?"

She sucked in her lips and closed her eyes. Her body went stiff.

"I see. And all the slaves are treated this way?"

Her nod was barely perceptible.

"How large is this facility? Is it the only one in this colony?"

"Tacesh, that's the name of this colony and the planet. It was my home." She took a shuddering breath and let it out.

"Do you want to leave? I can go on from here on my own." It hadn't occurred to me that returning here might be as traumatic for her as walking in the ruins of the Council's compounds had been for me.

"No. My presence here with you will mean a referral reward for my Mast...I mean, the Premier."

"He's plenty rich already. Do you want to leave?"

She shook her head. I didn't know her well enough to know if she did so because of her conditioning or if that was really her choice.

"This is the only compound I know of," she said as if nothing was wrong. "It's big enough for the staff, the trainers and the slaves, those ready to sell and those still training."

"So around a hundred then?"

"What are you planning to do?" she whispered.

"Something stupid, undoubtedly."

I hadn't been able to save those who'd served in grey with me when the High Council bases had been destroyed. Though most of us had likely had a hand in earning our fate, they'd died without any hope of rescue. From what Buria said, none of these women had a choice in being here.

Tacesh, being far from the Narvan, meant I could act without jeopardizing the goodwill of Jey or Kess. No one knew me out here. It had been well over a month since I'd had the chance to let loose, not to mention the whole shit pile with the Arpex before that—it had definitely been far too long. I could do something good here, something that might make up for some of the deaths I'd caused when the Council bases blew.

Committed to action, my body itched to get to it.

"How long are we supposed to wait?" I asked loudly.

Minutes later, the door creaked as the hinges swung inward. A woman dressed similar to Merona walked in. The narrow skirt of her outfit restrained her strides. I glanced to Buria.

"Some of those not suited as guards are trained in hospitality and administration, like Merona," Buria informed me in a level tone. She turned to the woman. "I have brought a prospective Master."

"Very good. I will note your owner's name. You will remain here."

Buria offered the woman a submissive bob of her head. "Please see that his needs are well met."

Leaving her alone here in this place where she'd suffered seemed cruel. "My needs would be better met if you remained with me."

Buria looked surprised and more than a little flustered.

"That will not be necessary." The woman bowed. "I am Untami. It will be my pleasure to see to all of your desires."

"And I'm sure you'll do a fine job, but I'm rather attached to Buria. She will be joining us."

I reached out and grabbed Buria's unresisting hand. It was warm, calloused, and had slender, strong fingers like another pair of hands I was intimately familiar with, but it was also darker, younger, and attached to a woman I very much wanted to see smile again. I placed her hand on my armored arm.

I just hadn't quite decided yet on what plan of action to take to make that happen.

Untami smiled pleasantly, and ignoring Buria, focused all her beaming attention on me. "What type of slave are you searching for so that I may best serve you?"

"I'm looking for a guard, but I may be interested in others. I would like to see all that you have to offer."

She did glance at Buria then, who offered Untami a tight nod. It seemed I had the funds to make giving me the full tour worthwhile.

"Untami, are you to whom I should be speaking if I wish to make an offer on the contract of one of your slaves?"

Her face flushed. "Oh no. I am no Master. If you see a slave suited to your needs, I will guide you to a Master right away."

It wouldn't hurt to take the tour while I shored up the details of what I wanted to do here. "Lead on then."

Buria walked sedately beside me.

"Are you all right? You can leave at any time," I said quietly.

She nodded, her lips pinched tightly together.

Untami brought us out of the atrium and into an open room with bright lights and a floor covered in a surface that offered a little give yet allowed for traction. "The women train here in various disciplines."

"No men then?"

"The only men here are Masters," Untami said quickly.

"Are there women masters as well?"

The pressure on my arm answered before Untami confirmed it. These men had never met Stassia. I didn't bother to contain my chuckle. They could make of it what they wanted.

With light steps, I followed Untami through one of the doors like the one in the atrium that lined the training room. After a brief pause and a pointed look at a camera by Untami, the door clicked. She pushed it open. A hallway brought us to another door. Another pause. Another click. Double security. They had a clue of what they were doing, and if they were monitoring our general movements through the complex, we were likely under direct observation. Best to put on a convincing show then.

The second door opened into an expansive room. Three massive beds with curtained sides of a semi-transparent cloth filled one half of it. Clusters of chairs and couches sat around a pole of prism glass lit from within on the other half. Lighting, pleasing, natural, and not overly bright, illuminated the clean space filled with expensive-looking fabrics and furnishings. An artificial fire rose from a stone circle at one end of the room. Flames licked at blackened logs that didn't burn. Eight women rose from their various perches, all dressed in a manner that made it immediately clear what need they were trained to serve.

None of them ignited the arousal that Buria did. I supposed that was a small positive as far as narrowing down why my bond was faltering.

"We offer an array of pleasure slaves. Though all of our slaves have a measure of training in this area, these particular women are experts. Would you like a demonstration?" asked Untami.

I couldn't get the words *all the slaves* out of my head. Some of what I'd seen in Buria's mind became painfully clear.

"That won't be necessary."

Untami bowed her head. "Then we shall continue." We backed out of the giant bedroom and returned down the hallway to wait at the door to the training room.

Once we were released with the door unlocking thanks to the observing masters, we headed off through another door to another room. This one had one open hall with partitioned rooms along the other side of the otherwise long and bland open space. All the women here were dressed similar to Untami and Merona.

"Perhaps you need assistance with your household or business?"

At the sound of our entry, eleven women hurried over and formed a line, staring forward, straight and tall like the best of soldiers. Like the pleasure slaves, they varied in race, color, and shape. All were neatly dressed and clean.

"We've all been trained in accounting, management, and hospitality." She joined the end of the line. "You may ask us anything."

Figuring I should put on a convincing show, I considered what to ask. "How old were you when you came here?" I asked Untami.

"We prefer not to discuss our lives before. We are far better off now, skilled and useful. We are dependable and can be trusted with any task without complaint."

"That's good to know."

They were well-trained. It was a shame they hadn't had the luxury of doing so at an academy or university somewhere else.

"I've witnessed one of you at work before. I think we're good here. Shall we resume our tour?"

Untami removed herself from the line and it dissolved, the women melting back into their modest chambers. "This way, please."

When we again passed through the training room, twenty-some girls of ages varying from Ikeri to Untami were divided into two groups. The younger working on physical training, defense, it appeared. One of the girls got up from the mat, shook herself loose, and went to the back of the line. The next stepped up. She was already wincing before the instructor struck and from the force with which she went down, it did not appear that he was holding back. Maybe it wasn't defense, but how to take a blow.

The older girls were talking to men, one on one, sitting on mats on the floor. One of the men reached out and slapped the woman in front of him.

She flinched, but only minimally. There were no tears or even a gasp. She merely bowed her head and waited for him to speak again.

Another of the men struck a woman. Without thinking, I started for the nearest couple.

"Please. You'll only make it worse for her." Buria begged, using our newly forged linked connection. Her clear discomfort at using the link to speak, that she'd resorted to it despite that, and her plea were the only reasons I allowed her to steer me after Untami.

"They're learning," Untami said, her voice devoid of emotion. "You will appreciate this training when your own slaves serve you without question."

I didn't appreciate the training one bit. There had been a few hard cases back when I was in school, kids who didn't take to the military hierarchy and earning-their-way-up mentality, but even the roughest of those hadn't faced what these women were subjected to.

Untami brought us through another door. Another hallway. Another pause and click, reminding me that we were being watched. If I went off now, I might be throwing away my chance at doing some good here.

The next door opened. The familiar sounds of physical training beckoned me inside.

"The majority of our slaves are guards. They are the specialty of the house." Untami led us into a cold, open room. Two rows of narrow, open-ended chambers, one on each side of the main space, provided beds and minimal privacy for the women. A handful of them, dressed much like Buria, were exercising in the middle. The heavy thwacks of two women sparring with short wooden sticks echoed through the room. All appeared in good health, muscled, and focused on their tasks. None of them were smiling.

"You lived here?" I asked Buria.

She nodded.

If any of the women recognized her, they gave no sign. There was no conversation, no laughter, no sense of camaraderie among any of them. My thoughts wandered to the squad of Artorian pilots stationed on Frique. They'd essentially been banished out there, together in their plight, alone in a strange and unwelcoming place, but they made the best of it. They'd bonded. They took care of one another. These women had none of that. Had Buria been just as solitary before Fa'yet bought her?

Untami motioned us to a grouping of chairs just inside the door, well away from the practice area. We sat, Buria remaining close but no longer touching.

"Do they do this all day?" I asked, watching them join up in the middle of the room, various pairs forming, practicing, and then separating to form new pairs or exercising along the edges.

"Except when we are taken into the main training room and given further instruction from the Masters in this or other fields," said Buria like she was reciting from a manual. All spark of the personality I'd enjoyed had vanished.

Untami nodded, resuming her sales pitch. "Our guards keep a rigorous training schedule to maintain their best physical form. They are both beautiful and deadly. They are kept to strict standards of conduct to keep their minds and bodies suited for their job. All of our guards have received elements of our other branches of training, both in pleasure and hospitality. However, our guards are surgically barren so that they may maintain their positions for as many years as possible."

"Is this true?"

Buria nodded sharply.

My fluid plan took a sharp turn. Even the slaves on Merchess were treated better than this, given choices about their fate.

"And those that don't wish to be barren?" I couldn't help but ask.

"We are here to serve," said Untami. "The Masters know our strengths and we obey."

Buria joined Untami in a quick head bow upon this proclamation. My skin crawled, and for a split second, I was back in the confining observation room with Arin telling me that I wasn't special and to just do my job.

"Are there other slaves?" I asked, trying to keep my head clear and temper in check.

"These are the three fields our house specializes in."

"Then I have seen enough. I would like to speak to your Masters about a purchase."

"Of course." Untami bowed yet again. "If you'll follow me."

Buria hurried to my side the moment we stood. Her hand returned to my arm as if it had never left. "If I might make a suggestion? That woman." She pointed to a short woman with skin the same shade as mine who was knocking two others onto the floor with a series of powerful kicks.

"I've made up my mind." I patted her hand. "I think you'll be pleased."

A look of terror flashed over her face. She bowed quickly and kept her head lowered. "Please be careful. Don't anger the Masters. I don't wish to see you harmed."

Could she stand beside me and face the Masters, who had ingrained this subservience into her? Would she dare act against them, even to protect me? My confidence in that answer dwindled with every second that her head remained bowed. She wasn't ready for that yet.

Reluctantly, I took her hand from my arm. "Please wait for me where we arrived. I'll find you when my business is complete."

That she didn't protest, didn't even look up to convey any further warning, that she just did as I asked, saddened me greatly. I'd been where she was, crushed and broken.

I'd come back from it, recovered who I was, and by Geva, so could she. I took in the room full of enslaved women.

So could they all.

FOUR

Untami led me out of the wing where the guard slaves lived. I missed Buria's presence beside me as we passed back through the central training room. She must have Jumped right after the door closed behind her because there was no sign of her ahead of us and I didn't see any other route to the atrium.

The young girls were now running laps, sweat dripping from their faces and seeping through the lightweight white clothes they wore, all the same, without ornamentation, all hint of personality erased from them.

The older girls were now practicing removing a more elaborate outfit of muted colors enticingly for each of their Masters. Imagining Buria enduring this training made my blood boil.

"This way," Untami said, leading me to one of two doors off the large room that we hadn't used before. She gave the camera above it a victorious nod.

The lock clicked. When this door opened, she stood aside.

Glad to be rid of the simpering slave, I went in. The room was more of a standard size, but perhaps was just an office set up in a wide passage way, as another door stood at the opposite end of the room. A wide table made of stone and polished to a glossy sheen sat in the middle. Plush chairs lined the long sides. Artwork hung on the walls which were beige with rust trim much like in the atrium.

A man, dressed as the others who had been tormenting the girls in the main room, entered from the rear door. He straightened his rust-colored, waist-length jacket as though he'd just pulled it over the white, high-collared shirt before entering the room. He wore his short hair slicked back, oiled so heavily that it glistened in the overhead lighting. A smile broke out on his weathered face that reminded me of Kess. Maybe it was the signature smile of all slavers, heavy on the charm, overly friendly, with a side sneer of condescension.

He held out both hands, offering me a seat and greeting simultaneously. "Welcome to Tacesh. I trust you have found what you're looking for?"

"I have."

"Wonderful." He sat. "Absolutely wonderful. You'll find our prices affordable and our product obedient and willing." He reached under the table.

I automatically slid a gun through one of the slits in my coat, but kept it under the table for the moment, aimed and ready.

His hands came up with a large datapad between them, the size of four standard pads built together, more like a flat portable vid. He tapped on it for a moment. The brightness flickered as images and text slipped across the screen.

"Here we are. Our contract." He held the screen up so I could see it, though the words were too small to read from across the table. "You speak Trade very well, but our policy is to provide the documentation in your language so that you have no legal issues when you take your purchases home. Preferred language?"

"Artorian."

He tapped again. "Very good. We have that translation on file. One moment." After more tapping, he pursed his lips. "It appears that transporting slaves to Artor is prohibited, at least according to the last policy review. Are you prepared to offer the necessary bribes to get your purchases through import processing?"

"I've got it covered."

"Wonderful." He slid the large datapad over to me. "Here is the pricing for each area of specialty. As you see, we offer a discount package on three or more."

The prices were outrageous, but having seen Buria and Nena demonstrate their skills, I had no doubt the other specialties were equally worth the credits. No wonder Fa'yet had come home with three.

Kess didn't know what kind of profits he was missing. If he could have gotten away with charging this much per head for his entire line of stock, he would have been rolling in credits somewhere far from the Narvan and the Rakon and not lifting a finger for the rest of his life. Then again, Kess likely had no desire to put in the time to train them. He was more about the fast turn-around of the general stock and long-term reuse of his dancing whores.

"Three it is then."

The salesman nodded. "Great choice. The skill list is on pages two through four if you would like more detail than the tour offered. Did you have anyone particular in mind? Otherwise, I can help you select those that you would enjoy most."

"I have my eye on a few." I sat back, giving myself plenty of room to move. "You've got quite the impressive operation here."

He rested his empty hands on the table, sliding his fingers together as if he couldn't wait to get his hands on my credits. "I'm glad you think so. We do offer referral bonuses if you know anyone else who would be in the market for a slave."

"As a matter of fact, I do know someone who has a market for slaves."

He cocked his head, eyes narrowing as if deciding whether to call me out on my misinterpretation.

"It must take quite a staff to train them all," I barreled onward before he got the chance.

"For many of our Masters, this is an enjoyable second job or hobby, you might say. We have an investment buy-in system. Eight of us are full-time, living in the compound to keep the operation running smoothly."

"A job not without its perks, I'm sure." I made a show of skimming over the skill pages. "Your prices are quite reasonable when you also take the security and housekeeping staff into account. And acquisitions, of course. I'm sure there must be a good deal of overhead to cover with this large compound."

"A man of business, I take it?"

I gave him a non-committal nod.

"Then I'm sure you know others." His face grew more animated. "The slaves are taught to clean up after themselves and to cook. We do make every effort to provide a well-rounded, finished product."

"How thoughtful of you. They don't maintain their own security though."

He chuckled. "No. We employ locals for that. As you said, there are abundant perks. We can keep their wages minimal."

"So these slaves I'm about to purchase, they've been through the mill, so to say?"

He paused, licking his lips. "You were seeking untouched product?"

"Do you have such a thing?"

"Only at the untrained stage. We do have a couple of recent acquisitions. They are being treated for their feistiness. Perhaps you'd enjoy such a trait?"

"How old?"

He reached for the datapad. I slid it back to him.

After a moment of flicking through files, he held up the screen. There were no words this time, only two side-by-side night vision vid feeds. Two young girls, naked, alone, and huddled in the darkness. I swallowed hard.

"One is eight. The other twelve. They have both been cleansed and vaccinated. The older one would need to be sterilized before we could sell her."

"I thought only the guards were sterilized?"

He leaned forward, voice conspiratorial. "They all are. Only the guards are aware of it. It made sense in their line of work. The others, well, we've found they serve better when they have a bit of hope left in them." He returned the contract to the forefront of the datapad. "We can't very well have clients angry over impregnated slaves. A man, such as yourself, likely has a family or public image to consider. We want you to be able to fully enjoy your investment."

"Very thoughtful of you. Can that be reversed?"

"I suppose that might be possible with the right medical expertise. Though I can't imagine why you'd want such a thing."

"Just curious."

He shook his head. "We do ask that you keep your slaves for yourself. Our vast experience shows they serve better if not passed around, if you take my meaning. More loyal. If you are displeased with them or lose interest, you may return them for partial credit toward a new purchase. Unless you've taken it upon yourself to fix them. That would void all offers."

Was it the passing around that had set so poorly with Buria in Kess's club? I supposed there was some degree of consolation in only serving one person rather than being whored out to anyone.

"Now then, are you interested in seeing the younger two or shall we proceed with choosing three from the trained stock?"

"I would very much like to see the younger two first."

"Wonderful. This way then." He stood, leading me to the room from which he'd come. "We don't offer a full facility tour, but I think you'll appreciate the efficiency of our operation upon seeing the back end while we walk."

The only thing I was going to appreciate was killing him. But that would have to wait until he let me skulk through the backside of the facility and led me to the girls.

The next room was where he'd been observing me on my tour. Vids lined three walls and a comfortable-looking chair outfitted with a terminal on one arm stood in the middle of the viewing space. A half-eaten meal set the small table beside it, along with a bottle and an empty glass. Perks, indeed.

Trying not to be obvious, I hazarded a glimpse of the feeds. They seemed to cover the entire compound, including several angles within the rooms I'd already visited. The one view that I locked onto was Buria sitting calmly in the atrium, both feet on the floor, back straight, hands in her lap, no hint of what might be going on in her mind apparent on her face. They had trained her well. It was the whole process of which that I disagreed with on every level.

"Through here." My guide hurried me along. The back-end tour consisted of a maze of hallways and doors. Several of the open ones appeared to be living quarters for the men who ruled here. We passed two of them, seemingly off duty by the lack of uniform. There were signs on some of the closed doors, but I didn't recognize the language.

We exited the maze through a heavy door, different than the others on the interior. I noted that the Master had to authorize the opening of this particular door with a fingerprint on a scanner. The lights came on as we entered, illuminating a massive storeroom. Three mover units stood idle, their standby lights blinking. The farther we got into the room, I started to realize just how big it was, nearly half as large as my warehouse at Dugans on Veria Minor. That reminded me that I should find time to touch base with Rosh, who I had left in charge when we'd left our lives behind there. It had been far too long since we'd talked.

"We keep the new product in a separate building," my guide said as he used his fingerprint to access a door at the end of the room.

We walked over what appeared to be a landing pad, though it was unoccupied. Another sizeable building stood a four-minute walk away. He unlocked the door and let us in. Again, automated lights kicked on, this time revealing eight rectangular shipping containers arranged in a semicircle in the middle of the otherwise unoccupied space.

He walked up to one of the containers and pounded on the smooth metal front beside the door. A shriek came from inside.

"This is the younger one," he said, swiping his finger over the reader next to the door.

The door creaked open. It was pitch black inside but for the warehouse light shining through the doorway. And then suddenly it was brightly lit.

A thin, naked girl huddled in the corner. Her hair had been shaved close to her brown scalp. She buried her head in her arms that were wrapped around her knobby knees.

"Why keep them in the dark?"

"They are being conditioned for obedience." My guide strode into the container and over to the girl. He put his hand on her shoulder. "Are you hungry?"

The girl shied away.

"As you will then, Eris. Another day without food for you." He shook his head and returned to the doorway where I waited. "If she is compliant, she gets fed. This is the first stage in the training process."

"How long has she been non-compliant?"

"Eleven days. Don't worry, we're not cruel. She's been fed every three days, though we do make them unconscious for the feedings."

"You tube feed them, then? Isn't that invasive? Uncomfortable?"

"Conditioning isn't intended to be comfortable. We offer compliant slaves."

I nodded. Words weren't a wise choice at that point. I switched slits in my coat. A simple shot to the head was far too kind for the Masters.

"Do you want to see the other one? Colata is a beauty for her age," he said, closing the container door.

"If I were to take the younger one, you wouldn't sterilize her?"

"We can, if you would prefer. However, we've found that it's unnecessary. Younger stock, such as this, isn't all that hardy after frequent use by one such as yourself."

The thought of him thinking I might do such a thing was enough to make me end the charade right there. I slipped a stunner out of my coat and hit his unarmored ass with a burst powerful enough to drop him to an unconscious pile on the floor.

Not knowing if another Master would take up the vid room post after seeing this one take me on an extended tour, I made quick work of exchanging the stunner for a knife. With a severed Master finger in hand, I unlocked the container in front of me and then two others before I found the second girl.

"If you'd like to leave, come out here into the light. Both of you. And hurry."

One of them sniffed. Feet shuffled across the floor.

The younger girl crept silently out of the container. She clutched the doorframe, staring no higher than my boots.

"I'm not going to hurt you, Eris."

Eris stayed planted in place.

The second girl came to the doorway of her prison. She stood there, arms wrapped around herself, shivering. Small dark bruises lined her arms like someone had pinched her repeatedly. A fading bruise on her face and more on her ribs attested to other methods of conditioning.

I wished there was something I could give them to cover up with, but the room was empty other than the containers and both girls would have collapsed under the weight of my armor.

"Please, I just want to go home. My mother needs me," she said.

"Colata, right?"

She nodded.

"Sorry, home will have to wait. Right now, I need to get you out of here. Hurry." I urged them forward.

Colata took one step.

"Don't. It's a trick. They'll hit you again," warned Eris from the safety of her doorway.

I pointed to the stunned Master at my feet. "I'm not one of them."

"My mother needs her medicine. I need to go home." Colata hurried toward me.

From the various colors of her bruises, she'd been there awhile. Considering what I'd seen in Buria's mind and what she'd told me of how the women had been sold as children, I didn't know if this girl had been stolen or her mother had sold her for whatever medicine she needed. Hells, her medicine could have been plain old street drugs for all I knew.

"Eris, we need to move. Now." As much as I wanted to grab the girls and go, that didn't seem like the way to gain their trust given what they'd been through. "Both of you are going to follow me. If there is a fight, if you see anyone with a gun, including me, you hide. Got it?"

Colata held out her hand to Eris. After one last hesitant look at me, Eris darted out and took her hand.

I took a few seconds to hoist the limp man into the container where he'd kept Eris and locked the door. He could enjoy the darkness for a while.

The girls watched with wide eyes. When I started for the exit, they followed silently and at a distance.

Out of their view, I used the severed finger to open the lock on the entry door. Pushing the door open a crack, I spotted the shadow of a nearby guard.

"Keep the door open, but stay inside until I tell you to come out."

The girls nodded, taking the door from me. Chilled air flooded inside in my wake. Leaving them behind, I slunk over to the shadow, moving along another outbuilding. The dome above projected an evening sky with a few half-hearted stars. The lights of the complex had dimmed to the night setting and were few and far between.

The guard must have been there for the benefits because his skill topped out at having two eyes, two legs, and shoulders to hold up a shirt. The knife slitting his throat was met with no more resistance than his flesh had to offer. He dropped to the ground. I set him up against the warehouse away from the edges of the nearest light. For my sake, I hoped the rest of the staff also ruled with fear rather than ability.

"Come on." I waved to the girls. They scampered out of the storage building without a second thought even though they were naked.

Eris caught sight of the severed finger as I unlocked the door to the warehouse of the main building. She let out a shriek. Colata clamped her hand over Eris's mouth.

"Like I said, not one of them. Come on."

Colata nodded, pulling Eris along with her. Hurrying through the aisles, I sought out a row of clothing racks I'd spotted on my slightly more leisurely tour. I found two white shirts that hung near the knees of the girls and only took moments to put on. We didn't have time for more.

"Things will get more dangerous from here. I'm going to take you to a friend who will watch over you while I help the others."

We'd just stepped into the first hallway from the warehouse when one of the Masters shot me. Thankfully, he was used to dealing with wealthy businessmen rather than men like me.

A scattering of bare feet on the floor behind me let me know the girls had run back into the warehouse.

He went for another shot to my chest. My coat deflected that while I put a bullet in his head.

Shrugging off the distant throbbing from the impacts, I got as far as, "You can come—" when two more men burst through the same door the Master had come from. These two weren't taking any chances, filling my vicinity with a storm of bullets. I threw my arms over my head and prayed the girls were far from me.

One of the bullets hit my hand. My skin slowed the impact, but the bullet still hurt like hell. Blood dripped down my face. I wiped it away and barreled toward the guards. They scattered, disrupting the flurry of bullets. I still had the one pulse pistol set low and tight. That took out one guard without too much destruction to the building. The other suffered my giant fist to his face with a satisfying crunch.

Even with the bullet-bloodied hand, I felt better than I had in months. My body sang with energy. This was what I'd missed. The thrill of a simple job. The quick and easy stuff I used to do with Stassia back when we'd done contracts that the Council decreed, or ones she'd picked that suited her plans for the Narvan. But now, I was doing something good. Something I chose to do. No one was paying me.

"Come on," I called over my shoulder.

When the girls didn't walk through the door, dread hit me hard. I ran back into the warehouse. A cry cut short caught my ear.

I found a Master with one of the girls' arms in each hand.

"You are not welcome here," he said. "You'd best leave before we find a place for you in one of our containers. We do have a market for male slaves. You'd fetch a high price."

I took the two girls into account and then gauged the distance between us. His hands were tied up with restraining his captives. What he expected to do to me other than toss threats wasn't apparent. I chalked it up to stupidity, slipped the stunner into my hand, and raced at him full bore.

A bullet hit me square in the back, signaling the arrival of more angry staff. Another bullet hit my right shoulder. My coat deflected them both. The distance from which they were fired turned them into only a minor annoyance thanks to my hardened skin.

Stunner blasts came from both sides. Thanks to my coat, my skin, and the rush of the job, the charges made me twitch but didn't slow me down. The Master in front of me darted left and then right, taking only a couple steps in either direction. His gaze was far more erratic, seeking help from his armed associates.

He grimaced and let go of the girls. Eris and Colata ran down one of the rows of shelving. Two men chased after them. I hazarded a glance behind me. How fucking many guards did they have on staff at one time? I still had four more and the Master immediately after my ass.

Another set of stunner charges hit me. One of the girls shrieked. Another spray of bullets pounded on my back, higher-powered and from close range. That slowed me down and pissed me off. How dare they ruin my enjoyable time here? I'd endured the tour of their torture factory. It was my turn now.

I dropped the Master with a stunner blast to the head and caught one of the other annoyances in the chest before another spray of bullets knocked the breath out of me for a second. The sharp twinge between my shoulder blades signaled that all of those shots had worn down the weave of my armor. A much sharper pain a few seconds later let me know that my skin might be minimalizing damage, but it wasn't impervious.

I hit one more with the stunner and then exchanged that for a more deadly solution. They got another shot into my breached armor before I dropped the remaining two. The adrenaline rush convinced me I could ignore the damage for now. I went on the hunt for the girls.

Colata had quite a mouth on her now that she was free and made it quite clear she had no intention of going back to her prison. All her cursing and protesting made them easy to find. It didn't occur to me until after I'd sighted and dropped their two accosters, that perhaps killing them in front of the girls hadn't been the best idea. Eris screamed. Colata pulled her away and wrapped her arms around the younger girl.

I spun around, watching the entry door to see how many more men Eris's scream was going to bring down on us. Ten breaths with nothing happening assured me that I could take a second to turn around to check on the girls.

They both stared at me with bald horror.

"Sorry about that. I didn't mean to…"

Colata pointed to drops of blood next to my boots on the plascrete floor. Oh. Maybe it wasn't the bodies, but the possibility of me joining them that had the girls so unsettled.

Rather than focus on the blood dripping beside my boots, I did a quick count of the staff compared to what the helpful salesman had conveyed to me. I had to have most of the hired guard subdued. It was the Masters who taught the guard slaves that might pose a problem. A problem, because while the wound didn't feel like anything critical, it was definitely high on the pain list now that I had a moment to think about it. Thankfully, with my new heart, avoiding stims was more of a choice than a necessity.

"I'll be fine." I waved the girls over to me and found my stim tin in my pocket. Once they'd unfrozen themselves from their spots and I had the promise of energy sliding down my throat, we hurried into the warehouse.

A niggling thought that had been politely waiting its turn on my priority list, made itself heard. How the hells was I going to transport all these slaves and the captured Masters? We navigated the Master's labyrinth without issue. When we reached the room with the vid screens, Colata finally confronted me.

"You're bleeding."

"I tend to do that. Nothing to worry about at this point."

Eris gave my torso an incredulous look. "You're bleeding a lot."

If I didn't focus on the sharp pain in my back, the stim would carry me through. "Enough about the blood. I need to know exactly where Tacesh is." The vids offered some clues, but it was the Master that burst into the room would likely be of more help.

I grabbed him before he had a chance to add to my growing list of wounds and dove into his mind without remorse. Rampaging around, I got the coordinates as well as the jump gate series from the nearest trade route.

Once I had what I needed, I dropped him onto the ground where he rocked, holding his head and squeezing his eyes shut. Stunning the rest would provide a quick solution, but this whole operation was going to take time. If I didn't want to repeat the hunt, I'd have to restrain and contain along the way. A quick search of the office yielded enough wiring to fashion suitable restraints.

Flipping through the vids, I tried to figure out my next move. I spotted Buria still waiting in the Atrium. The girls would be safer with her.

"Come on." We made our way through the room where I'd met the first Master and back out into the empty training space.

The hallway to the Atrium was clear. It wasn't until we'd stepped into the room, that my nerves sensed danger. Buria shot to her feet.

"What have you done?" she demanded.

"Well, I was trying to do something good for you. Why?"

She shook her head. "You've endangered them all."

"How so?"

"Without the Masters, they won't find their purpose. They'll go back to what they were. They'll die."

"The Masters want you to think that. It's not true. There are plenty of jobs for all of you. Jobs that pay. You don't have to serve anyone. Ever."

"But that is what we're meant to do," she said tightly as if it were obvious and I was an idiot.

Years of brainwashing couldn't be undone in a few minutes. "Trust me. Your Premier does. Is that good enough for now?"

She looked uncertain, but she nodded.

"Good. I need you to take Eris and Colata to the Premier's estate. When Ikeri arrives, ask her to perform Etara's memory balm for them. She'll know what that means. I'll forward the intake records to the Premier. If the girls were stolen off the streets, you can return them home. If they were sold, the Premier is to find them new families far from here."

Concern crept over her face. "You're bleeding."

"That's the rumor."

"No, you're bleeding." She pointed to the drops on the floor. There weren't as many as before. Either I was going to pass out, or it was clotting up on its own and I'd be fine. The stim would take care of me until either outcome came to pass.

"Yes, I'm aware." I gestured for Eris and Colata to go to Buria. "She'll see you to safety."

"But I must stay with you," said Buria. "I am here as your guard. The Premier will not be pleased that I have failed to keep you unharmed."

"Oh, he'll get over it. He's failed to keep me unharmed a time or twenty himself. You're welcome to remind him of that if he gives you any shit."

Her mouth dropped open. "I could never speak to him that way."

I snorted. "Maybe not, but you're not his slave either. Not anymore. That, I will make sure he understands. Now go."

Buria gave Eris a long look over, it wasn't near as long as the one she'd given me. Then again, a young girl in nothing but a shirt likely posed far less of a challenge than I did when it came to holding a Jump. The two of them left.

Colata gave me a pitiful look.

"She'll be back for you shortly."

Before I could run off, she grabbed me around the thighs and hugged me tightly. "Thank you."

For a moment, the arms around me were Ikeri's. Tears welled in my natural eye. Had I known I'd be cut off from her hugs so early in her life, I wouldn't have taken them for granted.

I blinked the tears away, patting this girl who wasn't my daughter on the shoulder. "I'm sorry these people hurt you."

"I'm sorry they hurt you too," she said.

"I'll be all right."

She let go. "Then I will be too."

For all the determination in her voice, her lips quivered and her hands shook. I hoped she was right.

Buria reappeared. I left the two of them and returned to the vid room. While I scanned the feeds, looking for the remaining resistance, I reached out to Gamnock.

We hadn't spoken since his father's funeral.

"I have a job for you, and I'm in a bit of a rush."

"Advisor Ta'set?"

"I'd hope you don't have a host of people who hit you with imme-diate jobs by link."

"Not usually. I have people for that. What do you need? I'm kind of in the middle of something right now."

From what I gleaned from our linked connection, that something involved two women, a bed, and a good deal of sweat. Appreciating the situation, I kept my request short.

"I need immediate transport for around ninety-five people." I gave him the coordinates and jump gate trail.

"I assume we'll be discussing my compensation at a more conve-nient date?"

"Let me know when."

"I'll do that." He cut contact.

With a ship on the way, Buria caring for the girls, and my back and hand throbbing if I thought about it too much, I continued into the Master's private rooms. On the way, I mulled over what to do with the complex once I'd emptied it of Masters and slaves. The slaves weren't going to want to come back here. The Masters weren't going to get to.

While I was distracted with that, my body went through the motions of subduing and restraining two half-asleep Masters in their beds. The fact that the other rooms were empty snapped me back into the present situation. If they had been alerted, and it appeared they had because their beds were a mess like someone had jumped up and left in a hurry, they were now probably armed and sweeping through the complex to find me. If they were smart, one of them would have barricaded himself in the vid room to communicate with the others. Before I headed back there, I paused to apply most of a tube of healing gel that was sitting on a countertop in the last of the bedroom suites I'd searched. The pain in my back eased greatly. I took care of the hole in my hand as well. The tank would take care of the rest later.

In the midst of attempting to infiltrate the local network to access the vid feeds through my link, Stassia slipped into my head, sounding tired and annoyed. *"What's got you all excited?"*

"Shouldn't you be sleeping by now?"

"Answer the question."

"I'll fill you in later." The answer certainly wasn't going to do anything toward making up for missing Ikeri's farewell dinner, but I didn't exactly care at the moment. Despite the pain, I was enjoying myself.

"You better."

"Get some sleep. I'll be home soon."

She sent a burst of aggravation and then went silent. As annoyed as she was, giving her more time to cool off or at least be sound asleep by the time I got there would be in my favor.

Had I given in to Stassia's wishes and stayed home for Ikeri's dinner, I wouldn't have had the chance to get to know Buria. Buria would have still been a slave to Fa'yet, and I wouldn't have been any wiser. Those girls would become slaves, and everyone else would eventually be sold off while the Masters counted their credits. This little time apart from Stassia was a good thing, and not just for me.

I tried to get into the vid feeds again, but the network here was unfamiliar and would take far more time than I had. Ready for opposition, I burst into the vid room. It was unoccupied. I allowed myself a moment to again scan the feeds. There were at least two Masters mid-tirade at the guard slaves. That room was going to be a challenge. Though I didn't spot any other men, I didn't know if that meant their numbers had dwindled that far or if it was because they knew where the cameras were and how to avoid them.

Deciding to give the gel time to work before facing the armed guard slaves, I located the door controls and unlocked them all. Then I went for the pleasure slaves. They hurried out of their beds and came to stand in the open area by the door.

"How may we serve you?"

"You can grab your clothes and follow me."

"These are our clothes." One of them bent low to further illustrate the mostly sheer, not-enough-even-there-to-be-considered-clothing that she wore.

"That's all you have?"

"We need nothing more. How may we serve you?"

"You can follow me." I turned back to the door.

"We are not allowed to leave this room, but we can entertain you here. Which of us would you prefer? Perhaps more than one?"

Thank Geva Stassia wasn't in my head just then. I muffled our connection as much as I was able. If she'd sensed my emotions before this, I certainly didn't need her to get an update.

"While that does sound intriguing, how about we focus on getting out of here?"

"But we can't leave."

"Sure you can. The door is open. I'll show you where to go."

They looked at one another but didn't move.

"This isn't a test. No Masters are going to beat you if you follow me."

They'd just started to shuffle forward tentatively when I heard someone come up behind me.

I spun around to find another Master standing there. Since he was far too close for me to draw anything to shoot him with, I opted to punch him instead. My formerly grey hand worked well for such tasks. The Master fell backward into the doorframe with a loud thump. He scrambled back to his feet with a metal rod in his hands.

The women shrank back.

That didn't bode well. I gave the rod some space and drew my stunner. As I fired, he lunged forward, slamming the rod into my leg. He fell to the floor and stayed there. My calf went numb. While that was annoying, it didn't hinder me from rummaging around the room until I found a couple silken ropes to tie him up with.

"Come on. I'd rather get to safety before I happen across another one of them."

The women stared at me.

"How are you still on your feet?" one of them asked.

"Should I not be?"

She shook her head and pointed to the rod on the floor. "They make you numb all over with a single touch. The Masters can do anything to you and you can't stop it."

I supposed that was one more thing I had to thank Nan and her Arpex-fusing for.

"I'm special, I guess." Or something. Special, made it sound positive. While the end result of the process had been useful in unexpected ways, I still wasn't ready to call it anything good. There were too many memories and whispers to remind me of the truth.

"Did you feel it at all?" asked another one, reaching down to run her hand over my leg.

"Part of my leg is numb, but that's it. Why?"

She smiled. "I wish I had skin like that."

"No, you don't." Then again, considering what she'd been through, maybe she did.

"As much as I'd like to talk more about this numbing rod weapon, we need to go."

"Where?" asked one of them.

"First stop is the warehouse so you can find some real clothes. If you get on the ship dressed like that, the crew is going to be far too distracted to rescue you."

"Rescue?" They looked at each other as if the word was out of the realm of possibility.

The reminder of utter hopelessness hit me like a punch in the gut. I shuddered as a wave of grey memories rushed over me. It would take time, but they too would learn to hope again.

"Yes. I have a ship large enough for all of you on the way." I headed to the door, not waiting to see if they were following. Their bare feet didn't make much noise and their clothing made even less. Not that going into a fight nearly naked was appealing to me, but I had to admit that it was pretty damn silent.

We met another Master in the large training room. He held one of the high-powered, rapid-firing rifles and aimed at me. I'd much rather he'd have had one of the stunning rods. However, I had a grenade in my pocket and it had been altogether too long since I'd used one of those. The women had frozen upon seeing him. I activated the orb and tossed it. It exploded right in front of him. There wasn't much left, which was damn handy, but eventually, someone was going to have to clean that up and replace some flooring. The distant part of my mind made a note of it.

One of the women threw up. The others huddled around her.

"Let's keep moving," I said.

We got to the warehouse without further delay. They eyed the rows of racks and shelves with amazement.

"Take what you want, but only what you can carry. Start with clothes. You'll need them where you are going."

"Where are we going?" one of them asked.

"Somewhere safe for now. We'll sort out the rest later."

"Are you our new Master now?" asked another.

"Not exactly." I counted them, making sure they were all there. "Keep an eye on one another. If one of the Masters finds you, work together and you can overtake him."

"He'll use the rod."

"He can't use it on all of you at the same time, can he?"

She shook her head.

"There you go then. Like I said, stick together. You will all be getting out of here. Don't let him stop you."

"Yes, Master."

"Don't call me that."

"Yes, Ma... What should we call you?"

"Advisor will work for now."

They nodded and set upon the clothing racks like rabid animals.

I went back to the messy training room and crossed to the unlocked door leading to the hospitality slaves. Untami saw me the moment I entered their room and strode over as quickly as her tight skirt allowed.

"You've come for one of us?"

"No, I'm getting all of you out of here."

Her perfectly manicured brows rose. "You're purchasing all of us?"

"Sure, yes. I purchased all of you." If it would make this go faster, I'd tell them what made more sense to their brainwashed minds.

"Now, gather up your things and follow me."

"We aren't allowed to take these things with us. They belong to the Masters."

"They said it was all right."

She put her hands on her hips. "The Masters didn't say so."

I cursed the men here and what their actions were making me have to say. "I own your contracts now. I said so. Take what you want and let's go."

One of them looked ready to ask a question.

"Don't question me. Move. Quickly."

They bumped into one another in their hurry to fold blankets, don clothes, and gather up their few things, most of which appeared to be personal care items. Not one of them had anything of value. At least they were slightly better off than the pleasure slaves.

Everything was going great until my traveling line of well-mannered slaves spotted the splattered Master bits on the training room floor. Even that wouldn't have been so bad, except his head had remained generally whole and therefore identifiable.

"What happened to this Master?" Untami gave me an accusing glare.

"I'd appreciate it if you didn't look at me that way. I'm trying to save you."

"Steal us, you mean."

"I did almost sign a contract, and I still could if that would ease your conscience. Let's agree to call your ownership a grey area for now."

She shook her head. "We can't go with you. We will be punished."

"Does it look like he's in any condition to punish you? Let me worry about the Masters."

"It's not your body they will beat or use," said another of them.

"They won't be touching any of you again."

The slaves mumbled amongst themselves.

"If you don't mind, the pleasure slaves would probably like some assurance that I'm not dead yet. Can we keep moving?"

"You've released them from their chamber?" Untami asked, her face incredulous.

"Yes, of course. I'm releasing all of you."

"I see."

For being rescued, they certainly didn't appear pleased about it. Maybe they'd take to the idea once they also got to fall upon the supplies in the warehouse. That had livened up the pleasure slaves.

She waved the others to follow. We arrived in the warehouse without further incident. The pleasure slaves seemed happy to see the new arrivals. They hurried over to show them what all they'd found from the shelves. The hospitality slaves watched the pleasure slaves with disdain and muttered amongst themselves.

I didn't have time to deal with the slave hierarchy. They were all going to be the same level of free soon enough.

"Stock up. All of you," I commanded.

Untami, the only one not scowling at the babbling pleasure slaves, worked her way over to me. "You are aware they have other training?"

"What kind of other training? You didn't mention that on the tour." And I'd been too busy getting information out of the salesman to pay actual attention to the lengthy skills lists he'd put in front of me. Sure, he'd mentioned that all the slaves were cross-trained to a degree, but the hostile edge in Untami's voice made my nerves tingle.

"They have triggers, making them just as deadly as the guards," she said with a smile as if she were suddenly back on her sales pitch tour. Her voice rang out clearly in the vast space. "A dog obeys."

The eight pleasure slaves dropped their gleefully gathered goods and turned their full attention to Untami. The other women backed away.

"Him." Untami pointed at me.

As much as I may or may not have fantasized about a bunch of nearly naked women running at me, a warehouse in some back corner of the universe wasn't the setting I'd envisioned. Nor did it involve their faces transforming from welcoming and teasing to extremely focused or adopting stances that meant I was going to have to fight them. Then again, that did sound like how one of my dreams would have gone if it was based on the reality of my generally unpredictable life.

"Oh come on. I'm trying to help all of you."

Untami held up her hand, pausing their advance. "You're trying to get us all killed."

"Think about it. The Masters wouldn't kill you. You're an investment they've put a lot of time and effort into."

"We can't leave. Our place is here," Untami said adamantly. "If you've truthfully purchased us, show me the contract."

She shook her head again before I had a chance to say anything. "You're lying. A Master would be accompanying you. He would help you pick the right slave for your needs. You are trying to harm us." She stood back, cautioning the others to remain behind her. "I will protect us all. I will be rewarded for my service."

"You definitely will not be rewarded by me unless you turn them off."

"Only a Master knows how to deactivate them. Otherwise, they will return to their natural state once you have been terminated." She lowered her hand and nodded toward me.

"I'm not fond of that outcome." I started backward, recalling the turns and distance to the door that led back to the Master's maze of rooms.

The slaves closed in. Several of them had located weapons from the shelves. One of them fired into my chest.

I worked my way through the corridors in reverse, keeping my exposed back out of view of the scantily-clad sleeper assassins. This caused two wrong turns before I found my way to the room where I'd left one of the subdued and restrained Masters.

"You're going to call them off," I informed him. "Or I'm going to kill them all."

He remained silent and decidedly smug. Thankfully the size and layout of the room prevented them from coming at me all at once. I was able to knock them aside without causing any permanent harm.

"Call them off."

He sat there, smiling.

I sent one of the women flying across the room. She hit the wall and didn't get back up. The next one encountered my fist, the natural one, and dropped like a rock at my feet.

By the time the fourth one fell, his smile had vanished. The fifth one came at me with a knife, but rather than a satisfying slash to my neck, the blade left only a scratch. The Master paled and his mouth dropped open.

"What are you?" he asked.

"Annoyed, verging on really pissed off. Now, call them off before anyone is seriously injured."

"What guarantee do I have that you won't kill me the moment I do?"

"You were included in those not being seriously injured. We both have investments to protect."

He uttered a few words in a language I didn't know. The three slaves still on their feet stopped, looking around as if lost.

"See, that wasn't so hard," I said to the Master. "The rest of you, drop your weapons, gather up your friends and let's get out of here."

"Where are you taking them?" the Master asked.

"Don't worry, you'll be coming too."

The slaves turned to regard me with terror-filled eyes. "You're taking the Masters too? You said we would be safe."

"And I meant it. He can't harm you right now, can he?"

They shook their heads slowly.

"Nor will he later. Not if he wants to live."

"You can't do this," said the Master. He struggled within his bindings to sit up straighter against the wall, trying hard to gain an ounce of authority. "We have backers, investors. We have a contract with the government. They're a good customer. You think they will let you live?"

"I don't think they have any say in the matter. Now, unless you'd prefer to be unconscious or I try out one of those nifty numbing sticks you so enjoy using, I'd suggest you keep your mouth shut."

I still didn't have feeling in my calf. How long would that last and would it be less for me given my alteration? I made a note to myself to confiscate a few of the rods for further examination.

We left the Master in his room on the floor, and I helped the conscious slaves carry the others back to the warehouse. Gamnock contacted me briefly to let me know the ship was about five hours out and that I owed him.

The five hours was a pleasant surprise. We weren't that far out from the Narvan then, or maybe it was just a straight shot with the jump gates. But that meant I had five hours to make sure the Masters stayed contained, and I had yet to approach the guard slaves. Best to clean up my existing mess first so I didn't have Masters coming at me from both sides.

Untami needed to be dealt with before I could leave the slaves alone. Whether she'd acted out of misguided loyalty to the Masters or she was one of their pets, she couldn't be allowed to walk free. I didn't want to hurt her until I knew which side she was on. I checked my stunner to see that the charge was getting low. It wasn't a weapon I normally had much call for, but if I meant to keep as many Masters alive as possible to answer for their actions, then I was going to need all the charge it had left.

I settled for escorting Untami away from the others. We walked through the storage room to the outside so I could make sure the guards and Masters I'd left outside were still unconscious. They were, but the first of them was beginning to stir.

Before Untami got it in her head to fight back herself, I whipped her arms around behind her back and hauled her inside the storage building where I'd found the young girls. She must have remembered the place because her uncooperative steps came to a dead stop.

Her voice shook. "What are we doing in here?"

"You're going to wait here and reconsider acting against me." I shoved her into the container next to where Eris had been kept and used the severed finger to lock it. Then I went out to collect the waking guard and the rest of the men I'd subdued. I could get the ones I'd already restrained once the guard slaves had been taken care of.

I'd just tossed the last of the men from outside the storage room into a container and double-checked the locks on all the filled units when a bullet hit me between the shoulder blades, right in the damned hole in my armor. Despite my skin absorbing the brunt of the impact, all air evacuated my lungs.

Gasping, I spun around, ready to fire, when I realized it was one of the guard slaves I'd watched practicing earlier. The one Buria had pointed out.

"I don't want to hurt you," I said.

"Put your weapon down." She watched me with the intensity of the sleeper assassin slaves, but she was fully alert and aware.

If she thought I was a threat to her sisters, to her family, as Buria seemed to consider these women, she wasn't going to be easily convinced of my intentions. People didn't just barge in and attempt to rescue these women every day. Or ever. No matter how much they may have dreamed about such a thing when they'd first come here.

Hells, I hadn't really expected Merkief or Jey to help free me from the High Council either, and I'd known them for years beforehand. I was a stranger here and how long had these women been here undergoing thorough training?

"I'm trying to help you. All of you," I said calmly.

"You're invading our home."

The captured men inside the shipping containers pounded on the walls. Their muffled shouts encouraged her to kill me quickly.

She took up a solid footing and gauged the distance between us, her gaze flowing over me in a clear estimation of armor and kill shot possibilities. She reminded me of Neko a few years ago, determined to do the job no matter what the cost. He was comfortable enough to give me shit about the cost these days, but he'd been dead serious about the work back then.

"Buria was here with me. You remember her? She recommended that I purchase you."

"You're not purchasing anyone. You're stealing. The punishment for theft is death." She aimed for my chest and fired three shots at the same point. She was testing my fucking armor.

While I did appreciate that she hadn't gone for my head, I was sore enough already, dammit.

"You didn't purchase Buria either. She belongs to another. Did you steal her too?"

"No. Please, put the gun down. I'm getting all of you out of here. I'll take you to Buria. You can talk to her yourself."

I glanced around, praying she was alone, that the other guard slaves were still safely back in their quarters. My odds against the remainder of the Masters and a couple guards was one thing, but twenty-some well-trained and armed slaves gunning for me was quite another. And I didn't want to harm any of them. They were only doing what they were trained for.

She watched me, taking in every detail with a calculating gaze. Maybe I was getting somewhere.

"I'm not a danger to you."

The pounding inside the containers intensified.

Her finger rested on the trigger.

"Please, don't make me shoot you."

"Your actions are your choice. You must be punished for them."

She aimed for my head.

I went for cover, but the bullet grazed my temple. No matter how modified my skin was, taking another chance of her hitting her mark was out of the question. So was walking away from all the other women I could rescue.

Making my own peace with letting Jey and Kess sacrifice one life each to prove the futility of the Arpex modification was one thing, but now, staring at the one life here, one I was going to have to take to save the rest, I felt sick. This was nothing like the contract jobs I'd done early on in my service to Anastassia or to the Council.

I hovered there behind the shipping container, thoughts racing. The innocent people I'd killed in service to the Arpex had haunted me for years, in fact, I sometimes still saw them in my sleep. Could I add this woman to their number?

Did I have a choice if I wanted to get me and everyone else out of there alive?

Filled with regret, I listened hard for her location and then swung out from the container to fire.

She went down with nothing more than a gasp, and then it was over. I approached her slowly, not wanting to see the light dim from her eyes but unable to look away.

"Please let this be the only one," I muttered to Geva and anyone else who might be listening.

FIVE

"Vayen?" Stassia's voice crept into my head despite my stifling our connection.

"I'm fine."

"Actually fine or the fine where you mean fuck off?"

"Honestly, a bit of both. Really though, when was the last time I told you to fuck off?"

"In words? A couple of weeks ago, but you've been saying it without words nearly every day."

I'd never been a good patient and my recovery had seemed like months. Long, incredibly boring months of Stassia hawking over my every move.

"Sorry, it's just..."

"I know. I get it." I felt her reaching out a bit more, examining with the remnants of her Seeker abilities. *"Are you hurt?"*

"Nothing serious."

She sighed. *"This is why I didn't want you to leave the house. Do you want Neko?"*

"Stassia, please. I'm fine."

"If you say so."

She still had that annoying Seeker tone down. Why couldn't the Arpex have taken that? But at least she wasn't demanding a jump point to send Neko after me whether I wanted him or not. She was just tired and aggravated. Those were Stassia traits I knew how to deal with.

"I'm waiting on transport for a valuable shipment. I may be a while."

"Just come home in one piece, all right? Neither of us can take another recovery period any time soon."

"I will."

I cut contact and moved the dead woman out of the main walkway. Taking a deep breath, and went back into the warehouse.

"Did Idra find you?" asked one of the pleasure slaves.

"Yes, she did." And now I had a name to go with the face I'd be seeing in my nightmares.

"Oh good. She wanted to make sure the guards were involved in your plan."

They were involved all right, but I didn't want to kill any more of them. They deserved to earn a good salary from the training they had been put through. Something positive had to come of the years they'd been tortured by the Masters.

I left the slaves in the warehouse once again and went through the training room, down the hall to the guards' wing. Taking a second to focus, I got the stunner ready in one hand and a pulse pistol in the other. No telling whether I was going to have to defend myself against all of them at once, in which case drastic and unfortunate measures would be called for, or if I could pick off a few by simply knocking them out and reevaluate from there.

I hit the panel on the wall by the door with my elbow.

Four Masters stood against the far wall, fully dressed and armed. It seemed those remaining had chosen to make a stand where they had adequate backup. One of them addressed the crowd of guard slaves. "Prove yourself and you will be rewarded. Go."

Four women detached themselves from the group, coming at me, two on each side. I hit two of them with a stunner blast. The other two fired into my coat.

The Master swore, his tone clear even though I didn't know the language. Then he switched to Trade. "No. Fools! Don't aim for the armor. Aim for the head." He waved another two to proceed from the side that I'd already dealt with.

All four aimed at my head. There wasn't any cover. The only option was to perform the quickest Jump I could manage. My default go-to was the tank room on the ship. I arrived there without any bullets in my head, for which was I was grateful. However, I needed to get back and figure out a way to deal with the slaves that wouldn't harm them.

It occurred to me that we had an armory on the ship where I could resupply. I exchanged a few of my usual weapons for three fully charged stunners. They weighed less, making my coat feel off-balance, but one new face haunting my sleep was plenty.

I Jumped back but had to start from the point I knew in the atrium.

That meant working my way back through all the halls, the training room, and into the guard slave chambers that I'd so recently vacated.

"He's fast. Don't let him escape again," the Master shouted.

With no time to waste, I slipped a stunner into both hands and hit as many of the guards on both sides as I could. Two of the Masters also went down. With half the threat unconscious on the floor, I felt better about the odds.

"Use the spray," a Master said, using forceful gestures to urge the remaining eleven guards to attack as though he would have shoved the women at me had they had been in reach. One of the two Masters joined them, his eyes filled with rage and a snarl on his lips.

I discharged both stunners on the oncoming threat. Most of them fell. Those that didn't, rushed at me, intent on knocking the stunners from my hands. That was a foolish goal since both were empty. They needed to stop me from drawing the third one.

"We don't need him alive." The Master fell back into his own language for a moment, ordering something, or maybe the same thing, then seeming to notice that half of the women didn't understand him, he slipped back into Trade. "Eliminate. Now."

Yet, for all the yelling about aiming for my head and eliminating me, the guards were taking their time in doing so. Not a single one made eye contact with the others, not giving any impression that they were working together to disobey their orders. Yet, that appeared to be what they were doing. At least, I thought I might have them secretly on my side, until one raised a small canister in my face and released a spicy perfume scented yellow mist.

I waited for the room to start spinning, my skin to start bubbling off, to gasp for air, or any number of other unpleasant things. Instead, the room took on soft edges, as did the women around me. I didn't feel any hostility from them. It was almost like they were watching me with interest. Like maybe they expected me to do something like keel over or go raving mad.

The Master who had approached with them raised his gun. I hit him with the new stunner. He dropped to the floor.

The women glanced openly at each other then. One looked from me to the Master. The one closest to me shrugged, more with her brows and a tiny dip of her chin than anything else.

The two standing nearest the remaining Master parted, giving me a clear shot. I took it without question.

"I assume you have been trained in methods of restraint?"

The one who had signaled the others nodded.

"Bind them and bring them out to the storage building." I gave them directions, assuming they hadn't been allowed outside. "Find an empty container and store them there." I pulled the severed finger from my pocket and held it out. "You'll need this. Our ride will be here in roughly four hours."

"Ride where?" asked one of the guards as she hesitantly took the finger between two of her own.

"Somewhere safe from these so-called Masters, where you can decide what you'd like to do once you've had a chance to explore some options."

They stared at me blankly. It occurred to me that options were something they'd thought were long gone. "I'll lay out your options later. For now, store the Masters." I waved them onto their assigned task, figuring they were used to following orders.

I was starting to get a lightheaded, and despite the threat that had just been eliminated, my muscles relaxed and the rush that usually accompanied this stage of the job remained distant. A pleasant warmth unfurled in my veins like I'd had two too many drinks. On the further plus side, the weight of Idra's death tucked itself away in the box deep inside where I buried all my other nightmare fodder. I was sure it would slip out again, but for now, I'd enjoy the reprieve.

Several of the women huddled around each of the Masters. They bent over, securing the four men in restraints. Their uniforms accented their backsides with great care. I blinked the thought away. Eight of them carried the men out of the room.

The others strolled closer, their hands empty of weapons.

"You're not hiding any more Masters in here, are you?"

"No, we heard them say they were the last ones on-site. They had hoped to hold out here until reinforcements came in the morning."

"Good. I think I might need to lie down for a few minutes."

"We have many beds to choose from. Would you like company?" Two women appeared on either side of me, their hands stroking the sleeves of my armored coat. I wished it was my skin. Their eyes were bright, their skin, these two a similar brown tone to mine, appeared edged in a hazy glow.

I shook my head. "I need to get back to the warehouse. The others are waiting."

The one who had shrugged came up in front of me, a soft smile on her full lips. "We have hours to wait, yes?" she asked in broken

Trade. Her voice held an accent I couldn't place but I wanted to hear more of it.

"Yes." I glanced at the door where I'd come from, where I needed to go.

"You're wounded," said a concerned voice behind me. "Let us help you." She spoke to some of the others in their own language. Footsteps drifted away.

"I put gel on it. I'll be fine."

"It should be cleaned and bandaged. We have plenty of time." The two women at my arms guided me toward the nearest bed.

"I need to make sure all the guards and Masters are secured. The other slaves need to gather supplies for the trip. Maybe eat something. I think I forgot to eat. I feel odd."

"We'll take care of it. You've done enough."

"Maybe he'd like some privacy. Some of them are like that," whispered the one on my left.

"Use my bed," said the one behind me.

"Mine's closer. We can just send the others away when they wake up," said the one in front of me while tossing a pretty smile over her shoulder.

"Any flat surface will do," I said. "I just need to catch my breath for a minute."

"How did you do that? Transport yourself so quickly? You vanished," said the one on my right.

I vaguely realized we were now sitting on the edge of a bed large enough for three of me. "Lots of practice. You were going to shoot me." I eyed the four of them, giving them all a taste of how annoyed that made me.

"If we wanted to shoot you, we would have been faster about it." One of them tugged on the sleeve of my coat.

"What are you doing?" I asked, not really protesting.

"Making you more comfortable. It's not often we get men like you here."

"The last one, that one who bought Buria and Nena, he was a fine one. Remember him?" asked one of the others.

She giggled. "Buria and Nena were very lucky."

Buria. "I came here with Buria. She asked me to help you."

By the sudden jerkiness of their removing my coat, I gathered that news had caught them off guard.

"I need my coat on. Leave it." But I didn't really, not with the

Arpex-altered skin. And they'd already taken it off. Now they were busy oohing and aahing over my host of bared weaponry.

One pointed to my pulse pistol. "I've never seen one like this before. How does it work?"

"Figures they wouldn't let you have those here. They're very powerful. Lots of damage."

The four of them found spots on the bed around me, their bodies rubbing against mine as they examined everything. Their uniforms were silken soft and form-fitting. Every touch sent a shiver through me. I wanted more.

"Saka, we need to get his shirt off to look at his back."

The one with the mesmerizing accent said something to one of the others who handed her a white plas case. She set the case on the bed and opened it to reveal assorted medical supplies.

"Do you mind if we take these off?" Saka asked, tugging on a holster strap. "It will help us make sure you're properly treated. No one wants to buy damaged goods."

"He's not for sale, Saka. He's the one buying us, remember?"

I lost my focus for a long moment, bewitched by Saka's pale blue eyes. "I'm not buying you. I'm freeing you."

"Shh." A finger brushed over my lips. "We'll take good care of you. You did overtake the Masters, after all. It's the least we can do."

"You had weapons. Why didn't you overtake them yourselves?"

They looked at me like I'd lost my mind. "Harming any Master is forbidden."

The blissful haze beckoned me to relax, but thoughts kept distracting me. "But you have the numbers. And weapons."

The one with the accent shook her head. "Hurt one, all are punished. All." She nodded toward the door that led to the rest of the complex.

Saka nodded. "We only see a few Masters at a time. There are always more. Besides, where would we go? Here we are cared for."

Being cared for was nice. Their hands drifted over me.

"I'm glad you're not like the others. They were upset that they weren't going to be sold," I said.

"When they are sold, they spend the rest of their lives managing a household, serving a family, entertaining a new Master." Saka rose on her knees to slide her hand under one of my holster straps, positioning her breasts right in my face as she slipped the strap over my head. "We are safe here. When we're sold, our job is to defend our

Master, to give our life for theirs."

"There is that, I suppose." I considered tearing my attention away from the view, but more of the same surrounded me. This was far better fantasy enactment than the near-naked women attacking me in the warehouse.

I cleared my throat and attempted to focus on what I needed to do. "Can you post someone in the atrium room? The one where customers arrive? Buria will be back at some point and she needs to know the situation."

I could have found her contact connection through my link, but it was too much work. I was enjoying myself in the now without having to think too much about anything further.

When the last of my web of weaponry was removed, my shirt vanished a second behind it. The four of them let out a collective gasp.

"Don't mind the scars."

"That's a lot of scars," Saka said, tracing a long one on my chest with her finger.

"I've been through a lot of shit." But I didn't want to think about that right now either. The four warm bodies clustered around me, their soft voices filled with concern and awe, their warm hands on my skin.

"Why don't you lie down here so we can clean up your back. I'm afraid it might hurt. It's a bit messy back there."

"I'll be fine."

"From the looks of you, I don't doubt that a bit."

One of them giggled. "He's much bigger than the other one."

"I can hear you, you know."

"You're much more resilient too." She ran her hand down my neck to skirt the dipped scar from the Arpex barb. "I've never seen anyone resist the spray before."

The spray. A drug. A drug that had a distantly familiar effect. The mist had looked yellow, so much like the golden bottle the High Council had forced upon me years before. While it didn't have the same take-on-the-world sensation of their version, the pleasure and craving of touch were certainly in full force.

Stassia wasn't going to like this.

She certainly wasn't going to like hearing how I was in bed with four women. But they were treating my back. She wanted me home in one piece. No one was in my head doing the things Stassia excelled at.

"What is the purpose of this spray?"

"You feel the effects, surely?" asked one of the two who sat behind me.

One of them was working on bandaging the wound on my back. Saka lazily traced lines of scars with a touch that left eddies of tingling warmth. Geva, I could feel her touch. Really feel it, not the distant sensation of touch my Arpex altered skin had left me, but like before.

All the skin-to-skin contact was making it hard to keep my focus on anything but the enticing daze of pleasure that begged me to let go for a little while.

Dammit. Letting go wasn't an option. I needed to keep talking. "Yes, but why do you use it on customers?"

"The Masters wish you to be satisfied with your purchase. No one wants to be returned for poor performance."

"I can imagine that wouldn't be a good thing."

"No, it's not." Saka stroked the skin beside the bandage, creating wonderful tingling spirals that made it hard to think. "Under the influence of the spray, inhibitions are removed and sensation is heightened."

Another ran her fingers through my hair. There was nothing wrong with that, was there? Stassia would probably tell me there was, but everyone other than me was fully clothed. There was no harm in enjoying myself a little.

"We see what you want, what you like," said the one with the accent. Her every word made my stomach flip.

"What we'd be in for, if you get my meaning," said Saka, with her fingers in my hair, her lips so close to my ear that her warm breath made me shiver.

The other two tugged at my boots.

"What are you doing?"

"You'll be more comfortable if we take these off."

That was true. I would indeed be more comfortable. Nothing wrong with taking my boots off. No one was going to be excited by my feet.

"Have the other women been taken care of? They're safe, right?"

"Yes." The fingers in my hair moved to my neck. "They're being watched over. Someone is taking them to the kitchen to eat."

"Good. Very good." I wasn't sure which I was happier with, the news or Saka's strong fingers working kinks out of my neck.

Then there were two more sets of hands working on my feet. People got massages all the time, hells, Stassia used to give them as part of her Seeker treatments. There was nothing wrong with relaxing.

"So, what do you normally see with this spray?" I asked to distract myself from the swelling sensation that had nothing to do with relaxing.

Geva, that wasn't supposed to be happening. First with Buria and now this. No denying it, my bond was definitely not in full force like it used to be.

One of them giggled. "We've seen a lot."

"We've seen a man grab the nearest woman and have at her. Another worked his way through most of us before he settled on one he liked best because she screamed loudest."

"Men who enjoy hurting, choking, restraining."

"Or that one who didn't want to be touched, but wanted us to have at each other."

"Watch you have sex?"

"No, fight."

"Well, that's different."

They laughed.

Did I want to know? I didn't. Not really, but the words came out anyway. "What about the one who bought Buria and Nena?"

"We don't know. He looked us all over, talked to a few, and then picked. He never touched them, not here that we saw."

That brought me a measure of peace. I thought I knew Fa'yet after all these years, but he'd always been a private man. "I think he's been good to them."

"This makes us happy," said the voice that made my insides quiver.

"If you'd like to roll over, we can continue," whispered Saka.

Rolling over. That would be most welcome given the straining going on in my pants. Yes, please. I shifted onto my back. The four of them came into focus. Their uniforms were gone, leaving them only in sheer undergarments.

Without a second thought, I rolled off the bed and scooped up my shirt. "When did that happen?" I waved at their nearly naked bodies.

They looked at one another, laughter barely hidden under their wavering grins.

"No seriously. Put your clothes back on."

I yanked my shirt on to show them how it was done.

One pointed at my pants with raised brows. "Are you sure you want us to get dressed?"

They were all very pleasant to look at, sturdy, muscled, not waify like Jey's wife. They'd earned their form with training. Training I was going to employ throughout the Narvan. The Narvan that I'd built with Stassia. Who was home waiting for me.

"Yes. Dress. Now."

Saka and the two that had brought me to the bed hesitantly reached for their clothes where they lay on the floor beside the bed. The other stood, stalking closer, each step accentuating her every curve.

"You are sure?" purred the voice I couldn't resist.

"Marta, give it a rest. He's not into us."

"Do you like men?" asked Marta.

I shook my head, trying to make words happen, but she was right there. All I had to do was reach out and pull her closer. I'd never had physical sex with anyone other than Stassia. What would it be like? Was it the same no matter the partner, or were they all different?

The others had paused, all still in various states of undress. There were four willing and consenting women right here. That take-on-the-universe feeling began to surge. Oh Geva, I'd missed this. I had no idea how much until just then. It was as if the very air around me was alive, invigorating and electric. I was free of everything that held me back, held me down.

"There it is." Saka grinned, pulling her uniform back down and tossing it on the floor. "Took long enough."

The other three gathered in front of me.

"So, what do you like?" asked Marta as she stroked my chest through my shirt. No, her hand was under my shirt.

Two took my arms. They started toward the bed again. "One at a time? All at once?" asked one of them.

Fuck. I wanted to go there. Really wanted to. But a shrill panicked voice broke through all the glow and tingle to scream at me to stop. I planted my bare feet.

"No. None," I distantly heard myself say. Fucking conscience. "Get dressed."

Saka cocked her head. "Really?"

"Yes." I dislodged myself from them one at a time and then forced myself to step back.

"One of you toss me my boots." I didn't trust myself to be close to them until they'd hidden all of their very appealing assets.

"Did we do something not to your liking?" one asked, her body draped across the bedcover in a languid pose.

I rubbed a hand over my face. "You're all very...good. There is much liking. If I weren't joined, I'd be on that bed right now."

"What is joined? We didn't learn that one," asked another, slowly bending over to pick up her uniform.

"Married? Contracted? I don't know what you call it out here."

The one on the bed chuckled, her lips drawing into a wicked smirk. "You've got a woman, and that's stopping you?"

"Oh yes." I slipped on my boots and buckled them securely. Dressed. I was dressed, but I needed more of a barrier. I needed my weapons. All of them. On my body right now.

"I'd like to meet this woman," said Saka.

"I'm sure you will. I just hope it isn't while she's killing me."

"That would be a definite shame. Would you like us to prevent that from happening? We would be happy to serve you," said Marta.

While I liked the sound of that and my body was very much on board with their offer, that annoying voice in my head was vehemently against it.

"Not doubting your abilities, but if she wanted to kill me, there is no number of you that could prevent that from happening."

"Now I really want to meet her." Saka's pale blue eyes danced merrily.

They were beautiful, like the water in a tide pool on a clear calm morning. I could fall into them and drown.

Drowning. Dying. Stassia was going to kill me if I didn't get out of here. A gurgling cough worked its way out of my throat and brought me back to reality.

"I'm going to go get some fresh air. Could you make sure everyone stays together? Post a few guards out by the storage building. Maybe a few inside too. We don't need the Masters getting out."

"Aren't they also restrained?"

"Most of them. But if they're familiar with the restraints and the containers, they may have tricks to get out of them."

Saka nodded. "You can stay. We will leave you be."

"While that might be true. I don't know as I would leave you be. It will be easier if I'm not in the same room."

She grinned. "So it isn't us then?"

Don't look at her eyes. Don't look.

I paused on her lips instead. I wanted to feel them on me. Right now. I started toward her before catching myself. Great Geva, I needed to leave before I got myself into more trouble than I already was.

I hadn't been bonded when I'd been in the throes of the drug before and it had allowed one to form without me giving any direct thought to it. Now that I did have a bond in place, one of my own accord even, it didn't seem to matter. The bond was still there if I bothered to look, but that seemed so much effort with all the willing and eager stimuli at my fingertips. The only thing keeping me in line was that damned voice of reason, but I had little doubt I could strangle it if given enough incentive. And there was far too much of that in front of me.

Then again, even without the spray, my bond with Stassia seemed less compelling than before. Maybe the self-induced bond wasn't as strong as the one Chandi's drug had imposed on me. I also hadn't been out of the house to encounter this problem since the Arpex conversion had been dialed back. Whatever the cause, this whole sudden freedom and awareness without some manic crisis to distract me into over-worked mode, was exhilarating. And so damned tempting.

After arming up as quickly as possible, I grabbed my coat, not bothering to take the time to put it on. For a moment I considered Jumping somewhere else, but with the haze of the drug in full force in my system, I didn't trust myself not to Jump right into the bedroom on Artor and convince Stassia to help me out. The job here wasn't done. More Masters or other armed parties could show up at any time and punish the women for my actions. I wouldn't let that happen.

I spent the next couple of hours walking outside in serious discomfort. Each step was a constant reminder of what had nearly happened. No matter how hard I tried to focus on anything else, the temptation that had been laid out before me kept echoing and building until it was all-consuming.

Saka stood by the storage room, alert and armed, her back straight against the wall, long hair pulled back from her welcoming face, I completely forgot what I was going to say. All I wanted to do was be with her immediately. Out here in the open and up against the building was just fine.

Saka seemed to sense my torment and let me hang for several minutes, her eyes twinkling with mischief. I couldn't take it anymore. Words refused to form.

"Did you need something?" She stepped closer, hand wrapping around my neck.

I nodded.

"Lucky me."

All I could see were her lips, and I wanted to kiss them very badly.

No reason was going to interfere this time.

"Go ahead. No one is watching."

I glanced around. She was right. She wasn't tricking me, not entrapping me. Maybe a kiss would help ease my torture. I still had two hours before the ship would arrive. Two hours until I could corner Stassia in the bedroom and find real relief.

Saka kissed me. It wasn't me. She started it. Sure, I could have ended it. I could have walked away. Limped away, maybe, at this point. But I didn't want to leave. I wanted to be right here with my hands wandering of their own accord. It wasn't until I hit flesh with fingers that reason popped back online.

I pulled away, breathless and pissed off. How could I let the drug lull me into this? It didn't own me. Not like it had before. My mind was sound. My body was sound. But the only sound I focused on was the throbbing pulse in my body and the soft moans of Saka again pressed against me with her fingers tangled in my hair.

"No one will know," she breathed in my ear.

"I'll know." And that was something I didn't want hanging over my head even if Stassia never found out.

"Then maybe you should go walk somewhere else because I'm not inclined to take no for answer after all that."

Before I could back away, her lips had taken over mine again. We tangled there for a few minutes, or half an hour, I wasn't paying attention. Even though I didn't find any actual relief, mauling a very willing Saka did serve to distract me from the discomfort of the whole situation. I was too busy enjoying myself to be worried.

"Enough. Either we're doing this or you need to go somewhere else before I take what I want," she said.

"Like I'd let you."

"If I have my mind set to it, you will."

"Oh really." If she made a move to take control, I didn't trust myself to put up any defense. In fact, the idea of her forcing the issue had me glued on the spot.

She let out a little gasp and her face flushed. "So, that's what you like. Your eyes, they changed when I said that."

"Sometimes," I admitted. Only Stassia knew, and she knew when I wanted to be equals and when I wanted her to take command. We had an unspoken understanding, one that was so natural that even not fully remembering me, our sexual activities had fallen back into place.

"Are you daring me to try?" Her fingers toyed with my pants.

"Maybe." Could I have that sort of trust with anyone other than Stassia?

"You're not not daring me either."

"You're not wrong."

She licked her lips. "I see how much you like this game, but it is not one we were taught. Maybe you could talk me through it so I can understand what you want?"

Of course the damned Masters wouldn't teach the women to be anything other than submissive. The reminder of what she was, of where we were, cooled the excitement of what she'd started.

I pulled away. "Maybe another time. Right now I need to take a walk before I get into more trouble than I already am."

"That may be wise, as much as I'd like to serve you, I don't want your wife to kill me."

"I don't want that either."

She grinned. Dammit, why couldn't she be ugly, or at least not smiling, and not edged with the soft glow and a promise of blissful release?

Taking a walk, that's what I was going to do. I got half a step away before turning to ask, "Do you, the slaves, I mean, use the spray too?"

"Only once so we understand it. The Masters use it to evaluate where our strengths lie."

That helped kill more of the effects of the drug. Anger didn't fuel sex. At least not for me. I knew it did for some.

"I have some ideas about what to do with the Masters, but what are your thoughts?"

She stood back, her mouth hanging open a little. Or maybe she was still panting. Her lips were certainly calling to me. "You want to know what I would do?"

I moved to stand beside her, trying like all nine hells to soak up the cold from the plascrete building through the palms of my hands. Not touching and not looking at one another helped a fraction. A very minute fraction.

"Yes. How long have you been here?"

"Eight years give or take."

"How did you come to be here?"

"I was sold, like all the others. I worked for my father, but he grew frustrated when I didn't earn enough. He eventually decided that one big payout was better than the trickle I was bringing in."

"What did he have you selling?"

She gave me a sideways stare.

"Oh." Here I thought young girls were off going about normal lives, training for careers, and giggling about boys. My complicated kids weren't typical, but they were safe. I made sure of that. Too many of the children here weren't. I couldn't fathom whoring out my child.

"Yeah, oh. It wasn't that I couldn't earn more for him," she said with a hint of defiance. "It was that I chose his beatings over pleasing men most nights. My life here isn't much of a change, except now I can defend myself."

"You are employable."

"I was employable before."

"Not like you are now."

Now she was a grown woman, mid-twenties by my guess. How young had she been when her father handed her off to other men? Thoughts of Eris and Colata and what the Masters had done to them brought the driving desires of the drug haze down to a more manageable level.

"I suppose not. But really, it's more of the same."

"Saka, you are not more of the same. The Masters made you think so, but that's not how it has to be."

She huffed. "If that's so, how do you explain yourself?"

"Umm, well, you sprayed me with a drug that makes me want to screw everyone in sight."

"There is that, I suppose."

"Yes, there is that. I don't normally kiss any woman I see."

"I'm not any woman."

"You're not helping."

She laughed. "You're easy to tease, you know."

"Not normally. I haven't kissed another woman in ages. We can never speak of this again."

"If it will keep your wife off my back, then I agree."

I wanted someone on their back. I wasn't even all that particular about who it was. Saka was right there, not even an arm's length away.

Dammit. I would not be ruled by the drug. I took a step to the left to allow a little more room for sanity.

"Tell me more about what you'd like to have me do with the Masters."

"Anything?" Saka's fingers swirled lightly over the rough surface of the plascrete behind us. I wished they were on me and that I could stop watching them, but the movement was mesmerizing.

"Not saying I will do what you suggest, but I'm open to ideas."

"I do like you," she said.

"If you hated me, I'd still ask you. And if you could pretend to hate me right now, that would be really damn helpful."

"I would like to make them suffer as I did. As we all did. Especially the ones who came here young. They suffered the most," she said.

"How did you suffer?"

"I was in the container for weeks."

"I'd imagine most were."

"You'd be surprised." She let out a weary sigh. "Some only last a couple of days. The darkness gets to us all eventually."

"So you want me to lock them away in the dark for a few weeks?"

Saka nodded. "That's a start."

"What else?"

"Numb them and set some wild animals on them."

"Wouldn't that damage the merchandise?"

She gasped.

I laughed to myself. Setting wild animals upon them was fine, but enslaving the men who had done the same to her was going too far?

"They're going to be sold, and I know just the market. I hope they're good at dancing in confined spaces."

"You'd make the Masters dance?"

"They don't just dance, but yes."

"Will they get the benefit of the spray? That would make it easier for them."

"You want it to be easier for them?"

"Well, no, I suppose not."

She was quiet for a while. The dome gradually shifted cycles overhead. "How many slaves do you own?"

"None. I have employees. A lot of them. They get paid just like you'll get paid, wherever you decide to go."

"I can choose?"

"Of course."

"Can I work for you?"

"That wouldn't be a wise idea, given, you know..." I gestured toward her and my pants.

"But you will take some of us? You did come here to buy someone didn't you?"

"Actually no, I came here because Buria asked me to help her sisters. However, I may have a few job openings."

"I would like that. If you need a guard, that is."

"There would be rules that pertain to everyone in my household."

"I can follow rules." She said eagerly.

"You don't even know what my rules are."

She shrugged. "I have a feeling you'll be fair. They can't be worse than our standard contract."

After hearing Buria and all the things that were prohibited, I nodded. "Let me think on it when I have a clear head."

"How many of us would you like? Do you need either of the other two specialties? I could recommend some women."

Buria's voice echoed the same offer in my head. Now Idra, a well-trained woman who had endured all this without tasting freedom, was dead.

"I'll make my own choices."

She slipped into a submissive head bow. "Of course."

"I'm going to try that walk now. How long does this drug last?"

"Usually a few hours. But you've been different so I don't know with you."

"Great. Story of my life." I left her there before I was tempted to continue where we'd left off. The talking had helped break the single-minded focus of the drug, but I still wanted much more.

On the way to check on the others, I concluded that it might be wise to attempt to take care of this predicament myself. After knocking on a few doors and getting no response, I cautiously entered a room and activated the light. The room was empty, except for a metal bedframe. Making sure the door was locked, I switched the light back off and let my mind play out what I'd wanted to continue with Saka. No matter how hard I tried to imagine it, my hands were not her hands and none of the motions were satisfying. The soft hazy feeling of the drug refused to indulge me with the same intensity now that I was alone. Frustrated, I worked myself back into my pants.

Jumping to the tank was an option, though not a very gratifying one. And that would take time, time I'd have to leave the women on their own to defend themselves if anyone showed up in the next couple of hours to reclaim the operation. If another shift of Masters or guards arrived on site, I didn't trust the women to stand against them. Though the few guard slaves had stood aside to allow me to shoot the remaining Master, they hadn't taken the shot themselves. Their training was too ingrained.

And even if I dared slip away to the tank, there would be a record of why I went there. Jey and Stassia could read the logs. Jey had been livid the last time I'd been addicted to a version of this drug. If he got wind that I'd taken it again and tried to hide it, I'd be in for a whole lot of grief. Even worse, Stassia might not remember my addiction, but Jey would be happy to fill her in. That would ignite doubt and mistrust in our reforming relationship. I couldn't take that chance.

Resolved to letting this play out naturally, I made sure my coat was closed to hide my blatant issue before leaving the room.

The sound of women chattering guided me to a room filled with tables and chairs. Most of the stunned guard slaves had woken and had gathered with the other women. An open window to a kitchen covered one wall with a counter along it. More plates filled with food sat waiting.

"What's for dinner?" I asked, hoping food might serve as a distraction from my discomfort.

"Breakfast," corrected one of the pleasure slaves. She jumped up to grab a plate and offered it to me with a bow that put her sweet-scented hair right under my nose.

I paid the utmost attention to the ceiling as I took the plate and sat in an open chair facing the wall. The hushed chatter behind me was too loud. Half was speculation on what I intended to do with them. The other half involved what they wanted to do to me. All of it made the ache in my pants worse than my encounter with Saka.

A wicked voice in my head suggested letting them have at it so we could all get it out of our systems.

Talking myself out of my indiscretion with Saka was going to be hard enough. I didn't entertain any thoughts about Stassia forgiving me for falling into bed with the whole lot of them. The more I tried to focus on Stassia, the more the pressure grew. I knew what she liked, even the things she liked that she didn't remember yet. And she knew what I liked and didn't need to be talked through a damned thing. Fuck, I needed that ship to get here so I could get home.

I didn't know these women. For all I knew, they'd screw me into a stupor and ransack my brain. But they wouldn't. They weren't the Council, not Chandi who screwed me over in every way but physically. None of them seemed aware of probes or even natural speech. They were simply normal women looking to show appreciation for their newly gained freedom. Women who were working up the nerve to approach me. Who were standing right behind me. In fact, I was pretty sure there was a pair of breasts brushing against the back of my head. All I had to do was turn around.

A hand reached for the plate I'd emptied while my thoughts were elsewhere. Another brushed over my wrist.

"Did you treat the Masters like this?" I forced myself to ask, hoping to channel some of the anger that had helped in dealing with Saka.

The hand pulled back. "We didn't seek to touch the Masters."

"Then why do you try to touch me?"

"You act like no Master. We would thank you."

"There are other ways to thank me."

That sent a titter through the crowd. I sighed. "Everyone, back away."

I stood up and faced them. "Here's how this is going to work. You're not going to bed anyone. Sex is not a means to express gratitude. It will not be your field of employment. When the ship gets here to transport you to my system, you will not entertain the crew in your beds, or their beds, or on any surface on the ship. Is that clear?"

They all slowly nodded, some glancing and whispering to one another like I was perhaps crazy.

"If I hear that you disobeyed this order, I will assume that vocation is one you enjoy and you will be sold with the Masters."

That shut them up and brought them to attention.

"I have a lot of contacts. These contacts all have households. I will find you employment."

"Are we to be celibate then?" asked one of the pleasure slaves. "What do you expect us to do?" She gestured at the women around her.

"You have had other training that doesn't involve a bed. And no, I don't expect celibacy, but I do expect that you'll follow my rules. You'll find them much more agreeable than the Master's contract."

"So you own us?"

"For now, let's say yes and keep this simple."

Buria's peeved voice cut me off. "I thought you didn't own slaves?"

Spinning around, I found that she looked as pissed as she sounded. In the haze of the drug, she was breathtaking, even angry. Maybe more so because she was angry. I'd always been enthralled by Stassia's fire too. Maybe she was on to something with this type she claimed I had.

I pointed Buria to the door. "Outside, now."

I told myself that I needed to get her away from the others because she posed a challenge to the authority I was establishing over them. For their own good, no less. I was trying like all hells to be good.

The hallway was too confining, too close to all the others who could overhear us. Their curiosity was too ripe for that not to happen. "All the way outside."

Her annoyance deepened, but she kept pace with me without a word and joined me out in the cool air away from prying ears.

"I don't keep slaves," I hissed at her. "You might not know me well, but you do know me better than that."

"But you said..." Her anger slipped into uncertainty.

"I said what I had to so I can keep them in line until we get this situation sorted out. They haven't been outside this complex in years. They don't yet understand the opportunities that await them."

"I don't even understand."

"You will."

I glanced around, making sure none of the guard slaves were posted nearby. Without a second conscious thought, I pinned her against the wall and resumed with gusto where I'd left off with Saka.

Though Buria played the willing partner, it wasn't the same as it had been with Saka, the heat was not reciprocated. Buria's hand pressed firmly against my chest slowly registered. I broke away and found her watching me closely.

"They sprayed you, didn't they?"

"Yes. I..."

She nodded and stepped out of my arm cage, putting distance between us. "When you told me you didn't want that earlier, I didn't believe you. You've looked at me like you are now, but not as openly. The spray always brings out the truth."

"I've been trying hard not to. This drug makes everything so hard."

She chuckled. "I felt that too."

Her accelerated breathing, the curiosity in her gaze, the laugh, all said that she wasn't disagreeable to what I'd started, only hesitant.

"It was easier to resist you before the damned drug, but you're right." Geva, she was so damned tempting. And so close. And I did know her. Fa'yet trusted her and so did Stassia. So could I. All the hesitation I'd had with the other women vanished when it came to Buria. "Maybe just this one time, to help work the drug out of my system, to clear my head so I can concentrate on getting everyone out of here safely."

One step put me directly in front of her again, her body only inches away. I backed her against the wall where we'd been before her escape.

Her gaze locked onto mine. "Would you be satisfied with just this one time?"

Fucking hells. All I wanted to do was touch her and have her touch me. On second thought, I wanted a lot of things.

"Advisor, would you?"

"I don't know. I've never been inclined to find out before I met you."

Buria smiled, the one I'd been wanting to see since we'd talked to Kess at his club. She slid her hands up the front of my armor and then rested them on my shoulders, holding me away with the slightest pressure.

"I do not wish to anger you. You understand this, right?"

I nodded, imagining all the things we could be doing that wouldn't make me angry.

"You are under the influence of a powerful drug. What you want right now, you may regret tomorrow. I would not put that on you, knowing it may have massive consequences for not only me, but your daughter's care, and the Premier himself. He's mentioned how angry you can get."

Fa'yet needed to shut up. For being the quiet man he used to be, he sure talked a lot to his staff. Then again, I supposed my wrath was a good deterrent for not fucking up with Ikeri under their watch.

"When the drug is gone, if you still have the same desire, I will not stop you."

"I don't want you to feel you need to stop me, Buria. If you don't want me to touch you now or then, just say so. No consequences. I don't own you. No one does."

Buria's warm hands slid to the bare skin of the back of my neck, pulling me closer. Her armor rustled against mine. She planted a soft kiss on my cheek that left eddies of warmth behind when she leaned closer to whisper in my ear. "I never said I didn't want you to touch me."

"Now you're just being evil, woman. Back away."

She laughed as she stepped out of reach. "How have you managed to control the urges this long?"

I rubbed my face and took a deep breath, turning away from her. "Talking about things that make me angry helps. The girls, Did you got them to the Premier's estate?"

"Yes. Merona is watching over them."

Frightened kids sounded like a perfect sex deterrent. "Can you show me how they were when you left them?"

"Like before when you were in my mind?"

"Yes."

Her voice trembled as she asked, "Can you promise me that's all you'll do?"

I turned back to her. "What do you mean?"

"You're like the Premier." Her gaze dropped to her hands. "You take enjoyment in the minds of others."

"Only with a willing partner, and only if that partner also has a mind like we do. What are you getting at, Buria?"

"When the Premier chose us, he was also under the influence of the spray. He didn't touch us, not like you did just now. He touched us in here." She pointed to her forehead. "He said we were special, that he could make us work."

"You have a degree of telepathy."

She shrugged. "I've never heard anyone in my head. I don't speak that way." Buria's fingers intertwined until her knuckles turned white. "We're supposed to please our Masters, to do what they wish. But you said we won't have Masters anymore?"

"Yes." I wanted to reach out and comfort her, but that would only lead to me doing far more than comforting.

"When he fills my head with thoughts, feelings, images, it's over-whelming. It hurts. He takes over and I'm gone. I don't like it." She shook her head. "Can you make him stop?"

"Or you can. Tell him you don't like it."

"He will be angry. He chose me because of this gift he says I have. If I don't let him use it, he'll find another who will. Then what will I do?"

"You'll be a guard and not have to share his bed unless you wish to."

"I would much rather share your bed."

"Buria, you're not helping."

She smiled. "Sorry, just being honest. But if we do that, you'd protect me from your mate? We'd make sure she never found out? The Premier warned us about her anger too."

My mate. Right. "Heed that warning. If she ever found out, there'd be a bullet for both of us. I'll make you a deal, I'll talk to the Premier if you can tell me how to get this drug out of my system so I'm not a walking sex bomb."

Buria laughed so hard that tears ran down her face. It was a beautiful sight to behold even if I could only enjoy it from a distance. When she finally pulled herself together, she shook her head. "Other prospective buyers would have worked it out of their system by now. If you're going to continue to resist it, I don't know how long it will last."

"Then I need to get somewhere where I can be alone until the ship gets here."

"So you can…" She waved at my pants.

"That didn't work," I said, not hiding my frustration.

She shook with barely restrained amusement.

"Go. Quit tormenting me." I pointed her back inside. "I'm going to wait this out in the observation room. Alone. If you need me, find a camera and wave."

"How will I know where the cameras are?"

Hiding the truth wouldn't do them any favors. Who knew if the Masters distributed feeds for profit or if one of the women would run across it at some point. "They're everywhere, Buria. They watched all of you. Always."

Her merriment vanished. "You'll talk to the Premier?"

I owed her that much. "I will." As awkward as that conversation was going to be, it was the least of my worries at the moment.

She gave me a head bow and went inside.

I gave her a couple minutes to get out of my sight before I went back in and made my way to the room full of vids. The chair was quite comfortable, and after a little experimenting with the control panel, I started flipping through the feeds to verify that all the men had been subdued.

Having a task helped me ignore the drug-induced urges. Once I was sure the men had been contained out in the storage building, and noted that someone had tended to Idra's body, I worked through a few more of the vid controls to find the local news feed. A man was mid-reporting on the rising costs of plascrete and then moved onto a mine explosion that had killed fifty-two workers on some nearby colony I had no knowledge of.

As long as I could keep myself busy in this room, keep my hands off Buria and everyone else, I was in control. The drug didn't own me like before.

The interior feeds showed the women, both those I was coming to know and the younger trainees, meeting each other in various rooms, comforting one another, and guiding the timid ones into the large training room where most of them had congregated. I did my best to skim over those, not seeking out the two I did want to see. They were all safe, that was what mattered. They would all get out of this prison alive and learn how to be free. I was doing something good. Something, that perhaps, my disdain-filled daughter might find redeeming.

I found the feed of the port landing pad and stared at that until my eyes started playing tricks on me, making me think I could see the dusty disruption of a shuttle coming in for a landing. There was nothing there. I went back to the local vid feed, doing some digging of companies and landmarks to better figure out where we were and what the colony was about.

What had started as an exploration base had expanded into a mining colony, which had been mined out, but then manufacturing moved into the bargain-priced, pre-built colony. That had thrived and failed in bursts until the right mix had moved in, employing what population was left. The most successful businesses now focused on entertaining and services for bored employees. The government was something Kess would have been proud of.

This complex had once been a bustling manufacturing plant with offices, a small on-site staff, and plenty of storage space for components. A quick check of the local markets turned up a few similar buildings that were empty and not yet in poor repair. Prices were low. Tacesh was right off the trade route. The complex wasn't as big of an operation as Dugans on Veria Minor, but it could be if I bought up a few more surrounding warehouses. I lost myself in the local network and sketching out plans on the large datapad the salesman no longer needed. Maybe I could turn this place into something good too.

SIX

When the shuttle bearing subtle Cragtek markings did arrive, I was deep into my plan of what I could do with the complex once it was no longer a slave factory. It was a flurry of activity in the interior feeds that pulled my attention out of distraction mode and brought the full awareness of my still-drug-infused body back online.

A knock on the door and the feed of Buria standing outside it brought the aching need back up to a desperate level.

"Go away, Buria."

"Is this your ship that has arrived, Advisor?"

Right. I hadn't told them what to watch for. That explained why they were all scrambling.

"Sorry, yes. Get everyone on board. They'll take you somewhere safe. Go."

She stood there, wriggling her hands.

"What?"

"They would feel safer if you went with them. Even if you could walk them to the shuttle? They don't know where they're going or what will happen to them. It's all..."

Overwhelming. I recalled how long it had taken me to want to talk to anyone, to even want to leave my room on the flight to Pentares after we'd taken out the Council.

I left the safety of the observation chair. Anger was my best defense. If I could maintain that, I could stay in control. And if I appeared angry, like the men they were used to dealing with, maybe the women would quit throwing themselves at me. Compiling a quick list of immediate things that pissed me off, I opened the door and glared at Buria.

She took a quick step back. "You're in a fine mood. The Premier mentioned your moods."

"Did he now?" I added Fa'yet's big mouth to my list.

Despite my snarl, she smiled. "He said all of them were shitty except for one."

"Accurate, and you've seen what trouble the good one gets me into."

"The spray is to blame for that or your wife would never let you out of the house. Speaking of which, is that out of your system yet?"

"No," I snapped. "The Premier shouldn't talk so damned much."

"He's quite fond of you, of all of you. Half his sentences start with, 'This one time when I was working for the Advisor.'"

Why wasn't she cowering or at least far more sedate? But no, Buria kept her smile and pleasant tone as she effortlessly matched my pace. Fucking Masters and their training.

"You'd think he didn't have a life before he lived with us."

"Not much of one, by the sound of it," she said.

If I kept talking to Buria, I was going to calm down and that would only lead to one thing in this condition. Maybe I could piss her off enough to give me some distance. She would find out eventually anyway.

"Did they tell you about Idra?"

That sobered her up quickly. I waited for her to let me have it.

"That the Masters sent her after you? Yes. I'm sorry you had to do that. She thought she was doing the right thing."

Dammit, I didn't need her understanding. Not that I didn't appreciate it, but her sympathy didn't help negate everything else I was feeling. Then again, given my reaction to her being angry earlier, my tactic may have had a serious flaw.

Ignoring her, ignoring all of them, was my only defense.

Reciting the litany of anger in my head, I entered the training room. A host of women turned their attention to me.

Masters. Slaves. Fa'yet's running mouth. Facing Stassia. All the endless pings for my attention on Narvan business while I was out here. Jey and Kess's demands. The damned spray. The bruises under my armor. The half-healed hole in my hand and back. Untami triggering the scantily-clad sex slaves.

No, that was a bad one to have on the list. Fuck.

I stared past all of them to focus on the back wall with the two doors that led to the guard and hospitality wings. "My ship has arrived. It's safe. I'm going to go meet with the crew, and then, when Buria tells you to, you will file out to the landing pad with whatever belongings you can carry and board the shuttle. It will take a couple trips to get you all on the ship."

"You're coming with us?" asked one of the women.

"No. But I will see you soon. You'll be taken to lodgings that I own on my homeworld. You'll be safe there."

While the women murmured uncertainly and quietly protested me leaving them with strangers, I turned to Buria. "Stay with them. I'll let you know when to send them out."

She nodded.

Making a quick escape from the room full of women, I bolted for the back exit through the storeroom to the landing pad where the shuttle waited. Ten people in plain clothes stood outside the open bay door with weapons drawn. One of them stepped forward from the rest as I approached.

"You the Advisor?"

I nodded.

"Any resistance we need to be aware of?"

"Not currently."

"Are the goods ready to move?"

"Yes. Waiting inside." I ran over the plan for the complex that I'd formulated while waiting for them to arrive. "How large of a crew do you have?"

"This is it. We were on another run and were the closest. Lucky for you, we'd just wrapped up our other job when Gamnock contacted us. There are two more keeping an eye on the ship in case of outside resistance."

"Expecting to grab and run?"

He shrugged. "Gamnock said it was your job and to expect anything."

"Fair enough. There are containers in the building there." I indicated the far storage building. "You will extract those contents, keep them under guard and contained. Store them at Cragtek. I will retrieve them within a few days. One of the women inside has the key to the locks. Fair warning, it's a finger."

His brows rose. "You're...not kidding."

"No. Everyone else is to be treated with respect and is under my protection. I would be very displeased to learn they had been touched, approached, solicited, or harmed in any way. Is that clear?"

From their fervent nodding, I gathered Gamnock had also warned his people about me.

I passed along delivery instructions for the women and gestured for the crew to get to work. After a quick link contact with Buria to let her it was time to move, I contacted Gamnock.

"Would you be interested in leaving some of your crew behind to hold an investment opportunity?"

"Can you give me some specifics?" He sounded much more interested and less distracted than the last time we'd spoken.

I gave him a quick rundown of the complex and the inventory.

"And this fell into your lap, I take it?"

"More of an acquisition by force."

"That, I'd believe. Will you also be taking part in manning and funding this venture?"

"Not taking part, heading it. But I'd like to discuss your role in this as well."

"And you want someone to hang out while you get your venture sorted so someone else doesn't acquire it."

"Exactly."

"And my people are there and yours are not."

He truly was a cut and dry man. *"Yes."*

"You will already owe me. You sure you want to go that deep?"

Normally I preferred arrangements the other way around, but I'd had a good working relationship with his father and I hoped to continue that with Gamnock now that we were on speaking terms.

I conveyed my general assent. *"I may have some incoming staff for you as well. We can discuss that when I see you. I need to sleep on all of this first."*

"Deal. I'll let Nacen know to leave half the crew behind."

"Thank you."

Seeing Buria and two of the crew approach with a line of women following behind, all of them with their arms full of goods, reminded me that I had a few things I wanted to take with me as well.

I offered the women a reassuring nod as I passed by and then hurried inside, hoping to miss the next wave queuing up in the storeroom. Geva was on my side as it was only occupied by one of the crew doing a quick scan of all the goods, likely relaying the feed directly to Gamnock. After making a reminder to get a copy from Gamnock later, I moved onward to grab the giant datapad on which I'd been outlining my development plans, two of the numbing rods, and all of the spray I could find. I needed to figure out how to market and manufacture that stuff, preferably in a toned-down version able to be sold in small doses. There had to be some chemical manufacturers on Artor who would be eager to please me. The drug would pay for itself within the first few days of sales.

Gunfire outside gained my instant attention. I contacted Buria. *"What's going on?"*

"It's taken care of," she said with satisfaction. *"Two Masters arriving early for their shift. They must have noticed the unplanned shuttle."*

"Stay on alert. There will likely be more." Would a handful of men be adequate to hold the whole complex? *"Choose five of the guards to remain behind for a few days. They'll join the rest once this complex is secured."* Even if I didn't trust them to shoot on sight, they could perform watch duty. Gamnock's crew could take care of the rest.

"Yes, Advisor." She cut contact.

With my horde gathered, I retreated to the observation room where I could keep an eye out for more threats. I caught the shuttle lifting off with the first load of freed women and smiled to myself.

Buria and her chosen guards readied the next batch of women while the crew patrolled the perimeter. They took out eleven more men before the last shuttle containing both women and the captured Masters had readied for departure. Two of the crew had sustained injuries. I offered to Jump them back to Cragtek to swap them out, but they declined.

"We've got this," Nacen assured me. "After seeing the inventory and the overview, Gamnock is sending another ship to assist in holding the complex."

I nodded, glad he'd seen the same value that I had. Leaving them to it, I gathered up my treasures from the observation room.

Buria found me before I could Jump. "Thank you for what you did here."

The sincerity in her voice and the earnestness on her face took my breath away. I nodded.

"You'll take good care of them all?" she asked.

"There will be people waiting to help them at the hotel when they arrive. Counselors and therapists, people who are equipped to help them process all they've been through and understand their new freedom."

"Is there more I can do than just say thank you? It doesn't feel adequate."

"Make sure nothing happens to my daughter."

She nodded solemnly. "I should return to the Premier so I can rest before she arrives. Will you be delivering her?" The hope in her question was plain on her face.

"Neko will see to that. Goodbye Buria."

Her second nod was even more solemn than the last. "Goodbye, Advisor." She closed her eyes, as one who was new to Jumping usually did, and then was gone.

With nothing left to keep me there, I Jumped to the bedroom on Artor and the promise of finally finding relief.

Stassia was asleep in bed. Perfect.

After quietly setting my horde down, I shed my coat, weapons, and boots into a pile she would yell at me for later. While a shower sounded good, jumping into bed and onto the willing body who knew me, sounded even better. I slipped under the covers.

I'd barely gotten past pulling her against me when she woke fully and smacked me on the chest.

"Where the hell have you been?"

"Doing some business with Buria."

She sat up and caught me in the full focus of her narrowed gaze, as though she knew I would see her glaring with my artifical eye even though she couldn't see me. She solved that by using her perpetually nearby datapad to turn on the lights.

"Turn those off and come here."

"Not until you explain where you've been." Her mind brushed up against mine. "And what the hell you were doing to work you up into such a frenzy?"

Her hand found my frenzy and squeezed in it a dangerous manner that might have been a threat, but under the thrall of the drug, made me quiver rather than cringe.

"Buria and I went to meet with Jey and then Kess and then we got to talking and it turned out Fa'yet purchased her along with Nena and Merona."

"And this was your business how?"

"Purchased, Stassia. They were slaves."

"Isnar wouldn't buy anyone."

"He did. All three of them."

Her grip loosened to a more agreeable pressure.

"Can we talk about this later? I'd very much like you to turn off the light, or leave it on, whatever, just keep doing that."

"Did you kill Isnar?"

"I haven't even talked to him yet."

Her hand vacated its post. "So where have you been all night? I waited up for you."

"I told you I would be a while. I had a shipment to take care of." I'd had enough talking. Rolling her onto her back with little resistance, I used my link to kill the lights. I let our connection swell.

She gasped. "You're going to do a lot of talking later, got it?"

"Sure."

"Do I want to know what you're on?"

"Tomorrow." I made sure she was too busy moaning to form any other words.

"Enough. She pushed me away. "I need a few minutes here. How can you not need a little recovery time?" she asked, trying to catch her breath.

"I might."

The drug was subsiding, the glow not as intense, fatigue gloating on the edges of my awareness. It was going to be a while before I'd be in any shape to pay a visit to Gamnock or Fa'yet or anyone else. Geva, then there was the whole experiment at the University that I'd been putting off checking up on. By the fact that Jey and Kess had already been demanding my attention, I gathered they were pissed about the results. I'd been too wrapped up in Stassia to care.

"Don't you need to sleep?" she asked.

"Later. I pulled her close again even if only to just appreciate her warmth on my skin.

"Really now, what are you on?"

"I don't think we've recovered that memory for you yet." That was one I hadn't wanted to return to her. It had been a dark time for both of us.

"So you've done this before."

"Similar but not voluntary. This time wasn't either, but I think it's safe to say we're both enjoying it regardless."

"Can you share it?"

"The memory or the drug?"

She kicked me lightly. "The memory, idiot. Neither of us needs more of whatever that was right now. I don't think I can get out of bed as it is."

"Good." I held her tightly.

"Vayen."

"All right, fine." I opened my mind to her, reluctantly revisiting Chandi's experiment, Shoulders' abuse, the threats against Stassia, and all I'd done to keep the tank safe.

When I finished, Stassia kissed me, erasing all thoughts of Saka and Buria. This was what I wanted, what felt right. The bond was again in the forefront of my thoughts, assuring me that the spray had indeed worked its way out of my system. What that meant for us would remain to be seen, given it had been right there when I'd been toying with Buria before the spray.

"So this drug, it's like the one you were on before?" she asked.

"Not exactly."

I reached for the case where I'd stored the mist canisters and pulled one out. Handing it to her, I rolled onto my back. While we'd been busy, the gel and my altered skin had finished their work, leaving only mild discomfort where the wounds and deepest of bruises had been. Stassia rolled onto her side against me, examining the canister in the dim light from the single window high above the bed.

"So what does it do that's different?"

Thankfully, it couldn't be as addictive as the initial batch had been or the Masters wouldn't have used it on their clients.

"Someone managed to filter out the addictive effects. I imagine you're very familiar with the positive end of the reaction by now."

She snickered. "So it enhances the sex drive and stamina."

"It also lowers inhibitions and generally makes you want to screw everyone in sight."

She stiffened.

"I didn't, by the way."

"I would hope you didn't manage that and yet come home with that much energy left over."

"That would be a pretty spectacular performance, but no."

She ran her fingers over the smooth surface of the canister. "Where did you happen upon this drug?"

"Buria and I were talking, as I said. She mentioned being a slave and you know how I feel about slavery."

Stassia leaned over me to put the canister down. "Do I?

"I don't approve."

"So the whole time I ran Merchess with the economy based on slavery?"

"That was your choice, not mine."

She pulled the sheet around her and settled back in beside me, chin propped up on her hand. "You ran Merchess without me, as I recall being told."

"It was a necessary evil." Which was probably her excuse too, lame as it was. The economy had been in place for generations before she'd taken over. "After having to serve the Council in grey, I'm far more against it than I used to be, if you need further clarification."

"Oh," she said softly.

I shook my head and brushed her hair out of my face. "This isn't about Merchess. Buria brought me to the compound to show me where she'd been kept and trained. I thought I might find a couple guards like her for us, or even maybe for Jey. He could use a few, don't you think?"

"Quit trying to distract me."

Damn, I was hoping for a few more minutes to dole out the truth of the matter slowly. "I may have liberated all the slaves."

"By yourself."

"Maybe."

"Vayen."

"What? I've been sitting home for far too long. I needed some excitement. And look," I held up the blankets, "I came home all in one piece."

"Yes, you did." She patted me on the head.

I swatted her hand away.

"And just what do you plan to do with these slaves and the complex you liberated them from?" she asked.

"The women are staying at a hotel here on Artor."

"Who is paying for that?"

"No one. It's one of mine."

"I wish I remembered all of your assets."

"I wish you did too." I stroked her shoulder in the way that always made her sigh contentedly.

"I've sent over a host of therapists from one of the health clinics I also finance. They're working with the women to start deprogramming the mess the Masters made of them. Two specialists from the University are erasing hidden cues used for specialized training. Those women would be deadly if someone uttered the wrong word." I shuddered, imagining the sleeper assassins accidentally being activated. "I'll have someone put together a presentation on job options in a few days once they all get settled in. They need to know there are plenty of things they can do outside of what they've been forced into."

"Sounds like you have everything under control." She snuggled closer. "And the complex?"

"I'm going to turn it into a waypoint for Gamnock and our own shipments. It's right off the trade routes, mostly ready to go. It will take very little in the way of investment and might open up some new trade options outside the Narvan."

Stassia smiled against my chest. "It's good to hear you enthusiastic about something."

It felt good too. A straightforward project for once. I hadn't had that since Dugans. Simplicity had chafed me then, but I sure as all hells appreciated it now.

She'd handled the liberated slave endeavor pretty well, I figured I might as well dive into the Ikeri situation while she was in a good and satisfied mood. "Ikeri get on her way?"

"Neko transferred her to Isnar a few hours after you got home. You could stop by and see her."

"I was thinking it would be best to give that a few days. Maybe some distance will help?"

"Yes, maybe," she slurred, drifting off.

With Stassia draped across me and having expended every remaining ounce of energy in pleasurable pursuits, I closed my eyes and let the oblivion of sleep take me away.

An insistent voice in my head slowly brought me awake. Jey sounded angrier than before. I checked the time, only to find it was afternoon on Artor. If I didn't answer him soon, he'd likely show up at the house, livid as all hells. The boys didn't need to see or hear that. I acknowledged his contact.

"Did you know?"

"Know what?"

I rubbed the sleep from my eyes, groaning as my sore muscles protested moving my arms. I hurt all over. Either I needed to employ that drug for a frequent and thorough workout of muscles not included in my regular routine or I needed to never touch it again. Particular muscles shouldn't be overworked.

Stassia was gone, but a quick check of our connection assured me she was nearby.

"Are you at the University or not?" Jey asked.

"I'm in bed. What the fuck are you ranting about?"

"My dead volunteers. Kess's too."

I sat up slowly. *"Let me get moving here and I'll see what I can find out."*

"I'm telling you. They're all dead." His voice dropped to a threat level that raked over my nerves. *"That's why you only wanted us to send one. You were going to sacrifice them to try and shut us up. You had no intention of sharing the alteration."*

"I told you this was an experiment. I wanted to minimize the risk."

"We both sent good candidates, a wide selection. If your University minions were doing a legitimate test, at least one of those should have taken. Instead, they're all dead."

"Were any of them Artorian?" I asked.

"Why would we send you your own people? You've already proven they can be altered."

"Because that would have been a legitimate baseline to send along with your volunteers. You have a planet of Artorian citizens at your disposal. Any one of them would do."

"We want our people altered. Not yours."

"They are yours."

"Are you deaf or just playing stupid?"

"I told you it only works on Artorians. The University has been doing studies on others. We've been trying to do as you and Kess asked. I'm not ignoring you, but those studies haven't shown any success. Yet you both insisted we go through with this experiment. Nan's team held out hope that live specimens might react differently than their tests indicated, but that wasn't the case. You disregarded my warnings and the preliminary data I sent, and now you're pissed the experiment wasn't successful?

"You have three worlds of people under your control, one of which is filled with Artorians. Why not use them to patrol your planets? For that matter, you already have some of the altered hunters in your half of the Narvan. We haven't seen a new Arpex threat. This whole alteration issue isn't a priority."

He again employed his threatening tone, *"So you are playing stupid."*

I took a deep breath through my nose and let it out. *"I have some business to attend to first, but we can meet later to go over the initial progress with the work integration program and the handful of proposed adoptions. I don't have to tell you to keep the results of the testing quiet, do I? We don't need any fuel to undo the progress we've made."*

"It's already out," he growled.

"How? The University should have reported directly to you. There should have been no opportunity for a leak."

"There was a documentation crew. Kess and I wanted to see the process. You owed us that, even if you didn't think so."

"You sent a documentation crew?" And the University allowed them in? Heads were going to roll over this. I began to form my tirade to Nan and her team while digesting everything Jey was throwing at me. *"Wait, did you or Kess leak the feed or was it the crew?"*

If it was the crew, I'd hunt them down and terminally punish them myself. I didn't want to consider the implications of either Jey or Kess initiating the leak.

"You can't hold this alteration for your people only. You will share it, even if we have to reconstruct it from the feed ourselves." Jey cut contact with the finality of a fist upside my face.

"Vayen?" A wavering note in Stassia's voice had me up in seconds and into pants, sprinting out of the bedroom to find the cause of her distress.

She sat on the edge of the couch, staring at the local vid feed, arms clasped across her chest. Jalvian protestors lined the streets of Syless. The feed cut to a crowd of them marching outside the University on Artor, chanting that their people had been murdered. My face was everywhere.

SEVEN

I stared at the vid feed of Jalvians slandering my name. Jey had undone everything we'd worked for in a matter of hours. A rush of terror sped through me.

"Where's Markus?"

"On Prime with Neko and Daniel."

I prayed Ikeri wasn't seeing any of this. Who would she believe?

I dropped into the chair across from the vid. "What the fuck were they thinking?"

Stassia slid off the couch and crouched in front of me, placing her hands on mine. "They weren't."

"I wasn't even there. I told them to only send one person. They demanded to send more, totally disregarding my warning and all the data the University provided. Jey and Kess brought this on themselves."

"Now it's our problem." She stood. "Get dressed. We have work to do."

I'd barely gotten a shirt over my head when Fa'yet contacted me. *"I'm going to need your help with damage control."*

"Where's Ikeri? Is she with you?"

"Do you need her to be? She's practicing something on Nena right now."

"No. I'd rather she isn't in the same room if I'm going to be there."

His surprise was tangible. *"Are you two really that bad off?"*

"Focus, dammit."

"Yes, of course, I'll be in my home office. Alone."

I finished dressing and armed only moderately, figuring I'd be in public figure mode rather than working. Leaving my armor behind, I let Stassia take the role of armed and dangerous. We Jumped to

Fa'yet's estate on Karin.

Merona met us in the foyer with a quick bow. She brought us to Fa'yet without a word. The three of us sat, going over the various vid feeds of protests throughout Karin and Artor. The downside to our recent work initiatives was that there were far more Jalvians on Artor and Artorians on Jal than there had been in centuries. They didn't have to wait to take a ship here to start a protest or riot, they were already in place.

One particularly large mess had erupted on the steps of the capitol building on Artor. I didn't like how my people were beginning to congregate around the edges of the Jalvian protestors, yelling back at them. One brandished a stunner. Law enforcement took him away. That got the Jalvians going, mocking the Artorians, which only escalated the tension in the crowd.

I stood, leaving Stassia with Fa'yet. Before she could argue, I Jumped to the nearest point I knew.

"What the hell are you doing?" Stassia yelled in my head. *"What happened to taking me with you?"*

"I'll be back shortly. The last thing this situation needs is more weapons. Fa'yet can Jump you here if your presence is necessary."

"You better be in one piece when you get back here." I sensed the glare that accompanied her words.

The crowd had more than doubled by the time I'd made my way to where the Jalvians were now surrounded by an angry mob of my people telling them to go home with a good deal of profanity and the occasional thrown object, one of which had been sharp enough to cut the forehead of one of the female protestors.

I forced my way through the crowd and got up on the steps. The Artorians in the crowd quieted and watched me expectantly.

"What happened this morning was unfortunate. However, we knew this process was still in the experimental stages," I announced.

A vid bot hovered near my face. I tried not to look directly at it or swat it out of the air. The downside to being a living public figure was now being subjected to their frequent presence. Others hovered on the outskirts of the crowd. I spotted another high above us. Damned things.

"We knew this process had a high chance of failure on others, but we were willing to try because we were asked under no uncertain terms to do so, despite our warnings. I am not pleased with the loss of life, but it does not come as a surprise. It was not a travesty of justice." I glared at the Jalvian who had been spouting those exact words earlier on the vid feed.

"The deaths were an unfortunate result that could have been avoided had your leaders and the other advisors heeded our warnings. Your anger gains you nothing. Go home."

A pulse blast tore through the Jalvian protestors, shredding them and the Artorians who had been close by. Stassia shrieked in my head.

The invisible wall hit me hard, sending a shockwave through my bones and knocking me on my ass. Though my ears were ringing and my vision went fuzzy, the alteration at the root of the conflict allowed me to get back to my feet. I'd have to evaluate the level of damage to myself later. Right now, I needed to continue this far too public display.

Fa'yet and Stassia arrived a second later. Buria appeared just behind them. Fa'yet shook his head in my direction and then vanished. Stassia and Buria bolted for me. I held up my hand and pointed them toward the woman holding the pulse pistol amid the scattering and screaming crowd. Whatever had been said about me, she hadn't expected my quick recovery because she hadn't made any move to hide or melt into the chaos.

The security on site rushed in to shove the remaining stunned masses away from the carnage. Several of them ran at me with horrified faces. I waved them off.

The woman stood tall, her voice rang out over the confused and scared crowd. "That is what we're fighting for." She pointed straight at me. "You have no right to hold this tech for yourself. Tyrant!"

A vid bot swooped down near her. Others sped through the gruesome scene surrounding us. Murmurs flowed through the people that hadn't fled as the bots again gathered closer to hear us. I wiped at the blood dripping from my nose and onto my shirt.

Stassia and Buria wove their way through the crowd, aiming for my attacker from different angles. There were too many moving targets between us for me to take a shot, and given that I'd taken the brunt of the pulse blast, I wasn't all that confident in my aim just then. I concentrated on keeping my voice steady and trying not to waver on my feet. Stassia needed to stay focused on the target, not be distracted by worrying about me.

"I'm not holding it for myself," I announced. "Others share the enhanced abilities from this procedure. They protect all of you from the Arpex. That is why we have this modification, not because we wanted it for ourselves, but to protect the Narvan as a whole."

The remaining Jalvians eyed the crowd. I wasn't sure if they were gauging their situation or considering how to cover the attacker's exit. The Artorian exodus had halted upon me regaining my feet and speaking. Murmurs passed through them in waves. Had I further set myself apart by not acting more wounded or was I portraying a strong image as their leader? Only Geva knew which they wanted. There was no question what the Jalvians wanted. Their sharply focused hatred burned into me.

One of the Jalvians stepped into the edge of the bloody mess, the only open space, and raised his face to the crowd. "The Narvan is not whole." He pointed an accusing finger at me. "You have brought this fracture upon us. Stealing one of our children. Misleading our Prime and Advisor. Lulling us all into this dream of a unified system while you fill your ranks with invincible soldiers. The day will come when your true goal shines forth and then all will see what you truly are."

What the fuck was I supposed to say to that? What a huge pile of paranoid propaganda. That was the truth that would come out. But first I needed to find where the shit was spewing from.

"Take him into custody." I hissed to the security team anxiously awaiting orders while also looking at me as though they expected my imminent collapse. "Arrest any Jalvian here that refuses to disperse. They've caused enough violence for one day."

Security infiltrated the crowd, aiming for the Jalvians. I left them to it and sought out Stassia through our bonded connection.

She sent one word back, *"Busy."*

I tried Buria instead. *"We've captured the Jalvian woman. She's undergoing interrogation now."*

So that was why Stassia was busy. She'd find out if someone had sent them or they were acting on their own. My credits were on Kess. Jey wouldn't have mowed down his own people. He wasn't quite that pissed yet. At least, I didn't think he was.

Two of the security team approached me. "Sir, do you need to sit down? We can clear a path for you, find somewhere safe."

The vid bots spun overhead, taking in the whole mess from every angle. I wished they'd collide and crash to the ground, but they maintained their coordinated dance.

"In a moment. Concentrate on dispersing the crowd and cleaning up what's left of the pulse victims. Respectfully. We don't need to give the Jalvians more ammunition."

They nodded and hurried off. Blood still dripped from my nose. Now that the shock was wearing off, every muscle ached and my head was spinning. I reached for my stim tin only to remember I wasn't wearing my armor.

Jey hit my link, ranting about the men and women who had been killed in front of me.

I cut him off. *"We have the woman who fired the pulse. I'll know who's behind this mess soon enough."*

"You put her up to this. You know as well as I do that a pulse wouldn't harm you. Cleaned up my people quickly, though, didn't it?"

My hold on remaining vertical of my own accord was starting to falter. I needed to get away from the vid feed before Jey and Kess had hard evidence that I wasn't as impervious as they'd thought now that Nan had dialed back the alteration. Wishing I'd taken the agents up on their offer of safe passage, I managed a somewhat graceful stumble through the milling public to the side of a nearby building.

"She killed a lot of my people too," I said. *"Do you think I'm that callous?"*

He made a non-committal grumble, but his fury was clear enough.

"Maybe have a chat with your pal, Kess. See what he thinks about her performance.

I tilted my head back, trying to get the nosebleed to stop. Three members of the security team spotted me and lingered close by, doing a good job of further deterring anyone from getting near me.

"Turning us against one another isn't going to work," he said. *"You're just as bad as the fucking High Council."*

That hurt, but I couldn't let him goad me into making this debacle any worse. *"We're all on the same side. Why would I do that?"*

"No telling what endgame you have going on in your head. You've had weeks of sitting on your ass to think about it while we've been busy cleaning up the Arpex mess."

"The only thing I've been pondering for weeks is how to avoid this damned situation. I've been working too and you damn well know that."

Stassia ventured into my head, blocking out Jey. *"Vayen?"*

"I'm still in one piece. Near where I was. What did you learn?"

"We'll be there in a few minutes. Hold on."

Jey's rant continued, *"...Karin in your pocket. Anastassia taking half the workload. That leaves you plenty of time for plotting with the University."*

Gawkers had joined the growing security wall between me and where the attack had happened. Vid bots gathered over where they'd congregated. Once in the public eye, it seemed there was no escape.

There were too many people watching me and standing weak-kneed and bleeding in public wasn't doing anything for my concentration or mood.

"Let me know when you're ready to be logical about this." I cut contact.

Security seemed to be having a fit about me loitering in the open. Given what had just happened, and the lingering crowd watching, I thought it might be best if I listened to them. One detached himself from the wall to approach me. A vid bot followed him.

"Captain Le'rin here," he addressed the bot that buzzed nearby, no doubt covering me from every fucking angle. "We'll be taking the Advisor to the University for treatment of his injuries."

"I'll be fine," I muttered to him when we were out of recording range. If I had time, I would have visited the tank. More likely, I'd be dealing with this shit and be damned sore for a couple days instead.

"Maybe you should pretend that you won't be fine, sir," Le'rin said, glancing at me sideways.

"I suppose that might be wise. All right then, I'll go make a scene at the University."

"Best you let us transport you. There's another mob over there."

"I can get there on my own."

"Just a suggestion, sir, but being seen as more average might be in your best interest at this time."

I sighed. "Where's the transport?"

Le'rin signaled a horde of security to surround us, effectively hiding me from any further close-up vid bot harassment. They moved quickly and efficiently, shuffling me into a secured transport.

"We will wait here until my mate joins us. She's on her way." I updated Stassia on my location and then rested my head on the seat and closed my eyes for a moment.

Jostling brought me back to alertness. Stassia dropped into the seat next to me.

Buria poked her head into the transport. Thank Geva they were both all right.

"Are you well?" Buria asked.

"Well enough," I assured her, noticing the fine spray of blood across her face. "And you?"

"Better than your attacker." She looked to Stassia. "Do you need anything else?"

"I'll take it from here. Thank you, Buria."

Buria nodded, gave me another worried once-over, and then backed away from the transport. Le'rin and two others crammed in across from us. He punched our destination into the panel on the door and then sat back.

Once we were speeding toward the University, Stassia took my hand. "How are you really?" she asked.

"Sore as all hells."

"And all the blood?" she nodded toward my shirt.

"Nosebleed."

"After taking on a pulse wave. I'm so jealous right now." She squeezed my hand gently and then increased the pressure. "And also pissed. You should have taken me with you. I might have spotted her and taken her out before this mess erupted."

"Noted. What did your interrogation yield?"

"She was promised a link if she fired on you, and she wasn't the only one. Sounds like agents have been planted throughout Artor."

"Who sent her?"

"Kess."

"She gave him up? His quality of help is going downhill."

Stassia raised one eyebrow. "Maybe my interrogation skills are that good."

"Or that."

She shook her head. "Really though, whatever Isnar paid for Buria was well worth it and you should probably thank her when you're feeling up to it. I was wrapped up in getting answers and being pissed that someone dared pulse you. I never saw the sniper on the rooftop."

My breath caught in my throat. I wrapped my aching arms around Stassia and pulled her close. A testament to how shaken she must have really been, she barely resisted, letting me have a moment despite our audience in the transport.

"Tell me the sniper was there to silence the Jalvian and not you."

"Both," she whispered. "Buria knocked me aside and took the bullet square in the back. Her armor held. The next shot silenced your pulse attacker. A second later, Buria shoved me away and took out the sniper with a shot right between the eyes. I know this because he fell from the rooftop to land on the ground in front of me. I recognized him as one of the assassins that used to work for Marin, you know, from the guild that Kess now runs."

"He's sunk to that level then. Got it. This means I get to kill him now, right?" I asked, already planning how I'd go about it.

"You can't. We're barely holding the Narvan together. We can't advise the Rakon too. Maybe drive the fear of Geva into him? I don't know."

"Stassia, his man almost put a bullet in your head."

"Yes, but Kess wouldn't have authorized that. He might not have known who I am. Maybe he was improvising. We'll never know."

Her faith in Kess was seeded in a messy past that she might remember, but in my opinion, it was sorely misplaced. However, she didn't welcome my opinion on matters of Kess.

"We should send one of the security team out to retrieve the sniper's body so we can firmly pin that attack on Kess. We can't afford to have this level of hostility festering between Jal and Artor."

She shook her head. "Kess will claim he wasn't involved, that the sniper was hired by some outside anonymous source. He'll have his tracks covered. He's been in this business longer than you have."

That didn't mean he was better at it. I stewed on that for the last few minutes it took for us to arrive at the University.

Le'rin hadn't been exaggerating. The crowd was even bigger than at the capitol building. He summoned several other security agents already on-site to the transport where they made a show of escorting me inside through the crowd. To go along with his suggestion of appearing wounded, I didn't bother to hide my discomfort, and I walked at a far slower pace than normal. I hoped Jey and Kess thought it was an act, and maybe Stassia too so she wouldn't worry. She was on high alert, one hand clamped onto my arm and the other hovering over a gun.

Word of the massacre had already spread in the barely half an hour since it had occurred. The Jalvian protestors here had intermingled with the Artorians on-site, chanting, but much more subdued, staying with the bulk of the crowd, clearly not wanting to be easy targets.

"Go home," I yelled over my shoulder, wishing I could do more, but the agents beside me had matched my pace and kept us mostly contained. If anyone else got it in their head to pulse me to prove a point, the people around me would be obliterated. I didn't want that on my conscience.

Once we were inside, I sent the agents off to watch over the crowd to try and prevent anything else from going wrong. Le'rin sent the majority of the agents outside but he and a handful of others stood patiently waiting for me to continue onward.

"I'd prefer if you were all outside making sure our people are safe," I clarified.

"I understand that, Advisor, but the Premier has asked us to do the same for you."

Of course, the Artorian Premier want me alive. We had far too many newly launched initiatives in progress. The man wouldn't want to have all that fall into his lap alone, not in the wake of the Arpex mess.

"Would you like to make a public address from here? It may be more effective than going from one hotspot to the next," Le'rin suggested.

"That's the Premier's job."

He shuffled his feet. "He wasn't sure how you'd prefer to handle this, being a personal attack, sir."

Life was so much simpler when I was mostly invisible to the public, when the Premier and I had only met behind closed doors.

"I'm wounded, right? He can make the damned address. That's what he's there for."

Le'rin nodded, likely conveying my response to the Premier.

An alarm went off in my head. I hunted through the flood of notifications pelting my link to figure out what the unfamiliar notification was: The house.

"Someone is attacking our fucking house."

Stassia swore under her breath.

"I'll send a squad over immediately," Le'rin said.

I was almost going to ask him how he knew where the hells I lived when I realized anyone could know with an ounce of digging. We were living public figures now, thanks to the adoption of Markus and my efforts to do the best I could for my people. Now they were attacking me. Or someone was.

"That would be appreciated. As would a clean shirt." Stassia said, pointing at the bloody mess on the front of my shirt.

Le'rin nodded.

"There's no one inside the house. It's just a security system alert," I explained.

"Still, sir, we're sending enforcers over. You'd prefer any damage minimalized, I'm sure?"

"They're not getting inside."

"They pulsed you out in the open, sir. Will your home withstand pulses or a bomb for that matter?"

This wasn't the shit I was used to having to worry about. He was. I had to trust that he knew how to do his job. "Send them over."

He went distant again, relaying orders.

While he was occupied, I checked in with a couple contacts and verified that Fa'yet's estate was not also under attack.

"Ikeri is safe," I assured Stassia. "And the boys are far from the Narvan."

She nodded, but the worried creases on her forehead didn't ease.

"Let's find Nan and see what exactly happened during this experiment beyond what the newsfeeds featured," I said.

"What about the leak?" Stassia turned to Le'rin. "If you want to be useful, we need a full investigation into who provided the feed to the news outlets. It was supposed to be classified. I want a name as soon as you have it."

"I'll do my best," he said, and after a curt nod, left us with an escort of two.

We passed through two security checkpoints with no issue, the staff there having recognized us. In all honesty, I wouldn't have minded a little break while they made a few calls to verify our identity.

"You're moving slowly. Are you sure you're all right?" Stassia asked.

"Stassia, I got pulsed. I fucking ache all over. I'm lucky to still be standing."

"I know. Sorry, it's just that you seem to either be impervious or unconscious. There's very little in between."

I chuckled despite the pain. "Fair point. Do you have a stim on you?"

Seeming grateful for something to do, she fished her tin out of her pocket and offered me one of the tiny tabs.

"Thanks." I swallowed it and waited a moment for the invigorating rush. When it didn't hit me, I started walking.

"Better?" she asked.

"Yes," I lied. I could breathe easier and each step didn't hurt as bad, but I was a far cry from better. Hopefully, the enhanced healing capability of the Arpex alteration would offer me more relief if I gave it some time.

After three more checkpoints, we made it to the level and section where Nan worked. Having likely received word of our impending arrival, one of her team rushed to meet us.

The young woman looked markedly relieved to see me. "We were hoping you'd come. With all the chaos out there, we didn't want to bother you with one more thing."

"Another thing beyond all the test subjects dying?"

"Nan is ill."

"Ill how? Why do you need me for that?"

The assistant hurried us through the hallways and into a room filled with medical equipment exactly like the one where I'd been confined in for weeks. Nan lay in the bed, pale and sweating. Tubes ran from the equipment to her body, exchanging and administering various fluids.

"What's all this? What happened to her?" asked Stassia.

"She seemed fine, upset at the loss of life, but otherwise fine when the last subject expired. We notified Advisors Te and Atta of the results as per our instructions and dismissed their assigned documentation team."

I held up a hand. "About that documentation team. I thought we had a strict policy against them? Who authorized an override on that?"

The assistant's eyes went wide. "You did."

"Definitely not," I said firmly.

"They had the forms. Your approval was on them." She shook her head. "We had no reason to question their validity, given we were dealing with all three of you Advisors."

"Who are they supposed to trust, if not the advisors?" Stassia grumbled in my head. *"What a fucking mess."*

"I'll deal with the falsified forms. For future reference, I would never authorize outside documentation teams. Ever."

Nodding fervently, she said, "I'll make sure everyone knows this." She glanced between Stassia. When no futher censure was forthcoming, she continued. "Both Advisors arrived in short order to observe the results and go over the report with Nan. Soon after they left, she fell ill. It's grown worse in the hours since. At this point, I'm told only the machines are keeping her alive.

"Sounds like poison," said Stassia.

The assistant nodded. "We think so, but we've been unable to identify one yet."

I looked the irritating yet brilliant woman over. Nothing obvious presented itself. "They'd use something subtle, applied to the skin most likely. Nothing she'd feel immediately like an injection. They don't have access to her food. It wouldn't be in the air or others would have been exposed. Give me a datapad."

I ransacked my brain for names of the poisons Jey and I had used over the years. Geva only knew what Kess may have gotten his hands on in the Nebula. I handed her a list of possibilities.

"You know of many options. Do you study this sort of thing?" she asked.

"You could say that."

Stassia smirked but kept any further commentary to herself.

"Do you think either of the advisors would try to kill her?" asked the assistant. "Don't they need her to make the soldiers they so desperately want?"

"Her research is here, as are you. We can pull the process together if need be. But if Nan is gone, it would slow us down, giving Jey and Kess time to experiment with the process on their own with whatever their documentation team captured," I said.

"But that could mean many others dying while they attempt to get the process right, a process that will likely never work on a non-Artorian anyway," said Stassia. "It's such a waste of lives."

"Agreed. I need to watch the footage to see what exactly happened so I can deal with this. Show me what they saw with Nan and then show me the entirety of it."

The assistant nodded curtly. I gave Nan one last look, her bright mind trapped in a dying body, before following the assistant to a room I recognized as one of the labs where Nan had examined me previously.

"Have a seat. I'll get the test footage and reports," said the assistant.

When she returned, she handed me a new shirt and a damp cloth. Le'rin had come through on Stassia's request. She looked pleased when I cleaned my face and removed the stained shirt, assuring her that I wasn't hiding any further visble injury.

We spent the next several hours watching the process at double speed. Six Jalvians and five men and one woman of mixed blood from the Nebula were all injected with the spike of one of the Arpex taken down by the hunters Nan had created. They used the same spike for the Jalvians, another for Kess's lot.

"We found that each spike has multiple uses and doesn't need to be left in place as it was with you," said the assistant. "It's like an injector, firing a solution of eggs and an activator, mixed upon impact with flesh."

The back of my neck itched. I ran my fingers over the scar

-tissue-covered indent and shuddered.

Stassia gave me a concerned glance.

I shook my head and focused on the footage.

The men and woman from Kess's lot were made to lie down in the chamber Sa'cota had used for me. They were packed in pretty tight, but they weren't sweating profusely and they were all conscious.

"Couldn't you knock them out for this part?" I asked the assistant.

"We found that sedating the subject has a higher rate of failure."

While the subjects waited for their skin to erupt in welts, the implications of what she'd said sunk in. "Are you telling me that some of our Artorian volunteers didn't make it?"

"That is correct. Sedation saw only a forty percent success rate. Letting the process run its natural course yielded an eighty-seven percent success rate."

"Do we have footage of those subjects as well?"

"We record everything, sir."

"Good. We will need that when I haul Jey and Kess in here."

The subjects screamed and cried out for mercy as the first of the larvae chewed their way out. Suited-up staff members entered the room, collecting the larvae and taking several of the subjects out on stretchers. The assistant switched the feed to another room with four beds set up in it. The subjects were placed on those beds where each was then sedated to the point of acquiescent quiet. They were injected at multiple points with blue fluid. A few more larvae made their way out. One of the subjects suddenly sat up and screamed. Larvae violently burst through his skin as though they were trying to escape whatever had been injected into the subject's body. He died moments later.

The larvae in the woman went still, as I understood they were supposed to do. Unfortunately, so did she. At least she died more peacefully than the first one.

The third man went into a seizure, larvae dropping from his body onto the floor. They rolled and crawled for freedom while the staff hurried to collect them. His monitors pinged madly and then went silent.

The fourth seemed promising, no larvae bursting through his skin. He opened and closed his eyes, moving his head a little, perhaps half-alert and trying to see what was going on with the others. However, the welts didn't subside. The movement continued and grew more frequent. Was this what the process was supposed to look like?

It wasn't until he began to scream that I realized something was wrong. The movement became more intense. Rather than escaping to eat, the larvae were eating him alive from the inside. When it was clear there was no turning back, which was several minutes after I would have called that point, he was again given an injection. He went still. The larvae followed suit soon after.

"Would you like to see the other results?" the assistant asked.

"Are they similar?"

"In varying degrees, yes. No result was identical, but all test subjects failed."

"I don't suppose you only released the peaceful death of the female subject?"

"As you saw, that was hardly the common reaction." She shook her head. "We wanted to make it clear that this was not a wise line of research to pursue, especially in light of their blatant disregard for our preliminary data. Besides, they had their own footage to examine, though we did keep their crew at a distance."

"For what little that's worth," Stassia grumbled.

"We also showed them the bodies, though we didn't let them remove them from the University. They are contaminated."

"Both with the Arpex larvae, which I'm assuming are all dead, and more importantly, the fusing fluid, which we don't want them to have."

"Exactly, sir."

I nodded. "At least we're on the same page there."

"Maybe we should just let them have it," said Stassia. "Whatever they do with it would be on them, and their people could hate them for it rather than you."

"They'd kill too many trying. I don't want that on my hands." I turned to the assistant. "And the report you gave to them? So I can maybe understand why they are leaping to conclusions about us killing their people?"

She handed me a datapad containing documents and the snippet of the vid with the violent death. Stassia and I watched the entirety of it.

"They wanted someone to blame. That's it," said Stassia. "They're toying with starting a fucking war rather than accept that they can't have something because it isn't possible."

She sounded as disgusted as I felt. "Seems like it, yes."

I returned the datapad to the assistant. "Thank you. How are the other hunters?"

"Two have come back for therapy. One seems to have readjusted well enough, the other is still here."

"Readjusted how?"

"I understand the experience of the fusing can be considered traumatic."

I nodded. "Hearing and speaking to the Arpex can screw with your head too."

"Perhaps you might drop in to speak to him when you have time? I realize now might not be optimal."

It wasn't, but the longer I stayed here, the more time my body had to heal. "Do you mind?" I asked Stassia. "If we can help, I'd rather he be out and working than living off the University."

She nodded.

The assistant brought us to a nearby wing and then to a small room meant for a test subject during their stay.

"Let me know if anything changes with Nan," I said to the assistant as she turned to leave.

"You will be notified."

I nodded and entered the room with Stassia right behind me.

A tall man sat on the narrow bed, his back against the wall. His eyes closed, lips downturned. He wore loose, plain clothes, possibly issued by the staff, with no weapons or armor.

I recognized him from our brief training session. "Ha'guris, right?"

His eyes flew open. Upon recognizing me, he sprang to his feet. "Yes, sir."

"What seems to be the problem?" I asked.

He glanced around me to take in Stassia. "Both of you? Geva, I don't mean to take up your time. I'm sure you're both very busy."

"Safer down here," Stassia said. "You've heard about the protests?"

He waved his hand around the room. "Not much available to keep up on things in here."

"No link?" I asked

"Didn't want one. One alteration is enough."

I nodded. "So what's going on with the one you have?"

"They didn't call you in to talk to me, did they? I don't mean to be a bother to anyone."

"I was here on another matter."

He sighed and dropped back onto the bed. "I can't get their voices out of my head."

"You can hear them now?"

"Always." He rubbed his temples, looking miserable.

"But they're gone from Artor. Gone from the whole Narvan, as far as we know."

"I'm imagining it. That's what I keep telling the staff."

"Did they do tests?" I asked.

"Lots of them. I don't want to be poked anymore, and I'd like to keep all my fluids from now on. I just need them to give me something to make the hissing voices stop."

"I'm going to need a minute," I said to Stassia.

She went to stand by the door, keeping her attention both on me and the hallway.

To give my slowly recovering body a break, I sat down on the bed next to Ha'guris. "Do you see images too or just hear voices?"

He seemed startled to have me so close. "Both, why?"

"Did you always have both?"

Ha'guris nodded.

"What are they saying?"

"Nothing concrete. It's all just noise and a blur of images."

"Does it feel like it should be something or it is repeating what you've experienced with them before?"

"No, they were always clear before. It's like," he rubbed his hands over the stubble on his head, "leftover conversation, like a channel left open after we killed them. Am I hearing dead Arpex? Will it never go away?"

"Can I try something?"

He nodded.

"Would you consent to me hearing what you hear?"

"What's one more in here?"

The defeat in his voice ate at me. I reached into his mind, trying to be as light as possible, but still meeting with resistance. As gently as I could, I attempted to infiltrate the thick walls he'd erected to keep the Arpex out. Now they seemed to be holding the Arpex in. The more I tried to get through his defenses, the more discomfort I sensed from him. He didn't need more pain. I backed off.

"You need to let me in."

His voice was edged with desperation. "I'm trying. They don't want you to know they're there."

I pulled out of his mind entirely, shaking my head as I came back to myself. "They're telling you this?"

"I feel it. I can feel them." Desperation overcame him. "Oh, Geva, this isn't a memory. They're really there." He grasped his head, his fingers digging into his scalp. "I don't want to feel them anymore."

"I know how uncomfortable that is." I resolved myself to what must be done with a deep sigh. "I'm going to bring someone here to help you."

"Ikeri?" asked Stassia.

"Yes."

"While you do that, how about you bring me back to Isnar's? I'd be of more use remotely working with Le'rin on tracking down that leak. Buria can stand here. Isnar was lucky to find her. If the rest of the women you liberated are as good as she is, I can't wait to meet them."

I could wait a very long time for her to meet them. And I didn't have it in me to clarify that her buddy Isnar had chosen Buria not for her abilities, beyond what the group demonstration had illustrated, but for the fact that she had a faint degree of telepathy.

"Sure." I stood and held my hand out to her.

She took it and squeezed lightly. "Thanks. You know standing around drives me crazy."

"I do." It wasn't my favorite activity either, but I could stay busy on my link. She didn't have that luxury.

I Jumped us to Fa'yet's foyer on Karin.

EIGHT

Merona met us with a surprised look.

"I'm here for Ikeri. I have a job for her," I explained.

"I'll get her," Stassia offered.

Relieved that I had a willing intermediary, I waited in the foyer with Merona.

"Buria tells me that you shut down Tacesh," she said.

"I did. Everyone should be arriving on Artor soon. Is there someone you'd like to see?"

She shook her head.

"I also promised Buria to speak to the Premier for the three of you. You will be free as well."

Panic lit her otherwise sedate face. "We will be allowed to stay? To serve the Premier?"

"Yes, of course. I mean that you'll be paid. You may also say no if there is anything personal you do not wish to do for the Premier that does not directly pertain to your duties."

"I see. Thank you, Advisor."

She didn't sound particularly thankful. I doubted Fa'yet would either, but that was a problem for later. While we stood in silence, waiting for Ikeri, I tried to decide if I should stick to why I needed her or attempt to be fatherly like I wanted to be.

Ikeri's dull tone answered that for me. "Father."

I couldn't look at her. Not straight on. I'd want to hug her and she was having none of that. On to business it was.

"There's someone I hope you can help. One of the Arpex hunters."

Ikeri nodded, standing still, not touching me. The bright swirling tattoos on her bare head invited me to take her in fully. I tried not to give in but I was weak where she was concerned.

She wore her new Seeker robes with confidence, looking every bit as natural in them Seeker Tomias, her teacher, did. The gold geometric patterns reminded me of the golden hair she no longer had. The deep red fabric made her skin, the same tone as Stassia's appear stark and hard. She was no longer the soft slip of a giggling girl that used to sit on my lap with a head full of curls that tickled my cheeks.

The disapproval on her face brought the hateful words she'd written vividly back to the forefront of my memory. My gaze slipped to the floor where I would only have to see her peripherally.

"He's on Artor at the University," I said.

She just gave me a dry stare.

Buria joined us. "Your mate has asked me to accompany you?"

"Thank you for saving her earlier today."

"Of course." She offered a solemn head bow.

"It will be easier if I Jump us all."

Buria placed her hand on my arm without question.

"Are you ready?" I asked Ikeri.

She merely nodded. I missed when she used to hold her hand out to me, when she'd hold my arm, or for Geva's sake, when she liked me. I put a hand lightly on her shoulder and Jumped. We arrived in the heart of the University. Even at my slower than usual pace due to every muscle in my body still aching, it took only minutes and two security points to get back to Ha'guris.

Ikeri finally addressed me directly. "Where's Neko? Are Markus and Daniel safe?"

"They're all on Prime with Tomias."

Seeming to accept that answer without further disdain, Ikeri turned to Ha'guris.

"He's hearing the Arpex, but they're all gone from the Narvan," I said.

"Lie down. I need you to relax." Ikeri turned to Buria. "Turn off the lights."

The lights went out, leaving a good deal of the institutional brightness coming in from the hallway through the open door. Ikeri didn't seem to mind.

Buria took the spot in the doorway where Stassia had been. I stood back against the wall beside her in the hopes I could cut the contempt emanating from Ikeri so she could work with a clear mind. She stood beside Ha'guris, her hands on his temples, gazing down at him with the radiant peace I missed surrounding me whenever she was near. The little goddess of peace that Stassia and I had somehow created.

Maybe Ikeri was one of Geva's cruel jokes.

Hours passed with Buria and I standing side by side. My mind wandered between Narvan administration tasks and distraction. Though the drug was long gone and I knew my bond with Stassia was in place, I envisioned nuzzling up Buria's neck to see where that got me. Probably a swift kick in the groin. I laughed. Out loud, apparently.

Buria gave me a quizzical look. Ikeri ignored my outburst.

"Just thinking about you kicking me," I said quietly.

"Is that what you find enjoyable when you're not on the spray?" She snickered.

"Not usually, no. Today, I'll be happy if that's the only thing I encounter between now and when I hit my bed."

"It *has* been a rough morning for you," Buria conceded.

"You could say that." I was about to continue the light-hearted conversation when Ikeri's gaze settled on me with enough force to squash any hope of happiness in the next century.

"What did you find out?" I asked as neutrally as I could manage.

"He's not crazy. He is hearing Arpex. I think they're too far away to be clear. Like he's got an open channel."

"Can we use him to find out where they are?"

"He's not yours to use," she declared.

"Yes, I am," said Ha'guris, sitting up slowly. "If it wasn't for you, we'd be at the mercy of the Arpex right now. Whatever you need, I'm in."

As if she couldn't bear to concede the loss, Ikeri penetrated my head. *"Does mother know?"*

"Know what?"

"About you and Buria."

"That's none of your business, and not what you think."

"I can see quite clearly what it is."

While I would have liked to boot her out of my mind, I knew that wasn't possible and even trying to do so would confirm what she accused me of. Instead, I just stood there, as open to her as ever, which was pretty damned closed to anyone who didn't have her gift.

"You blame a drug for your actions," she said flatly.

"I don't blame anything. I'm bonded to your mother, and I would never intentionally hurt her. You know that."

Buria let out a gasp and ran out into the hallway. Her boots came to an abrupt halt several yards away.

I glared at Ikeri. "What did you do?"

"Told her the truth." She stood there, patiently waiting as if nothing had happened. "I'd like to go back to my room now."

It wasn't like I could ask Buria to take Ikeri after what she'd just done. I didn't want to touch her either. I was too angry, and I was sure she could sense that before the confirmation of my vice-like grip, but she didn't seem to care. She was much like her mother, stubborn and spiteful.

Ha'guris watched us, clearly confused as to what had just transpired.

"I'll be right back," I said.

I Jumped Ikeri back to Fa'yet's and barely let go of her before Jumping back. I didn't trust myself to hold back my tirade if I stayed in her presence a second longer.

Maybe we would never get back to what we had been. In that moment, maybe I didn't want to. Acknowledging that thought filled me with self-loathing.

When I again reached the room where Ha'guris was staying, I found Buria waiting outside, her back against the wall and tears in her eyes.

"What did she say to you?" I asked, making an effort to tone down the rage in my voice that I felt toward my daughter.

She wiped her eyes and took a shuddering breath. "I think it would be best if you took Nena from now on, if you need someone."

"I don't want to take Nena. I like working with you." Hells, even Stassia liked Buria. There was a small optimistic part of me that wondered if I could make that work somehow. It was common practice for Jalvians to have multiple wives. And we were all the same at the core, weren't we?

Buria looked away, her lips pinched together. "Please, Advisor Ta'set. I appreciate all you did for my sisters, and you say I won't be a slave any longer, but the Premier will fire me if he learns I've caused a rift between you and your mate. With a termination from the Premier, I will have a hard time finding another position."

"She's blackmailing you? Holy Geva, she really is my daughter." I wanted to laugh and cry at the same time.

"The Premier told me what you and your mate were like when you are separate. He was trying to explain how Artorian bonding works. I do not want to be the cause of a separation or what might befall others because of it."

I looked down to see her hand on my sleeve. I didn't mind it there at all. In fact, I very much wanted her hand to stay there. However, Stassia and I needed to have a serious conversation before I could consider offering to fix anything with Buria.

"Please. Take Nena from now on," Buria said.

I nodded reluctantly.

"Will you please try not to get killed for a few minutes on your own? I think it would be best if I return by myself."

"I'll go visit my sons for a while. I need somewhere quiet to think."

She was gone seconds later.

I checked in with Ha'guris, letting him know that I'd be back soon to speak with him so we could examine the opportunity his problem offered. Learning his problem would be useful brought about a significant positive transformation in his demeanor.

Before leaving Artor there was one more task I felt safe doing on my own as no one would expect me there. I Jumped to my point closest to the lab where I'd had Neko deliver the canisters of spray for development and took a public transport from there. No need to be too reckless. When I entered the lobby of the tall, plaz-lined building, hushed whispers erupted. The stammering man at the front desk pointed me to a private lift and assured me that the scientist I had chosen for the job would be waiting for me on the fifth floor at the room number he quickly provided.

Tara Ja'rul was indeed waiting with an eager smile, empty hands atop her desk, and a pair of tiny plaz vials waiting for my inspection.

"I've isolated and separated the product as per your request." She nodded to the vials. "Here are two samples of the endorphin booster. The sex stimulant is also ready for production."

"You've run trials? Made sure both are safe?"

"We have. Other than fatigue and soreness, no ill effects were reported."

I was intimately familiar with both of those side effects. Picking up the two vials, I examined the enticing golden fluid inside.

"The effects should last three to six hours, depending on activity level and body mass. I think you'll be pleased."

I tucked the vials into my pocket. "My cut of the profits will please me."

Tara smiled. "Of course, Advisor. Distribution is already underway, both prescribed and street varieties. All security precautions will be taken. Your name will not be associated in any way. You should see credits in the account that was provided in a matter of days."

"Thank you. Good work."

She beamed. "As per the agreement, you have only to let me know and a secure courier will deliver as much as you need."

Whether I'd need any or not remained to be seen, but having the option available eased the edginess that haunted my nerves since I'd lost the full Stassia and then Ikeri. One hand slipped into my pocket to caress the vials and their promise of wellbeing, even if it only would last for a few hours.

With that profit stream set up, I made a quick Jump to the bedroom at our estate. Ducking into the closet, I stashed the vials in the pocket of a pair of pants toward the bottom of a stack I rarely wore.

I controlled the drug. It would not control me.

Maybe just one drop to test Tara's work myself. I reached for the pocket.

No, if I showed up with that in my system, I might be able to fool Markus into thinking I was just in a good mood, but Daniel and Neko would know something was up. I sighed. What kind of screwed up life did I live where being happy was cause for suspicion and scrutiny?

Leaving my emotional safety net behind, I Jumped to Veria Prime and made my way to Seeker Tomias's home.

Neko had made a jump point within the Seeker's sanctuary, but I refused to use it unless it was an emergency. I liked the walk through town. It gave me time to breathe and, usually, to clear my head. That wasn't happening today.

When I arrived at the red door and knocked, an acolyte opened it. They all laughed at me for knocking, but for as many times as I had been there, walking in still felt wrong.

The boy, wearing a shirt two sizes too large and pants above his boney ankles, smiled. "They are in the yard behind the training hall, Advisor Ta'set."

"Thank you." I didn't remember this one's name. There were many children here and they came and went, staying with one Seeker to learn their specialty before moving to the next. Some stayed longer than others. A few had been here since I'd first visited with Stassia years ago, like Etara. But now she was a Seeker of her own accord and off serving the Verian people, probably in some town like this one.

Neko sat in the grass behind two rows of children of various sizes. They were going through the common Verian stretching forms. I'd seen Stassia do them a thousand times. She claimed they kept her thin and flexible. I liked watching her hold them, one form moving to the next in a smooth flow.

Neko caught sight of me and started to get up. I motioned for him to stay put and went to sit with him. Settling into a position that let my sore muscles relax as much as they were able, I breathed in the fresh air and let it out slowly.

"Rough day, boss?"

"You heard?"

"No, you just have that look about you, you know, more pissed than usual."

I gestured toward the boys who sat side by side in the front row facing away from us. "How are they doing?"

"Good. They're both listening without complaint and learning. Daniel helped make lunch, which was very good by the way. Markus is keeping right up. Spry little kid."

"I'll take two out of three today."

"Ah, the other one then?"

"And a lot of other things."

"We missed you last night."

I didn't miss his accusatory tone. "Long story. Most of which was ignored, the important parts anyway, and now I'm the number one hated person by every non-Artorian in the Narvan and Nebula."

"Wasn't that on your to-do list?"

"No, smart ass, it was not."

He gave me a wry smile before returning to watching the boys. "So what did Ikeri do?"

"That's not important right now."

"I sense a not important theme building."

"Why do I talk to you again?"

"Because no one else listens like I do, boss."

I sighed. I'd been doing a lot of sighing lately. "If you don't mind, I'd like to keep you and the boys here for a few days. I'd prefer you with me, but I need to know they're safe here and you're the one I can trust with doing that."

"Who's got your back then?"

"I borrowed Buria last night."

Neko's brows rose. "Isnar's guard?"

"Yeah."

"How'd that go?"

"Great, actually." I smiled, remembering our time outside the complex on Tacesh and our conversation in the University doorway before Ikeri had ruined it all.

"You're not stealing her from Isnar, are you? I heard he paid quite a lot for the three of them. At least make an offer."

"I don't pay for people."

"Not saying you do," he said quickly. "It's just how things are done in some corners of the universe."

"Not in my corner."

He nodded slowly. "So if you're not stealing Buria, and I wouldn't recommend Nena..."

"Why not? Has she done something I should know about? She's watching over Ikeri now."

"Don't doubt her skill a bit, boss. Relax. It's just that, well, she looks at you. In that way. If you know what I mean."

"Does everyone notice that?"

"Other boss definitely notices that."

"So I've heard. I guess that means I hire someone."

"Now, in the midst of being the most hated man? Kind of a rough place to start someone, isn't it?"

"Has there ever been a good time to ease someone in?"

"There were a few quiet days in there somewhere. As I recall, eleven in a row. Wasn't that the record?"

"I think so, yes." I picked at a blade of grass. "What are your thoughts on Buria?"

He tore his gaze from the boys to look at me. "I thought we just said you weren't taking her from Isnar." He let silence stretch on for a few moments. "I don't have thoughts about Buria, but I'm starting to think you do?"

How much did I want to tell him? I knew I could trust him not to run to Stassia, but did I want to put him in the middle? Dammit, I didn't have anyone else to talk this through with and Stassia deserved a clear conversation rather than my uncertain rambling. "I do."

His mouth dropped open. "But you... The bond... I thought..."

"Yeah, me too. But it's not like it used to be. I mean, it's still there, and I'm not saying I'd let Anastassia go by any means, but—"

Neko's mouth gaped further. "You'd go Jalvian? Is that even acceptable on Artor? Would Ana go along with that? And you're the Advisor of half the Narvan. Do you think it's wise to set yourself even further apart from your people? Gods, think of the threats that would bring on." He shook his head, silently ticking off supposed threats on his fingers.

Fuck. He was right. I sighed. "All right, yes, bad idea."

"On so many levels."

His gaze darted between the boys, the surroundings, and me.

"What?" I finally asked.

"Don't bite my head off, but seriously, if your bond is faltering, you need to talk to Ana about it. She deserves to know."

I thought about facing the hotel full of liberated slaves with Stassia at my side. "Oh, she'll know soon enough. How would you feel about adding a female guard?" I asked. "One that isn't Buria."

"I'm not opposed as long as she's good."

Watching the boys go through the forms would have been relaxing on any other day, but my nerves were still humming from Stassia telling me there had been a sniper on the rooftop, and the riots, the pulse wave, bodies flying apart in front of me, Jey's accusations, and the incessant barrage of contacts and requests pinging my link. I took in the gardens around us, the breeze blowing through the leaves of the voluminous tree overhead and the encouraging voice of the instructor. Everyone around us moved with grace, joy clear on their faces. Neko and I sat side by side, two stark, armored forms, full of weapons and clearly having no place here. Yet, here we were.

"I may have acquired twenty-some guard slaves like Nena and Buria to pick from."

His forehead creased. "I swear I just heard you rather vehemently tell me that you don't buy people."

"I said acquired. Liberated. That work better?"

"Boss, you did not happen to liberate those slaves from an old mining colony called Tacesh, did you? Last night?"

"Maybe, why?"

He whistled quietly. "Because the investors are pissed. And they're big. And I would anticipate they'll figure out who you are. We'll be hearing from them."

"How do you know?"

"I have connections. Ex-Cragtek remember? Maybe you don't. Sorry, I lose track between both of you sometimes."

I considered punching him, but in light of the rest of my day so far, I let his teasing go. "I do remember that, yes."

He snickered at my dry reply. "We dealt with them on occasion, good location on the trade route. My contact on the colony sent me an update this morning. That's where that shipment went that you asked about last week."

"One of these days we need to sit down and go over your contacts. I have the distinct feeling I'm not using you to your fullest potential."

"In your spare time, boss."

At least he wasn't opposed to being used. If anything, he seemed to thrive on it.

"Yes, exactly." I chuckled. "So this contact, he seems to think I'm in trouble, does he?"

"I'm telling you you're in trouble. But that's nothing new. We'll deal with it."

"These investors, what kind of force do they have?"

"Give me a few hours, and I'll see what I can find out."

"Just make sure you're keeping an eye on the boys while you're at it."

He nodded solemnly. "Of course."

"Is Tomias here?"

"Don't think so. I heard he was out on a call to a family with several sick kids. There was talk of a virus that they didn't want to spread. It's hit several homes nearby already."

"That doesn't sound good. Feel out what it might be and if they want help. I can have doctors here in a matter of minutes if they'll accept it."

"Will do. Where to next for you then?"

"I guess I'm taking Anastassia to meet the liberated slaves so she can choose a new guard and we can have some version of that conversation you recommended. I'm probably going to be sleeping on the couch for a week or two if she doesn't kill me first."

"Let's hope for the couch, shall we?"

I smiled weakly. "I'm also trying not to get pulsed again today."

His attention snapped back to me. "*Again?* Boss, please don't get pulsed again today. You're killing me here. I know you want the boys protected, but I should be with you. I don't think I can take another month of the other boss running things. She's not—"

"Easy to work for like me?"

Neko snorted. "You read my mind."

"I'll do my best to avoid it then." I stood.

The class finished. The boys noticed me and ran over. Enveloped in hugs, some of my agitation over Ikeri faded. Two out of three, I kept telling myself.

"You're picking that up quickly," I said, ruffling Markus's hair.

He flashed a beaming smile. "It's fun."

"I'm glad you think so."

My subconscious suggested that there might be another reason I was here on Veria Minor, here in the sanctuary of Seekers. While I'd grown comfortable talking with Neko, an outside opinion on dealing with Ikeri might be more helpful.

Stassia had served as a confidant and counselor to most of our colony while we'd lived on Veria Minor. Geva knew I needed one of those about now. Talking to Tomias would be awkward, but there were alternatives. "Do any of you know where Etara got stationed?"

"She's here," said Daniel. "I saw her this morning. She's been helping the acolytes while Seeker Tomias is gone."

"That saves some time then. I need to see her." For my own sanity.

I left the three of them on the lawn, Markus doing his best to knock down Neko, who was on his knees. I wished I got to play with them.

No rest for the wicked.

A quick inquiry to the acolyte at the door sent me to Etara who was up in the open training room where Stassia and I had recently shared our memories thanks to Ikeri's memory menders. It was also the same room where I'd lost my temper with Ikeri. Where I'd driven her away. Even though the space was open and full of light, being in that room made my teeth grind together.

Etara smiled when she noticed me. It was hard not to, with my boots clomping up the wooden stairs despite my attempts to be quiet in the echoing space. She dismissed her students and came over.

"Can I help you with something?"

"Can we go outside?"

She nodded, following me down the stairs. The sunlight washed away the dirty feeling from the room above.

"You like it here," she said, nodding toward the garden.

"I suppose so."

She stopped, the peeved look I was accustomed to her wearing resurfaced. "You owe me a favor for the memory balm, yes?"

It figured that today of all days she was going to collect on that. I sighed, wondering at the fact that I had any air left in my lungs to do so. "I do."

"I would collect a vow from you as payment then."

What would she ask of me? To never return, to stop killing people, to do no harm? A hundred other impossible demands plowed through my head.

"You will be honest with me, always."

"Ah."

"Indeed. You have a lot going on in your head. How you keep it all straight, I can't imagine. It will help to both of us if you can be honest." She held up a hand. "It's not your nature, I understand that. You have to hide your true opinions and feelings behind what is expected and what is best. But you and I, we will be honest with one another. Agreed?"

"Yes, all right. You may not like it though."

"I don't have to like your truth and you do not need to like mine. But lies won't help either of us."

A warm breeze blew through the deep green leaves above. The acolytes, released from their exercises laughed and tumbled in the grass, trying to use what they'd learned on one another. Daniel knocked down a young man with little effort and then another. Markus ran around them all, dodging between sparring pairs of older children with a wide grin on his face, all of them harmlessly burning off excess energy so they could focus on their studies later.

"Let's start again then. Do you like it here?"

"Outside in this green space, yes. Up there," I pointed to the building where we'd been, "no."

"That's better," she said, using the same tone she'd used on her students. "Why don't you like it up there?"

The truth was personal. I'd lost Ikeri in that room and it was my own fault. We could have patched things up between us, returned to who we had been to one other if I'd not gone too far.

"I showed Ikeri who I was there, what she had to fear for one so prominent in her status at such a young age. She hates me for it." Unable to stand still with everything tumbling around in my head, I started to walk.

Etara walked beside me, slowly, calmly, holding me to her pace as we circled the students at a distance. Some began to drift away toward the dorm hall, taking their joy with them.

"You did what needed to be done, clearly explained what we couldn't," she said finally.

"What?" Surely she didn't condone what I'd done.

She turned her head up to the white clouds high overhead. "Ikeri is so very young. More powerful than any of us. She thinks she's invincible. Tomias did his best to dispel this notion, but neither of us leaves Prime often, and even then, only to assist on Minor. We hear rumors of the horrors in the wider universe. Life has its difficulties here, but it is peaceful. We knew she would not be able to stay on

Prime. Rumors of the youngest Seeker have made their rounds thanks to visitors. Some of the rumors and visitors are not that friendly."

"I'm sorry to hear that. Would you like someone to assist the acolyte that is posted at the door?"

"Someone like you?"

"Not exactly. I have a large number of trained women who need employment. They've suffered at the hands of others, some since childhood. I can cover her wages if you would like a little security."

"In addition to your guard?"

"Since we're being honest, Neko's priority will always be my children."

"I understand. I'll take your proposal to Tomias when he returns. But as to Ikeri, I'm not sure how you could have proceeded other than how you did. It was necessary."

"I'm sure there must be a kinder way. I'm not known for delicacy."

Etara cracked a smile. "While that is true, the universe is not a kind or delicate place. She needed to know, and who better to explain it to her?"

"She has asked me not to speak to her or to be near her."

"And this pains you." Etara studied the patterns on the sleeves of her robe as though looking me in the eye would pain her too.

"Greatly," I admitted.

"Why?"

I knew the tone of a therapy session from Stassia's time of practicing on Veria Minor, but hells, that's why I was here. I dropped down onto a stone bench under the tree where we'd started, now having come full circle.

"Her mother and I, we're working through a lot of things. It hasn't been an easy process."

"The Arpex-induced memory loss?"

"Hers and mine, yes, among other things."

Etara nodded.

"Ikeri has always been a source of calm for me. She's the center of it all, I guess."

"This makes you uncomfortable, talking about things that are important to you."

"You could say that."

Etara settled onto the bench next to me. "Where your mate was once your center, she is not quite so anymore and this makes you uncertain, sad."

I was about to scream at her for being in my head without permission, for violating my privacy, but before the words left my mouth, I encountered a burst of calm from Etara. Not one that felt as though she was trying to manipulate me into letting her roam through my head, but just enough to let me know it was all right, that it was simpler to just show her and let her talk.

It was easier for her to speak the words I didn't want to say.

"Ikeri filled that void for you, and now you have neither of them at your center."

"Yes."

"Does Ikeri know how much her actions have hurt you?"

I could only give her a dry stare.

"Of course she does." Etara sighed. "As bright and talented as she is, she's still a young girl. She's lashing out."

"If you say so."

The calm from Etara grew until it held me like Ikeri used to, like she had that last time when I'd come here to introduce them to Markus. It brought tears to my eyes.

"She will come back to you. You are as important to her as she is to you."

"You think so?" The words slipped out before I'd had a chance to censor the raw emotion from them.

"We are being honest. Yes."

I nodded, feeling a small weight lift from me.

"When Ikeri first came to us, I worked with her quite a lot. Our skills were closely matched. I spent a good deal of time in her mind." She held her hands on her lap, studying the grass just beyond our feet. "Your minds are similar, full of fast-paced thoughts. But where you have the vast knowledge of the reality of things, she has only a faint idea, an idealized version."

She turned to look at me. "You brutally crushed her reality. Once she comes to see what is true, that you showed her those things because you care deeply, she will be back beside you."

"I'm afraid that will be a very long time from now."

"We will see." She stood. "Until then, if you feel the need for calm or counsel, find me."

While I gathered that she'd spoken to me this time out of duty, or maybe to diffuse the chaos in my head that a Seeker could surely sense, her offer stunned me. I stared down at this young woman who had been a point of ridicule at one of the lowest points in my life. She was everything I was not.

"Why would you help me? This isn't a favor to Ikeri."

Etara chewed her lower lip for a moment. If I hadn't known better, I would have thought she was struggling with our pact of honesty.

"I have seen into your mind. Once, like Ikeri, I was repulsed by what I saw there, but I've come to understand that you are a complicated man. A necessary one, I think. My life is given in service in return for the gifts I have received." She looked at me levelly for the first time, her standing and me seated. "I've never considered that my service should end on Prime."

Etara turned and walked back inside. Neko and the boys had gone to whatever was next on their schedule. I sat there alone for a few minutes, caught up in the quiet and calm Etara had wrapped around me. But I couldn't stay there all day. Reluctantly, I returned to Fa'yet's estate to collect Stassia.

Merona brought me to the common room where Stassia sat curled up with her datapad in a stuffed chair large enough for both of us. Her armor and several weapons sat on the low table in the middle of the room. I sat down beside her.

"Making waves all over the system today, aren't you?" She glanced up from her datapad and immediately switched off the screen to set it down.

"Not intentionally."

"Ikeri stormed off to her room when she got back. Buria wasn't much better, and now you show up with an aura of weird rolling off you. What's going on?"

"Besides the obvious?"

She idly stroked a finger over the back of my hand. "Other than the Jey and Kess disaster, and nearly getting killed this morning, yes."

"One thing at a time. Get anywhere on finding the source of the leak with Le'rin?

"So far it's looking like a member of the documentation crew. Le'rin's team found his body a couple hours ago on Artor. My gut is telling me this is another Kess move, and he's cleaning up just like he did with the woman who pulsed you along with whatever other agents he had in that crowd to stir up a riot."

Nena walked by, the heels of her boots clicking on the tiled floors. She didn't look our way. I pondered Stassia's pale finger against my skin, considering the implications of her opinion.

"I'm with you on that one. My bigger concern is whether Kess was in it with Jey or if this is him laying groundwork for sewing enough distractions to make a play for the whole Narvan for himself."

She grimaced. "You think he'd do that? He's got the nebula to run."

"And he has it in hand. Beyond keeping the Merchessian families from killing each other, the Rakon is easy. He just has to be feared enough to rule. He's got that down. Jey has the Fragians tamed with his truce. We're the ones over here struggling to meet the needs of our people without being dictators and without the plentiful funding."

She dropped her head onto my shoulder. "Let's hope you're wrong."

One could hope. "I should eat before the next crisis strikes."

"I got something earlier." Stassia called out, "Merona?"

Seconds later, Merona showed up. "What can I get for you, Advisor?"

I shook my head. "I can get something to eat."

"It's no trouble," she said.

"Why did you have to do that?" I asked Stassia. *"I don't need anyone to serve me."*

Stassia shrugged. *"It's her job."*

"A job is something you get paid for."

"That's Isnar's business."

"I'm fine, thank you, Merona," I said as politely and yet dismissively as I could manage.

Merona bowed quickly and left.

"Now you made her uncomfortable," said Stassia, uncurling from the chair and stretching her legs.

"The fact that he's keeping slaves makes me uncomfortable. Speaking of which, I need to speak to your pal Isnar before we go."

"And where are we going?"

"To Artor, to see about getting another guard or two."

"As long as they're like Buria, I'm in."

"Similar, yes." I was starting to get a taste of Jey and Kess's frustration about things they wanted but were impossible to have.

"What did you do to Buria, anyway?" she asked.

I held up my hands. "That was Ikeri, not me."

"They had a falling out?"

"You could say that."

Stassia shook her head, irritation seeping through our connection.

"I'll explain later." I wanted to enjoy Etara's peace a little longer. Stassia would learn the truth of it all soon enough. "Why don't you get suited up. We'll leave in a few minutes. This conversation with

Isnar shouldn't take long."

"If you truly feel you need to say something, at least keep it civil, will you? He's gracefully agreed to tie up his guards with watching Ikeri for us."

"I will." I walked away with her dubious look drilling into my back.

The Premier of Karin sat in his private office, the lights of his ornate liquor cabinet lending a familiar glow to the room. It was good to see he had brought something from his other house.

For as much stress as running a world put on a person, though he was quickly becoming a master of delegation, he still appeared more relaxed than he had when he'd worked for me.

"How's retirement treating you?" I asked, closing the door.

"Great, until you walked in. What's on your mind that's about to be my problem?"

"Your slaves."

He scowled. "What did Buria do?"

"Buria is fine. They're all fine. My issue is with the fact that they are slaves and that you bought them."

"They weren't cheap. They had years of training, all of them. How else was I going to find a staff with no other allegiances on short notice?"

"I know exactly what they cost. Call it a loss and start paying them a fair wage."

He blanched. "You can't be serious. I bought them perfectly legally."

"And if you'd kept them on Tacesh, I'd have no say in the matter, but you're here in my system and we don't do slavery."

"You and Ana had no issue with profiting from the slave trade on Merchess."

Geva, not Merchess again. Would that be thrown in my face every time this issue arose? "Merchess isn't part of the Narvan."

"Oh please, what about Kess? His entire fortune has been amassed from the slave trade."

"Kess also does not operate in the Narvan. And I've never liked him, even before taking his business ventures into consideration."

"So because you like me, you're going to toss my credits out the door and make me pay my staff a fair wage even though their contract expressly forbids me from paying them."

"The moment you brought them into the Narvan that contract became invalid. Oh, and their operation is no more so it's also null everywhere else."

"Is that what Buria was upset about when she came back?"

"No, that was an entirely different matter. I'm also going to ask that you don't expect your staff to jump into your head or bed."

He shot up from his chair. "That is absolutely none of your fucking business. I put up with your chastity-inducing job for years. I'm retired. I will enjoy what pleasure I want in my own damned house."

"Then find an Artorian to do it for you. These women might have a whisper of telepathy, but using them as you do hurts them."

"What?" His angry tone faltered. "They never said a word about that."

"Do they have the freedom to say a word? Complaining is expressly forbidden in their contract."

He stammered and then sat down abruptly. "How did you come to know this?"

"We talked."

"Since when did you start being friendly?" he snapped.

"Don't worry, I don't make a habit of it."

"With Buria or in general?" He gave me an accusing glare. "I'd appreciate you not monopolizing my staff. I did purchase them for a reason."

"I'm aware of that. I appreciate you letting Ikeri stay here and having the benefit of your *employees*."

He grumbled. "Fine, I'll pay them. I hope you and Ikeri get over whatever is between you soon. Surely you can do that, being the adult? She's just a kid, for Geva's sake."

"I assure you that it wasn't my choice to have her leave our home."

"It was Ana's. The tension between you and your daughter has been hard on her in light of her own situation."

"I'm aware of that too. You also know Ikeri is much more than just a kid."

"I do." He eyed his cabinet.

"Good. I have other fires to attend to, and I'm hungry. I'm taking Anastassia with me."

He nodded.

"One more thing, you'll want to put Nena on primary Ikeri duty rather than Buria."

"Duly noted." He got up and headed for the liquor.

I left him to drink alone.

NINE

I tore into the warm bread pocket filled with smoked fish and cream sauce like I hadn't eaten in days. With Stassia beside me, my nervous energy needed the distraction of food while we walked the one block from my jump point to the hotel filled with the very friendly and grateful women that I'd freed. This was a smaller city with nothing of great importance, which is why I had invested in the hotel and a handful of other businesses here. I preferred to keep my holdings off the radar so they didn't stick out as glaring targets for angry Jalvians or anyone else to wipe off the map. I didn't even spot any Jalvians here, though I kept an eye on the rooftops and for any roving vid bots that might report our presence.

"So how many are there?" Stassia asked.

"Twenty-some guards, eleven hospitality, and thirty-some who were in training." I took a big bite and chewed it thoroughly. "And eight sex slaves."

"I'm sorry, did you say that you plan to employ sex slaves?"

"Not personally," I said quickly. "The women are all cross-trained. That just happens to be what they're best at."

People on the walk near us gave us a wide berth, whether that was because they recognized us, or because of the pitch of Stassia's voice, I wasn't sure.

Stassia's eyes narrowed. "And you would know this how?"

"Part of the tour."

"You took a tour."

Though I kept my eyes forward, I could feel the laser-like burn of her gaze. "I needed to have information about the business before I took it down."

"Did you take the crazy sex drug before or after meeting the professional sex slaves?"

I didn't particularly like how her voice dropped to that level tone that made me worried for my safety. "After. And I didn't take the drug. I was attacked with it."

"So were you drugged by the casually-trained sex slaves in hospitality or by the bodyguards?"

I savored the final bite of my meal in case it was my last. "The guards."

"Of course you did." She walked faster.

I hurried to catch up. "They sprayed me with it when I was trying to take out the remaining Masters. It's not like we were all hanging out on a giant bed, naked, and basking in drugs."

She smiled, but it was the dangerous kind. "We'll see what they say about that."

I held my breath as I entered my override code to open the side door to the hotel and let her in ahead of me. Showing fear would only put her even harder on the scent.

"Which floor?"

"Third. All of it. Thought it best to keep them isolated for now."

She headed up the stairs, not bothering to wait for a lift. Great, she had plenty of energy to burn. I nearly had to run up the stairs after her. We made it to the third floor in record time.

Stassia hit the first closed door in the long hallway with a fist. As soon as it was answered, she loudly demanded that all of the occupants gather in the hallway. She continued pounding on doors down the row and around the corner until everyone had spilled out into the corridor.

Curious stares traveled from her to me. My heart started to race when Saka stepped forward. Good thing the heart was new. My old one might have given out.

I'd hoped that my reaction to Buria earlier was because we were more acquainted. We were working together. But there was no explaining away my near magnetic attraction to Saka. Apparently, the drug wasn't required for that. Fucking hells.

Saka looked at me with her tide pool eyes that were just as beautiful without the drug. "Is this your wife?"

I nodded, not trusting myself to speak.

"It's so nice to meet you," Saka said in an utterly Merona-like voice. I wondered if they all learned the tone or if it was a coincidence.

"Is it now?" Stassia eyed her suspiciously.

Saka cast me a smile so bright that her eyes twinkled. "I see what you meant, she would definitely kill me."

That made Stassia laugh. Hard. A sudden wave of warmth flowed through our connection. I much preferred that to the alternative but had a feeling we'd be back to that in no time.

I cleared my throat to get the attention of all the women, which was rapt and too admiring for my comfort in Stassia's presence.

"I have several possible positions. My wife will be interviewing you until she finds what she wants."

As I feared, their disappointment was blatantly obvious. Stassia's ominous gaze cut through me.

"You're going to stand by your story that nothing happened while on that drug with this entire gaggle of trained sex slaves who are hanging on your every word? I'm not kidding when I say half of them are drooling."

I backed up a step. *"I didn't say nothing happened. The damned drug all but erased our bond. What I said was, that I didn't have sex with any of them."*

She nodded slowly. *"How many of these women did you not exactly have sex with?"*

"Depending on the scale of not exactly, four or one."

The barb she flung at me through our connection was well aimed. I'd hoped my relative honesty would gain me some leniency, but maybe I should have tried lying. I'd gotten better at that over the years.

She left my side and stalked down the hallway. The women hastily formed a line, thinking they were being assessed for employment. Their years of being beaten down by the Masters lent them blank and obedient expressions even in light of Stassia's judgmental gaze. I supposed they were used to being shopped like this regularly.

"You wouldn't have gone for a bed slave. That's far too easy." She continued down the line. *"The hospitality slaves are too nice. You have your moments, but you don't do nice. It's awkward and uncomfortable for you."* She again looked from me to the line of women. "A guard then," she said out loud.

I cringed. I didn't want to see any of them hurt, certainly not Saka. "Stassia, leave them be. It was the drug. It didn't mean anything."

Saka again stepped forward, keeping her gaze stoically locked on the generic still frame on the opposite wall. "If you're looking to blame someone, it was me."

Stassia huffed. "That's no surprise. I was hoping to torture him a bit longer."

Saka paled. "How did you know?"

"You blushed when he walked in."

Saka bowed her head and remained that way, clearly waiting for her punishment.

"Please," said one of the other guards who had been on the bed with us. "The drug is all but impossible to resist. It wasn't his fault. He held off the effects more than we've ever seen."

Marta also stepped forward. "He could have easily had all four of us when we were in bed together."

Stassia turned her steely glare on me.

"I was clothed. Mostly. And none of them have any telepathy. Fa'yet took the ones who do."

"He refused us," said the first one. "It's unheard of. Sometimes they'll pick one of us over another, but they never outright refuse."

"So you're telling me that this drug effectively erased our bond and you were in a bed with four of these women and you got up and left?"

"I did, but I did happen across Saka outside later and the drug was in full force at that point."

"But you didn't screw her in the head or otherwise?"

"No."

Stassia stalked towards me. *"Why not? They're all exactly your type and I assume she was willing and able in one way or another."*

"Because she's not you."

It was the safest answer I could throw at her. And it was mostly truthful. Thankfully, Buria hadn't been as agreeable as Saka, or I'd have been feeling a whole lot guiltier.

"Damn." Her stalking came to a sudden halt.

"What?" Could she sense my omission? I held my breath.

"I have no comeback for that." She turned back to the line. "How many do we want, and how many can we afford?"

"They don't expect to earn anything, but they will if they are in our service. As long as the wage is fair, there's no need to get extravagant."

"Glad to see you're still approaching this logically. Though it's the how I'm rather amazed about."

What could I say? I'd already used the best answer and acknowledged that the bond had been erased while under the influence of the spray. 'I told you that you didn't have anything to worry about' was all I had left, but that seemed too flippant. And a total lie.

"You're lucky that I trust you given what they've said, or you'd be bleeding and on the floor right now." Stassia turned back to her task, leaving me to sweat and wallow in my guilt in silence.

At the end of a two-hour-long agonizing evaluation, for me anyway, because I wanted to make sure she wasn't waiting to kill me until later, Stassia picked three of the women.

I did my best to keep my face blank when it was clear Saka was one of them. My best didn't fool Stassia.

"Is that going to be a problem?" she asked.

"Not exactly. Uncomfortable, yes."

"Good. You deserve that." She smiled sweetly. "At least I know she's even worse at lying than you are." Pinning me in her gaze she asked, "Since we're on the topic. Are there any other women not in this room that something happened with?"

This was only going to get more awkward. "I may have mauled Buria a little."

"A little?"

"She wasn't having any of it." Sort of. At least not at that moment and certainly not now while Ikeri had leverage.

"I knew I liked her."

Though it was somewhat of a relief to have the truth out in the open, I did really like Buria. On many levels. And now I was going to have to be on my toes at all times with Stassia on the scent of my weakness with her and Saka. Worse, I'd have to be around them on a daily basis, or at least Buria as long as Ikeri stayed with Fa'yet. I didn't foresee any sudden reconciliation happening with Ikeri despite what Etara thought.

"Perhaps we could talk about this later, in private?" Neko was right, she deserved to know about the faltering bond.

"Oh, we will," she said, the high threat level clear. "Why don't you get these three to the house. I'll wait for you here."

"What next?" I asked with all the enthusiasm of a convict waiting for their sentence to be revealed.

She pulled out her datapad and started typing. "I'm inviting Jey for a hiring spree."

That wasn't so bad. Annoying, but not directly related to me.

"Make sure you have him out of here before I'm back."

"No, I'm waiting for you. You two need to work this shit out before it escalates any farther."

"Sure. Yeah."

If she thought she could play negotiator and make it all better, she was welcome to try. This wasn't going to be as easy as switching our shifts to minimize the mutual awake and insult times like when she'd first hired us. We were a whole lot past that now.

"Your sarcasm is showing," she said.

"It's logic, Stassia. But have at it."

"I will." She waved the women toward me and kept watch as I gathered them into my mind to perform the Jump to our home.

Saka, I knew quite well. The other two took a couple moments. All of them had the tanned skin prevalent among the whole lot, though of varying shades. The hospitality slave had a softer, rounder build than the two guards, full cheeks, and long, straight dark hair that hung to her waist. The second guard looked to be one of the youngest of the fully trained bunch, maybe early twenties, with a heart-shaped face, and pale blue eyes like Saka's.

Taking the time to Jump them individually would have been a far better bet, I considered as I arrived in the foyer with the three of them, but I just wanted this day done already. The more I could accomplish at once the better.

I rubbed my temples. Fa'yet might have been onto something with his need for a drink.

"Are you unwell?" asked the hospitality slave in a red dress. She looked quite unwell herself. Saka and the guard beside her also had a green cast.

At least none of them made a mess on the floor. I had to give them credit for holding the nausea in. Not many people could manage that on their first Jump.

"Can I get you something?" the woman asked.

On a normal day, I would have said no and gotten whatever it was myself, but with what still lay ahead, taking the easy road, just this once, held a certain allure. "I need a drink."

"Of course." She started to the left and then to the right, "I'm sorry, I don't know where that might be found yet."

"What's your name?"

"Hedvika, Advisor."

"All of you follow me." I brought them to the kitchen. "Food is in here. Drinks are there." I pointed to the cabinet where Stassia kept our stash.

I sat at the table with my head in my hands. "Glasses are to your left."

"Would you like something to eat, Advisor?" asked the young guard.

"No. Just a drink."

"Ice?" asked Hedvika.

"No."

"Today or always?"

All the questions. I was not in the mood for them.

"Are you coming back?" asked Stassia.

"Not immediately. Give me a few minutes to recover from Jumping the three of them."

"Maybe you shouldn't have been showing off for the new help by Jumping them all at the same time."

"I wasn't," I snapped. My head was really starting to pound on top of the soreness from the morning pulse blast. Her needling wasn't helping.

I realized I'd not answered Hedvika. "Unless we're on Frique, no ice."

"Yes, Advisor." She opened the cabinet. "What would you like?"

"Anything strong. The red wine is for Anastassia. No one else."

"Of course, Advisor."

I was going to get sick of that quickly. Did we need a staff?

She set a glass that was only a quarter full with liquor in front of me.

"Fill it. Always."

"Of course, Ad—"

"And no more of that. Just do it and we'll call it good, all right?"

She started to say something but snapped her mouth shut and bowed instead.

I swallowed half the glass and waited for the warmth to blossom in my throat. When it finally did, I exhaled.

"That's better. Saka, what's your sister's name?"

"Meera."

"I will likely forget your names for a few days. There's a lot going on. Don't take it personally."

Saka gave me an odd look.

"Not yours. That's kind of ingrained in my head. Just do whatever you can to stay on her good side, will you? Anastassia can be hard to live with."

"I will do as you say."

The bland acceptance of their situation made me wince. I hoped that, in time, they'd all find themselves again. I'd do my best to help them.

"Saka, it would be wise to pay me no special attention. Especially not in her presence. You do realize why she picked you?"

"I do." She bowed her head. "I'll do my best."

"Good." I finished my drink and gave standing a try. The throbbing in my head had subsided somewhat. "You three will stay here and get settled in. There are extra rooms down that hall." I pointed them in the opposite direction from our bedroom. "Neko will be back in a few hours, probably before we are. Do any of you cook?"

All three nodded.

"Daniel isn't going to like that. My son likes to cook. However, he needs some nights off so you can figure that out with him, Hedvika. Saka and Meera, you two will be trading off. Neko will figure out your schedule. You will answer to Neko first and then to me. Clear enough?"

They all nodded. "Good. Also, we were attacked this morning so pay no attention to the scorch marks on the outside of the house. If there are more attacks while I'm out, the house systems will alert me. None of you will be able to contact me until you are linked. Neko will explain that when he gets here."

Neko was going to have a lot of explaining to do. I contacted him. *"You now have a staff of three. Congratulations on your promotion."*

"What if I don't want a staff of any size?" he said sounding like I'd just handed him a grenade. *"When you suggested hiring another guard, I didn't realize—"*

"It isn't an optional promotion."

"At least you didn't screw me over as bad as Fa'yet," he grumbled. *"Did you? Seriously, what does this mean for me?"*

I imagined him gritting his teeth. *"It means you're off Veria Prime duty and back beside me once they get linked and trained. Your first priority is getting them linked and trained."*

"That sounds like a lot of headaches." He was quiet for a moment but when he spoke again he sounded more resigned than annoyed. *"As much as I like your kids, I'll feel much better about watching your back personally."*

"Didn't think you'd mind in the long run."

"Oh, boss?" The waver in his voice set me further on edge.

"What?"

"Those investors in the Tacesh operation you halted? They've got a few ships. It's a similar-sized operation to Cragtek but spread through several systems. Might take them a bit to get their forces together and get after you."

"Thanks. I'll figure something out."

"I know you will, boss." He cut contact.

I eyed the bottle Hedvika had left on the counter but decided it was best to see Jey with a relatively clear head. I returned to the hotel and Stassia to discover that she'd moved everyone to one of the meeting rooms on the ground floor.

She tucked her datapad into a pocket and gave me an unimpressed once over. "Jey will be here momentarily."

"What's he interested in?"

"Beating the hell out of you, from what I gather. Are you sure you want to offer him bodyguards?"

That lit a flame of inspiration in my head. I felt a smile forming.

I got everyone's attention and addressed them. "I told you I would find you employment. You're no longer slaves, but you will answer to me in return for your freedom. If you have an issue with your employment, let me know. I am here to help you. You will report to me with information if I ask for it. You will never act against me or any of my family or staff. If that becomes a conflict of an order given by your new employer, let me know and I will take care of the problem. Am I clear?"

"Are we to be spies then?" asked one of the guards.

"I prefer contacts."

"And how will we report to you?"

I turned to Stassia. "Set up a secure address and give each of them the information."

"You sneaky devil," she said with an appreciative look. "A whole influx of new contacts loyal to only you."

"And you."

She snorted. "Only by association. I'll get on it. Jey will be here any moment."

"This particular employer is a business partner and we are currently not on the best of terms. He has a family. I expect that they will be protected no matter what should happen between him and me."

The women nodded.

Loud footsteps announced Jey's entrance. He strode over to us, the medals on his uniform loudly jangling with each step. "You have the nerve to suggest that I might need protection?"

Stassia stepped forward to intercept him in the hallway just outside the room. He wouldn't harm her, so I let her have at him as long as she stayed in sight. I moved closer to the end of the line of women so I could hear the two of them.

"If Kess was willing to plant someone on Artor to pulse Vayen, then yes, he might do something similar to you and try to make it look like we're acting against you. Or someone else might take a shot at you. You're not exactly popular around here today."

He stared down his nose at her. "My popularity isn't your concern."

She didn't give an inch. "It is. You think what happens in your half of the system doesn't affect us?"

"I think your people might want to get off my worlds until this is resolved. I can't assure their safety."

Using that threatening tone with me was one thing, but I wasn't about to have him continue throwing it at Stassia. I joined them in the hallway. "Can't or won't? Are you telling me that you don't have control of your populace, or are you sanctioning violence against my people?"

"I have as much control as you do," Jey spat. "You allowed your university to put my people to a gruesome death yesterday and my people to be obliterated by a pulse this morning. What are you going to allow tomorrow?"

"I had no part in either of those things," I said adamantly.

"You knew you'd be safe from a pulse. We tested it, you and I. Your little show might have fooled your people, but I know how you work. You wanted that protest to end and pulsing everyone was the quickest solution."

Stassia jabbed him in the chest with her finger. "You think I would have allowed him to take any part in that plan you imagined? Really? After all the grief you've given me for treating him like he's made of glass this past month?"

His rock-solid ire dropped a notch. "You and I both know that he doesn't always listen to you. He likes to do stupid and crazy shit on a whim."

Stassia glanced from the waiting, silent crowd of women to me.

"Like leaking the documentation footage that ignited this whole mess?" I said, hoping to get a feel for the true leak.

"I didn't leak it," he said tightly.

"You had a hand in generating the false documents that allowed for your damned team to get into the University to get the footage," I said. "You used my name and you knew I'd find out, but you did it anyway. What am I supposed to take from that?"

He looked at the floor. "We needed to see for ourselves. University provided footage could be altered."

"Why would we want to show you the horrible deaths of your people if that's not what happened? You can saw how well that went over even when it was the truth. How are we supposed to trust you?"

"You can," he said, meeting my gaze for a second.

"Kess was behind the pulse attack," Stassia snapped. "Artorian enforcers recovered the body of both the woman who pulsed Vayen and the sniper sent to take her out after the job was done. They're working on confirming their identities, but I know the sniper from Kess's guild. We'll publicly pin this on him soon enough. Would you like to go down with him?"

Uncertainty flashed over Jey's face. "You're sure?"

Was he asking because he wanted to know who he was really aligning himself with or because he wondered if ties to himself would also be uncovered? I missed the days when I could trust him implicitly.

"We are," Stassia stated. "Which brings us back to the reason I asked you here. Vayen, through one of those stupid, crazy whims, has acquired these skilled women and thought you might be interested in employing some of them."

I trailed behind as she led him into the meeting room. She'd always been adept at handling Jey. Both of us really, but I more appreciated her manipulations on someone other than myself.

While the two of them went down the row, discussing what needs he might have, I skirted around them and established personal contacts with several of the women. I had a few in mind to place in certain positions by the time Jey had made his selections.

It shouldn't have surprised me that he'd selected one of the bed slaves, but yet it did. They wouldn't offer him anything beyond the obvious. Perhaps attracting another woman of any beneficial social standing would be difficult when he already had the top prize of the Jalvian Prime's daughter.

And maybe I was a little jealous. Not that I had any desire for a bed slave, but that his people wouldn't think anything of him having one or a second wife or even a third. It was normal, totally acceptable. Though Jey and I had initiated a slow exchange of culture to attempt to bring the Narvan fully back together, Neko was right, my people would have a serious issue with me leaping on that practice.

Assuming I dared even broach the topic with Stassia. She already wasn't going to like that I, for some Geva-forsaken-reason, had the inclination to entertain the idea given that we had a bond.

Stassia must have caught wind of my wandering thoughts because her narrow-eyed gaze had honed in on me. I detached myself from the milling women who were starting to talk quietly now that it appeared Jey had made his selections. I crossed the room to join Stassia and Jey.

"Dayana will appreciate having help around the house," Jey was saying to Stassia in regards to the hospitality slave he'd chosen. "The guard will ease her mind too. She's been on edge since that Arpex showed up at our door."

And the bed slave would take care of him, I grumbled to myself.

"Speaking of the Arpex, I may have a lead on them," I said.

That caught Jey's attention. "How so?"

"One of the hunters thought he was going crazy, but it turns out he has a connection that is stuck on open."

Jey scowled and shook his head. "How is that helpful? Are they able to talk through him? Are we negotiating? Are they spying through him?"

"No to all three. Ikeri thinks he's an open channel. I'm going to have her do another session with the hunter to see if we can work the channel to our advantage somehow."

"Your hunter," he said snidely.

"Our hunter. They work for the whole of the Narvan."

"Did you see what your people did to my volunteers?"

"The experiment that you demanded happen despite my warnings? I did see the results. They were quite horrific. I'll give you that."

He scowled. "They wouldn't even give us the bodies to return to their families."

Stassia stood on standby as though she were ready to get between us. I very much did not want her to do that. She'd only get hurt.

"They're contaminated. It wasn't done as an affront. The staff was merely following procedure. It was all explained in the documents your people signed when they gave their consent for the experiment," I said. "You know how the University is, they're all about the fine print and procedures."

He let out a frustrated snarl. "Fine. I'll deal with the families, but what am I supposed to tell my people? That they will have to rely on your hunters for safety? Are we just supposed to trust that you aren't building an army of them?"

There had to be a way to reach him that wouldn't launch us into further hostility.

"How many years have my people relied on yours for safety?" I asked.

"And they got fed up with that and started a war. Remember how that went?" he threw back at me.

I looked to Stassia, having no clear answers of my own.

She nudged him away from me and back toward the women he'd selected. "Why don't you get these women home and we can address the other issues tomorrow after we've all had time to calm down?"

"I'm not going to drain myself with all three." He put his hand on the bed slave. "I'll be back for the other two tomorrow."

"Vayen will help you. Won't he?" She gave me a pointed look.

"Sure." I gritted my teeth. Not like I was still getting over Jumping the last three or taking a fucking pulse blast.

Jey left with his bed slave. With my head still aching, it took me a few minutes to commit the other two to memory and form the Jump. When I arrived at Jey's house, Dayana was waiting in the foyer. There was no sign of Jey or the new slave.

"Where is he?" I asked.

"Busy." Though her face was composed, the tightness in her voice told me exactly how she felt about the new situation.

It appeared he hadn't consulted her on his choices, but for this being a regular practice among Jalvians, she seemed quite aggravated. Then again, he hadn't wasted any time.

By way of some level of apology, I motioned to the two women with me. "He also selected some help for you."

"So he said, briefly, on his way to the bedroom," she said through clenched teeth.

"Sorry, this was not my choice, but I thought this was common here?"

Her ire turned into a pained smile. "It is. I just thought... I'm not used to having to share anything."

Right. The Prime's daughter. "You are within your rights to set up similar arrangements of your own, aren't you?"

Her shoulders slumped. "I am. I guess I just thought we were good how we were, that we hadn't reached this point yet. Our marriage contract isn't that old."

"I see."

"Artorians seem so much more civilized with your joining system. You would never consider putting your mate in this situation." She let out a wistful sigh. "I think it's every Jalvian girl's secret dream to have a man bonded to her alone." She chuckled. "Don't tell Jey I said that."

My dream was to be blissfully bonded too, but Geva had ripped that away and left me little better than Jey. "Your secret is safe with me.

A giggle erupted from the rear of the house. Dayana looked up to the ceiling and sighed. "It's not like this is the first time. Our arrangement has always been that he be discrete. I suppose keeping a whore under our roof isn't a direct violation."

"They all have training in multiple areas that could offset the annoyance of the situation." I nodded toward the dark hallway. "Maybe they can make you more secure and comfortable?"

She nodded. "Maybe."

"They will require regular payment and housing."

Dayana the annoyed wife vanished and Dayana the Prime's daughter took over. "Yes, of course, Advisor Ta'set. Thank you. Will there be anything else?"

"I'll leave you to it." I turned to the women I'd brought. "Remember what I said about their safety."

They both nodded.

Dayana's attention switched to the two women I'd brought with me. "Let's get you settled in then."

I offered Dayana my best imitation of Neko's apologetic smile and returned to the hotel on Artor to collect Stassia. She stood in the middle of the meeting room where I'd left her. The last of the women were filing out.

"Anywhere else we need to go before we have that private conversation?" Stassia asked.

Since we were now alone here and by the fact that she was allowing for further delays, I gathered that despite her threatening bluster, she wasn't looking forward to what I had to say. Neither was I, but delaying wasn't going to help either of us.

"Le'rin has his people monitoring the protests. They've remained mostly peaceful since the pulse massacre. We'll deal with Kess tomorrow, hopefully after we have identity confirmations to throw in his face. Home for now, it is," I said.

I held out my hand. She took it slowly, her hand cooler than usual. I Jumped us back to our estate on Artor.

The house was quiet when we arrived, the lights low. Saka sat at the security station, her face lit by the soft glow of the vids. She jumped to her feet and bowed.

"Good morning, Advisor."

"Good night, Saka."

She checked the vid beside her. "It's nearly morning."

"Actual time here is irrelevant for the most part. We're going to bed."

She did her curt head bow and returned to her seat.

"Are the boys here?" asked Stassia.

"Yes, madam. Asleep upstairs. The little one is very sweet."

Stassia grimaced. "Kill the madam."

Saka bowed. "How do you wish to be addressed?"

Stassia looked at me.

"Your call." I wasn't stepping into that minefield, especially not when Saka was involved.

I could see she was running through the options, all of which were long and formal and likely made her grimace just as badly. Neither of us liked titles. We'd never needed them before. At least Advisor was short. Stassia was technically just as much entitled to that address as I was, but she deferred it to me for the sake of clarity.

"Ana. At least then I'll know who you're talking to."

Both Neko and Fa'yet used that, but I was surprised she'd chosen such a familiar address for the new help.

"The bedroom then?" Stassia asked, slipping her hand out of mine.

For all the good things that occurred there, our bedroom was also the one place in the giant house where we could talk without being overheard. I nodded, leading the way.

In no big rush either, I stepped into the cavernous closet off the hallway leading to our bedroom to remove my coat and weapons. When I went in, Stassia was just coming out of the bathroom, also minus her armor and weapons. She stood with her arms crossed as the door sealed behind me.

"You could have told me what you did before we were standing in the room full of women leering at you."

"I could have. I'm sorry." I sat on the edge of the bed, my sore muscles needing a break. "Stassia, you were right—"

"How far did it go with Saka? And don't you dare tell me it was all because of that spray, because I saw how you looked at her when she walked into that hallway at the hotel."

"I kissed her. That's all."

She thrust her hands onto her hips and stared me down.

"I kissed her a lot and there was a good deal of groping involved. Is that what you want to hear?"

"No, it's not what I *want* to hear," she said quietly. "But at least have the decency to tell me the damned truth."

I clutched the sheets, bunching them in my fists on the bed we shared in the room that was ours alone. The dark brown walls were bare of any ornamentation. The floor, a low pile, unpatterned ivory carpet. Thick pillows sat propped against the headboard. No clothing on the floor, the doors all closed. Nothing of interest in the room but the woman standing opposite me.

"I keep reading about the bond we're supposed to have and thinking about the memories of it that you've shared with me. It isn't like it used to be, is it, like it's supposed to be?"

I took a deep breath and let it out slowly. "Not exactly, no."

"Not exactly," she scoffed. "You might not have slept with Saka, or Buria, or any of the rest of them, but you're certainly thinking about it." Stassia tapped her temple. "I can feel you getting all hot and buzzy when they're around, like you get with me. I thought when Buria and I got to the transport after you'd been pulsed, that the feelings over our connection were only for me, but they weren't. The same thing happened when Saka walked into the hallway."

"The bond is still there, it's just not whole like it used to be. It's not focusing my attention solely on you, not blocking the urges like it's supposed to."

Stassia swallowed. "Is the bond weakening because you regret being with me now that I'm not who I was, now that you know there's no true fix to getting back the person I used to be?"

I stood and closed the gap between us, wrapping my arms around her. "I don't regret bonding with you again. What I do regret is all the shit that has happened since then that's made life less than ideal for either of us."

How much had we recovered of what we'd been before? Not near enough, mostly the highlights.

"Our bond has never been the full deal. It will never be because you're not Artorian. What you're researching doesn't apply to us."

"What are you saying?" she asked in my ear, her arms hanging at her sides.

"I've heard that a second bond never quite replaces the first. Before I had first-hand experience, I thought they meant that they couldn't replace the mate they'd lost, but as it turns out, they meant the bond. It's not as all-encompassing this time."

I held her tightly, wishing she would reciprocate, but she didn't. "I still feel the same way about you. The peace I feel near you is the same. I want to be with you."

She pushed me away, her arms back to crossed over her chest. "If I said it was fine, would you leap out of this bed and into Saka's?"

Leap was a strong word. I gave her another few seconds to hang just because she'd brought it up. "Not unless you were legitimately fine with it, but unless I've totally overlooked something about you in all the years we've been together, I'm pretty sure you'd never be on board with that."

"So if I said yes, you would." She shook her head. "The correct bonded answer is: no, absolutely not."

"I had plenty of opportunities to explore other beds while on Tacesh, but as you heard today, I didn't. Even with the weakened bond and on the damned spray. I came home to you."

"And I do appreciate that." She pointed at me. "It's the fact that you're still attracted to other women, to the same degree that you are with me, that I have an issue with."

"Not all women, just Buria and Saka."

She rolled her eyes. "That you know of. You've hardly been out of the house since we bonded again. And now one of them is living with us."

How dare she throw that at me. "You put her here. We could place her anywhere else."

"At least if she's here, then I know you're not sneaking off to be with her when you're not with me." Her voice trembled as she asked, "Do you want out?"

Was she listening to me? "No. We don't need the bond in full force, Stassia." I tried to find something logical to talk her down with. "Your people don't bond and they stay together."

"You're not my people. And you lived on Pentares long enough to know that most of them don't stay together whether they said vows, signed a contract, or bastardized some other ceremony."

Well fuck. I hadn't paid much attention to any of that beyond figuring out their general social system.

"All right, then I guess I'm asking you to be patient while I figure out how to deal with the bond that we do have."

Her brows shot up and her volume rose. "Or maybe you just need to figure out how to control your fucking urges. Literally."

"I've never had to," I yelled, matching her volume. "The bond always blocked them."

"Welcome to exercising some self-control like the rest of us." She punched the control panel on the door and stormed out.

TEN

The meal we'd shared had been quiet except for the bantering of Daniel and Markus. I'd barely slept and if Stassia had, it hadn't been in our bed. Neko came in to collect the boys, seemed to gauge the tension level in the room, and made a quick escape with them.

Just when I thought we were alone, Hedvika wandered in and started clearing the table.

"Meera will come with us to meet with Kess. Will that be a problem for you?" Though Stassia maintained a civil tone, the barbs over our connection relayed her true mood.

"Meera isn't a problem." I prayed no one else was either. This was all already complicated enough.

"Good. I've set up appointments for their link procedures, but it's going to be a few days. The protests have the University on high alert."

"I can handle the double Jump."

"I'm sure you can." She pushed her chair away from the table. "I checked with Le'rin. We've got the sniper tied to Twelve, but of course, there's no documented link to the guild so that's as far as that goes. The woman who pulsed you and two of the other surviving Jalvian protestors are also from Twelve, but also without any direct ties to Kess."

"So we can point at the nebula for instigating the violence, but that's it." I shrugged. "Not what I'd hoped for, but I'll take it. I'll get with the Artorian Premier on making a formal public address."

"I've already sent him the information," she said coolly. "I thought it was a better defense if you aren't seen pointing any fingers yourself."

"All right. And Jey?"

"Behaved while you were peacefully sleeping."

"It wasn't peaceful and I didn't do much of it."

Stassia stood and ran her hands down her armor. "I hope you used that time productively then?"

Like she expected me to come up with a magic fix for the bond overnight? "Stassia."

Meera walked into the room, a smile on her young, energetic face. "I think I'm ready, Ana. Thank you for the additional weapons. I'm looking forward to learning how to use them properly."

"Neko will train you with those as time allows. For now, use what you know." Stassia turned to me. "I believe we're finished here?"

She seemed to think so. I wasn't going to get anywhere with her in a mood anyway. I Jumped the three of us to the point Kess allowed at the former assassin's guild. We were escorted to his office.

The lack of music and questionably artistic sculptures, like those in his club offices, were welcome. His sour attitude, in addition to Stassia's, was not.

"Your people murdered my volunteers," he said as soon as the door closed behind us.

I approached the desk where he sat with several data pads arrayed before him. They were all switched off. Stassia and Meera stood behind me.

"They weren't murdered," I said. "The experiment failed. I told you quite plainly that the results had no guarantee."

He slammed his fist on the desk, making the datapads bounce. "We need that modification. We have a right to it. You can't monopolize it."

"He's not," said Stassia, stepping up beside me. "Let's discuss your documentation crew and their footage."

"Mine?" He shook his head. "It was a Jalvian crew."

"There are plenty of Jalvians living on your worlds. Like the ones you sent to Artor to inflame the protests into all-out riots," I said.

"And the ones you ordered to pulse Vayen if they got a shot," Stassia added.

I leaned over his desk to get right in his face. "And the ones you have out there cleaning up your agents after they complete their assignments, that almost took out Anastassia."

His gaze flickered to Stassia and lingered there a moment before returning to me. Meanwhile, I became aware of the gun in his hand, pressed directly against my armor. If he fired, it wouldn't penetrate, but it would hurt like all hells.

Meera was around his desk and had her gun to the back of his head a shallow breath later.

"Perhaps we should all calm down," Kess offered, lowering his gun. "You have proof to back your accusations?"

"Enough that the Premier of Artor is firmly laying blame at your doorstep as we speak," Stassia said.

Kess scowled. "That's a bit premature. I thought we were all working together?"

"I thought so too," I said, nodding for Meera to stand down. "It would seem that I was mistaken."

For all the trouble he'd caused, he appeared relaxed as he leaned back in his chair. "You both look well enough, far better than my volunteers. No harm done, I'd say."

"Oh, would you?" Stassia said. "Just because we don't have a direct tie to your name, doesn't mean we don't know who was behind this political nightmare. Consider yourself on thin ice."

For a split second, he appeared abashed, but his signature slimy smile covered it an instant later. "Will we be attempting the procedure again then? In the near future? With more favorable results?"

I shook my head. "We will not. You have what you need from your crew. Hunt your own Arpex to harvest a barb from. Perfect your own procedure. You've manipulated your way out of a welcome at the University."

His smile slipped away. "It almost sounds like you're saying that we're no longer working together. Do you want the Rakon as your enemy? I have plentiful resources and many friends."

"Jey has access to the entire Fragian empire who are right at your back, plus the Jalvian fleets and I have mine. Don't make empty threats."

Kess leaned forward, planting his elbows on the desktop. "But do you really have Jey?"

"Do we"? asked Stassia.

No matter how pissed Jey might be with me, he wouldn't want to hand half the Narvan to Kess. He had ample experience with being tied to an unpredictable partner. And no way in all hells would he hand over the entire Narvan.

"Yes, we do. So call off whatever other shit you have planned before you completely talk yourself out of our alliance."

"You're certainly embracing this whole mutant tyrant thing. That's what they're calling you, isn't it?" He picked at nothing on his sleeve. "You don't hear people say that about me. Maybe you're doing the advisory position wrong."

"We were doing just fine until you fucked things up," Stassia said.

He gave her a doubtful look.

"Before we get the guns back out, I have some slaves I need to move. Are you interested?" I asked.

Kess turned to me so quickly I thought his neck might snap. "You? Slaves? Did all your nine hells freeze over?"

Stassia cast me a surprised glance. *"You weren't kidding about the degree with which you are opposed to slavery."*

I shook my head, answering them both. "Not exactly."

"How many? What are they?" he asked.

"Eleven men. One woman."

Kess looked to Stassia. "Is he kidding?"

She shook her head, stepping back and letting me have at it. Meera stood beside her with the slightest of smiles on her thin lips.

Kess finally seemed to notice her. "And who's this?"

"New help. One of several. If you're in the market for employees, I can help you out there as well."

"What kind of employees?"

I filled him in on the skill sets of the slaves.

"Sounds intriguing. Did your partner also take you up on that offer?"

"He did."

Kess sat up, a calculating look on his face. "Well then. Let's take a look at your slaves and then we can talk about these employees."

"I'll retrieve one. Where would you like to meet him?"

"The hallway is safe."

Meaning it was unmarked and generic enough to not provide a solid location for a jump point.

"I'll be back in a few moments. Meera, perhaps you can further expound on the abilities of your sisters."

"Yes, Advisor."

I Jumped to Cragtek and found Gamnock in his office, cleaning up for the day. "I wasn't ignoring you."

He shrugged. "I heard you were having some issues."

"You could say that."

"Neko mentioned you might require some defense?"

"Did he?"

Last I knew, I was taking care of that. I sent Neko a burst of annoyance that he ignored.

"He thought you might be a bit too tied up to deal with that particular issue."

And then I regretted my annoyance. All the time Neko had worked beside Stassia while I'd been recovering had encouraged him to take more initiative. Maybe that wasn't so bad.

"Your assistance would be welcome, but I'm here for a piece of the shipment."

"That's in containment on the second level," Gamnock said. "I'll let the guards know you're cleared."

"Thank you."

"As to payment—" He gave me an appraising look.

"I'm working on it. Can I get a copy of the inventory list that was relayed to you?"

He nodded, tapping a quick note on one of the datapads on his desk.

"We're splitting it equally. Feel free to move your half. Leave mine. The storage unit where that shipment was contained is yours for holding sensitive items or whatever you need."

"I'll require a bit more than that for my trouble."

"I said I was working on it."

He held up a hand. "As long as we understand one another then."

"We do."

"Good luck with your business, Advisor."

"And with yours." I left him and went to the second floor to retrieve one of the Masters. He was bound and gagged, still dressed, unsoiled, and unharmed. He smelled quite ripe though. Not much to be done about that on short notice.

After taking him in, I Jumped the two of us to Kess's jump point and brought him to the specified hallway. The Master's eyes went wide when he saw Meera. She dropped her gaze to her feet. Kess regarded us with interest.

"This is one of them. Sorry about the smell."

I held him by one arm while Kess circled him. "Looks healthy, relatively clean. What skills does he have?"

"Meera, care to elaborate?"

She went on in length about his hand-to-hand combat skills, his preferences in bed, the languages she knew he spoke, what he preferred to eat and how he liked his drinks served.

"She knows the details on all of them?" asked Kess.

"Do you?" I asked.

"Some more than others. I didn't spend as much time with the bed slave masters."

Kess's eyes lit up. "I would be very interested in those."

"I'm sure you would. These men are new to their lot in life. They'll take some training in servitude and time to learn their place." I warned him.

"For someone who claims to be against slavery, you've got this down."

"Do you want them or not?"

"I do."

I knew the mention of bed slaves would reel him in. That was his most profitable line of entertainment.

"Do they have any papers?"

"No prior owners."

"Perfect." He pulled a credit chip from his pocket and ran it under the reader on his desk. His gaze beckoned me to take note of the amount.

I nodded.

He tossed me the chip. "Delivery?"

"Where would you like them?"

He flashed me a location.

I considered whether I wanted to owe Gamnock another favor for transporting the stock or to deal with the headache of jumping them myself. Better to have this business concluded and off my perpetually endless list.

"I'll have them delivered today."

"Now, these employable ones. They like her?" He looked to Meera.

"Some, yes."

"I'll take three of her."

"No bed slaves?" Stassia asked with an edge.

He smiled at her. "I don't pay for my entertainment. Protection, on the other hand, has better results with monetary incentives."

"Make sure you plant women here that you trust. The last thing we need him to have is more actual security," Stassia said.

"Planned on it."

She gave Kess a stern glare. "I mean it. Thin ice."

I placed a hand on Stassia and Meera, Jumping us all back to the Artorian estate before things with Kess devolved any further.

"I'll work on political damage control from here while you move slaves. Swap Meera for Neko for a while. He can help you with the Jumping," Stassia said before marching out of the foyer without a backward glance.

"Did I do something wrong?" Meera whispered.

"You handled the situation quite well. She's pissed at me. That happens a lot. You'll get used to it."

"Thank you." She watched Stassia walk away. "I like her."

"So do I."

Meera giggled. "You should buy her something nice. Maybe that would help?"

"I doubt it." Unless I could buy a bond fix from some secret department at the University. "Come on, I'll introduce you to the quiet life of Veria Prime. You'll be spending more time there with the boys once you get up to speed."

In anticipation of having Neko beside me again soon, I spent an hour showing Meera around the Seeker compound and introducing her to Etara and some of the other instructors before we found Neko and the boys. Markus and Daniel took to her right away, dragging her to the kitchen to try whatever Daniel had just finished baking.

Before they got far, I ran and caught up with them, pulling Daniel aside. "Any idea where I can get some of that way too sweet candy that sticks to your teeth that your mother liked when we lived on Minor?"

"Is she mad at you again?"

"Maybe."

He grinned. "There's a whole container of it in the kitchen. We get it donated a lot, people think the acolytes like it, but you're right, it's too sweet."

I followed them to the kitchen where he poured half of the contents of the large jar into a white paper box that likely served to store leftovers. Just as I was about to take it, Meera darted in from outside with a long blade of grass and a yellow flower. She tied the grass around the box and looped the flower stem through it.

Daniel handed me the box.

"Thanks." I nodded to Meera who was busy with a blathering Markus. "She'll do just fine watching over the two of you, but she doesn't have a link yet. Let me or Neko know if anything big happens."

Daniel nodded. "Good luck."

I collected Neko and we Jumped to Cragtek. Leaving Stassia's gift there, the two of us Jumped the remaining ten slaves to Kess. Then we went to the hotel on Artor to select three guards. After giving them instructions on their new boss, we also Jumped them to Kess. Once that task was complete, I retrieved Stassia's gift and then the two of us returned to the house. I got as far as the common room before I dropped into a chair.

The ache in my head and body must have been visible because Hedvika set a full glass in front of me a few minutes later. She stood back with a nervous smile while I drained it.

She looked to Neko who was walking toward me from the kitchen. He shook his head. I realized he must have been the one to order my painkiller.

"Hey boss, since yesterday was quite a day and that was a lot of Jumping unfamiliar people, why don't you relax for a bit? I'll hang with other boss for now."

"I'm fine."

The pinched look on his face told me he wasn't buying it and that he was also suffering from the link strain. He glanced toward the office down by the foyer where Stassia was working and spoke quietly. "Though we both know she'll never say this to your face—"

"What did she tell you?"

"Enough to know you were wise to bring that home." He nodded toward the box. "Look, she realizes she pushed you too hard with all the Jumps yesterday, especially after getting pulsed, and after Jumping all the slaves just now..." He shook his head. "I get that with the mess out there you don't want to be stuck in the tank, so please, rest."

The earnestness in his voice got to me. "All right. I'll hang out here for a little while." I waved him off.

"Thanks, boss." Neko tossed a stim into his mouth and then headed for the office to collect Stassia.

Hedvika lingered nearby.

I held up the empty glass. "Bring the bottle."

A stim might have put me back on my feet, but I was trying my best to avoid them. I'd grown too reliant on them over the years, and as my original heart could attest, stims hadn't done me any favors in the long-term. Another glass or two like that and I could take a long nap and wake up ready to go. Stassia would wake me if anything dire required me before then and a stim would kick the effects of the alcohol if need be.

Hours later, Stassia's fingers on my forehead brought me back to the waking world. I'd found my way to bed. The box was beside my hand.

"We do have other ways of dealing with headaches that don't include draining half a bottle of liquor."

"I'm avoiding those."

"I noticed." She settled onto the edge of the bed. "We just stopped back in to eat for a few minutes."

Though she didn't mention it, I could feel her concern through our connection. Figuring now was my best shot at forgiveness, I handed her the box. The flower had wilted.

"What's this?"

"You know I love you, right?"

Stassia took a long sniff of the flower and then opened the box. She smiled and tossed one of the candies into her mouth, chewing slowly. Not that there was any other option with that sticky stuff.

Once she could talk again, she said, "Neko and I are heading to Syless. They're having issues with being under our control in light of the current issues with Jal."

"I'll join you." I started to sit up.

She put her hands on my shoulders and pressed me back onto the bed. "Your face is better off here for the time being. Neko doesn't want to have to Jump us both."

"Come on, if a pulse can't take me down..."

The pressure on my shoulders didn't ease up. "The pulse may not have taken you down, but it didn't do you any good. I don't want to see you back at the University or in a bloody mess in the tank. Please just stay here. If your headache cure worked, work through your contacts. Let them be the ones in the public eye."

"I liked it better when we weren't public knowledge."

"I did too." She leaned over and kissed me. "And yes, I know."

Taking the flower and the box of candy, she turned the lights back off and quietly sealed the door behind her.

The rest of the day passed with me flat on my back in the dark, deep in a link trance, doing my best to quell the civil unrest on Syless while Neko and Stassia worked there in person.

Shortly after they returned, I smelled food. I emerged from the bedroom to find Stassia and Neko having dinner with the boys. The flower, looking resurrected, sat in a vase in the middle of the table. Upon seeing me, Daniel jumped up to get me a plate. I settled in to eat with them, the boys entertaining us with stories about their day on Prime. My gaze kept wandering to the empty chair where Ikeri usually sat.

"She's doing well with Isnar," Stassia said over our connection so as not to interrupt Markus who was giggling his way through how he'd defeated Neko in mock combat that afternoon. *"He said she was working on a couple young girls you had Buria stash at his house?"*

"Good. They need it."

She smiled warmly and then returned her attention to Markus.

It was only when the boys started clearing the table that I realized that Hedvika, Saka, and Meera were all absent. I gave Neko a questioning glance.

"I figured it would be easier for both of you to not have that particular sore spot present this evening. The new hires are enjoying a meal of their own in their rooms. One of the counselors that was at the hotel today is stopping by in an hour to have a session with them."

For not wanting the responsibility of a staff, he was taking to it easily enough. *"Thank you, Neko."*

He nodded and then excused himself to take up his post at the security station until Saka had her session with the counselor.

Stassia shooed the boys off to their rooms and me into ours. Ignoring the constant pings on my link of political fires, reports, and financing requests, I settled into bed with Stassia tucked in beside me, content in knowing that, at least in my own house, and at that moment, no one hated me.

ELEVEN

The Artorian Premier's address two days ago had taken a little heat off of me, but the vids of me getting up after being pulsed and the gruesome failed alteration documentation were still circulating. Prints and defaced still frames of my face with *mutant tyrant* written boldly across them still littered windows and sides of buildings. The one blessing was that some of the hostility had shifted to the degenerates of the Rakon Nebula and its Advisor. However, this also managed to reflect poorly on me for not protecting my people from said threats. I was supposed to be working through my link, but I couldn't resist the morbid fascination of watching my image utterly destroyed across all the local newsfeeds.

"I'm starting to think there is no actual winning," Stassia said over my shoulder. "Maybe we just need to wait for this to fade away."

I shut the newsfeed off and twisted around on the couch. "Suggestions on how to make it fade quicker? Another Arpex invasion to distract everyone, maybe?"

She chuckled. "Let's not get that extreme. Jey promised he'd make a public statement condemning the violence and to show his support for us. It's scheduled for tomorrow. Can you stay out of the public eye until then?"

"Thanks for talking him into doing that."

"I made it clear he owes us after taking part in starting this mess."

"I'll stick to working by link here, but I do need to get to the University to see if Nan's team has had any epiphanies either with her health or the alteration process. I'd also like to do another session with Ikeri and Ha'guris."

Stassia sucked on her lower lip for a moment. "I need Neko with me if I'm out in public. The boys like Meera. Hedvika might know how to fire a gun, but I'd feel better with you having a full guard at your back, considering what we're dealing with. Can I trust you with Saka?"

Neko had Saka on the sleep shift, doing his best to keep the poor woman out of Stassia's face. I hadn't spoken to her since the first night she'd come to work for us. To keep the peace between me and Stassia, I could do this.

"Yes."

"Prove it." She gave me a challenging stare before turning on her heel and marching over to the hallway where the staff bedrooms were. She knocked on Saka's door and when Saka answered, brought her over to stand in front of me.

I kept my full attention on Stassia.

"Look at her."

Praying Geva would protect me if my body reacted even though I was begging it not to, I tore my gaze from Stassia to look at Saka.

Don't look at her eyes. Don't look at her lips. Not her hands either. Skimming from head to boots, I gave her a quick nod and turned back to Stassia.

"All good."

Stassia cocked an eyebrow. "At least your making an effort. I will attempt to be patient, but please get your bond figured out?"

Knowing there were no quick or easy answers on that front, I merely nodded and stood there while Stassia hesitantly walked away, leaving me alone with temptation.

"She doesn't like me," Saka said.

"You'll win her over. Eventually. Hopefully, I will too."

Saka smiled. I tried not to notice.

"We're going to the University where you'll get your implant in a couple days. I need you to be extra vigilant, and for the love of Geva, please help me be good."

Saka's smile lit her eyes. "Neko told us what to watch for. As to your other request, I will do nothing you do not ask for."

"That's not exactly helping, Saka."

The twinkle in her eyes faded as she performed a quick head bow and stood waiting.

Maybe this would be easier if we were both busy. I Jumped us to the central University jump point. We stopped at the next security station to clear Saka for future visits and then proceeded to Nan's territory. Lab workers buzzed around in the several rooms where the Arpex studies were taking place. Tanks of blue fluid and racks of plaz tubes covered counters along with jars of what I guessed to be pieces of Arpex. The cots that had been in the experiment feed were all empty.

The abrupt shattering of glass made me spin around wildly, seeking out the threat. Saka stood in front of me, weapon drawn, doing the same. Someone in the lab swore loudly. A male voice launched into a tirade about clumsiness and the scarcity of Arpex matter to study.

"I think we're safe for the moment," I said, forcing my breathing back to normal.

Saka laughed nervously but didn't fully stand down. She kept her eyes on everything that moved while we made our way to the room where I'd last seen Nan.

A man in a lab coat stood at the side of her bed, alternately running a scanner over Nan's torso and taking notes on a datapad. He glanced up at me and realizing who I was, stood there gaping.

"Any improvement?" I asked in an attempt to put him at ease.

"I think we've found the culprit. Thank you for the list you provided."

"Would the cause help figure out who did it?" Saka asked.

"No. We've all used poisons from that list. I'm more concerned with getting Nan back on her feet."

"She's hanging on. We're devising a treatment strategy," said the man.

Nan might be hanging on, feisty little wench that she was, but she looked awful, deflated. "Maybe do less devising and start treating."

"Yes, Advisor." He offered a shaky smile and hurried out of the room.

Assured Nan was still on this side of Geva's doorstep, I headed to the next wing over to see what I could do with Ha'guris. Now that I knew what was going on in his head, I hoped it would be easier to get in to see the open connection. Saka assumed her position in the doorway while I sat with Ha'guris.

As it turned out, knowing had little impact on my abilities to penetrate the shield protecting the damned Arpex connection. My probe again failed. I didn't really want to involve Ikeri, but it seemed the only way I was going to make progress.

I contacted Fa'yet, who said he would send Buria with Ikeri after she was done with whomever she'd been treating. I excused myself to the hallway where I worked through my link with Saka beside me until they arrived.

"They're here," Saka said, tapping my sleeve as I had instructed her to do.

Buria matched Ikeri's shorter stride just as perfectly as she'd matched mine. She smiled upon seeing me. I ignored her, focusing instead on my daughter, who was doing her best to ignore me.

We went inside, leaving the double helping of temptation in the doorway. The two of them talked quietly. I ignored that too.

"How are Eris and Colata doing?" I asked Ikeri.

She looked at the wall beside me rather than at me, but at least held a civil tone. "Lots of nightmares. They don't want Uncle Isnar anywhere near them. They're staying in my room with me."

She'd never had friends to visit or friends at all, really. This might be good for them all.

"Thank you for helping them."

"It is my job." There was the snide tone I'd not missed. "I've talked to Etara about at least temporarily placing them with families on Veria Prime. They would benefit from some of the other Seeker treatments that aren't my specialty."

"That's a great idea."

For a second, I thought she might smile, maybe even at me, but she gave herself a little shake and got down to business. "What did you need me for?"

"May I observe how you get into his mind so that I can better understand if his open channel can be of use to us?"

Ikeri scowled but nodded. She had Ha'guris stretch out on the bed and then sat on the edge next to him. I sat on the floor beside her.

"Show me how you are trying to get inside," she said.

With two guards in attendance, I allowed myself to relax enough to sink slowly into the probe. The walls in his mind were just as high and solid as before, preventing any degree of penetration.

"You're trying too hard," Ikeri said with all the patience of an entirely frazzled instructor. "More like this. Lighter, smaller." She reached right into my probe, reducing my nudge to the force of a wisp of smoke.

"How are you doing that?"

"Lots of practice. Now focus." She indicated a nebulous point on the wall. "Here."

"I don't see what you're seeing."

"Look closer." On this crazy ride-along, she pulled me into her vision, where everything was so close that it blurred, but then suddenly became clear like looking through a microscope.

In the nothingness of our three minds attempting to be one, she blew the grey smoky haze into a hairline fracture on the wall. And then we were on the other side. The hissing was deafening. I tried to put my hands over my ears, but I had neither hands nor ears.

A light, warm touch settled on my hand. My heart lurched into my throat as I realized Ikeri was touching me. Comforting me of her own accord.

"You're making the sound louder than it is. Imagine it quieter, like a whisper."

And then, as if her voice had the power to make it so, the hiss grew quieter until it was only white noise. Ha'guris let out a sigh of relief.

Clouds of bright greens and yellows danced around us. I stepped into one to look around.

Ikeri yanked me back. "Always stay in the shadows. You can be sensed in the lighter spots."

So that was how she did it, traipsing through our minds, lurking in the shadows as nothing but a wisp.

"I can't do anything here other than listen to the static. If we're going to use this connection, I need to see what is on the other side," I said.

"Be careful," she whispered, sounding like the young girl she was.

I stepped into a green swirl of pulsing light. The static became a crackle. Knowing I had Ikeri to anchor me, I let go of the sensation of my body to focus on only the sound. The crackle became words. The light became images.

Tall trees, an immense green space surrounded me. Arpex voices argued, shoving words and images back and forth in each other's minds. They wanted food. They wanted young. When I saw my scarred face, I forgot to breathe and then reminded myself that I didn't have a body here.

The Arpex wanted me dead. They wanted my kind dead, and they were willing to sacrifice a lot more than the eighteen Arpex we'd hunted down to make that happen.

Filled with dread, I sought out anything of significance around me, every detail I could commit to memory. We had to strike at them before they came for us. I wouldn't allow them to venture into the Narvan again, especially not with a large force.

Ikeri tugged at me, trying to pull me away, but I needed more. More information, more details. The light flared, clarifying my surroundings, every leaf, each blade of grass, the black moss-covered rocks to my left, and the yellow striped bark on a tree bigger around than Jey and I could have spanned. Sunlight glistened off the blue shells of the Arpex surrounding me. Their claws clacked wildly. The air grew heavy with their fury at my intrusion.

Could they see me as I could see them? They made no move to reach for me but the pressure in my head began to build. They were trying to get in, all of them at once. I reached out along the threads that they cast into my mind and let loose my rage, the loss of Stassia's knowledge of me, Sonia's death, my own lost memories, the lives they'd taken with their memory tricks throughout the Narvan, the thousand that had perished on the space station when their ship had self-destructed. I thrust my wrath down those threads and into the strange workings of the minds around me with the force of a fist to the chest, reaching in and crushing anything I could get my fingers on. Fluid dripped from my hands.

The Arpex fell back. The pressure ceased. The threads snapped. I floated there in the green that had lost its focus, glimmering like a jewel through freshly rubbed eyes, a sense of something beautiful but too far away to touch.

Then I was sitting on the floor beside a bed with Ikeri beside me, her face locked in a look of terror as though I were one of the Arpex. She scrambled off the bed, away from Ha'guris. Away from me. I stood, reaching for her, filled with the need to comfort her, to let her know I was all right, that I was proud of her, of what she'd helped me do.

Ikeri skirted my grasp and ran to Buria. She backed herself against the tall woman's legs like a small child seeking safety from a mother. Buria's attention locked onto my daughter and then they were gone.

The room began to spin. I dropped to my knees and clutched at the edge of the bed but my fingers lost their strength. Saka rushed toward me, her arms outstretched. The blankets and mattress floated out of my grip. The lights arched overhead, trailing in my vision like a slow-motion comet. My head slammed into the floor with sudden force.

❧

I woke to see light streaming through a window high overhead. I spent the next several minutes trying to figure out where I was. Not enough beeping or activity to be the University. There was no hushed throbbing of the air scrubbers on the ship deep under Friquen soil. The ceiling was wrong to be my bedroom on Artor. It didn't smell like Fa'yet's estate.

Saka's voice broke the silence. "You're awake!"

Footsteps raced away.

I tried to sit up, to rub my aching head, but my body was sluggish like I'd just woken from a long, deep sleep. Thankfully, not the same sluggish as half-baked from the tank. Relieved to know everyone else was all right, I sank back into the comfort of the pillow.

Waking enough to further consider my situation, my brain began to click information into place. I was missing the weight of armor. Not restricted by the web of my usual load of weapons. The air was clean, fresh, home. Our estate on Artor.

The security station, empty at the moment, sat to my right. Yet, I was on a bed. That didn't make sense.

Pushing back the single blanket draped over me, I found I was wearing a long shirt and loose pants, clothes I'd worn on days I didn't go to work when we'd lived on Minor during those few peaceful years. I moved everything and found nothing injured.

Saka came back into the room, standing beside the security station. Stassia, pale and with dark circles under her eyes, and wearing her usual black and grey work clothes but no boots, stumbled in. She blinked in the bright sunlight and shoved away a lock of hair that had escaped her braid.

"Do you know who I am?" she asked.

I tried to answer but coughed instead. Why was my throat so damned dry?

Hedvika hurried over with a glass of water. I worked my way to sitting, gulped it down, then handed the glass back.

"Stassia, I'm fine. What's going on?"

A tired laugh burst from her lips. As if summoned by her weary cheerfulness, Neko slogged his way toward her with the stiffness of a sleepwalker's legs.

"Do you know everyone here?" Stassia asked.

"Yes."

"Do you know your children? Jey? Kess?"

The way they were all staring at me like I was some kind of scary miracle and the need to know what in Geva's name was going on made me angry. "Yes, and you're not holding up any fingers. Why the hells am I in a bed in the middle of the damned house?"

"Yeah, he's back," said Neko.

Stassia made her way over and grabbed my shoulders, staring at me intently. "Do you remember what happened at the University?"

"Ikeri and I were trying to get a lead on the Arpex through Ha'guris's connection. She showed me how to get into minds like she does. Stassia, we were actually working together." I rubbed my temples, which were starting to throb now that I was sitting upright.

Her eyes glistened and her hands trembled. She let go of me to wipe at a tear that escaped down her cheek.

Neko was suddenly right beside her, looking for all the world like he might have hugged her had I not been right there glaring at him to keep his hands off my mate. What the hells was going on between the two of them?

"And then what happened?" he asked.

"We got through to where the Arpex were, to where I could hear and then see them. I might have a jump point." What I'd seen and felt rushed back to me. "I attacked them, I think. Through the channel. Ask Ikeri if she felt that too. If I can do that again, if we can figure out how to do it on a larger scale, Ha'guris may be our secret weapon." My mind raced with possibilities. "Is he all right?"

"He's fine. Worried about you. We all were," Neko said.

"I'll be fine. Just had a dizzy spell coming out of what Ikeri and I did. Being in a mind like that with her and him and the Arpex together, it was quite disorienting."

Waves of distress hit me through my bonded connection with Stassia, igniting my nerves. "How did I get here? And really now, why is there a bed in the middle of the house?"

The two of them stood frozen, exhausted and disheveled. Anxiety rolled off both of them even though I was awake and right there.

Saka stepped forward. "You fell unconscious. At first, I thought it was because you got dizzy like you said. You hit your head hard on the floor. I called for help but before anyone from the University staff got there, the Premier arrived. Buria had sent him. He said he would help, and I didn't have my link yet so I let him take you."

That all sounded well and good enough, but I didn't remember washing off the tank gel or changing into these clothes. I wanted my regular clothes back, my armor. I had work to do and Arpex to hunt. I slid my legs off the bed and started to get up.

Neko blocked me, forcing me either to sit back down or go through him. I sat.

"Isnar got you to the tank, but when the cycle was done, you were the same, unconscious. The log didn't show anything wrong." Neko shook his head. "That was twenty-seven days ago. You've been in this bed since then."

I blinked and replayed what he'd just said. My tongue forgot how to work for a moment. "That doesn't make any sense," I finally managed to say.

Despite my second warning glare not to, Neko rested his hand on Stassia's shoulder. She nodded and cleared her throat.

"It took all of us to convince Ikeri to see you. Whatever the two of you did scared all your hells out of her. I had to beg her to get into your head, to bring you back like she did last time." Her voice cracked. "She said you were lost inside your mind, that she couldn't help you. That she wouldn't. That you deserved it."

I sighed. "She's said worse."

What little progress I'd made with her was gone. Having tasted that little glimpse of hope, the weight that settled over me at losing her again was even heavier than before.

"Where is she? I need to talk to her."

Stassia let out a sob. Neko gently guided her onto the edge of the bed next to me.

She grabbed my hand and gripped it tightly. "Ikeri is gone."

TWELVE

Blackness edged my vision. I was glad for Stassia's hand to anchor me to my body. Like Ikeri's hand on mine when we'd entered Ha'guris's mind.

My daughter was gone.

Neko's calm voice penetrated the black fog in my brain. "Five days ago, Ikeri was working with the Prime on Jal, restoring memories for him that she'd taken from Jey the day before."

I tried to ask how that was possible, how she could hold memories that long and transfer them later, but though my mouth was moving, nothing came out.

"There was an attack at his office. The Prime and Buria weren't seriously injured, but whoever it was took Ikeri. We think she was the target, but there's been no contact for ransom or demands."

My heart thundered in my chest. The people of the Narvan had seen that a pulse couldn't take me down. Was taking my daughter the next step? Were the scenarios I'd made her see that day before she'd become a Seeker coming true? The warnings she hated me for had prevented nothing. Not even having a guard with her in the Prime's own office surrounded by his security had kept her safe.

Anger started to melt the numbness that had taken hold of me. "Five days. Who has her? Has she contacted any of you? Do we know if she's all right?"

"We can go over everything we have when you're feeling up to it," Neko said.

"You need to rest," Stassia added, still holding onto me.

I wanted to cry and strangle something. Maybe kill something. No, I definitely wanted to kill something.

"I need to get dressed. Now." I shook off Stassia's hand and staggered a few steps away from the bed before landing gracelessly in one of the nearby chairs before my wobbly legs deposited me on the floor. I'd done enough resting.

"Someone hand me a damned stim." When no one rushed to comply, I tried to get up again.

"Vayen, please. Sit." Stassia begged. "You need to recover from whatever happened with the Arpex. Stims are not going to help with that."

"How is Ikeri missing if Buria wasn't seriously injured? How the hells did all of the Prime's security fail?" I was snapping and I didn't care. I was days behind whoever had taken my daughter, and dammit, I needed information now.

"They were knocked out," said Neko. "Ana probed them both but got nothing but a headache for it."

"I expected more from Buria." Surely she couldn't have let someone get close enough to knock her out. Her standing orders were not to fight with Ikeri present but to grab her and Jump. "Where is she?"

"Contained," said Stassia. "Isnar has her in one of his cells."

"He has cells? Do we?"

She shed a weary smile. "It would seem the Premier needed private cells. They were there before Isnar. We do not, but we do have a full Artorian security team two minutes away and they can detain anyone we want."

"There is that. Where was Jey during all of this"?

"Meetings. There are witnesses," said Neko.

"And Kess?"

"In one of his clubs. Also with witnesses," said Stassia. "However, their people are loyal and not to us, so their statements are meaningless."

"Daniel and Markus, they're safe?"

Stassia nodded. "Upstairs, where they've been since Ikeri vanished."

Thank Geva. I planted my feet firmly and gave standing another try. "One of you, help me get dressed. I don't care who."

"If I help you get dressed, will you promise to stay here?" Stassia asked. "You've been off your feet for weeks and we can't afford to have you go down again."

The closer I looked, the more her exhaustion showed. Her shoulders slumped, her eyes dull, even her voice was worn. I'd been asleep for weeks. It was her turn to rest.

"Let's see if I can manage to stay on my feet to change and take it from there."

She nodded, putting one arm around me to help me to the bedroom. I didn't remember our hallway being so long. She reached into her pants pocket with her free hand and came out with her stim tin. Stassia held it out to me.

I opened it to find a single pill inside. It wasn't like Stassia to be strung out on stims. That also explained the haggardness and Neko's wooden motions. They must have both been on them since Ikeri vanished. I tossed it into my mouth and swallowed.

She brought me to our bed, motioned for me to sit, and then went back out of the room. When she returned a moment later, she set a change of clothes beside me. The stim started to hum through my veins. I pulled off the clothes I'd been sleeping in and slipped into the ones that made me feel like myself again.

"Your armor is in the closet."

I stood. "I thought I wasn't leaving the house?"

"I've asked but evidently you're not going to listen." She wrapped her arms around me, resting her head on my shoulder. "We've been looking for days. That stim will only get you so far. You need to take it easy. Seriously. You scared the hell out of me. Again."

I hugged her tightly. "I'm sorry. Wasn't intentional, I swear."

"As much as I want you to run off and fix this, I can't lose you, not with Ikeri missing. The boys need you too."

"I'll be careful."

"Your version of careful and mine seem to vastly disagree."

She did have a point. "I need to do something. Let me at least take a couple steps into this. I promise I'll be back to rest soon, all right?"

She nodded. "Canelli Ra'net, your personal attendant from the University, will be by in six hours to check on you. I'd recommend you be back in that bed when he gets here."

"I have in-home service now?"

"We didn't want you at the University with the uprisings and attacks."

A knot formed in my gut. "You can fill me in on all that when I get back. Is Meera here?"

"She's with the boys upstairs."

"You and Neko need to sleep. Even if it's only for a few hours. Hedvika can watch the security station. I'm going to take Saka, if that's all right? How are they with the links?"

"Still getting the hang of all of it. None of them have any degree of telepathy so it's all new territory for them. Neko set up their tank profiles, but they don't have a jump point there yet. I wasn't ready for that step. You can make that call."

"I'll evaluate that later. At least they can reach out to Neko or Fa'yet if we need the tank."

She nodded against my chest. "I don't want to move."

"Get into bed. Sleep, for Geva's sake."

Stassia must have truly been dead tired because she didn't argue. She let go of me and collapsed onto the bed. As I covered her with a blanket, she closed her eyes. By the time I'd leaned over to kiss her forehead, her breathing had already slowed. I turned out the light and went to find my armor.

After assuring Neko that I would take Saka with me if I went anywhere other than Fa'yet's, I ordered him to bed. Like Stassia, he didn't argue. Then I ventured upstairs to let the boys know I was awake and alive, and after receiving hugs from both of them, I Jumped to Fa'yet's estate.

Merona met me in the foyer two seconds after my arrival.

"Do you ever sleep?"

"I have a bed right there." She pointed to a bench just outside the foyer.

"He didn't give you a room?"

"Yes, Advisor. I'm not comfortable using it at this time."

"He's not still harassing the three of you, is he?"

"No, Advisor. With your daughter gone, we've had frequent visitors. I wish to be ready and available if needed."

"I see. Thank you."

She bowed. I noticed she no longer wore the red dress that marked her as a hospitality slave. Instead, she wore a simple moss green shirt and tan pants. It suited her well.

"It makes me glad to see you back on your feet, Advisor. My sisters and I have been concerned for you."

Her sisters. It hit me that I still had a hotel floor full of slaves that needed employment. Had anyone been checking on them? Had they been fed? Were they even still there? "How are your sisters?"

"Well enough, Advisor. Your wife has found positions for many of them. The Premier has also placed some. There are only a handful of the younger ones left at the hotel."

"That's good to hear. Where might I find Buria?"

"Follow me."

We went into an area of Fa'yet's estate that I'd not been in before. A door led to another door, which opened to reveal a lift. We went two levels underground and exited. An open square revealed four cells, two smaller ones ahead and two larger on either side. The air was cold and the lighting harsh in the open space. There were no lights within the cells themselves.

Merona pressed a button on the wall, turning one of the cells' fields translucent.

"She can hear you now."

"Thank you."

"Do you wish for me to stay or go?"

"You may go. The Premier may need you."

She bowed and returned to the lift.

Buria sat on the floor, knees drawn up against her chest. She was missing her armor and boots, wearing only a sleeveless shirt and pants. The knots of her hair had come undone, leaving two long tangles of hair to spill over either shoulder. Even disheveled, she was beautiful.

"Buria?"

Her eyes lit up for a second upon seeing me, but then she cowered there on the floor, hands over her face. I'd seen before in her mind how the darkness was terrifying, how it brought her back to her initial containment by the Masters. She'd been here for weeks.

"Buria, I need you to show me what happened."

"I had no part in it, I swear. Please be swift, I beg you."

"Show me what happened."

"It hurts."

"I will try to be gentle." Unless I saw something that made me inclined to be otherwise.

"I have failed in my duty. Please, I've waited for your judgment. Do what you must."

"No need to get quite so dramatic about that just yet. If Anastassia and the Premier didn't find anything concerning in your mind, why are you down here?"

"My employment has been terminated." She stood, coming to the doorway with her head bowed. "They knew you'd be angry. My punishment was in your hands if you woke, and if not, I would stay here and dwell on my failure. Whatever you have said about my freedom, it seems I belong to you."

Sadly, that could never be the truth.

Using my link, I shut off the field so that I could lay my hand on her chilled shoulder. "Relax if you can. I'll try to be quick."

If she had it in her to attack me, now would be the perfect opportunity, but other than trembling under my grip, she didn't move.

I attempted to duplicate what Ikeri had shown me, the delicate touch of a wisp of smoke. I entered Buria's mind, tiptoeing through thoughts of terror and embarrassment, of nightmares and imaginings of the fate that awaited her now that I was here. In one of those, she kissed me and offered restitution in several intriguing positions until I forgave her. In another, I ripped her in half and tossed her onto the floor in a bloody mess of entrails.

I tried to calm her mind. Whatever it was to be, it would be neither of those extremes.

Her terror eased and the trembling subsided. Her shoulder grew warm beneath my hand. "You were in the office with Ikeri and the Prime. She was working. Show me."

Ikeri stood, robes and tattoos as brilliant as any of the treasures in the Prime's office. Her face stilled in concentration, small hands on his balding head just behind his ears. She spoke softly to the Prime, probably prompting him to expose the next hole so she could insert the memory.

There was a knock at the door. The Prime's secretary came in looking anxious. Buria went on alert, starting for Ikeri.

One Jalvian man in a business suit came in behind the secretary. There was nothing overly distinctive about him, no physical trait that stuck out, pale skin, blonde hair, blue eyes, a round face, his tan suit of common fashion on Jal, no drawn weapons, but there was an air of something off that Buria had sensed.

The Prime was busy having a memory inserted. Ikeri was deep in the process. Buria was only three steps from Ikeri when the man slipped an object from his sleeve, a cylinder the size of a finger, and gave it an abrupt jerk. It expanded to the length of his forearm. He squeezed his eyes shut. A bright beam of light sliced through the room along with a barely perceptible sound. Buria reached for Ikeri but the room blurred and then went black.

I withdrew from her mind and back into my own. The stim had taken the edge off the sluggish feeling permeating my body, but

Stassia was right about taking it easy.

"Did you find what you were looking for?" she asked.

"Maybe. Have you seen a weapon like that before?"

"No." She bowed her head again. "I didn't even remember seeing it until you slowed it all down just now."

"Then I'm done here." I started for the lift, deciding what my next stop would be. "I'll ask the Premier to hire you back into his service.

Her head remained bowed. "No. I did fail my task. I do not deserve this position."

As much as I liked Buria, it didn't change the fact that Ikeri was gone. Fa'yet wanted to distance himself from that failing by cutting his losses. He was well-acquainted with my wrath. There was no way in all the hells, I would get away with bringing Buria into our house. Stassia would question the fuck out of that and my resolve to honor the bond to her, despite its weakened state, screamed that this was a terrible idea. I might be able to control my urges around Saka, but I was far less inclined to want to control anything around Buria.

"I'll find you a position elsewhere."

She wrapped her arms around her chest. "Why would you help me?"

"I have a lot of enemies. I don't think you're one of them, at least not at the moment. You're currently an asset, and I take care of those as best I can."

"I need my daughter returned unharmed. If you wish to prove yourself, you'll help make that happen."

Buria bowed low. "Anything you need. Always. Any time."

Filing that offer away, I took her arm and Jumped us to Cragtek. Gamnock sat in his office, appearing only mildly annoyed when I walked in without knocking.

"I don't have anything on your daughter, but I'm glad to see you back among the living."

"Thanks. Anastassia's been working with you, I take it?"

"Neko, actually. Good man that one. I'm still a bit bitter that you stole him from me."

"He is. Thank you for letting him be stolen." I gestured toward Buria and then back to Gamnock, "This is Gamnock, the man who transported your sisters to freedom."

Gamnock nodded to Buria before turning back to me. "Ah, so you stole her too. We repelled a few ships bearing the markings of Tacesh a couple weeks ago but there have been no other reprisals. Maybe they've been adequately subdued?"

"One can hope." I was just glad that any fallout over Tacesh hadn't also landed on Anastassia to take care of while I was comatose. "This is Buria. Your new assistant. Guard, whatever you need. There are a few more like her that I would like you to take on. Anastassia has been too busy to place them. They have skills, that with a little additional training, could make them valuable to Cragtek. Buria can fill you in."

The two of them took measure of one another.

"Buria and these other women will require living wages and lodging. The rest I'll leave to your discretion as you feel they merit. Buria is linked. She knows how to get in touch with me. A mutual agent, if you will."

Gamnock regarded me with a raised brow. "And you'll want private lodging for her when you visit?"

I looked to Buria and then back at him. Damn, that would be easy. Not like Jey at all. Nothing would be under Stassia's nose. She rarely had any in-person business at Cragtek, instead, handling transactions over her datapad.

Buria watched me intently, lips parted, her cheeks flushed. My brain dove into a high-speed replay of our encounter on Tacesh.

"That isn't necessary," I heard myself say. If I wanted to indulge myself with Buria, I could make that happen anywhere. I didn't need to hand Gamnock a neatly wrapped tray full of leverage.

As if Buria could somehow see the truth in my head, she offered me one of her little bows and a smile that I'd seen in her memories, the one where I'd exacted my punishment on her on a bed, among other places.

Damn, I needed to lock that away somewhere before it got me into trouble. Her too, for that matter.

Gamnock let out a deep bellow of laughter. "Already sampled that one, did you? Do you two need a minute before we get to business?"

"I think we're good. Buria, could you please wait outside?"

She nodded and left us alone.

Once the door closed, Gamnock grinned. "So, the pretentious Artorian finally joins our ranks."

"And exactly what ranks would those be?" I asked, gauging his level of insult.

"Those of us who don't hide our true nature. We were never wired to only have a single mate. That was an artificial dampener your stuffy ancestors hobbled you with." He didn't bother to wipe the grin off his face. "Is Buria in the running for second wife or are you just sampling the goods?"

"Only a light sampling. It's a long story." I sat down across from him, feeling a bit lightheaded from the stim running through my otherwise empty system. "Anastassia fell victim to an Arpex before the extermination. She forgot me and that voided our bond. I formed a second one, but It's not as...dampening as the first time around."

Gamnock sat back, chuckling. "Welcome to being normal, or at least, not near as brainwashed as you used to be."

"I'm not so fond of normal. It's distracting as all hells."

Gamnock banged his palm on the desktop and laughed. "Can you imagine Anastassia's face if you brought up a second wife proposal?" He threw his head back and laughed even harder.

"I'm glad you find some humor in this, but unless you have something helpful to offer on the topic of getting my brainwashing back, I have more important issues to deal with."

He drew a deep breath and wiped tears from his eyes. "Sorry, no. The brain isn't so tricked into submission a second time. You'll just have to learn to live with what leash you've got left."

I glared at him. "Leash?"

"I'll take these women off your hands. That's all I can do to help. If you choose to visit Buria in her off time, that's no business of mine."

"Thank you." Which part of his offer I was thanking him for was undecided.

It was a miracle Jalvians got anything done at all and weren't overrun with children for as physically promiscuous as they were. At least my people kept their raging hormone years to Artorian sex. Geva, that was exactly it, I was a teenager all over again but now with the ability to have physical sex. With anyone.

Fucking urges, indeed. I sighed.

"Rough day?" he asked.

"I just woke up a few hours ago and learned my daughter has been taken or is missing, or Geva, we don't even know."

Gamnock sobered quickly. "If there's anything else we can do, just ask."

Neko often knew things from his time working with Cragtek. Maybe Gamnock could be a similar asset. "May I show you something? A weapon that was used? Maybe you know it or where it comes from?"

He grimaced. "This is one of those mind jack things, isn't it."

"A memory of Buria seeing it is all I have to work with, so yes, I suppose it is."

"You know we hate that unnatural shit, don't you?"

"If I had another way to show you, I would."

He nodded but didn't look at all happy about it.

One concession I could give him was that I now had Ikeri's soft touch for slipping into minds. I kept it quick, sliding in, flashing the few pertinent seconds of Buria's memory, and slipping back out.

Gamnock paled. "We've seen a couple of those turn up on the market recently."

My heart began to beat faster. "Where do they come from?"

"Jal. The project has been in development but was fast-tracked when it was clear that the hunters you made wouldn't be Jalvian. Some felt we needed a weapon of our own." "

Fucking hells. A weapon from my own system used against me?

"It went into limited production just before the vomit-inducing feed from the failed experiment hit the news." Gamnock shrank into his chair. "Cragtek supplied some of the components, but I swear, I never thought they would use it on you, not like this, certainly not on a child."

"Thank you for being honest. Take care of Buria for me."

He nodded but seemed to be waiting for me to go on a rampaging tirade.

If I had been in full capacity, I would have Jumped to Jal and started pounding on Jey, but I wasn't, and for all I knew, he was waiting and prepared for just that. Instead, I Jumped home, leaving Gamnock to wonder how pissed I truly was. He deserved to be worried after laughing at me.

I spared a moment of thought for Saka, letting her know I'd returned from my business and would not need her for a while. I waved off Hedvika and went straight for the bedroom. Stassia was still sound asleep. Even me taking off my coat and weapons didn't cause her to stir. It wasn't until I pulled the blanket back to get in beside her that her eyes sprang open. She reached over and pulled me closer, settling in against me.

"Thank you," her voice was muffled against my shoulder.

"For what?"

"Coming home. I assume in one piece. I don't think I could take hunting you down right now."

Though I wanted to tell her about the weapon and the connection to Jal, and thereby Jey, the heavy waves of exhaustion coming off her convinced me that she wasn't in any better shape than I was. Maybe worse. She'd been at this for days without me. If getting Ikeri back could have been resolved by quick action, Stassia would have brought her home already. A few more hours of rest would hopefully give both of us the boost we needed to make some real progress toward that end.

I drifted off with the comfort of Stassia's familiar form against mine. In my dreams, Ikeri sat naked on the floor of a dark room waiting for a man to come and offer her food in return for unwanted touches. Touches I would kill him for, but I could only hear her crying in the darkness, crying for help that I couldn't give.

❧

I woke with a start, covered in sweat with Stassia shaking me.

"Is this an Arpex thing? You were having a nightmare. Do you need Markus?"

"No." I sank back into the bed. "How long before my University check-in?"

She paused to check her datapad and swore. "Half an hour ago." She climbed over me and got out of bed. "I'll meet you out there."

I took in her disheveled appearance. "You might want to change first."

"Canelli is plenty used to me looking like shit by now."

She was out of the room before I could say anything further.

I scrambled out of bed and went to join her.

A short Artorian man in a University uniform stood near the bed where I'd been until roughly seven hours ago. Stassia jumped up upon seeing me and rushed over as if I would need help. I waved her off.

"I'm fine."

"This is Canelli Ra'net," Stassia said. "He works with Nan at the University. He's been taking care of you."

"I wish you would have stayed in bed until I was able to be here," Canelli said. "It would have helped our research."

"How so?" I asked, fending off Stassia's continued efforts to guide me into the chair where she had been sitting. Instead, I maneuvered her into it during our subtle shifting of wills. I moved to stand behind her, putting some space between me and the research I'd been part of.

"We've been following the developments in your brain, shifting patterns, altered areas. It's been quite incredible."

"So happy to have been a source of entertainment for you." To keep myself occupied and out of reach, I loosened Stassia's hair from what remained of her braid and ran my fingers through it, combing it out like I used to for Ikeri...when she'd had hair and didn't mind me being near her. The tension ran out of Stassia's shoulders as she relaxed against me.

"Not at all, sir." He swallowed. "It's just that whatever you did, it started a process, activated something in your mind, made a new connection, if you will. We've checked it against the other hunters. None of them have what you do. Not yet anyway. You have been altered longer. We have the few hunters that are linked under observation in case they show symptoms of your condition."

"I have a feeling whatever it is in me, won't happen with them. I was working with my daughter at the time. We were able to follow the open channel through Ha'guris and find Arpex on one of their worlds. I'm pretty sure I attacked them through the channel. In Ha'guris's mind,"

"Fascinating." He jotted notes on his datapad. "Would you mind if I took my usual readings so we can see if being awake has changed your results?"

"In a moment." I braided Stassia's hair and tied it off. "There, that's better."

She caught my hand and squeezed it. "Thank you. Now go be a good patient."

"Never, but all right."

She grinned. "I'm glad you're back on your feet."

"Me too."

I spent the next hour and a half jumping through mental hoops for Canelli so he could get all the readings he wanted. If what happened to me wasn't triggered by Ikeri and hit the other hunters, I did want to help them in any way possible. The thought of having the whole team of them down for several weeks after I'd possibly antagonized the Arpex made me anxious.

What made me even more anxious was Canelli confirming that my body was still adjusting to the fusing with the Arpex larvae. Geva help me, there could be more changes and they could hit me without warning. We agreed to meet once a week for the next few months to track any other possible transformations, hopefully before they knocked me out cold this time.

Once he was gone, I found Stassia at the table, picking at a plate of Daniel's favorite seaweed noodles. There were always a few portions of them in the cold storage. She'd changed but appeared only slightly more awake. What she needed was a couple full days of rest to recover from her stim-binge, but we didn't have that.

"I'd tell you to get back in bed for a while, but I need you to come be my voice of reason," I said.

"Since I did change my clothes and attempt to look somewhat alert, I'll bite. Where are we going?"

"Jey." I told her what I'd learned from Gamnock.

She put her fork down and stared at me. "You don't think he'd take Ikeri, do you?"

"Kess was top on my list, but snatching a kid isn't his style. Pulsing me in front of a crowd of innocent people is."

I pulled her plate toward me and started picking at it since she appeared to be done with it. "Arpex would have simply made her forget me, or us, or gone for full impact and eaten her in front of me."

Stassia shuddered and shoved the plate fully onto my side of the table.

"It could be the investors of the Masters, but Gamnock says he's repelled the attacks from that direction. Which leaves Jey."

She shook her head. "He knows how upset I've been, that you've been down for weeks."

I got that she trusted Jey. She wasn't missing memories of him other than the early tensions that had been between the two of us. However, since the Arpex had shown up, he'd been less like the man we'd both known before we'd slipped away to Veria Minor or since our reconciliation before I'd moved out to Pentares. I'd trusted that man. This one, publically up against the pressures of his people and still suffering from hidden wounds Merkief had left behind, not as much.

"Has he been here helping you look? Did he meet you on Jal and offer to talk to the Prime's people?"

"He's been looking on his end. I've consulted with him several times since Ikeri was taken." She shook her head again. "Jey wouldn't dare do that to me."

"You and I are one in his eyes now that we're back in this. Would he do that to me?"

Stassia stared at the wall just over my shoulder. "I knew you'd accuse Kess. He's been our top suspect and Neko's been investigating him hard, but Jey? I've been giving him the benefit of the doubt because you two have this partnership going and all he did for us with Markus." Her gaze slid over to meet mine. "You don't trust him? You think he'd take Ikeri?"

"What I do know is that he's been developing the weapon that

Buria witnessed being used to abduct our daughter."

She clenched her fists on the table. "If he took her, if he's been lying to me this whole time, I'm not the person you want along to be a voice of reason."

"I'd like you to come along anyway."

She nodded. "Are you up for this?"

Truthfully, I didn't know. I felt better now that I'd rested a little more, but was I up for calling Jey out and possibly acting against him?

As angry as I was, I didn't want to believe he'd hurt Ikeri. The man I'd known before had been nearly broken by Merkief's accusation that Jey had killed his infant daughter. Would he really embrace that role now?

"I need to know the truth, to do something."

"Then get suited up. I'll let Neko know to watch the boys, she said."

"I'd like Neko with us. Saka and Meera can watch the boys."

She let out a mocking gasp. "Did those new brain connections short out your reckless impulses?"

"I doubt it."

"Too much to ask, I suppose." She pointed me toward the bedroom. "Get dressed. We're going to go get some answers."

THIRTEEN

Jey asked us to meet with him at his home. That seemed odd to me until we got there and saw Dayana and Dallarayn sitting next to him on the couch as if everything was fine. As if he had a normal family. As if his new guard wasn't lurking just around the corner out of sight when I showed up all fired up with Stassia and Neko, who were also both fully armed.

"What's this all about then?" asked Dayana.

They may have all been dressed in plain clothes, looking for all the world like we'd interrupted a regular family enjoying an evening watching the local vids, but the pinched look on her face and her rigid posture said otherwise. Dallarayn, who was normally quiet, was absolutely silent with her hands clenched together on her lap and her gaze locked onto the floor just inches from my boots. Of the three of them, only Jey appeared at ease.

"This might be better handled in private," Stassia said.

"You wanted to discuss the search for Ikeri?" Jey asked. "My family can handle a family matter, I would hope?" He gave Dayana a pointed look.

Neko stood three steps behind me. I knew that because his armor creaked the slightest bit, just enough to let me know where he was in case I needed to move and that he wasn't liking the situation.

Neither was I. It wasn't at all like Jey to hide behind anyone, let alone his family.

Stalling wouldn't get us anywhere.

"The weapon you developed in retaliation for my not killing your people with unneeded alterations was used to abduct my daughter. That leads me to believe that you or one of your people is involved. As you can imagine, and I can see that you are by your reaching for the gun you have in the cushion beside you—" I shook my head. "I wouldn't do that."

Jey's hand hovered over the cushion, gaze locked on me. "You seem to have forgotten those guards you delivered. I've been informed that all three have received weapons training."

"Boss?"

"Yes, I know. We need to get him out of here. Or them."

Thank Geva I had an answer for that. "Ladies?"

"Yes, Advisor?" One of them called out from around the corner.

"Now would be the time to protect those we discussed."

"Yes, Advisor."

Two of them came forward, one from a bedroom doorway, the other from the kitchen. They shot toward the couch, one placing a hand on Dayana, the other Dallarayn. Seconds later, they were gone.

Jey was on his feet in an instant with the gun drawn. "What in all the hells did you just do? Where did you take them?"

"I didn't take them anywhere. Your staff followed whatever orders you gave them regarding the protection of your family."

"I should have known you'd have overriding orders," he said.

"Wouldn't you?"

He glared at me.

"Where's Ikeri?" asked Stassia, sounding far more strained than I wanted to hear. Exhaustion and emotion were getting the best of her. "How could you do this to us?"

"You are withholding weapons from my people. Vayen refuses to see reason, and Kess's ploy didn't yield the results we needed."

They were in on that pulse attack together? The scene filled with shattered bodies flashed before my eyes. His people were dead right beside mine.

"So you abducted our daughter?" I asked. "The one helping your Prime? Your people?"

He stood his ground. "She was in on it."

Ikeri couldn't have fully understood what she was in on. She was young and she trusted Jey, who I'd inserted into her life. Clearly a poor choice on my part.

He'd used her. He'd used my daughter against me. Red crept into my vision.

"She wouldn't do that," said Stassia.

"She did do that. She is pissed at you," he said to me. "She's undeniably your daughter," he said to Stassia.

"So...she's unharmed. She's fine." Stassia's relief tumbled out in staccato words. "She can come home."

Then her anger began to kick in. "You almost started a war over this. You could have been killed. You know that, you rock-headed ass? You would tear the Narvan in half to get a weapon you don't need? Conspire to take our daughter from us for something we're already providing you with? What the fuck were you thinking?"

"I was thinking," his own suddenly strained voice said, "that if Vayen was out of the picture, you might be more amenable about giving me what I wanted."

Her mouth fell open. "After all I've done for you? After everything? You used my daughter to try to manipulate me?"

It was fortunate for Jey that she couldn't kill him with the deadly focus in her gaze. And also for me, because I planned on doing it with my bare hands. It was one thing to go after me, but using Ikeri to get to Stassia? Fuck goodwill and friendship.

"If that was the case, why not make an open demand?" she asked. "Why let me run ragged over the Narvan looking for clues? Why not at least be man enough to claim the deed yourself?"

"You're not the only one who's been running ragged," he said, keeping a close watch of the three of us.

"Boss, you doing all right there?"

He knew my cues and even standing behind me, they must have given my rage away. Too focused on Stassia and Jey, I didn't bother to answer.

"What the hell does that mean?" Stassia nearly spat. "Where is my daughter?"

My gut in knots and my knuckles aching from gripping the gun I'd not yet fully drawn, I waited for his answer.

Muscles along his jawline twitched. "We don't know where she is."

"Who is we?" Stassia asked.

I took two steps closer. Neko followed my lead.

"She was taken to a secure location Kess set up."

"If it was secure, why don't you know where she is?" Stassia demanded.

"Kess lost her?" I asked.

He nodded slowly.

I glanced at Stassia out of the corner of my eye. Shock seemed to be overriding her anger but her fists were clenched at her sides. I never anticipated that Jey would break his allegiance to Anastassia.

That, more than breaking his goodwill with me brought out a low threatening tone that sounded deceivingly controlled given that I wanted to tear him apart. "Let me get this straight. While you knew I was down, you manipulated our daughter into going along with your plan to con Anastassia, and then you gave Ikeri to Kess, of all fucking people? All to get an alteration that not only do you not desperately need but is currently impossible to give you?"

While he was distracted in trying to form an answer, I used what Ikeri had shown me to worm my way into his head. He started to say something. Whatever his excuse was didn't matter to me. All I needed to know was where they'd kept Ikeri. Her whisper-light touch made it easy to stand in the shadows and browse his recent memories as if I were nothing more than a distant observer inputting queries into a datapad. No trails, no need for force. He didn't know I was even there.

When I found the moment Jey had learned of Ikeri's disappearance, my soft touch began to waver.

Jey's eyes went wide. He spun to face me. "How are you doing that?"

"She's my daughter too," I said.

Desperate to know what had happened, I dove in with far more force before he could slam the doors on me, demanding a mental meal just like an Arpex. *Show me how you got Ikeri involved. Show me Kess's part in this.*

As if I were a magnet, words and images flowed to me. I couldn't take them away like Arpex did, but I could hold them, examine them. Once I'd seen his conversation with Ikeri and with Kess, confirmed the truth of what he'd said, I had what I needed. Not that it was much consolation. Ikeri was still gone.

He had been the one to approach her, to lay out the plan, to encourage her, convince her she'd be safe, that she was doing the right thing. And now she was gone.

Still in his mind, I squeezed and let loose my rage as I had with the Arpex through Ha'guris's open channel. If this attack landed me in bed for another three weeks, I didn't care. I stood there, unmoving, yet attacking with everything I had, pummeling his head from the inside.

Jey dropped to his knees. His gun fell to the floor as he reached up to grasp his head. Blood trickled from his nose.

"Anastassia. Please. Make him stop," he said between gasps.

"I have no idea what he's doing, but be glad it's him and not me."

She punched him in the face with enough force to knock him backward.

Neko circled around to watch us both while also keeping an eye on Jey. He glanced at Stassia but she shook her head.

With some experimentation, I found I could also grab Jey's mind, jabbing in certain places to cause intense agony, the likes of which I was very familiar with. He began to tug at his hair as though he wished to pull it out, alternately driving the heels of his hands into his temples and his eyes, moaning all the while as he writhed on the floor.

"Whatever you would like to do to him, have at it." Stassia backed up to stand beside me. She turned slowly and looked me in the eye. "Without limitation."

Stassia clutched her hand to her chest, rubbing her knuckles. "I'm out of reason and sick to my stomach. Neko, take me home."

Before I could pull out of his mind to ask her if she was absolutely sure, Neko grabbed her and they were gone. I continued ripping him apart from the inside for a few moments before it occured to me that Stassia would likely regret her decree once her head cleared.

Testing my new touch, I explored how much pressure it would take to make Jey lose consciousness. When his eyes rolled back and his giant form went still, I vacated his mind, returning fully to my own.

I found I was on the floor as well, and while my head hurt, I didn't feel as disoriented as I had the last time. The room remained in focus and didn't spin. I cautiously got to my feet, making sure I had them firmly under me before I stood. Going over to him, I knelt to assess what I'd done.

He was still breathing. I hadn't gone too far, but whether he would wake up or not was my next question. What to do with him hit me a second later: Canelli.

I Jumped Jey to the University. Lugging his giant ass around was more effort than I cared to put toward his wellbeing at the moment so I stood waiting in the middle of a corridor. University staff approached me. After a quick relaying of orders, they took Jey. I followed as they brought him to the room Canelli used for his research.

He gave me a questioning look over the top of the datapad he'd been working on. "What's this?"

I nodded to Jey's prone form on the bed where the others had left him. "He is to be kept sedated enough that he can't Jump or contact anyone. Is that clear?"

"Yes, Advisor." He got up and ran his datapad over Jey's head. "Is this Advisor Te? You did this?"

"Yes. And if you don't want me to do it to you—"

"Heavily sedated. Got it." He nodded. "How are you feeling?"

I sighed. "Scan quickly. I have things to do."

He managed to wrap up his testing in ten minutes. "I would advise you to get some rest. No stims, alcohol, or other drugs until the pain clears. We don't know what effect they may have on this new development."

"I'll see what I can do."

"See that you do, Advisor. Your mate needs you." He quickly stepped away and sought out an injector.

I left him to his work and Jumped to the house to do some damage control with the Jalvian Prime and his daughter through my link where I wouldn't chance straining anything further.

Hedvika met me in the foyer, pointing frantically to the common room. I ran in to find Stassia standing in the middle of the room, crying and cursing. Neko stood within reach, one hand out as if he were trying to calm her down or maybe catch her. As I got closer, I could see her shaking, her skin a sickly pale cast. Sweat dampened the hair at her temples.

The blatant relief on Neko's face upon spotting me didn't make me feel any better.

"Stassia?"

She turned to me. "You're all right."

"I am." The throbbing in my head didn't seem relevant at the moment.

Her gaze darted over me with manic speed. "No blood."

"I didn't kill him if that's what you're asking."

She nodded, took one step, and then collapsed in slow motion to heave the contents of her stomach onto the rug.

From what I could tell, she was about five minutes away from convulsions and a full-blown attack the likes of which she hadn't suffered since before Jey and Merkief had barged back into our lives on Veria Minor.

I scooped her up and took her to the bedroom where it was relatively dark and quiet. After putting her on the bed, I retrieved a cold, wet cloth for her head, which likely felt much like my own.

Whatever Ikeri had healed to get Stassia's mind speech going again hadn't fully addressed the underlying damage the High Council had inflicted on her brain. Exhaustion, stress, and heavy stim usage had returned her to this state that I'd hoped we'd left behind.

I sat down behind her and felt my way to the pressure points she'd drilled into me years ago.

"We've made progress. We're one step closer," I assured her.

"We're nowhere."

"No talking or I'll stop."

She made an assenting noise.

"Jey is being held in a sedated state in a secure room at the University. Canelli is studying what I did to him."

She mumbled something that sounded like, "How did—"

"Ikeri showed me how to get in softly like she does, stealthy. I don't know as she meant for me to actually learn how she does it, but I did. That and whatever this new Arpex ability is."

I changed finger positions. "And no, I have no idea what it did to Jey in the long term. He deserves it, whatever that might be."

After a few minutes, I asked, "Do you need your medicine, or is this helping enough?"

"Helping."

"Good."

We sat there for a long while in the dark, me pressing and massaging until I was sure she was asleep.

I sought out the link connection I'd used with Jey's wife Dayana only once before. "Are you safe?"

"Yes, Dallarayn and I are with my father at his estate."

"Good. Please let your father know that I will meet with him soon to discuss the charges against your husband. You and your daughter are free to go about your lives. Jey, however, will not be returning home until he answers for abducting my daughter."

"Yes, Advisor." Those two words conveyed a tidal wave of emotions.

I had my own to sort out.

"Be well, Dayana."

"You too, Advisor."

I cut contact, amazed she'd held herself together so well. It was clear she'd been raised to put on a public face. I wondered if Jey had taken into account what would possibly befall his family or his homeworld if he was caught. Hells, he'd seen my fury in action before with the University and my own damned homeworld. I supposed it was fortunate for everyone else that I'd lost my temper on him alone.

A chain of thoughts niggled at me, clawing their way up to smear itself over the idea of anyone being fortunate. Ikeri was still missing. I'd ripped Jey's brain apart. How was he supposed to help me get her back now? How much pressure had he been under to bring him to crossing us? Was there anything I could have said differently to sway him to reason? Something I could have done to help ease whatever or whoever he'd been against that might have prevented this?

Sitting there in our bed, I listened to Stassia's even breathing. I tried to synchronize mine with hers, to find some measure of calm, but the lump in my throat wasn't easily deterred. My eyes burned with tears I refused to shed for my daughter who was so against me that she'd been part of this plan and for the man I'd torn apart from the inside who had been my friend.

It was an hour later when I finally extracted myself from the bed and went to find Saka.

Everyone was in the common room talking at once while Hedvika scrubbed the rug. I supposed having a staff was, in this instance, worth the hassle.

I addressed Neko. "I gather you've filled everyone in?"

"Did Uncle Jey really take Ikeri?" asked Daniel.

"Yes, and not quite, but mostly yes. She went along with it, at least initially."

"Why would she hurt you and Mom like that?" asked Markus.

"She's mad at him," explained Daniel, nodding at me.

Markus's brows furrowed. "But she hurt Mom too."

"And a lot of other people," I said. "Keep that in mind if either of you gets it in your heads to do something stupid like this. Ikeri has now been taken by someone else, and we don't know who that is yet. So you two are still on lockdown. You know how this works."

They nodded solemnly. I wished they didn't have to do that. I wanted to hear their laughter in the Seeker garden again.

"Daniel, do you remember how your mother used to get headaches?"

He nodded. "Do you want me to go sit with her?"

"Yes, both of you. You can play games if you want to, as long as you're quiet. She needs to sleep. If you see her getting worse, you let me know right away. If you see anything, anyone not currently in this room, you let Saka or Meera know. Got it?"

They both nodded eagerly.

"Go on then."

They ran up to their rooms to find their games.

I addressed Neko, "Are you up for a visit with Kess, or do you need to rest? Truthfully, because I don't anticipate this going well."

"I'm good, boss."

Saka looked disappointed, but I much preferred Neko if this went as I anticipated. We worked well together, and he knew Kess.

"No one comes in or leaves until further notice."

Saka bowed.

I flashed the location I'd gotten from Jey's memory to Neko and then Jumped. He arrived a minute later. New jump points always took him longer. Thankfully, there was nothing immediately threatening. In fact, there wasn't much of anything at all. The etched symbols on the wall were the only decoration in the otherwise plain grey hallway. Even knowing Jey had said she wasn't here, my heart raced as I pushed the door open.

Much like the dorm on Prime, the room was fairly standard for a holding cell. A cot with a blanket and a stool. Nothing that identified that Ikeri had been there. Then again, if Jey was to be believed, she hadn't been there long before someone else had taken her.

The only door at the end of the short hall wasn't locked, but that may have been because there wasn't anyone there to contain. I pushed the door open. Neko followed a step behind me. We entered a bustling warehouse. Slaves, marked by Kess's brand on their necks shuffled items from crates to shelves or the reverse, followed by other slaves with datapads in hand, fulfilling orders. No doubt all the goods were stolen or gained as payment from his excess taxes and enforced protection fees.

"Didn't hide her far, did he?" asked Neko.

"He stashed my daughter in a fucking storage room."

Not that she needed more. She'd enjoyed the simplicity of Veria Prime, but the room Fa'yet had provided was far more what I wanted for her. It was who she was. Or who I thought she was. I still couldn't believe she would willingly cause the sort of anxiety she had just because she was mad at me.

What we'd done with the Arpex, that had scared her, no doubt about that, but to make her mother worry, that I couldn't excuse. For all she knew, I may have killed Jey and Kess while trying to find her. Assuming she'd anticipated me ever waking up. Maybe she hadn't.

Did I blame her for not trying to wake me when Stassia had asked? I'd been angry at Ikeri for forcing me back into the realm of the living last time, but she had to see what kind of stress Stassia was under. I had to believe she'd have enough spite to yank me back again just to please her mother. Unless she'd come to scorn Stassia too? If she had, we were both screwed. With one of us in her graces, we had a hope of pulling her back into our family. As powerful as she was with her gifts, I didn't want her working against us.

Dread crept in. What if she'd seen how to do what I did to the Arpex, just as I had learned how to sneak softly into minds from her? But would she use such a weapon? I hoped not. It would scar her forever in ways far beyond seeing the bad things I'd done in my memories.

"She's not here, boss. What do you want to do?"

"Strangle someone?"

He smirked. "In the immediate helpful sense."

"I guess we better find Kess, since it was his breach of security that led to my daughter vanishing."

"Glad I'm not Kess."

"Yes, you are." Without thinking, I reached for my tin of stims and popped it open. Canelli's warning came to mind before one ended up in my mouth. Mentally strangling Kess into a liquid glob of brains on the floor sounded like an excellent plan, and I didn't even think Stassia would mind now, but that wasn't within my ability at the moment. We'd have to do this the regular way.

I contacted Kess and got his current location. He didn't seem happy to hear from me. Rather than Jump to him, since we were already in his complex, we walked. I needed some time to clear my head of the throbbing. Another Jump wouldn't help with that.

"You all right, boss?"

"My head is rebelling. This new thing is going to take some time to get working smoothly. That's what Canelli said. Like working a new muscle."

"Strained it a bit, did you?"

"Maybe."

"Not planning to use it with Kess, I hope?"

I shot him a look.

He shrugged it off. "Other boss isn't here. Someone has to keep you in one piece."

"No, I don't think I'm up for using it on Kess."

"Good. One of you down at a time is enough."

"She'll be fine when she wakes up. Always is. She hasn't had an attack like that in a long time."

"She's been under a lot of stress. Too much going on at once, and she was really worried about you. Then Ikeri went missing. It's been hard."

"Thank you for helping her hold it all together."

"You're welcome, boss, but really, it was all her."

Knowing she had everything as under control as it could be, considering, brought me a flash of warmth. Despite the toll of our overwhelmingly eventful life, she was still the capable and intelligent woman I'd first fallen for and still loved no matter what condition my bond might be in.

We waited outside Kess's office until his new aide, one of the former hospitality slaves, signaled us to enter.

Kess at least had the grace to look worried. Jey likely had warned him we were onto them when our meeting had turned sour.

He stood behind his desk with three of the new guards flanking him. I couldn't believe my eyes when I saw that Untami was one of them.

"What is she doing here?"

"Untami? She works for me."

"No. I distinctly sold her to you as a slave. She was not of the batch that I asked you to employ."

"So she pissed you off. Get over it. She works for me now." Kess took one step forward. "I take it from your more unfriendly than usual scowl that Jey tried to blame this abduction ruse on me."

"No, he admitted his part in it. He did blame losing my daughter on you, though. After a look at her lodgings, I'm inclined to believe him."

"She was safe here. Safe as all my goods. Surrounded by my people."

"Ikeri is not goods. She's my daughter. Anastassia's daughter. You and I may not be on the best of terms, but did you consider what your ploy would do to her?"

Kess shrugged. "Anastassia has softened of late. Mellowed. More sentimental, maybe."

"Are you aware she gave me leave to terminate Jey?"

His bravado faltered. For all I knew, he was trying to contact Jey to confirm my announcement. I let him sweat. Jey wouldn't be responding any time soon, if ever.

Desperate for a lead, I tried to keep him distracted with conversation while I wisped into his mind. "You're utilizing Untami as a guard?" I asked. "You are aware her skills are primarily in the hospitality field?"

"We've covered all her fields and found them satisfactory."

The pain in my head doubled before I'd done no more than slipped in. I shelved the probe plan until I ran out of other options.

"I'm sure you have. The men she was with?"

"Don't concern yourself with them."

"I'd like to interview them."

"I'm afraid they're all on duty and I don't remember exactly where they've been placed. Maybe in my clubs? Maybe I sold some of them off? You gave up your rights to them when you sold them to me."

Damn him and his lack of any cooperation whatsoever. I'd have to come back and try the probe again another time if I wanted any chance of getting information out of him.

I didn't particularly like the way Untami was looking at me. *"Keep an eye on her,"* I told Neko.

"Already on it."

The others didn't seem overly concerned one way or the other, and I was grateful that they were standing behind Kess so he couldn't see their lack of interest. It would only tip him off that they were on my side. At least, I hoped they were still on my side. They hadn't informed me that Ikeri was here, or that Kess was working against me.

"And my daughter?"

"She was here and doing just fine. Working with a couple of my employees, in fact. They quite appreciated her visit. Remarkable kid you have there."

"And then?"

"Somewhere between going back to her room and being served dinner, she vanished."

"You have surveillance, surely?"

"Yes, of course."

"And?" I was fast losing what little patience I had. If I hadn't gone overboard with Jey earlier, Kess would have been babbling on his knees.

"Untami was with her. We have feed of her going toward the room where Ikeri was staying."

"Closet. You stashed my remarkable daughter in a closet."

"She said it was more than adequate for her needs."

"That's not the point," I said through clenched teeth.

"The point is that she is missing. I get it. You're pissed. I would be too."

"If you had children. Or cared about anyone, I might believe you meant that, but in all the time I've known you, I have seen no evidence that this might be true."

"I cared about Anastassia. Still do. As you well know."

"You have an odd way of showing it, abducting her daughter and hiding her here while Anastassia runs ragged trying to find her."

He had the grace to look away. "How is she?"

"Not well." I quickly consulted our connection to verify she was still sleeping. "And what did you hope to gain from this charade?"

"We knew you were down, possibly of a permanent nature."

"Are you aware of why I was down?"

"What do you mean?"

"Did Anastassia tell you why? Either of you?"

"She didn't know, she said. Only that she didn't trust the University to look after you full time and she had someone coming to you instead."

"The Arpex modification is why I was down. You grabbed Ikeri to try to get Anastassia to allow the University to continue the testing, but you know what? We don't even have solid long-term data on what the modification does to those of us who already have it. It's still changing us. It may hit all of us at once and leave the Narvan entirely defenseless as far as the Arpex are concerned. We don't know. Now do you understand why I am reluctant to create more hunters, no matter where they might come from?"

From the belligerent cast to his scowl, my point still seemed to be lost on him. "If you don't know what it does to Artorians, why not also find out what it does to anyone else?"

"It kills them. Or did you forget that already? It works with us because our minds already have the capacity for mind speech. If you have anyone who is naturally inclined in that direction, and no, links don't count, then we may have a chance. Still, I'd caution against it because it may also have a physiological element. Again, we don't know."

"Sounds like you have a lot of knowing to figure out."

Behind him, Untami smirked. I tried not to let her presence distract me, but the fact that she was there, free, grated on me badly. Refocusing on Kess, I left her to Neko's watch.

"We do, and despite acknowledging that, you still keep trying to force your demands. All you're doing is distracting us from the work we're trying to do so that we're all safe when the Arpex return."

"Who says they're going to return? We killed them all. Wouldn't that send enough of a message that they're not welcome here?"

"If someone showed you a warehouse filled with everything you could want that was only guarded by a force with sub-par weapons, would you maybe give it another go after your quick and easy method of taking it was thwarted?"

Kess grunted. "Maybe."

"No maybe about it. You'd gather up a larger force that had little chance of losing and unleash it to retrieve the prize."

"Yes, you're probably right."

"I know I'm right. I saw it in their minds."

"You could have just said that to begin with," he snarled.

"Why? You don't seem to listen to anything I say."

"That's not true."

"Then listen. My daughter is missing. She was under your roof when it happened. As angry as I am with Jey in going along with this plan the two of you came up with, you're left holding the larger part of the blame. Where do you think that puts you?"

"Wishing you were still oblivious to the universe and flat on your back."

Two fingers tapped on the desktop. I glanced up at the guards to see if that was some sort of cue, but they didn't move.

"No doubt, but I'm here."

"But you only brought one guard and I have four."

"I'm fine with those odds."

"A little high on yourself, aren't you? I mean, I know you've got that armored skin and all, but you're not entirely invincible."

He reached into one of the pockets of his coat. I let him, curious as to what he thought might be effective enough to elicit the smug smile he was now sporting.

"Boss, I'm not liking this."

"Stay behind me if he pulls something nasty."

"That's not how my job works."

"Just do it."

"Other boss will force-feed me my man bits and then kill me. She's said so on numerous occasions."

While we were busy making light of what was certainly going to be an unpleasant event, Kess came out with a grenade.

I laughed, which was a total bluff. "You think that will have any more effect than a pulse?"

"You might not think so, but I'm willing to give it a shot if it means I get to walk away."

"You won't be walking away. No one will."

The three guards behind him shifted nervously.

"Are your guards linked? I know you can Jump in a heartbeat, but can they? You willing to kill them already?"

"They don't need links, they'll be fine."

I shook my head. "The room is too small. If you toss that, everyone is going down."

"Not me." He depressed the button to activate it.

The guards looked at one another.

"Your willingness to kill everyone but yourself is duly noted."

Neko's anxiety skyrocketed in my head. *"Boss?"*

"I'm going to need you to get me to the tank. Can you handle that while making sure Anastassia doesn't worry about me and containing Kess?"

"I'd rather you didn't put me in this position."

"I'd rather not let Kess kill everyone in this room. If you have the opportunity, get that vid feed. I want to see Ikeri for myself."

"Sure, boss. And if you're going to do something stupid, now would be the time. He's going to toss it any second."

I slunk into Kess's mind, the force I wanted to use, severely throttled. It wasn't near what I'd used on Jey, but enough to slip in and take control of Kess long enough to deactivate the grenade and put it back into his pocket. Not daring to leave Kess's fate in the hands of the questionably loyal guards while Neko would be on his own, I made one swipe of my mental claws across his mind. The path leading back to my mind began to waver. I let go of Kess and found myself back in my body, on my knees, with the floor rushing up to meet me.

FOURTEEN

"Boss?" Neko hovered over me. He'd moved me to my bed on the ship.

"Yeah."

The tank had thankfully removed the pain in my head. Whether that was good or bad for this new advancement in my Arpex transition, time would tell. I tried to gingerly touch that part of my mind, but it was hard to pinpoint without actively using it. I meant to enjoy a pain-free head for a while. Testing could come later.

"Kess's guards helped contain him. He's sedated at the University with Jey."

"All the guards?" I sat up, pulling the sheet around me.

"Not the one. She tried to bolt. The other three grabbed her. She's in one of Isnar's cells."

He sat in the chair beside the bed. "I hit Kess with a stunner while he was busy screaming and clutching his head."

The thought of Kess screaming made me smile. "Untami, did you speak to her?"

He nodded.

"You got the vid feed?"

"Yes, and I also got her to talk. She had help. You're not going to like this."

That was a given. I didn't like a lot of things these days. "Let me guess, those Masters that Kess has working for him or maybe sold aren't all accounted for, are they?"

He shook his head. "I located intake records for all of them, and sales for all but two of them, to anonymous buyers of course. I'm guessing you hoped to dig into their brains for information?"

"That was the plan. Did Untami say if Kess was part of this?"

"Yeah, boss, he was. Saved the two assholes for just this purpose, I'd guess."

"Fucking hells. I handed him the perfect tools to torture me with." An oppressive yoke of guilt dropped onto my shoulders. This was my fault. I had to fix it.

I slid out of bed and gathered a stack of clean clothes. "How long was I out?"

"Only a couple hours. Ana is still sleeping. The boys are fine."

"Good." I left him to whatever he'd been working on and took a quick shower. Once I dressed, I nudged Neko.

"Home," I said.

Neko arrived right behind me.

"Get a few hours of sleep. I want Anastassia with us if she's up to it. We'll need to eat and then it's going to be another long haul."

"How do you plan on hunting down the Masters?"

"We'll start where I last saw them."

He nodded and headed to his room.

I went to sit with Stassia, waking her because I needed to hear her voice. "Kess has been dealt with."

She wiped the sleep from her eyes. She always woke slowly from her headaches rather than her usual spring-from-the-bed alert-and-ready. "Dead?"

"Not yet."

"Amazing restraint for you."

"I'm not *that* violent."

She scoffed. "Whatever you need to tell yourself. So he's also at the University?"

I nodded. "How are you feeling?"

"Nauseous, but better."

"The Masters have Ikeri." I shared with her what we'd learned, leaving out my trip to the tank.

"Retaliation?"

"Yes, and a nudge from Kess." I braced myself for the blame about to be hurled my way.

Instead, she said, "They never would have gotten to her if Kess hadn't handed them the opportunity."

While that might have been true, it didn't make me feel any less guilty.

"Do we know where they might be holding her?"

"Since Gamnock and I have possession of their previous operation, no. But I can try digging around in Kess's brain, and if that fails, we can trace their investors and work from there."

She nodded. "I'm going to get cleaned up and then we're going to find our daughter."

Her optimism filled me with the hope that I could indeed rectify this. So much so that I didn't want to wait for her to shower or eat or anything else. To stay occupied, I went to check on Daniel and Markus.

I stopped just short of the open door when I caught sight of them working on the exercises I'd seen them doing on Prime. Saka stood aside, offering pointers on their positions and some ideas of her own. Seekers might be healers but they needed remain strong and flexible to serve those in their charge. That sort of training was one of the redeeming aspects of having the boys there so much.

Markus, who Daniel was making an exaggerated spectacle of defending himself against, caught sight of me and lost his rhythm, allowing Daniel's fist to connect and knock him onto the floor.

"Are you all right?" Daniel was by his side in an instant, helping him up. "I didn't mean to really hit you."

Markus held his stomach and managed to nod.

"Good to see you're using your time here wisely," I said.

Daniel started. He backed away from Markus. "I didn't mean to hit him. Honest."

"I know."

I sat down beside Markus and whispered some suggestions to use against Daniel, who was much larger than him. Markus grinned. Distracted from his sore stomach, he got back to his feet.

Daniel's eyes narrowed. "Hey, what did you tell him?"

"Same thing I told you years ago."

"That's all right then. I remember what you told me."

"I may have told him a few other things."

"Why would you do that? It's not fair if we don't know the same stuff."

Saka shook her head. "That's how the universe works. Nothing is fair. Gather all the surprises you can, little ones, you never know when you will need them."

"Do you have a few surprises, Saka?" I asked.

"I might, Advisor."

"While we wait for your mother to get ready, why don't we go downstairs and see what you two can learn from observing."

I had way too much energy after coming out of the tank and far too much on my mind. I needed to take a bit of the edge off so I could focus on everything that needed doing.

Saka followed us at a cautious distance as we went into the lower level where we'd set up a proper training room similar to what we'd had in Stassia's homes long ago.

Stassia and I didn't often workout together like we used to. I missed that too, but maybe someday we would again. Or maybe someday we wouldn't need to, maybe we could relax like we had on Minor, staying in shape because we wanted to rather than out of necessity.

I shed my coat and stood on the mat-covered floor. "Come on Saka, you know how this works."

"I do, Advisor, but not with you. Wouldn't you rather I call Meera down? The three of you could observe together."

"I'm not the one who needs to observe."

She took a hesitant step onto the mat. "You do not wish to watch?"

"No, Saka, I do not. What you do isn't a pleasure performance. It's a job. One I'm paying you to do. So get over here and attack me already."

She bowed her head. "Yes, Advisor."

"Come on then, like you mean it."

Shedding the roles the Masters had drilled into her was going to take some time, but Saka made a valiant effort. She circled, calculating her options, and then made a rush for me. It took me a few moments to get a solid hold long enough to restrain her. We went again. It was interesting working with a woman other than Stassia. Saka moved differently and had a longer reach.

We went a few more times before I realized the boys were watching raptly. Daniel had observed Neko and I and occasionally Stassia and I, but this was apparently more interesting.

"Why don't you let her have a chance to win?" asked Markus. "We take turns in class."

"No one is going to give you a turn in real life. If you want a win, you have to take it," I said.

"But you're bigger than her," Markus said.

I made a grab for Saka and pinned her against me. She struggled to get free to no avail.

"Your mother isn't bigger than me. She's got the best of me plenty of times," I said, adjusting my hold to make sure I wasn't hurting Saka while she was working out how to free herself.

Markus grinned. "I want to see that."

Daniel nodded. "I don't think I've seen that either. When did she do that?"

"A long time ago, I'm sure." Stassia stood at the bottom of the stairs, with what may have been amusement or annoyance. It was hard to tell with the remnants of her headache lending her a weary tightness. Or maybe that was because I was still holding Saka against me. I let her go and quickly left the mat to get my coat.

Saka made a hasty exit with the boys, the three of them scampering up the stairs.

"Please tell me she let you win for the benefit of the boys. If she can't adequately defend herself against you, how is she supposed to keep our kids safe?"

"She's fine. Neko says so too."

"Of course he does. I'm sure you've noticed the way the four of them ogle each other."

"I think you're exaggerating."

Her brows rose. "I think you've been asleep for three weeks."

"You've worked with Saka and Meera. Hedvika, too, I would imagine."

Her scowl didn't lessen. "I have, and I can tell you quite honestly that none of them let me win. But will they stand up to a male attacker or are they trained to let them dominate?"

I hadn't considered that. With all the conditioning they'd undergone—but surely the Masters wouldn't have programmed them to fail in their duties because of the sex of their attacker.

"Maybe you are on to something there," I said. "Not with anyone, but with males who are in charge of them. It wasn't as if she put up no fight, not in the least, but you might be right."

"Did you enjoy that?" she asked, maintaining her distance.

"Enjoy what?" I didn't like the predatory gleam in her eye. She was in a mood and it wouldn't take much to fall victim to it.

"The fight, knowing you would win, that you could do anything and she'd let you."

"I was merely showing the boys a few things while we were waiting for you."

"Merely."

This was going to be a long day.

"Stassia, you're well-acquainted with what I enjoy and that doesn't involve always getting my way."

I pulled her against me, fully expecting resistance, but she didn't provide any. She slammed against me with more force than I'd anticipated. That threw off the kiss I'd planned to prove my point with and ended in her shoving me away.

"I liked it better when your affection didn't require a warm-up act."

"What are you talking about?"

She glared at my pants. "And don't bother scrambling. I spotted that as soon as Saka scurried off you.

"She wasn't on me, for Geva's sake." Had it been Saka rubbing against me or spotting Stassia all suited up that was to blame? I couldn't say for sure, but I did know that anything I said in my defense would be used against me. Silence only made it worse.

"Why don't we focus on finding Ikeri and fight about this later?" Preferably when she was exhausted or in a less hostile mood.

"Fine." She stood there waiting without looking at me.

"Neko or no?"

She gave me a pointed look. "Would you prefer Saka joined us?"

I took a deep breath and let it out slowly. She was the one who placed Saka in our damned household. I wasn't doing anything wrong. But I also knew how badly jealousy had eaten at me when our bond had been fresh—when Jey or Merkief would even be near her, and I'd known them for years before that. Stassia might not have the ingrained bond, but that didn't appear to affect the depth of her feelings. I probably would have ripped Saka apart weeks ago if our places were reversed.

"No, I would not prefer Saka. Maybe it would be best if we traversed this leg of the investigation alone."

"Do you think that's wise?" she asked.

"Yes." Though I didn't clarify that I thought so because no one else should have to deal with her when she was angry.

"If you say so."

Geva help me, it would be a miracle if we were still speaking by the end of the day, or by lunch, for that matter.

I wrapped my arm around her, mostly just to gauge where we were in the pissed off spectrum. She didn't pull away or stiffen. We weren't at the point of no return quite yet.

I formed the Jump to Canelli's room at the University. One of his assistants stood by Jey at the other end, adjusting a piece of equipment that was beeping slowly. Stassia stared in Jey's direction but remained by my side. A torrent of emotion rushed through our bonded connection.

"Neither of them will cause any further trouble," I assured her.

"I know." Her gaze dropped to Kess, the man who had once been her partner just like I was. "What you did to them," she shook her head, "It's no wonder they wanted the same ability for themselves. They were right to fear you."

The troubled look on her face caught me by surprise. "I don't go around doing this to just anyone."

"But you could. You said Nan made you into a weapon. We don't know how this alteration is going to fully affect you. What if you become too much weapon and not enough you?"

"It would be hard to lose me to that degree with the bond in place."

"We've lost the bond before. With these changes, who knows if it will happen again. And you've admitted that it isn't as strong as the first time." Troubled turned to outright emotional, right down to quivering lips, which was most unlike her. "Will it fade? Break? If it's gone, if you fall back into manic work mode, I'm afraid the weapon part of you will take over."

If Stassia was *afraid*, this was a very valid concern. "Then we better make sure our bond, in whatever form, stays in place."

She nodded but turned away. "Do whatever you're going to do to him so we can leave."

Having her out of sorts made it hard for me to concentrate.

It took a while to get myself calm enough to wisp into Kess's mind.

After some sifting, I found the memory of Kess talking to two of the men I'd sold to him. He suggested that they take Ikeri, that it would be the ideal way to punish me for what I'd done to them. My heart raced, digging deeper into that brief conversation, seeking out the details, hunting for follow-up conversations. There weren't any. He hadn't asked where they were going or how they would get there. Or what they planned to do with Ikeri. Nothing. He'd just planted the seed and sat back to watch it grow.

The disappointment, on top of the uneasiness between Stassia and I, invited the urge to resume flaying Kess's mind, to punish him for what he'd done to us. To me.

I grabbed ahold of the nerves that hurt most and flexed my mental fingers, picturing my fingernails as sharp claws begging to tear into his body.

But where was the gratification in that? He was already down. I could leave him to rot here indefinitely. I pulled back from his mind, returning my full awareness to my body and the fact that Stassia was watching me with a flicker of hope.

I wished I had something to give her, no matter how small of a detail, but I had nothing. I shook my head, letting her disappointment mingle with mine. At least that was one thing we both agreed on.

Feeling deflated, I held out my hand. "No luck here. Let's try their compound."

Her cold hand slipped into mine but she remained silent as I Jumped us to the atrium of my new warehouse on Tacesh.

When we arrived, I was glad to see a guard posted at the doorway. The staff I'd assigned here had already begun changes in the room to erase all the obvious decorations in order to prevent anyone who had the jump point from showing up.

"Any trouble?" I asked.

The female Artorian guard shook her head. "No one exciting so far. Just potential customers and a few suppliers, most by ship rather than linked. Everyone has been allowed to leave and has done so of their own accord without a fight."

"Good." We'd already made enough enemies with the investors.

"No sign of my daughter by chance?"

"Sorry, Advisor, not a word."

"My half of the stock remains untouched?"

She nodded again. "Still on the shelves."

"Good," I turned to Stassia. "I want to show you a couple things here before we move on."

We passed through the training room with the blood-stained, broken flooring and then through the vid room. She lingered there a moment, taking in all the rooms where the women had been kept before we moved through to the Master's chambers, which were now mostly shut and occupied by my staff and a few of Gamnock's.

We moved quickly through the back end maze and into the warehouse. The lights were on low, enough for the vids to pick up movement but keep costs minimal. I played with the panel on the wall until I got the unfamiliar controls to turn the lights bright enough for her to appreciate what we had here.

"This is our half."

"It's stuff, Vayen. I want Ikeri back. Now."

"I realize that. There are also weapons here. I was thinking we might use some of them."

"Assuming we can find someone to use them on," she said, eyeing the tall racks.

I led her to the shelves where the Masters had supplied their security team as well as themselves. After slipping one of the numbing rods into my coat, I handed one to her.

"I don't know how much of a charge they hold or how long they take to refill, but they do a nice job of completely numbing a body while keeping it conscious."

"I don't want to think about what they used this for."

Knowing the use, I only nodded.

We grabbed a few other things to fill out our mobile arsenal and then went outside.

"Have you gotten anything from Ikeri? Anything at all?" she asked.

I hated having to crush her hope again, but the truth was all I could offer. "No."

I had been getting used to having Ikeri gone from my mind since our quarrel. It hadn't occurred to me that she should have reached out for help. She'd proven she could do so from incredible distances. If she were in danger, she'd ignore her feelings for me and ask for help. Wouldn't she?

"You?" I asked, not wanting to hear the answer I already knew.

Stassia shook her head, her braid sliding over her shoulder. Her hair was longer than she normally let it grow. I didn't remember her cutting it since she'd lost her memories of me to the Arpex. It lent her some of the flavor of when she'd been Rhaine. If only she were calm and peaceful, maybe even smiling. But she couldn't be. Not now. I reached out and pushed the thick braid back where it belonged. She grabbed my hand and held on tightly.

For a moment, the tension between us faded, leaving only two despondent parents joined in grief.

"You don't think it means—"

"No one would have anything to gain by killing her. Kess made her identity and gifts very clear to the men who took her."

"Daniel hasn't heard from her either," she said.

No matter how Ikeri felt about me or Stassia, she wouldn't make Daniel worry needlessly. If she was maintaining silence with him, then she was unable to contact anyone.

"They're keeping her silent somehow. Geva only knows what their endgame is."

Stassia swallowed hard. "Where do we start looking?"

"We need a guide. I'll be right back."

I Jumped to Fa'yet's estate. Merona was more than happy to

retrieve Untami from her cell and deliver her to me. It wasn't easy forming a Jump with her while she was writhing and kicking, but my time in service to the Council's Arpex had given me plenty of practice with wrangling unruly people.

We stepped out of the void at the atrium jump point and made our way to the warehouse where Stassia waited.

"Can they talk when they're numb?" Stassia asked, holding the rod I'd given her.

Upon seeing the rod, Untami went still. Her momentary semi-co-operation allowed me to slip a pair of the restraints on her so I could free up my hands.

"I don't know, but we could find out," I said.

Happy to have a new target for Stassia to vent on, I let her begin the interrogation. She put the rod down and went the traditional route. Untami wasn't convinced to talk by Stassia's fists, but Stassia appeared slightly more relaxed. That worked for me.

Stassia stepped back and gestured me toward Untami. She'd stood against the warehouse wall and remained silent for Stassia other than a few grunts. When I took Stassia's place, she made a run for it. Stassia knocked her down before she got more than three strides away. Untami lay on the ground gasping.

The moment she got her breath back, she addressed Stassia. "I have some vid feed you may be interested in. Let me go and I'll let you have it free of charge."

"I'm not interested in any of your feed. Get up."

Untami stayed on the ground. "Maybe not of us, but what about of him? Everything here is recorded. Everywhere."

Fuck. I'd told Stassia that I'd had a moment with Saka, but it had been far longer than that, and I'd do pretty much anything to keep her from actually seeing it. It was one thing to suspect, to imagine, but living color evidence would be hard to swallow.

Untami craned her head around to look at me with a smile that belied her situation. "Give me five minutes with the system and I'm sure I can find some saleable feed of you. No one can resist the spray."

Stassia stiffened.

If she did see that feed, either by Untami's hand or her own, would she walk away from me? Especially not remembering most of who we were to one another?

She was absolutely not getting her eyes on any of that. Ever. As we stood there, I began infiltrating the Master's network through my link, seeking out where the vid files were stored.

I kept my gaze locked on Untami in case she got it in her head to run again. I hoped she did. Then I could shoot her before she said anything else.

But then she couldn't help us find Ikeri. Dammit.

The silence was killing me. I hazarded a glance at Stassia.

"If there is damning feed of him in the system. I'll find it on my own. I don't need you for that. Now, get up and start talking." She suddenly had the numbing rod in her hands again.

Untami went still, staring at the rod. There was one upside to the conditioning they'd endured.

"Where did your masters take our daughter?" Stassia asked.

"Somewhere far from here. Somewhere they could start again." She turned to me. "She's sitting naked in the dark, starving, because of you. Little thing like her won't last long before she lets them touch her, before she lets them do whatever they want so she can eat."

I dropped everything I was doing in the network to slam Untami against the wall and wrap my hands around her neck.

Stassia was in my head instantly, calming, trying to block out Untami's words. She was doing her damnedest to keep me from squeezing Untami's throat until she'd never speak again.

"We need her," she repeated on each wave of calm.

While she was right, Stassia hadn't seen those two girls in the dark containers, their terror and desperation.

"Where did they take her?" Stassia asked again, this time with the numbing rod almost touching Untami's chest.

"I only serve. It is not my place to know."

"You'd better serve me right now or I'm going to let him kill you," Stassia said.

Untami's pulse beat a frantic rhythm under my hands as she looked to me and back to Stassia. Her voice wavered. "I don't know." She closed her eyes and jerked upward into the numbing rod. Her body fell limply onto the ground.

Stassia turned the rod off and shoved it into a pocket. She gave Untami a swift kick in the ribs before turning away and rubbing her hands over her face.

"I could find out if she knows anything." Though I didn't know how my use of the tank after the confrontation with Kess would affect my new ability.

"Is this going to set us back another few weeks?"

"I honestly don't know. I hope not. It didn't with Jey or Kess."

Stassia took in the woman on the ground, the buildings around us, and the artificial sky above. "I assume I will need Saka or Meera to retrieve us if it comes to that?"

"They may have a jump point here, but I doubt it. Buria would be your best bet. She made the one here that I used today."

She forced a particularly terrifying smile. "And where is your dear Buria these days?"

I tried to keep my tone as level as possible. "Working for Gamnock."

"I don't have any contact with her, but I can get with Gamnock if I have to." She muttered something about blaming Buria for everything before her words dissolved into curses in her own language in which my name came up several times.

While I was grateful her venting didn't involve weapons aimed at me, standing around wasn't getting us anywhere. "Should I?" I nodded toward Untami.

"Yes, fine. Do it."

I sat near Untami, trying to calm myself enough to get the wisp of a probe working, but Stassia's muttering made it impossible.

"Enough, Stassia. I need quiet."

She sighed and came to stand over my right shoulder, placing her hand there so she could let me know if anything happened while I was occupied.

The wisp came easier with not only her silence but the comfort of having her close and the peace she brought even when she was angry. I sent some of it back to her, hoping it would calm her too. Our connection equalized as her hostility downgraded from its critical level.

Secure in knowing Stassia wasn't going to kick me while I was wandering in Untami's mind, I let go of my body and dove into hers.

Numb on the outside, Untami attempted to keep me from invading her mind, but she'd had little practice with that. Without links, Kess's guards had no need for learning anything in that field. They were for show more than anything. Since taking control of his territory, he'd been fond of portraying an image. I imagined he still had the remaining mercenary guards I'd encountered at his club on call should he feel the need for them.

Untami squirmed inside as I wormed my way through her memories. Once I'd found the area I was looking for, I didn't bother being subtle.

"Show me the Masters."

Her memories raced, touching on all the interactions she'd had with them, shuffling into the semblance of a timeline like soldiers quickly forming ranks. The most recent memory flashed by first. I latched onto the images, the sounds, hazy backgrounds, the hands and lips on which she'd focused, a compliment, a promise of reward for delivering Ikeri to the two men. She'd paid Ikeri herself little mind, only the shape of a young girl in red robes.

Pleasure flooded through Untami as the Masters smiled upon her. "We will send for you once we have established a new home. You have proven yourself worthy, Untami. Your service will be remembered."

"Where is the new home?" I asked.

Memories shuffled again, speeding backward and forward but settling on no solid line this time. Instead, they flashed by faster than I could keep up with, flickering to life and burning away before I got a full sense of each one. Written words in a language Untami didn't know, a map on the giant datapad the Masters had used, snatches of overheard conversation, faces of the Masters, and through it all, a deep longing to be with them.

"Did the others help you free these Masters?"

The burst of pride answered that question before the memory of her setting off alone raced by.

"Why give them my daughter when you could have given the Masters countless slaves from Kess's stock to refill their ranks?"

"She'll fetch a much higher price," Untami whispered, her voice ragged. "She was who they wanted. You need to pay for what you did."

"As do you." I tightened my hold on her mind, squeezing until all resistance was gone. It only took a few seconds.

A frantic shaking registered from my body. I pulled back to find Stassia staring at me.

"You killed her."

Untami's body lay still, her eyes staring up at the artificial light above. "Well, that worked then."

"Are you all right? Do we need to go to the University?"

"I'm fine." Though it did concern me that I'd not pulled out on my own even knowing that she was dying. If it had been a probe alone, all sorts of alarms would have been going off in my head to signal I should leave. Instead, there had only been a sense of satisfaction. I didn't feel sick or that her personality was lingering in my head. I certainly didn't get the impression that I was on an impending spiral into insanity, but maybe not realizing it was the first step downward.

"I am fine, right?"

She rested her hands alongside my face and peered down at me. "Your version of fine anyway, yes."

"It's getting easier to control. As much as I'm sure Canelli would like to continue with his data collection, we need to get back to Artor and consult the datapad I took. There's a map. They must have been planning to expand before I took them down."

She helped me to my feet and then nudged Untami with her boot. "What are we doing with her?"

"I'll have one of my staff take care of her. We need to look at that map while I have this all in my head."

"How is your head?" she asked.

"Not bad." Surprisingly, nothing more than a mild ache.

She gave me a skeptical look.

"Give me a couple minutes before we Jump home just to make sure." The moment she nodded, I dove back into the network, hunted down the stored vid feed, and erased every file I could find. Then I left a message for my Tacesh staff to destroy any backup files they might come across to protect the privacy of the women who had been held here.

After a convincing show of making sure I was all right, I held out my hand. Stassia took it.

Considering that as progress, I Jumped us to our estate on Artor. Hedvika met us in the foyer. I waved her off and we went directly to the bedroom where I'd left the datapad.

Stassia and I sat on the bed, side by side, while I went through all the files until I found a map. It wasn't the one I'd seen. I kept looking. The next three weren't right either. I began to wonder if I'd remembered wrong or if I'd imagined the map. A fourth file looked promising, but the details didn't line up and I was almost out of files. The last map turned out to be close, but again, not quite as I remembered. The three planets it showed were in different places, but the alignment was right even though the colors were also off.

I flipped between the fourth and fifth map. "It's one of these. I think."

"You don't sound very sure."

"I'm going on the memory of a memory of a picture a woman saw once. So no, I'm not very sure, but of the options on the device where she remembered seeing that picture, these are the closest matches."

Stassia got up and started pacing. "That's not good enough."

"I'm sorry, this is all I've got. It's more than we had when I was dead to the world in the middle of the common room."

"You mean, more than Neko and I were able to get." She kicked at a shirt I'd left on the floor. At least I wasn't wearing it right then.

"I mean, we're making progress. Even if it's small. It's something."

"Is it? We have a map. Maybe. Of three worlds with no coordinates, no names. What are we supposed to do, figure out where these worlds are and search all of them?"

"If we want Ikeri back, yes," I declared.

"If?" She glared at me. "Maybe I was wrong. You're already too far down this weapon path."

"Of course, I want her back. I meant—"

Her pacing took on a more determined stomp. "Why can't they just make demands? Ask for credits? Want to trade you for her or something logical?"

I set the datapad down. Maybe I'd imagined that we'd made positive progress. "You'd prefer they ask to trade me for her?"

"You wouldn't trade places with Ikeri if it meant she could come home?"

"Yes, but that's not what I asked."

"You survive everything." She gestured flippantly, her scowl in full force. "We just keep replacing parts and you're back at it. She's a ten-year-old girl who wants to bring peace to the known universe. She had no idea what she was getting into when she agreed to Jey's fucked up plan."

I stood, hoping to catch her and hug her until she calmed down. She was still exhausted from the stim-binge, not to mention having to take over everything while I'd been incapacitated for nearly a month and then the stress of Ikeri's kidnapping. I held out one arm, gauging the receptiveness of my approach.

"No, she didn't know. Stassia, Jey used her. And now he's paying for that. So is Kess. We will find her."

Her voice shook. "You heard that woman, what they plan to do to Ikeri." Stassia pushed my arm away. "They'll do the same thing they've done to all those women, to those girls you sent over to Isnar's. He brushed over their minds to make sure they were safe to have around Ikeri. He told me what they went through, asking for advice from my Seeker training to see if there was anything more he could do for them."

Her hands formed fists at her sides. "I know exactly what those men are doing to our daughter while we stand here with your maybe map and not a damned solid lead to go on."

I wanted to assure her that the Masters wouldn't hurt Ikeri, that they wouldn't damage the goods, knowing what she could do, but my gut knew that was a lie. Kess had handed them my weakness, knowing full well that what was in store for Ikeri would tear me apart.

"Stassia, I'll find her."

"What will be left of our daughter when you do? *If* you do?" She waved a finger at me as if it had the force of a pulse wave. "You took it upon yourself to attack these people. I know you think you were doing the right thing, but they never would have taken Ikeri if you'd have minded your own damned business."

"I know, dammit." Her accusation was true, so hearing her say the words shouldn't have hit me quite so hard, but they did. My voice rose. "So yes, if I have to search all the worlds on these maps myself, I will."

"You can't." Her voice rose to meet mine. "With Jey and Kess out of commission, the Narvan needs you more than ever. Not to mention the chaos of the Rakon now that you took Kess out."

The bedroom was of ample size any other day, but right then, it was far too small. We stood two steps apart, face to face, her's growing redder by the second. No matter how calm I tried to be, to find the peace of being near her, the fury rushing through our bonded connection drowned it all out and inflamed my own until we were all out screaming at one another.

"Should I have let Kess go about his business because his absence is inconvenient? He handed our daughter to monsters!"

"Monsters you brought into our midst. You couldn't just kill them, no, you had to punish them." She was no longer shaking a finger at me, but a fist. "Well, guess who's being punished now?"

"Clearly, I am. Geva be damned, Stassia, I'm trying to fix this."

"You wouldn't have to if you'd done the job right the first time and killed them like I trained you to do from day one!"

I wrapped my hand around her fist before she did let it fly. "What was it you said when we first met after losing your memories of me? You held the whole Narvan together without any help? Well, I'm sure you can do it again. I'm going to find Ikeri."

"You can't leave me here and run off to look for her," she sputtered.

"Who will then? You think we can pay people to search for her? We don't have a giant stockpile of credits. We barely have enough to keep our half of the Narvan running. You're going to have to dig down and find that person you used to be. She could handle this."

I let go of her hand and took a step away before I did anything I'd regret.

"Could she? I didn't ask to lose half of myself!" She picked up a boot and threw it at me.

The boot caught me on the shoulder despite my attempt to dodge it. "If you had listened to me, you wouldn't have," I yelled back at her.

"Oh, so that's what has been lurking in your mind all this time." She threw the other boot with even more force.

I knocked it aside. It hit the wall, leaving a dark spot and a dent.

"Why don't you just take Saka and go then," she screamed. "Get out! I don't need you."

A sudden pounding erupted on our door. I slammed my palm onto the panel to open it. "What?"

Neko stood there with Daniel and Markus close behind. "Everything all right in there, boss?"

"What do you think?"

Sick of everyone, I almost left, but then it occurred to me that I didn't want to lose another kid. I grabbed Daniel and Jumped.

FIFTEEN

Daniel stood beside me at our jump point at the Jalvian capitol. To his credit, he wasn't shaking or stammering or asking a hundred questions. He just stood there, watching me, gauging and calculating. He'd need to work on masking what was going on in his head, but overall, I was impressed.

"Your sister did something stupid because we tried to hide our reality from all of you. We thought we were keeping you safe, giving you a chance at a semi-normal childhood."

I started walking. He followed, doing his best to keep up but rushing along on his shorter legs.

"It's time you see who your parents are and how the universe works."

"Ikeri told me. Some of it anyway," he said.

"About us?"

He nodded. "She thought I'd be mad too, that I'd side with her."

I came to a halt in the middle of the busy hallway and pulled Daniel aside so we didn't obstruct traffic. "When was this?"

Daniel licked his lips and glanced around me as if seeking out possible help. "When she came home with her robes and tattoos."

"You don't sound too excited about her becoming a Seeker."

"I liked her being my sister. I liked helping her, watching out for her," he said sullenly. "She doesn't need me anymore."

I snorted. "Do you have any idea how big of a mess Ikeri is in? She definitely needs you. So you didn't pick a side then?"

He shook his head. "She tried to talk Markus into it too, but he doesn't like when she tries to show him things. He made me tell her to stop."

I realized I'd boxed him in and that's why he was acting so anxious. I backed off. "Has she talked to you since she went missing?"

"No. It's like she's gone." His lower lip started to quiver and tears pooled in his eyes.

"She's not gone. The men who have her intend to sell her or use her. They can't do that if she's dead."

"Don't say that," he growled, blinking his tears away. That was an improvement.

"It's the truth, and as I said, I'm done hiding that from you. Now, what's this about Ikeri and taking sides?"

"She had nothing good to say about you."

In the interest of expediency, I adopted Etara's pledge. "How about we make this truth thing work both ways."

Daniel exhaled loudly. "People are staring."

"People often stare at me. You'll get used to it."

"Doesn't it bother you?"

"Only when they're armed." I started walking again. "The whole truth this time. I know how she felt, she told me quite explicitly."

"She did?" he asked quietly.

"Why do you think I wasn't there for her farewell dinner?"

"Mom said you were too busy working. Ikeri said you were mad at her for becoming a Seeker."

I laughed. "I was working, but only because Ikeri made it abundantly clear she didn't want anything to do with me. I figured I'd give her the night with all of you."

"She said you killed people."

"You know that's true."

"But that you enjoy killing people."

"Depends on the person, but in some cases, I suppose that's also true."

He was quiet for a few minutes. We'd come to the Prime's secretary before he asked, "You don't think that makes you a bad person?"

"That alone? Probably. But if you take into account why I do all the things I do, it's more of a grey area."

"So you don't think you're good?"

I laughed again. "No, I don't think I'm good. Look what happens when I try to do something good?" I shook my head. "Pissed off people take your sister to get back at me."

His face lit up. "So you know who took her? You know where they are?"

"Very generally, yes."

"And we can go get her?"

"That's why we're here." I spoke to the secretary, gaining us a meeting with the Prime in short order. We stood aside to wait for his current meeting to end. There, next to a pointy metal blue statue of what might have been fish if I were drunk and stared at it long enough, I dropped my announcement. "When we're done here, we're going to the University and you're getting your own link."

His eyes about popped out of his head and a red flush raced up his face. "Are you kidding?"

"Do I look like I'm kidding?"

"Mom will kill you and then me."

"We'll deal with her later, just like we always have."

He shook his head. "This isn't wrestling in the dirt or making too much noise when Ikeri was sleeping. Are you sure she'll let me keep it?"

"She wouldn't make you go through the whole procedure again to have it removed. She'll only be pissed at me, and that's nothing new." I could still hear her screaming at me to leave.

"I won't have you hauled off by someone, unable to escape, like your sister. You're getting a link and learning to use it until you're as fast as Neko."

"I want to be as fast as you." He grinned.

"That would be fine too. The important thing is you learn to use it so you can help protect your mother, Markus, and Ikeri when we get her back."

His grin faded. "Are you and mom... Are you leaving?"

"I hadn't planned on it, why?"

"You were fighting. Loud fighting. We could all hear you."

It would seem that we'd exceeded the volume specifications for the soundproofing of our bedroom. I cringed, replaying the last things we'd said to one another that the boys might have overheard.

"Yes, well, we do that sometimes."

"Not like that. Mom is really mad. Like Ikeri was mad."

"I'm gifted that way, I guess."

His brows lowered and he frowned. "Why do you do that?"

"Do what?"

"Take all the blame? Seeker Tomias taught us that both sides of an argument share blame."

"Seeker Tomias never argued with your mother."

"He did so. They trained together. He told us stories about how the two of them didn't get along when they first met."

"I'm sure that was different. They weren't joined. When she forgot me," I shook my head, trying to find honest but censored words, "we've tried, both of us, to be patient, but it's been hard. There are good days and bad ones. Lately, mostly bad ones."

"But you're still bonded to her, right? You're not leaving?"

"I'm leaving to find Ikeri, not leaving your mother."

He had that lightly veiled look of disapproval that Seekers wore when they spouted 'as you say' in a forced neutral tone. Thankfully, he kept the words contained.

Daniel sighed. "I'm not going back to Veria Prime once lockdown is lifted, am I?"

"Probably not."

"Advisor," said the secretary. "He's ready for you."

"Thank you." I started for the door, only to realize Daniel was still standing by the fish-like sculpture. "Come on. You're by my side until I tell you otherwise."

The secretary's curiosity was clear, but she didn't ask and I didn't clarify. We entered the Prime's trophy room office.

"Don't touch anything."

Daniel was so busy taking in the visual extravaganza that I didn't know if he'd heard me or not. As we stood there before the Prime, I realized Daniel was wearing his favorite shirt that was stained and a size too small with a hole in the sleeve and the baggy pants he often wore to bed. He hadn't been planning on going anywhere. He'd been on lockdown for Geva's sake. I adjusted my position so I blocked him from view.

"Welcome Advisor Ta'set. Who is this then?" the Prime asked, peering around me.

"My son."

"Learning the ropes or being punished?"

"Neither. I have a proposal for you."

"Oh?" He lost interest in Daniel, looking up at me from under his bushy white brows.

"Your forces haven't had much opportunity for glory lately. I'd like to take a significant force into some new territory."

"What does Advisor Te have to say about this proposal?"

"He's not saying much since I learned of his part in abducting my daughter."

The Prime blanched. "I had no part in that." He began to stammer.

"I know that or you wouldn't be sitting here."

The Prime nodded vigorously. He cleared his throat. "This force, what sort of compensation should we expect?"

"I'm sure I'll find some incentive we can agree upon. Beyond that, I'll tell you that it's likely we'll have more Arpex on our hands soon. My hunters will be on high alert. I expect you'll offer them your full cooperation."

"You'll not be taking Artorian forces out of the Narvan?"

"Yours are better suited to the task at hand. Artor's fleets can assist in guarding the Narvan. I need the option of an aggressive approach to this particular task."

"I see." He shifted in his chair, finger tapping on his desk.

"If you're thinking about refusing, I will reconsider my stance on your innocence."

He drew himself up, and as only a Jalvian could, managed to stare down his nose at me even as I stood and he remained seated. "I understood we were allies. Yet, you stoop to threats."

"I understood you worked for me. If that's not the case, I'll be happy to take my hunters back, along with the cooperation of all Artorian worlds."

His voice rose. "You'd start a war?"

"My daughter was taken. By a Jalvian. Right here in this office. So yes, it seems a fitting place to start a war."

The Prime's bravado faltered, and suddenly he was only an old man in a medal-laden uniform. "I've seen enough fighting on my world. If you wish to battle with someone, let it be far outside the Narvan."

"I have your cooperation then?"

"You leave me with little choice."

"Is that a yes?"

"Yes." He shrank in his chair. "When do you need this force ready?"

"Two days."

"That's not enough time for the size fleet you ask for."

"Don't fuck with me. You keep your ships stocked and your men on call. You could have them ready to leave the system in a matter of hours." I leaned on his desk. "I'll not stand for your second best ships, your expendable crews, or your outdated weaponry. I expect half of your fleet ready and waiting in two days."

"Yes, Advisor."

I imagined him bowing his head like Buria and all the others and it just pissed me off more. Before I screwed up the deal by venting further, I reached out to lay a hand on Daniel and Jumped us to the University.

"Are we really going to do this?" Daniel asked, taking in the bustling staff of the inner University with wide eyes.

"We are." I flagged down an empty-handed employee and demanded a meeting with an LE.

"Should we ask mom first?"

"Do you want to ask her?" I asked.

"She'll tell me no, but with more words and much louder."

"And I'm telling you yes. Your choice."

"You'll protect me from her, right?"

"I will."

"All right then. What should I tell her? She wants to know where I am."

Activity bustled all around us, everyone going about their business with a level of focus and distraction that kept their attention off of us other than as a passing glance. I'd been in this area of the University enough that most everyone knew me on sight. Stassia might have her own contacts. She might know exactly where we were and what I was up to. But she wasn't in my head, berating me yet, so maybe we were lucky so far.

"While I don't condone lying to your mother, if you do want this link, I suggest you tell her you're safe with me and leave it at that. Tell her you'll see her as soon as I cool off. She knows how long that takes."

"I don't like lying to her." His gaze darted to everyone around us, more curious than anything, but I knew him well enough to see he was squirming inside.

"That's a good thing. But I'm sure this isn't the first time, is it?"

He'd run pretty wild when they'd been on Pentares without me. Not to mention, our departure from traditional parenting since we'd returned to the Narvan. He might have had Neko or Fa'yet or any of our other guards watching over him, but they weren't his parents. We were fortunate that he was a good kid.

Now I was putting him in the middle of me and Stassia, tempting him with what he wanted, what I wanted for him. I rubbed my hands over my face as guilt leeched away some of my anger with Stassia.

"If you want to go home and forget about this, I'll take you."

Daniel shook his head. "But Mom says Markus is upset you took me and not him too."

"Markus is too young for a link," I said hoping to sound jovial, but inside I was fuming that Stassia would use Markus to get at Daniel. Markus might well have been upset, but she didn't have to guilt Daniel with it. She could have kept it to her damned self.

"Tell her that you'll be home tonight and whatever you want about Markus. I'll make it up to him another time."

Relief washed over his face. "You can tell him when we go home. He'll be happier to hear it from you."

"I may not be going home with you."

Stassia and I had only fought that badly once before. I'd left then too. Not that she'd remember. I'd not returned many memories of our time on Veria Minor to her yet. It had taken weeks for both of us to cool down last time.

"Maybe bringing you there but not staying," I clarified, "But yes, eventually."

"All right," he said quietly. "What do I need to do to get a link?"

His choice then. I'd given him the opportunity to back out. Yet, even as I repeated that to myself, the guilt didn't go away. Good thing I was used to that eating at me. I distracted myself by explaining the link implant process.

Before I'd reached the end, an LE arrived and brought us to an examination room. There, the LE and her assistant berated me for wanting my twelve-year-old son linked. I let them say their piece and then told them to do it anyway. Daniel remained quiet but his excitement was tangible.

I stood outside the door, peering through the tiny window while the procedure took place, sweating at the memory of Stassia nearly dying in a room just like that one. Neko sent a couple attempts to contact me but none of them felt urgent. I didn't need his humor or his nagging. He'd keep Stassia safe and that was enough for now.

Daniel's procedure went quickly and smoothly. I followed them back to the room we'd been in and waited for him to wake up. In the meantime, I sunk into my link, checking in with Canelli and getting updates on Jey's condition. Kess remained sedated and without any notable signs of issues from my brief internal attack. Jey, on the other hand, was unresponsive. Alive, but on autopilot, his brain activity minimal. I did hope he would recover, if for nothing more than so I could pound on him from the outside too.

I notified Artor's Premier and Fa'yet of the possible Arpex invasion and the preparations they should take as well as my demand that they work peacefully with the Jalvian forces. The hunters were put on alert. The still tenuous government on Syless was given instructions on working with both Artor and Jal. It took longer to work through my contacts on Jey's other holdings. They encountered significant resistance when those they spoke to couldn't reach Jey, but I felt relatively sure we'd made suitable arrangements. By the time I'd touched base with my contacts on Merchess, Twelve, and Thirteen, which weren't as numerous as they once had been, my head was throbbing.

Daniel's eyes fluttered open as I was reaching for my stim tin. I left it in my pocket and checked him over.

"How are you feeling?"

"Weird." He blinked slowly and then closed his eyes again.

I called for the LE. She came in moments later and ran a scanner over him.

"He's still recovering. Don't rush him." Her brows drew together. "You understand this is highly irregular. We don't implant children."

"You've made your disapproval abundantly clear. Will he be all right?"

She consulted the scanner again. "Everything appears normal, but as I said, we have no baseline for children. Give him a few more hours. I'll check in on him in a bit."

"It shouldn't take this long." I'd witnessed the process for Neko and others. All of them had come out of the procedure by now. He should be talking and cautiously exploring.

"I'm sure there's no cause to worry," she said, clutching her scanner and backing away.

"What aren't you telling me?"

"Nothing. I swear." She held out the scanner as if I could decipher the data in her shaking hands. "Everything looks normal."

"Don't go anywhere."

"I'll be right outside." She scurried out of the room.

I moved my chair closer to the bed and looked down on the innocent version of my face. His body was unscarred, without the shooting aches up his back and down his leg like mine was doing just then. I shifted in my chair to find a more comfortable spot. His hand, two-thirds the size of mine, was warm but not soft as I held it. His work on Prime had given him some calluses and muscle on the arms that were covered in the fine hairs of youth. How long had it been since I'd held him? Since we'd rolled in the mud outside the house on Minor? It seemed like a lifetime ago. A different life. Now we were here, getting him linked, and in the back of my mind, I was contemplating what to dress him in for the days and weeks ahead.

I couldn't reconcile myself to the image of Daniel in armor, yet I wanted to keep him safe. The Jalvian academy uniform would get him laughed at by Jalvian officers. Typical Artorian clothes wouldn't gain him any favor with the Jalvian crew. I'd always skirted the issue with a mix of whatever caught my eye. Maybe that was the answer for Daniel too.

If he woke up. If he was all right.

Stassia would kill me if anything happened to him and I'd probably let her.

"Come on already." I shook him lightly and squeezed his hand. I started running through ways to tell Stassia that Daniel wasn't going to wake up, that this was my fault too. His hand remained in mine, warm but limp.

In the midst of the third time I pictured Neko shooting me in the back of the head while Stassia screamed at me, Daniel's fingers twitched. I shut off my imagination and focused on the waking boy in the bed. He opened his eyes, clearer and more alert this time, and smiled.

"It worked," he said.

"Oh thank Geva." I hugged him and then stood back to look him over.

He sat up slowly. "Are you crying?"

"No. Definitely not." I willed the excess moisture in my eye to evaporate and wiped my face dry as I turned away to call the LE back in.

She ran the scanner over him again. Her grip on the equipment relaxed. "There we go. His link is active and everything is still normal."

"Good. How long should he rest?"

"I can't give you a number. We don't implant—"

"He should rest as long as possible. Got it." I waved her away.

Once she'd left, I returned to my chair. "How are you feeling?"

"Tired, but good." He grinned, a sight I never grew tired of. "There's so much to see. How do you sort it all?"

"I'll show you, but right now, I want you to rest. Explore carefully." Which I knew was a stupid thing to say, remembering my initial excitement with the vast network before me. "I'm going to find you some suitable clothes, and then I'm taking you home."

"Can I Jump myself now? Can I?"

"Not today, but yes."

He slapped the bed and sat back on the pillows. "I'll never need a datapad again. Everything is right here."

"Remember to stay out of where you don't belong."

"I can get into places I don't belong? How? How do I know if I don't belong there?"

I sighed. "We'll cover that too. I'll be back shortly. Don't open the door to this room. Do you hear me?"

"Sure, yes."

Hoping he'd been listening, I locked the door from the inside and Jumped to one of my points on Jal near where I occasionally purchased clothing. On a regular day, I would have purchased it through my link under an alias and had it delivered to one of the drop locations I used, but today I was in a hurry. I walked into the shop.

A startled clerk gave me a single glance before reaching for the alarm.

"Don't do that."

He froze mid-reach. "Don't hurt us. We'll give you whatever you want."

A young woman stood nearby, folding shirts on a display table. Her hands shook. She dropped the shirt she'd been working on.

"I need several shirts, like that one." I pointed to a dark blue shirt that fastened up the front. "And that one." The black pullover with long sleeves might even reach Daniel's hands.

The woman hurried around the shop holding up various shirts. I nixed all the bright Jalvian favorites. Darker colors suited our skin tone better. That's when I realized she had them all in my size.

"Small. They're not for me. And those boots." I set a pair next to my own feet and picked the pair that best matched Daniel's feet compared to mine.

Three pairs of grey and black pants later along with, several shirts and various other items to get him started on a semi-adult wardrobe, I approached the counter and pulled out a credit chip under my legal name. I figured I might as well make a statement while I was there.

The woman's hand shook harder when she realized who I was. She dropped the chip. The young man grabbed it and completed the transaction. I forced a smile I didn't feel to round out my public appearance and left with the bulky packages. Safely away from the store, I Jumped back to the University and hurried to the room where I'd left Daniel. He was still grinning and laughing to himself.

My pounding on the door got his attention. He slid out of the bed and unlocked it.

"What's all that?" He asked, eyeing the packages.

"Open it and see."

He pawed through the contents with unbridled enthusiasm. "Can I change now?"

"I'm taking you home and putting you to bed so I can deal with your mother, but yes, if you want to. Just don't sleep in any of it. You'll need it for work."

"Work?"

"You heard me. I said you were by my side until I told you otherwise."

"We're going off with the Jalvian fleet? I'm going with you?" He looked like he might burst, and I couldn't help but laugh despite the rest of my day.

"Yes. Now change if you're going to. I need to get you home."

"You're the best dad ever."

"Hardly."

If his grin got any wider his face would split in half. "You're the best dad today."

"Your mother will not be sharing that opinion."

His exuberance diminished. "Give me a few minutes head start to get Markus up to my room and some loud music playing before you talk to her, all right? He was really upset when you were fighting this morning and he's not much better now with me gone."

That made my stomach drop. "You can feel him from here?"

Daniel nodded. "Not a lot, but yes. I learned how to use a mix of what we can do naturally with what the Seekers teach. I'm not as good as the other acolytes, but my reach is longer than theirs."

Etara said he was gifted, but I didn't think she'd meant in this way. In fact, I was sure she hadn't been talking about his abilities. Perhaps she just considered that normal for one of my children.

"Have you been helping him at night?"

"What little I can, yes. I figured it would help you with mom if he wasn't in your bed all the time."

"Thank you for that." I'd been so focused on Ikeri and working through everything with Stassia that I'd been neglecting my time with Markus. Even having him in the house seemed to be keeping my sleep issues under control, but his nightmares were still regular.

Daniel piled everything back into the bags. "I think you'll have enough to argue about without my showing up dressed like you."

"Thank you for that too then."

He nodded, still aglow. "I'm ready when you are."

There was no getting ready for facing angry Stassia. "Maybe I'll just go sleep on one of the Jalvian ships."

He elbowed me.

"All right, yes, let's get this over with."

"It's just mud. That's what you used to say."

"We're a bit beyond having played in the mud today."

Daniel shrugged, handing me the packages. "Still washes out."

I elbowed him back. "No more Seeker school for you."

With the clothes under one arm and my newly linked son in the other hand, I Jumped us back to the house on Artor.

SIXTEEN

Hedvika met us in the foyer, rushing toward us as if propelled by a gale-force wind. "Are you well? What do you require?"

"We're fine. What's all the hurry about?"

"We live to serve, Advisor. If there's anything I can do to make your day better?"

"I don't think so, no." Short of sending me back in time before I'd visited Tacesh, but that still wouldn't fix Stassia, or our relationship, or make Ikeri accept me.

"Perhaps Saka then?"

"For reference, that should never be an option you suggest."

"But, Advisor, it is no secret that you favor Saka. We are not offended by this fact."

Daniel watched us intently. I transferred the bags to his arms to distract him.

"Why don't you head up with Markus while the coast is clear? And rest, dammit. I mean it. I don't need your mother even more pissed than she already is."

"I will." He inched away, clearly hoping to hear more of what Hedvika was getting at.

"I don't favor Saka any more than Neko."

Hedvika bowed her head. "Oh, I see. I didn't realize you had open preferences, forgive me."

Daniel didn't even bother to hide his gaping twist-around stare.

"That is not what I meant. Not at all. No." I shooed Daniel up the stairs with a glare. "Post either Saka or Meera on the boys. Where is Neko?"

"With Ana, in your bedroom, Advisor." She bowed and hurried off.

I stood there, stunned and growing more furious by the second. What in all nine hells was she thinking? Was this some sort of revenge thing? I liked Neko, and he was the one man I didn't mind working with Stassia. I trusted him.

I replayed the memory of him looking like he wanted to hug her, how he'd reached out to her, comforting her when I'd rejoined the living in the common room.

Had trusted. Fucking hells.

I didn't want to kill him, but there was no way in the known universe that I was about to stand for this.

Whatever was going on in there, I came to the conclusion I couldn't bear to see it. *"If you value your life, you better be fully clothed when you get out here,"* I said to Neko.

I planted myself in the hallway to our bedroom, blocking his path of escape. The door opened and Neko stepped out, holding out a hand to me until the door closed behind him. He walked quietly toward me. There were far too many vivid scenarios of what he'd left behind in there playing in my head for me to form coherent words.

Neko approached, stopping inches away when he realized I wasn't moving to let him by. "Boss, it's good to see you." He released an outpouring of anxiety and urgency on me through his link. "I didn't know what to do, but I figured you were busy, and she didn't want you here. And I mean, *really* didn't. So I did the best I could to calm her down. We got some work done, but then she got that sick look again so I got her back here right away. She's sleeping now, but I didn't dare leave her alone."

All the anger that had been building vanished, leaving a dry hollowness in its wake. "Thank you for taking care of her, but you should have told me what was going on."

He leaned against the wall, fatigue plain on his face. "It wouldn't have helped if you'd known. You'd just want to be here and she wanted nothing to do with you, which would have made her worse."

"Good help is hard to find." I patted his shoulder. "I'm glad I don't have to kill you. I would have felt pretty bad about that."

"What?" Panic overtook him. Then he turned to the door and back to me. "Oh. Oh! No. I couldn't do that to you, not even if she ordered me to. I wouldn't." He stepped back. "Not that I wouldn't because she's not...I just mean I—"

"Neko?"

"Yes, boss?"

"Can you go give Daniel some pointers on using his new link while I enter the den of doom that awaits me?"

He stared at me, mouth agape. "You didn't."

"It's safer that he has one."

He grabbed my arm and then suddenly let go as if realizing what he was doing. "Oh thank you! I was going to suggest it a while ago, but I thought you'd flay me alive. I knew she would." Neko glanced back at the door. "I didn't want to sound like I was lazy, but yes, not having to Jump both of the boys will help tremendously, and knowing he can duck out himself or take Markus with him if there is trouble, that eases my mind a lot."

"Mine too. Remind me someday when I have excess funds to give you a raise."

Neko grinned. "Good luck in there. We can discuss that if you're alive in the morning."

"Thanks, but the raise may have to wait a bit longer." I backed off and let him escape before proceeding down the hall and through the door.

Stassia was curled into a compact ball, knees against her chest, dressed, but minus armor and weapons. Her boots sat on the floor beside the bed, still in reach if she had a mind to start throwing things again.

Her eyes remained closed and her breathing was slow and even. I backed out of the doorway and ducked into the closet to remove my boots, coat, and weapons. If we were going to attempt to work anything out, less ammunition would be in our favor.

My hand hovered over the stack of pants where I'd hidden the endorphin boosting vials. Knowing they were there, that I had a possible escape, even if only short term, made facing Stassia less daunting.

Armed with nothing but my clothes, I entered the bedroom and closed the door behind me. If Daniel had made good on his loud music, I couldn't hear it. Which was just as well. A sleeping Stassia couldn't behead me.

It wasn't until I'd carefully climbed into the bed from the end all the way up to rest beside her that I realized she hadn't stirred. Her breathing hadn't changed either. Willing to take the chance that she'd wake up yelling and punching, I sat up and looked her over more carefully. I hadn't been here to help her through the headache this time. I'd assumed she'd managed to fall asleep, but the injector I discovered under her arm revealed the truth. I could have sworn it had three doses left in it, but now there was only one.

"Stassia?" I tentatively touched her mind only to find her awareness

sluggish. *"Are you all right?"* My words fell into a thick blanket of silence, unheard and unanswered.

Taking her to the tank would clear out the drug, but the damage that caused the attacks was part of her profile, part of her now, thanks to the Council's testing. The stress that triggered her attacks wasn't going away anytime soon. Better to let her rest and work through it herself, but I wished she hadn't double-dosed. It wasn't like her to be reckless with medicine.

Neko had been right not to leave her alone, whether he was aware of her dosing or having taken the medication at all. The fact that the injector was in the bed with her and under the blanket made me think she'd hid it from him.

With nothing to do but sit beside her while she slept, I got comfortable and tried to think of a way to talk myself out of all that had been said that morning.

I woke to her hair tickling my nose and her back pressed against my chest, likely my doing rather than hers. Her breathing hadn't changed. The medicine had her down long-term.

The nagging of far too many waiting contacts and reports pinged in my head, but I ignored them. Instead, I sat back up and loosened her hair, finding the pressure points that offered her a measure of relief. With the medication already in her system, I didn't know if my efforts would help, but it was worth a try and it allowed me to touch her without fear of any more damage being verbally flung between us.

Slipping inside her head might offer me some clues as to what I could do to make her better, but the last time I'd done that, I'd managed to reopen the cascade of damage the Council had caused and sent her into a medically-induced coma for months. The wisp technique I'd learned from Ikeri might help avoid that, but the rest of my new mental skills were aimed in the exact opposite direction of healing and comfort. No matter my good intentions, it was better to stay out of her head for anything but our usual interactions.

Having done all I could, I got up and returned her injector to the bathroom cabinet, took a shower, and got dressed. When I returned to the bedroom for one last check before I went to see Daniel, she was awake. I probably should have backed out of the room and left, but that would just be prolonging the inevitable.

Stassia unfurled, shoving the blanket aside, and sat on the edge of the bed, hair falling around her shoulders.

"How are you feeling?" I asked.

"Like hell." She stretched her shoulders and neck.

Giving in to habit, I let the door close and went to sit behind her. Whether she was still angry or not, peace flowed through our connection as I rubbed her shoulders. She didn't exactly relax against me, but she didn't pull away either.

"You didn't take Saka."

"Did you truly think I would?"

"She is younger, and pretty, and totally your type." She made a disgusted grunt. "She tries hard to hide it from me, but I see her watching you like she wants to give you a full-body tongue bath."

"Tongue bath?" I couldn't help but chuckle. "While I won't say you're wrong on all those accounts, she's been conditioned to treat men that way. If she wants to bathe anyone, she'll have to give Neko a go. I'm sure he'd be agreeable."

She glared at me over her shoulder. "Are you trying to tell me that I'm imagining your gawking at her?"

"I didn't say that. I said you were right, and you still demanded she be in our house anyway. You knew about what happened between us. You knew, and you still put her here like a baited trap hoping I'd fall in so you could let me have it. But I haven't taken your bait, and I don't plan on it."

She eased against me a little. I enjoyed it, knowing it wouldn't last.

"I'm still pissed that you kissed her, even if you were drugged."

"I know." I kissed the back of her neck and got up, needing some space between us before she elbowed me in the eye or something equally painful. "I got Daniel linked yesterday."

Her eyes flicked into full laser mode, unblinking. "How could you do that?"

"We're not losing another kid to anyone. He's got to be able to protect himself." I backed up two steps, not liking the way she was scanning the room for a weapon. "No one will expect he's linked. He's just a kid."

"Exactly, Vayen. What the fuck were you thinking?"

"That he could Jump you if you need help and one of us can't. That he can watch over Markus, that he could protect himself."

"We have Neko and your slaves for that. How could you do this without consulting me?"

"Because he needs to know who we are. We kept it from them, and Ikeri turned against us. Me, anyway. I'm not lying to them anymore."

"Ikeri was mad at you, but she wasn't against you."

"Would you like me to share the letter she wrote?"

"Now you're in the mood the share?" She stood, shaking out her limbs like she might take me down.

I hit her with the memory of Ikeri's datapad before she lifted a foot. She sat back down ungracefully, disoriented by the memory I was shoving at her.

When I was finished. Stassia opened and closed her mouth, shaking her head. Eventually, all she managed was a sharp intake of air and a grimace.

I left her to gather her next stage of tirade and suited up in the closet where I'd left my gear. When I glanced into the bedroom, bracing for another attack, she was still sitting there. Deciding she was going to be a while, I went to find something to eat.

Daniel and Markus sat at the table, slurping up noodles drenched in what smelled like a savory meat broth. I filled a bowl from the pot on the counter and joined them.

"Do I get new clothes too?" asked Markus.

"Maybe. I'll have to give that some thought." If both boys were with me, I'd have to have Meera or Saka along. I couldn't watch out for both of them and work at the same time. Neko needed to stay with Stassia. He knew the Narvan and her moods. That meant immediately testing the fragile truce Stassia and I had come to on the Saka matter. I didn't know if I was up for that quite yet.

Markus pouted, shoving his bowl away. Broth slopped onto the table.

"You better clean that up," I said. "Little boys with bad tempers aren't allowed in the Jalvian fleet."

Daniel grinned at Markus, who jumped up and mopped up the mess with a cloth.

"We won't be going anywhere with the fleet for a couple days so you better make sure you both behave until then."

Markus nodded and sat back down. He proceeded to empty his bowl with vigor.

Daniel asked, "So how did she—"

"Not well," said Stassia, suddenly standing in the kitchen with her arms crossed and suited up, ready for work. "Why do you look like a miniature version of your father?"

Daniel scowled. "I'm not miniature."

"Smaller, then." She shot me a look. "I take it you took it upon yourself to dress him too?"

"Maybe."

"Maybe, my ass." She shook her head. "When is he getting armor? Is that on your agenda for today? Target practice tomorrow?"

"I couldn't very well have him parading around the Jalvian fleet in his pajamas."

"I met the Jalvian Prime yesterday." Daniel said proudly. "His office is—"

"A visual disaster," said Stassia. She pinched the bridge of her nose. "That's where you took him? Wearing clothes he'd been in for three days?"

I stood. "I didn't look at what he was wearing when we left."

Her eyes narrowed and her voice took on an accusing tone that put me on edge. "When you stormed off, you mean."

"When you told me to get out."

Daniel slammed his bowl on the counter. "Stop it."

I turned to see Markus staring at the table with tears in his eyes. "Come on." I picked him up. "Let's go see who is going to show you how to run the security station today."

"I get to help?" he asked, clinging to me.

"Yes."

I spotted Meera in the chair and handed Markus off to her. She straightened his shirt and adjusted him on the edge of the seat in front of her. "He's going to assist you today. Show him how it all works, will you?"

She bowed her head. "Yes, Advisor."

Stassia and Daniel remained in the kitchen, talking in hushed voices that came to an abrupt halt when they caught sight of me.

"Do you need help with anything before I go?" I asked as calmly as I could manage. When she didn't spit an answer at me right away, I looked to Daniel. "Why don't you wait for me in the foyer?"

He shot Stassia a glare and left.

"What was that all about?" I asked.

She muttered, "Damned Seeker school."

"I said the same thing yesterday." The smile I'd hoped for didn't make an apperance.

"After the fallout with Ikeri, I get why you want Daniel on your side, but I didn't agree to this."

"This isn't about sides, Stassia. I want him safe, for Geva's sake. You want to protect him from everything, but he needs to be able to protect himself."

"He's safe here, at home with guards to watch him."

"Guards didn't save Ikeri. He needs to learn. Now."

"And you think this is the best way?"

"This is the way I know. He couldn't stay at an academy and he has no interest in studies on Artor. I think we both agree that he's had enough time at the Seeker school."

"So it's take your kid to work day for the Advisor of the Narvan?"

"Technically, you're advising the Narvan. I'm off hunting Masters with half the Jalvian fleet. I gave those two maps to the University and they were able to locate the system where those worlds are located."

"That's good news, but I did not ask to be advising the Narvan," she hissed. "You threw it at me."

I put my hands on her shoulders. "You'll do just fine. You remember doing this before, before me. You don't need me."

She looked away. "You seem so sure of that."

"When I first met you, you didn't need anyone. You had the Narvan under your fist and everyone jumping to stay in your favor. I'll deal with the Nebula and Fragia. The rest is the same."

"I'm not the same, dammit." She shook off my hands. "I can't do a damn thing when my head is splitting open, and thanks to you, we now have three kids to deal with on top of everything else."

"The Council screwed you over. The Arpex did too. I'm probably to blame for a fair share as well, but you can do this." I reached out and caught her hand. She didn't pull away. "Neko knows how the Narvan runs. He can help you. Lean on him as much as you need to. He's up for it."

"I'd rather lean on you, even though I'm so angry I don't want to look at you right now."

I kissed her forehead. "A little time apart might help with that, don't you think?"

"Maybe," she said begrudgingly. "You'll still be coming home if you're swapping out Daniel and Markus?"

"I was going to put Meera on Markus duty. She can transport him as needed. That way you don't have to worry about either of them. You can put Saka on the off shift so both you and Neko can sleep."

"You've got it all worked out, don't you?" she said sullenly.

"Not in the least." I squeezed her shoulders. "The first time you and I were together it was because the Council forced it on us. This second time, I needed to be with you, and it feels like you went along with it because everyone told you to. We're both going through the motions, and thanks to the bond, I do need to be near you, but... I'd rather you make your peace with who you are now and maybe then we can work through the us mess if that's what you actually want."

"Why are you good to me even when I'm so damned mad at you?" She came closer to lean against me.

The words were hard to say, inadequate. I expanded our bonded connection and let her see why, let her feel why. Her smile, touch, laugh, the way she was pressed against me just then with armor between us, the focused determination she wore when she was working, the open concern she'd shown that first time I'd woken from the tank to find her beside me, how we moved together when we used to workout with one another years ago. All of it and more, flowing between us.

When she spoke again her voice was quiet and thick. "You'll come back twice a week at a time we can both agree on. We'll resume our sessions with a memory mender and then sleep. You have a tendency not to do that as much as you should."

She ran her fingers along the collar of my armor. "And if we're in bed, in the dark, sleeping, we don't have to talk, but you can be near me so the Jalvian fleet doesn't have to suffer crazy intense Vayen."

"For the good of the fleet."

"Yes. And so I can see Daniel," she added quickly.

"I can make that work."

"So you're leaving right now then?" Her fingers worked up my neck.

"Daniel is waiting. Besides, I thought you couldn't stand the sight of me?"

"It's dark in the bedroom."

"What happened to being so damned mad?"

"Nothing. However, I have no issue with you in the bedroom. As you've said, that's the one part we've got figured out just fine." She kissed me to the point where I didn't care what time it was, what I had to do, or that we were standing in the kitchen.

"Are we going or should I..." Daniel's voice registered, bringing us both to a sudden halt.

Stassia stepped back and straightened her coat. "He's going."

"I am?"

She nodded, the playful smile that made my heart beat faster teased her lips. "Daniel is waiting, you said."

"So you are still mad."

Stassia laughed, not with any hint of malice, just laughing like she did in the rare times we were happy together. "I'll expect you in three days then? For our therapy session?"

"I could make tomorrow work."

"Let's stick with three days. It will give us both plenty of time to think about what we want to share."

"I already know."

She laughed again. "Daniel, get your father out of here before we stumble onto another reason to argue."

I left the two of them to say their goodbyes and issued instructions for everyone else. Daniel emerged from the kitchen looking somber. Stassia followed behind but stopped short of us.

"You make sure to stick by your father," she said to Daniel. When she addressed me all the laughter and openness was gone, leaving only the steely tone of Stassia in full work mode. "You bring him back unharmed or this comes off for good." She held up her wrist and tapped on my joining gift. "Is that clear?"

I wanted to say that I wouldn't be around to come back if that were the case, but her tone allowed no degree of commentary. "Yes."

Satisfied, she turned and left us. Or maybe she didn't want to watch us leave. I chose to believe the latter, but in traditional work mode, the former would have been true to form.

"Dad?"

I dragged my attention from the empty spot where Stassia had been. "What?"

"Are we leaving? I know she said for me to take you away, but I don't know how to Jump yet."

"Right. We should set a point here for you." I turned one last time to where she had been standing, hoping to see her lurking there, but she was gone.

"Are we still doing the truth thing?" he asked quietly.

"Yes, why?"

"You're still mad at her, right?"

I nodded.

"And she's still mad at you. But you're both still..." he shifted uncomfortably, rather like a shudder gone wrong.

"It's complicated." I sighed and then pointed to the intricate pattern drawn on the wall. "Come on, I'll show you how a Jump works."

I spent the next half hour explaining what made a jump point and how to frame it in his mind to become the magnet of a gateway. Daniel might have been eager to learn, but his focus was scattered, as was to be expected from a young boy. It took him several tries before he got the point fully encapsulated in his head.

Searching for something easy, I pulled the Cragtek point from memory and went through that with him, detail by detail until I was sure he had it. Then I waited for him to calm down enough to form the point in his mind. It took a while before he managed to pull himself toward it. Three tries later, he finally vanished before my eyes. I Jumped to find him standing there, grinning.

"I did it," he said proudly.

"You did." I let him bask in his accomplishment for a moment before taking off for Gamnock's office.

"If you need help, you can come here. Commit that point to memory. I mean it." I punctuated the command with a stern look. "I'm only going to give you five points. Those are the ones you'll need to focus on, practice with, all right?"

"They'll let me jump here for practice? What about the guard?"

"Get to know the guards. Ask them questions, learn their names, what they like to do, but don't be a pest. They get ignored by almost everyone. They'll be happy to see you and get help if you need it."

"What kind of help?"

"If your mother is hurt, or Markus. If you can't reach any of us. There's a clinic here, ships, plenty of armed protection."

"If something bad happens."

"Exactly." Using my link, I let Gamnock know I was there to speak to him.

Daniel nodded. "Gamnock is good then? Not like Uncle Jey?"

"He's currently not on my shit list, so yes, we'll call him good."

"Do you have a long list?" he asked, carefully omitting the word he wasn't allowed to say.

I considered the current goings-on in the Narvan. "Yes, I suppose I do."

"How do I keep track of who is on it?"

"You listen. A lot. Pay attention. Observe."

"We learned to do that in Seeker training."

"Put your training to work then." I waited at Gamnock's door until he called out for me to come in.

Gamnock took us in from his desk and stood. "Well, that's an uncanny likeness. Starting him young then?"

"Necessity."

"Probably wise." He gestured to the chair I often occupied on my visits. There was only one.

I sent Daniel a quick visual of where he should stand and that he should stay quiet. He assumed the position.

Our meeting lasted well over two hours while we discussed preparing for more Arpex and additional opportunities for acquiring products during my excursion. I asked after Buria. Gamnock was happy with her performance, though she was out on an errand just then. When our meeting was over, I gave Daniel a quick tour of the facility.

"You still have an office here, don't you?" he asked. "I kind of remember it."

"No, Gamnock burned my things and repurposed the room."

"You said he was good."

"I said he wasn't currently on my list. He was on it for many years."

"This is complicated."

I laughed. "Most of life is."

We headed back to the jump point so he could take it in again. Next, we went to visit Fa'yet.

Fa'yet's appalled face needed no words. He, like Stassia, didn't approve. Good thing I was far past needing anyone's approval.

From there I sent Daniel home again but didn't join him. Instead, I flashed him the point on the ship, one he'd seen a hundred times before, then went there myself to wait. And I waited.

"Did your mother seize you?"

"No." Frustration flooded through our natural connection.

"Headache?"

"Yes," he whispered as if he was admitting a devastating defeat.

I Jumped home for the few seconds it took to put a hand on him and take him to the ship. "You've done well."

His shoulders slumped. "I couldn't do it. My head hurt too bad."

"When did it start to hurt?"

"At Uncle Isnar's."

"So your current limit is three Jumps. Keep that in mind. You'll have more stamina the more you do it."

The tank with its blue half-light of standby mode stood before us. "You feel comfortable being able to use this on your own?"

"On myself?"

"Or if you have to bring someone here?"

He swallowed, glancing from the controls to the tank platform and then to me. "I couldn't get you up there."

"I'll let you in on a secret. Neither can your mother. Unconscious people are heavy." I showed him how to lower the trusty gurney that had long stood at its post against the wall, and then how to raise it to match the platform. "From there, you can shove or roll."

"Do Saka and Meera know about the tank?"

"Not yet. They'll have to earn that privilege. If one of us is wounded, they have orders to contact Neko or your Uncle Isnar. I suppose I should add you to that list now."

Daniel beamed, his aching head forgotten for a moment.

We spent an hour going over the jump point there until he got it firmly pictured. By that time his ever-growing body demanded food. I Jumped us up to the Friquen house and let him do his thing in the kitchen while I rested. It was going to be a long day.

While I was stretched out on the couch with the sounds of Daniel going about his merry way with the meal setting me at ease, I sunk into my link and got some work done. I was in the middle of a conversation with a contact on Merchess, which was a mess without Kess, when a nudge on my shoulder registered. I held up my hand to let Daniel know I'd heard him and finished delivering my instructions to the Ka'opul heir. If he couldn't achieve order within his city in the next few days, I'd have to visit myself. I also let Stassia know of my conversation so she could concentrate her efforts elsewhere.

We ate in relative silence, only the faint songs of the birds outside disrupting the rhythmic clinking of spoons as we sipped our soup.

"When you're far away like that, are you ever afraid that you won't get back to yourself?" Daniel asked.

"It's not that I'm away, I'm deep inside. Like concentrating so hard that you forget about everything else but the thing you're doing—usually its many things at once."

"It seems like you're always doing many things at once. Like you're never really all in one place."

"What do you mean? I'm right here."

"But what are you thinking about? How many people are you talking to?"

"I'm not talking to anyone else, but I'm thinking that I need to get a jump point for us within the Jalvian fleet. That I should contact Uncle Jey's family and see how they're doing in his absence. That there are hundreds of things I should probably be taking care of but those things are in your mother's hands right now."

He put his spoon down and looked at me thoughtfully, far too much like Ikeri. "You're afraid she can't do what you asked her to do."

"No. She's done it before, and I very much want her to succeed now, but it's hard to step back and let her do it on her own."

He got up and put his bowl in the sink for the bots. "As you say."

"I say if you spout that Seeker shit again, you can sit here alone while I'm gone with the fleet."

In a tone that was all Stassia, he said, "You forget I can Jump myself now."

I put my bowl away and patted down my coat, making sure everything was in order, taking my time. "You go ahead then." I stood there waiting. "Going back home already?"

He shook his head. I could almost see him straining to get a Jump to work. Though I had no idea which point he'd pick, none of them would get him into trouble. I let him sweat it out for a few minutes, wondering how stubborn he would be in competition with what had to be a horrendous headache by now.

Pretty damn stubborn, as it turned out. Sweat broke out on his face and he ran for the bathroom. A retching sound followed moments later. I sighed and went to check on him.

"How about we stay here for the rest of the day. I'll get some work done while you recover from your first overtaxing of your link. Congratulations."

He wiped his face with the washcloth I handed to him and glared at me.

"So, no best dad ever award today?"

The glare darkened.

I tried not to laugh. "Go on," I nudged him toward the room he'd used when we'd lived here. "You'll feel better after you rest."

He stalked off, glowering all the way. I returned to the couch. How had Neko managed to wake up refreshed after sleeping on it? Then again, he wasn't as wide. I got as comfortable as I could and sunk back into my link.

The sky on Frique was full of stars when I came back to myself, stiff and sore. I got up to check on Daniel. He was deep asleep, the face of the mischievous little boy I'd played with on Minor warring with the one who would be fully grown in a few short years. I'd missed too many years of his life while locked away in service to the High and Mighties. I didn't plan on missing any more. For better or worse, he'd see who we were and what running the Narvan demanded. What he chose to do with that was up to him, but I'd be damned if he was going into his future blind.

SEVENTEEN

I woke sitting against the wall on the floor of Daniel's room with him looming over me.

"Why aren't you in a bed?" he asked.

"Beds are too comfortable. I prefer to wake up with numb legs and an aching back." I held out my hand so he could help me up.

Daniel laughed as I got up and stretched, making a show of grimacing and groaning, except it wasn't much of an exaggeration.

"How's your head?" I asked.

"Better."

"Good. Take it easy today. I want you to go home and change then Jump to the tank room. Think you can manage that?"

"Why can't I just bring my clothes here? Am I going to have to Jump home every day to get dressed?"

"For now, yes. Your mother might not want to see me for three days, but I have a feeling she'd appreciate seeing your face, even if only for a few minutes. So would Markus."

Daniel smiled at the mention of Markus. "But only for a few minutes."

I nodded. "I'll be waiting on you."

He drew a deep breath and closed his eyes and then he was gone. I went through the house and straightened everything so Stassia wouldn't have a fit next time she was there. Then I went down to the ship to wait. And again, waited.

Warmth flowed from Stassia through our bonded connection. She didn't say anything, but that was enough. I sat down, feeling slightly more patient.

Daniel arrived, freshly dressed, yet appearing out of sorts.

"How did that go?" I asked.

"Can we just go?"

I sent a silent question to Stassia.

"Markus didn't want him to leave."

"I'll take Markus tomorrow. Let him know to be ready."

She sent me a burst of gratitude and was gone.

I Jumped the two of us to the point I'd been given on one of the Jalvian ships. The room was big enough for exactly four people shoulder to shoulder. No invasions by large forces of Jumping soldiers would fit here. Not that I'd ever heard of that sort of issue, but it didn't surprise me that Jalvians were paranoid about it. While links were available to anyone with enough credits and the right connections, it wasn't a modification that a large population of the Narvan had taken advantage of. Many Jalvians viewed it as an Artorian thing and shunned it like our natural speech. Most Artorians had no need for it because they were tied to their jobs and mates and could already communicate with natural speech. They didn't require wide-ranging instantaneous travel nor did they have a need to speak with non-Artorians at a distance.

We stepped out of the room to be escorted to a door by four men. "Your quarters, Advisor."

"Thank you, but I need to speak to your commanding officer."

"She will be with you as time allows. She asks that you await her here." He held the door open to what appeared to be a sizable suite. "For our most esteemed guests," he added.

"It will do nicely. However, I will see her now. Where is she?"

"General Elenoi is currently occupied with getting the fleet through the next jump gate.

"Perhaps Advisor Te was accustomed to lounging around while his generals did what they wanted, but I am not. If General Elenoi does not wish to be in my service then she can find an escape pod and make her own way home. So, one last time, where is she?"

Three of them conferred in a round of uncertain glances. The fourth stepped forward. "I'll take you to her, Advisor."

"Good. Keep in mind that your treatment of me and my son, as well as your performance, will directly impact my goodwill toward your Prime, and thereby, your people."

"Is that a threat?" asked the first man.

"A statement, a threat, an explanation of reality, take your pick."

Daniel brushed up against me. He might not be saying anything, but his uncertainty beat its way through our natural connection.

"One step away, always. I need room to move. If you see me reaching into my coat, get behind me."

"They're all around us."

"Then hit the floor."

His voice dropped to a whisper even in my head. *"Mom isn't going to like this."*

"Your mother knows exactly what you're getting into. She works beside me, remember?"

That seemed to take him aback. His awareness shrank away. Leaving a whisper of fear behind.

The first man shouldered the helpful one out of the way. He rested his hand on the weapon at his side. "I'm afraid General Elenoi insisted that you wait here."

"It would seem that you need a better understanding of how this operation will be run." I wisped my way into the helpful one's mind, finding him unnerved by me. I didn't mind that at all. Pulling out of his head, I asked, "You, what's your name?"

"Frad, sir."

"Frad, you'll take my son over there and make sure nothing happens to him." I pointed to the far side of the room between a vase of tall reeds and a halfway decent painting of a shadowed plex against a sunset.

I sent Daniel a mental nudge to peel himself away from me and follow Frad. From where they now stood, I could keep an eye on them while still focusing on the others.

"Now then, I understand there has been an uproar about my Arpex hunters. You feel left out and now your Advisor is missing. He aligned himself with the wrong man and made a few other terrible choices, including knowingly killing your people while trying to pin it on me and then losing my daughter. He's now paying for those crimes and will never set foot on Jal again. Unless you'd like to suffer as he did, I'd appreciate your full cooperation with every damned request I might make."

Rather than backing down, the other two also reached for their weapons. The first one drew. Daniel was in my head in an instant, his fear raw and distracting. I shut him out.

"I see you're committed to ruining my morning." I'd not tried wisping into more than one mind at a time, but the opportunity to experiment stood before me. If Arpex fed on multiple victims at a time, I'd not witnessed it, but they were feeding, savoring, drawing out memories and emotion. My process had a different intent.

I reached into the mind of the one who had first drawn his gun. Jalvians were easier to penetrate, their resistance minimal. None of these three were linked. They had no reason to have built any internal defenses. I squeezed his mind, raking my ghostly fingers over the places I knew from experience hurt worst. Once the other two were distracted from their weapons by his sudden descent to the floor where he lay writhing, I divided my focus and reached into their minds.

Being divided was much more difficult. My mind strained with the effort. I'd find myself heaving over a toilet just like Daniel had if I didn't finish this quickly.

I needed these two to be able to talk once they recovered, to spread the word so I didn't have to make a repeat performance. While I did get them down on their knees and wailing, I didn't apply the extra pressure. In the back of my mind, I considered taking the first one to Canelli. It would be interesting to see his possible recovery compared to Jey's, but without being fully sedated. That would have to wait. After this expenditure, I wouldn't be Jumping anywhere for a least a day unless it was a dire emergency.

Daniel and Frad stood still, watching the writhing men. I caught Daniel staring at me like I was a stranger.

"Frad, you may wish to call for some medical assistance for your friends here."

"Yes, Advisor. I'll just leave then, shall I?" Hope lent his voice a higher pitch.

"Yes, but you'll be taking us to meet with the general now."

"I'm afraid I don't actually have clearance for that."

"Let me guess," I pointed at the unconscious one. "He was in charge?"

Frad nodded.

"Of course, he was. How about you consider yourself promoted for today and get me to her before I have to hurt anyone else."

Frad gave the men on the floor a good long look before straightening his shoulders and heading for the door. "This way then."

Daniel followed a few steps behind as we walked down the corridor and into a lift. Frad touched the pin on his collar and frantically chattered under his breath. I hoped whoever he was reporting to wasn't going to pose any more of a threat. Reaching into my coat as covertly as possible, I grabbed a stim out of my tin and popped it in my mouth. By the time we reached the control room, the headache was down to a tolerable level, though I still didn't have any urge to want to Jump anywhere or eat anything, for that matter.

Frad shifted from foot to foot, doing a poor job of appearing at all confident in my off-handed promotion. While we waited for those on the other side of the door to arm themselves in whatever manner they saw fit, I took a moment to seek out Frad's record of service. It was spotless and uneventful, him having only enlisted a few months ago. The second son of a third wife of a much-decorated mid-ranking officer. Five older siblings all had gained notice from their superiors and were steadily advancing in rank. Frad, sadly, was a nobody.

"How are you with a gun, Frad?"

"Advisor?"

"I'll take that as passable. How about you stay out here and keep my son safe while I go talk to General Elenoi?"

"They haven't opened the door yet, sir."

"I'm tired of waiting." I studied the locking panel and thanked Merkief for having the patience to show me how Jalvian tech worked because I sure as all hells hadn't been talking to Jey at that point in our lives. While touching the recessed override points on the sides of the panel, I accessed the internal workings through the ship systems using my link. It didn't help my head at all, despite the stim. However, the door did open.

With the obstruction removed, the bickering crew inside was revealed. A broad, grey-haired woman stood among six officers, all of whom seemed to be pleading their case at once. There was one person posted at the door, but rather than doing her job, she was watching the argument inside. Everyone else was scurrying around, calling out to one another with what I gathered to be the arrangements for proceeding through a jump gate.

Such disorganization on a Jalvian ship was unheard of. It seemed the Prime had disregarded my stipulation about not giving me the expendable crews. Their discordant chatter grated on my nerves.

As much as I wanted to yell at the officers to shut up, I didn't particularly want to be turned inside out if the crew screwed up the jump gate transfer. Instead, I quietly inserted myself into the bickering six. They fell silent and eyed me with a mix of terror and disdain.

"General Elenoi?"

She looked to the door, and finding no one to blame for my appearance, snarled at me. "You were told to wait for me in the suite that I graciously provided.”

“And I asked for the best of the Jalvian fleet. I guess we’re both disappointed. Now, if you’re done not being in charge of your crew, we need to discuss this mission.”

She bared her teeth and dismissed the officers with an abrupt wave of her hand. “I think you perhaps forget your place, Advisor Ta’set. This is the Jalvian fleet, not Artor’s.”

“Who is your second in command of this fleet?”

“Get out of my control room, you mutated Artorian tyrant. You have no authority here.”

I punched her in the face. It wasn’t my best diplomatic move ever, but my brain squeezing abilities weren’t available and my tolerance level had been reached for the day. Already. Maybe I needed to talk to Stassia about taking up meditation…once we were back to talking.

General Elenoi dropped ungracefully to the floor, clutching her bleeding nose and swearing.

“Are we clear of the gate?” I ask the gawking crew.

Enough of them nodded that I felt confident a few minutes of distraction wouldn’t kill us all. General Elenoi started to get up. I put a gun to her head, which stopped her on her knees.

“Now then, how many of you are fond of the General here? Do you feel confident that she’s the best person to lead this mission?”

The officers whom she had been plagued with upon my arrival quietly conferred with one another. The nods I’d expected from the rest of the crew were slow in coming.

“You’re not very popular, General.”

“Neither are you,” she muttered.

“Good thing I’m not the one on my knees with a gun to my head.”

With my other hand, I reached into my pocket and pulled out a numbing rod. I thumbed the activator button and tapped the rod on her neck. The General fell face-first onto the floor. I made no effort to slow her descent.

I put the rod and the gun away. “I am Advisor Ta’set and this is my mission. Your performance from here on out will directly reflect my goodwill toward your people back home. I would suggest that you do your jobs with the skill and efficiency that I know you are capable of.”

I turned to the still-open door. “Frad, get in here.”

The harried young man rushed in with Daniel right behind him.

“I’m guessing none of you know Frad?”

Murmurs to that effect moved through the room.

"Frad offered to be of assistance while his fellow crewmembers ignored my requests. They are currently in a similar state to your General." I surveyed my audience. "This mission is very important to me. I would like us all to profit from it. Be like Frad."

One of the officers took a step forward. "General Tellison is the next in command, sir. Shall I get him for you?"

"That would be appreciated."

"His ship should be through the gate shortly. I'll see that he is transported here as quickly as possible."

"He's not linked then?"

His blank stare was less than helpful. A jump point was probably also out of the question. I wasn't up for that anyway.

"Yes, fine, transport him."

The officer hurried over to one of the crew where they conferred. Before the others escaped, I directed them to confine the general and to get the three men in my suite to medical care. They quickly dispersed. Activity in the room fell into the rhythm I was used to from a Jalvian crew. A strained silence lingered, but I could live with that.

I sat in an open seat and called Daniel and Frad over. "You have a job that you should be doing right now?" I asked Frad.

"Yes, sir."

"Get to it then but check in with me later."

He nodded and hurried off. Daniel stood beside me.

"Did you kill her?"

"No."

"What about those men in our room?"

"They'll live. I don't go around killing people all day, if that's what you were thinking. I'm trying to make life better for all of us, and it's preferable that we all remain living to enjoy those efforts."

He rested his arms on the back of my chair and leaned down to talk quietly. "How did you do that, hurt them without touching them?"

"Part of the Arpex mutation. Ikeri helped me discover it, though not on purpose."

"It was very not on purpose. I think that's why she went along with Uncle Jey's plan."

"What do you mean?"

"Ikeri tried to talk to me about what happened the day after Neko brought you home. She said what you did, what happened to you, and what would happen to all of us because of it, was her fault."

"It's not. She said something like that in her letter to me too."

Daniel sunk lower as if he could hide behind me. "I thought she was just continuing her talking bad about you so I didn't say much. Maybe I could have talked her out of helping Uncle Jey. I should have listened to her."

"She made a bad choice, but what ultimately went wrong was entirely out of any of our hands. Except maybe mine. I should have killed Untami the first time she betrayed me."

I gripped the arms of the chair, wishing it was her throat I was crushing. "But I'd thought she'd suffered enough, that she was unwisely loyal to those she'd been conditioned to serve. If nothing else, I should have sold her elsewhere, a place she could have never reconnected with her Masters or fell in with Kess."

"You sold her?"

"I did. I've always told you slavery is wrong. It is. Both the buying and the selling. It only leads to trouble."

"But you did it anyway."

"It seemed a fitting punishment for the men who made a living from selling others."

He went silent for a moment. "You should have killed them all."

Taken aback by the certainty of his declaration, I turned to face him. "What would the Seekers say about your assessment?"

Daniel watched the crew work as they relayed information about the last of the fleet emerging from the jump gate. "That the life of another is not mine to take. But we're not Seekers. That woman took my sister and gave Ikeri to her masters, knowing exactly what they do. The Seekers say there is no true evil, but that sounds like true evil to me."

"Me too." I patted his arm. "We'll find Ikeri."

Daniel stayed behind me, quiet and subdued, until the announcement of General Tellison's arrival.

"Let's go meet this general and see if he's a little more agreeable."

Daniel skulked in my wake as we made our way to the room where the helpful officer said he would bring the general to meet with us.

General Tellison arrived in short order, sporting a few less medals than Elenoi. He was younger by several years and walked with a limp on his right leg. We met with mutual nodding and no words, gauging one another. Daniel stood behind me again, my coat brushing against him when I pulled out a chair to sit. There were other chairs around the table but Daniel made no move toward any of them even as General Tellison sat across from me.

"Bit young for a bodyguard, aren't you?" Tellison asked, his voice sounding hoarse as if he were ill or had a throat injury. It didn't bother me that he addressed Daniel first. It gave us both a chance to further observe one another.

Daniel answered clearly and levelly. "I'm not a bodyguard."

"An understudy then. Have you worked on a ship like this before?"

"I've never been on a ship like this before."

"Then you have a lot to learn. I imagine you'll be spending a good deal of time with your father. It might be wise to gain a solid understanding of the workings of this ship while you're here so you can be useful. No one gets a free ride."

"I would like that." Daniel's excitement flowed through our natural connection. "I did study at one of your academies for a while."

"So I've been told."

The officer had done some quick research and briefed the general. I made note of his name.

"Let's hope you fare better here where it counts, hmm?" Tellison's attention locked onto me. "It is an honor to work with you again, Advisor Ta'set. Your part in defeating the Fragians was inspiring."

"That was quite some time ago. Much has changed."

"It has. We're both a little greyer." He smiled. "I understand you're searching for your daughter."

"And the men who have taken her. We will be canvassing several worlds in the system where I suspect them to be. I would prefer casualties to be minimized whenever possible. I also expect resistance. No one likes an invading force."

"Are we an invading force?"

"Your people need an outlet. We could all use new opportunities for expansion and trade. I would like to pitch our arrival as assistive, a business opportunity."

"As expected from an Artorian," he said but managed to avoid making it sound like an insult.

"We both know how that pitch often is received. Which is why you're here instead of the Artorian fleet."

"So you acknowledge our superiority."

"In this field, yes, I do."

His smile grew. "And what of Advisor Te? Will he be joining us?"

"We will not be reenacting the Fragian war, General. Advisor Te is the reason my daughter is missing."

"I find that hard to believe. Are you sure? You have evidence?"

"I have his confession."

Tellison grimaced and spent a quiet moment studying his hands on the table. "That is unfortunate for him."

"Indeed. My mate and I have taken on the full Advisory position for the Narvan as well as the Rakon Nebula. Advisor Atta also played a large part in that plot. If word of this change in leadership has not already filtered through the ranks, it will shortly. The Primes and Premiers have been notified and have declared their cooperation."

"Were they given a choice?" he asked, his gaze back on me.

"No. I haven't had a lot of faith in the choices of others lately."

Tellison offered a tight nod. "Let's hope we can change that."

From my lack of an urge to hit anyone, I concluded that we could work together. "Will you be assuming control of this ship if you are now leading the mission?"

"If you wish. I can have my second take command of my own."

"Yes." We had a suite here, and a rough feel for the crew. It may have only been a small step forward, but I had no desire to start over.

"I understand you have bestowed your favor on a young man who serves on this vessel. Do you require his direct assistance?" he asked.

"Not at this time."

Tellison nodded. "These business opportunities, will you be leading negotiations?"

"I'll leave that to you, assuming you can round up a few suitable agents with friendly faces. Mine isn't so well-suited anymore."

He chuckled under his breath. "I'm sure there must be a handful of those somewhere within our fleet. Shall I send them to you for briefing?"

"Yes. Now, when we do come to an engagement situation, your cut of spoils is seventy percent."

"This is approved by the Prime?"

"The Prime isn't here. I'm dealing with you, unless you wish to join General Elenoi?"

He stared at me for a long moment. His gaze darted to Daniel and then he winked. "Eighty but you get first pick."

"What do you think?" I asked Daniel.

Daniel stammered. "I don't know anything about this."

"What do you make of him? Use what Tomias taught you."

Silence drew out, but I made no move to hurry Daniel. If Tellison grew uncomfortable, he hid it well.

"He respects you."

"I can see that. What else?"

"He's honest. He likes his crew and isn't happy to leave them."

"Will that be a problem for us?"

Daniel grinned inside at the mention of *us*. I waited for him to refocus. *"Well?"*

"He's excited but trying very hard not to show it. He won't end up on your list. I like him."

I laughed out loud. "You're fortunate, General. My son likes you. Seventy-five."

Tellison smiled at Daniel. "Seventy-seven then."

"Do we give him the two percent?" I asked out loud as a courtesy to let the general know we were discussing the matter.

"Why are you asking me? I know nothing."

"What does your gut tell you? Does he deserve more? Will he honor our arrangement? Will he live to see the end of this mission?"

The kid was starting to sweat. Though I couldn't see him behind me, I could smell it. Again, Tellison sat patiently, balancing on the precarious line of neutrality with no visible effort.

"He is willing to leave his crew for you. I'd reward him with more. As to the rest, I can't see the future."

"Correct. We can only use what we can see and the knowledge we have to make these decisions. They may turn into a rewarding experience or come back to haunt us."

"Like when you chose to let the people who took Ikeri live."

"Yes. Just like that."

"Give it to him," Daniel said.

"Seventy-seven it is then," I announced. "I'll prepare the contract, which we will both mark and then send on to your Prime."

General Tellison nodded. "I have arrangements to make then and our next jump gate transfer to oversee."

We both stood, our meeting concluded. At least I thought so, until he slowly reached for the pocket on the front of his shirt and came out with two of the standard-issue communication pins the entire crew wore.

"If you don't mind. In case we need to reach one another?"

I had to give him credit for being prepared. I hadn't thought that far ahead. Perhaps he did deserve his two percent.

After Tellison left us, I instructed Daniel in using his new means of communication and then we went to locate a meal. The kid needed a break and he was always hungry.

The crewmembers left us alone. Though there were plenty of hostile looks, there was also curiosity. I let them all wonder for now and stuck to the task at hand—shoving food in my mouth so I had enough fuel to get through the day. Without anything pressing to occupy my mind, the ache caused by straining my new mental muscles grew more prominent. I rubbed my forehead for the tenth time.

"You know how you said that resting makes you feel better?" Daniel asked. "We could go back to the suite. It will be hours before our next jump gate, right?"

"Try days, but yes, that might be wise. Can you stay out of trouble if I close my eyes for a while?"

"Will you sleep and not work?"

"I thought your mother was on Artor."

Daniel snickered. "Neko was right. Taking care of you is a thankless job."

EIGHTEEN

I woke to find nine hours had passed. Daniel lay on the other half of the bed, sound asleep. The lights were out. I reached into the ship's network and found everything in working order, our route proceeding in a timely manner toward the next gate. No messages were waiting from General Tellison. With nothing left to do there, I sunk into my link and sought out more information on the worlds to which we traveled. There wasn't much to find without the specifics but the University had provided a direction and confirmed trade reports regarding the colonies there, along with one fairly populated planet and a docking station for system trade.

With my distractions in that direction exhausted, I checked on Merchess and my Ka'opul contact. He was making slow progress. I let him be and touched base with my other contacts on Twelve and Thirteen and then on Fragia, leaving notes for Neko so as not to chance getting into a fight with Stassia.

"She's fine, boss." he assured me and then was gone.

I wondered if her fine was like mine, more of the fuck off variety given our current separation. I'd find out tomorrow during our therapy session.

Knowing Stassia and Neko were out working, I almost Jumped home to get Markus, but that would leave Daniel alone. Instead, I contacted Meera, and after a little carving on a wall, provided a jump point within our suite. No one needed to see us coming and going. The crew could assume what they wanted.

Meera arrived within the hour with Markus grinning from ear to ear. She'd dressed him as I'd instructed, in the clothes of a wealthy Jalvian family, as was his heritage.

"Stay with Daniel until he wakes on his own. I don't know how long he was awake while I was out. Get him something to eat and then meet us here." I showed her how to use her link to access a map of the ship and pointed out where we'd be.

Not that I was needed anywhere, but I felt I should make an appearance for an appropriate length of time to establish a unified front with General Tellison.

I kept Markus's hand in my own to keep him contained. When we entered the command center, his head spun around taking in the lights, sounds, and activity. Nothing of consequence was going on that I could tell. Tellison noticed our arrival and came over with an officer at his side.

"This must be Markus formerly of the Nytun's?"

"I'm a Ta'set now," he said proudly.

"Yes, you are. Don't let your new father alter you to look like one though," said the General.

"I hadn't planned on it," I said, not bothering to disguise my displeasure with his comment.

"It's just that you appear to have a penchant for alterations, what with the University at your disposal and all."

"They weren't by choice."

He offered a complacent smile. "Come now, Advisor, we've all heard the stories of the benefits of your modifications."

"They're just stories. I would think a man such as yourself would be smart enough to know what negative propaganda is."

Tellison conferred with the officer, standing his ground. "So you're telling me that three of this crew didn't suffer from your mythical modification benefits?"

"No, I'm telling you that I didn't suffer these alterations by choice. They were done to me. I did not ask for them. Is that clear enough?"

The officer cocked a brow, his lips downturned. "So you're a victim? Yet you've come out of all this with bulletproof skin, night vision, excessive strength, and can inflict pain with a thought. Sounds more like a wish list to me."

"You're going to want to sit down," I informed the officer. "I'll show you the truth, but you'll find this uncomfortable.

"I'll pass. It's clear you disagree with common knowledge."

"I insist." I stood and pointed to the chair I'd vacated.

The officer looked to Tellison. The general, seeming relieved I'd not put him in the chair, nodded.

Scowling, the officer sat.

"What are you going to do to him?" asked Markus.

"Show him memories."

Markus nodded sagely. "Relax," he said to the officer. "It makes it hurt less."

"You've hurt this boy?" asked General Tellison.

Markus inserted himself between us. "Not him."

I was thankful he didn't take it upon himself to kick the general as he once had Jey.

The officer eyed me, waiting. Tellison stood by his side.

I leaned down to speak to Markus. "If anything happens here, grab my hand, all right? I'm going to be busy for a few minutes."

Markus nodded.

I closed my eyes, endeavoring to keep my touch gentle and not let loose the urge to make my point clear by dropping the officer to his knees. I needed to be patient, but that wasn't one of my gifts even before the fusing. I wisped into his mind, past the utter revulsion of having someone in his head, and saw the reports, the propaganda Jey had launched against me. Perhaps not all of it had been him, but he had made no move to correct or block it either. He'd been there beside me through most of the trauma in my life. He knew the truth. Yet, his drive to get the Arpex alterations for his people had been more important.

Now he was unconscious on a bed in the University.

As carefully as I could, I tried to duplicate Ikeri's memory mending, but I had none of a healer's finesse. When I hunted down a memory, probing rather than prompting as the healers did, I simply rammed my version into place.

When the healers had done their work, my replaced memories had a different feel, someone else's emotions, a distance, but I had the knowing of what should be there. My version was a truncated hack job, but I hoped it got the point across.

It was awkward and uncomfortable to take my memory of Merkief blowing himself up, of the blast and the spray of shrapnel taking out my eye and covering me with scars. I shared the terror of the Arpex snipping off my hand as though it were nothing more than an offending hangnail. For good measure, I made sure to include a snippet of Jey beside me when I woke with my new hand and eye, which were less attractive versions of the modifications I now sported. Lastly, I took a little pleasure in inflicting the agony of the Arpex larvae hatching under my skin before vacating the officer and slipping back into my own body.

The officer blinked slowly and then began to heave. He ran out of the room.

"Would you like a turn?" I asked Tellison.

"I'll hear what Lieutenant Balcor has to say. I have a feeling that will be adequate."

"Good. Then if you don't mind, I'm going to sit down for a while and watch your crew work. Perhaps you'd like to give Markus a tour of the room."

"It won't be a very long tour."

"See that it is. It would be good for him to spend some time learning about his people."

"While that's true, and I do appreciate your thoughtfulness on the matter, I'm sure you can find someone better suited for that task? I have a fleet to oversee."

"And I have the entire Narvan, Nebula, and Fragia to oversee, the Arpex to hunt down, my daughter to find, and countless other obligations. I think you can handle multitasking for a few hours, don't you?"

He offered me a tight smile. "Yes, Advisor." He gestured for Markus to join him.

Once I had some space to breathe, I did my best not to slump in the chair. I had no idea how Ikeri and her memory menders managed all they did. My short session of memory shoving had wiped me out and the day was only beginning.

Daniel arrived with Meera in tow. From his fresh clothes, I gathered he'd gone home to change. He came to stand beside me. I dismissed Meera to get some rest.

"How is your mother?"

"Tired. She looks like she did when you were sick. Can you please go home and help her?" He looked around the room, smiling when he spotted Markus chattering at the general. "We don't need to be here yet. We can come back when they're closer. You said it would be weeks before the fleet got there."

"Ikeri is likely in transit unless they had someone to Jump them. We don't know. If there's any chance she might contact someone, it's probably going to be you who hears her first. We're going to check any ship using this same route that we come across in case she might be on it. You need to get comfortable here, learn about your link and how I work. This ship is a good place to do it."

"And I want to," he said earnestly. "But Mom needs you."

"Did she say that?"

"No. She didn't say much of anything at all. I think she was only at home to wait for me to stop in. She was distracted by whatever she was doing on her datapad when I got there."

"That's probably true. I'm glad she's seeing that working from home doesn't always work."

"You're not even listening to me," he grumbled.

"I am. Neko would let me know if she was getting too overwhelmed. So would she."

Daniel snorted. "She most definitely would not. I know you're both a little off in the memory department, but you do remember my mother, right? The one who would drop dead before she asks for help?"

I glared at him. She just needed some time to get her bearings being on her own. I'd been helping a little here and there through Neko, but I wanted her to remember who she was without me. We could work on us later. "I'll see her tonight."

"Therapy night?"

I nodded.

"Are we sleeping at home tonight then?" he asked eagerly.

"That's the plan, but we'll see how the session goes."

"I hope it goes well."

"Me too."

Daniel wandered off to see what Markus was doing. The General, in a clear effort not to be saddled with entertaining both boys, shunted Daniel off on a woman working in navigation.

With everyone occupied, I slipped into my link, though not as deeply as I would have liked, to get some work done. Keeping half of my attention on the boys kept me from getting much accomplished, but seeing them happily learning new things wasn't so bad either.

It wasn't until I was good and hungry that I dragged myself to full awareness to discover that both of the boys had been so occupied they'd not noticed we'd missed an entire meal. I'd have to remember to take better care to watch the time. Going hungry now and then wasn't anything new for me, but neither of them needed to do it. They were both growing. A lot. They needed every bit of food they could shove in their faces.

I took mercy on the general and took the boys off to eat and then went back to our room. With Meera up and watching over them while Markus played and Daniel explored the ship's network, I was much more productive with monitoring my contacts. Stassia and Neko were mostly tied up in the Narvan so I concentrated on wrangling Kess's part of the nebula and also Fragia and its holdings.

Jey's Fragian contacts were a challenge to hunt down, but I'd seen quite a lot while rampaging through his mind, details that, if I concentrated hard enough, I could harvest for my own use. Notifying them that they would now be reporting to me took some time. Convincing the Fragian leadership itself that I was now solely in charge of the truce between Fragia and the Narvan took a lot more effort. They'd been dealing with Jey since the truce had been reached. They knew of me thanks to my part in the war, but my lack of involvement since made my current solo status with them tenuous.

While I was confident Stassia and I could manage the Narvan and the few free worlds of the nebula, it took only a few hours for me to wish I had Jey around to consult on Fragia. He'd had them well in hand. I was relegated to polite tiptoeing so I didn't inadvertently drive our truce into the ground.

Before I could clear my mind enough to approach therapy with Stassia, my conscience demanded a visit with my Jalvian partner. After notifying Tellison that I'd be off-ship for a while, I had Meera take Markus home and had Daniel Jump himself, telling him I'd be there later.

It took a bit of throwing around of my weight to convince the Jalvian crew doctor to release the Jalvian crewmen who had suffered the brunt of my attack into my care. With him in hand, I Jumped to the heart of the University and got him settled in with Canelli. I gave in to Canelli's pleading look and let him do a scan to monitor my condition before asking about Jey.

"It's likely he will never wake," Canelli said solemnly.

People died all the time. I'd helped a fair number of them along. However, Jey and I had a lot of history, both good and bad. Much like Stassia and I. With all the thought I'd been giving to her lately, it was hard to ignore the similarity.

Jey had been blinded by doing what he thought was best for his people. I had no doubt that the Prime and many others in the higher circles put him under a lot of pressure to stand up to me. Kess was an ass, but Jey hadn't intended for Ikeri to vanish indefinitely.

I stared at the big man, his feet hanging over the end of the bed. I couldn't remember a time that he'd been in bed and I'd been the one standing beside him, urging him to wake. Conversely, I'd woken to him next to me too many times. Whether he was snarling threats or relieved varied, but he'd been there.

"Is there anything I can do?" I asked.

Canelli's forehead furrowed. "You put him here for a reason, no?"

"I did, and he will remain here until I say otherwise, but I'd like to know he'll wake up eventually."

"It's not for me to say one way or the other, Advisor. We don't fully understand your new abilities."

"Neither do I." I sat down in the lone empty chair in the room. "I did try my hand at implanting memories today."

"Like the Verian memory menders?"

"Not exactly. My subject hadn't lost memories, but I overwrote his incorrect ones with my own."

By the grimace that suddenly crossed his face, I gathered that was a clarification I probably shouldn't have made. "I've undergone the treatment enough times to have a rough idea of how it works," I said quickly.

He recovered his composure with a strained smile. "And?"

"That man is in better shape than Jey is."

"You weren't trying that process with Advisor Te, were you?"

"Not at all. Just thought I better mention it for your notes."

He rubbed his chin. "I wonder if we could bring in one of the Verian Seekers and see what they make of him?"

"Maybe at some point. I'd rather keep his whereabouts quiet for now."

"Of course, Advisor."

In truth, I didn't know if I could face a Seeker or even one of the memory menders, knowing how abhorrent my abilities would be to them. At least Etara would have her attention focused elsewhere when we met.

"I'd like to sit with him for a while."

"I'll be nearby if you need anything further." Canelli backed out of the room.

I did a quick check on Stassia through our connection and found she was still working too. She had Etara on standby on Prime for when we were ready for our session. That pledge of honesty was going to be much tougher with Stassia present. I sighed and settled into the chair.

The back was too low, more like a glorified stool, making my shoulders and neck ache. The tan faux prantha covering creaked with my every move to find relief. Not finding any, I left my aches behind and wisped my way into Jey's defenseless mind.

There was little need to wisp. I'd stomped all over, shredding and slashing thoughts, memories, and even basic functions. Had the Arpex I'd encountered on the tree world suffered the same?

Leaving Jey's mind, I tried the Jalvian crewman's. The damage there wasn't as wide-spread. If I could repair that, it would be good practice for working on Jey.

I spent what seemed like days trying to match up tattered ends in his mind, only finding a scant handful. Try as I might to make the two halves connect, they kept slipping loose, the connections lost. I needed real help, or at the very least, proper instruction.

I returned to my body, exhausted and thirsty. If I really wanted to help Jey and the crewman, the only place to get what I needed was Prime. I braced myself for honesty and Jumped into the garden in Tomias's home. It was near midnight, the stars bright in the sky above.

Etara was easy enough to find in the otherwise dark buildings. Candles lit the bench next to where she sat in the grass. Back straight, eyes closed, hands on her lap with her palms up. I approached quietly but her eyes opened before I'd taken three steps.

"Nice night, isn't it?" she asked.

"It is."

Mid-summer here, the heat of the day had given way to a pleasant evening. Bugs chirped, and somewhere up in the trees, a creature cooed softly. I sat in the soft green grass across from her.

"The candles should keep the bugs at bay. I thought you'd be more comfortable out here."

"Thank you." Meeting outside would also prevent us from waking the acolytes in the dorms behind us and those that slept in the main house.

"Anastassia will join us soon?"

I let Stassia know I was ready whenever she was. "Within the hour, she says. Until then, if you don't mind, I'd like you to show me a few things."

She cocked her head, the rest of her body unmoving beneath her robes. "What kind of things?"

I explained what I'd encountered in Jey's mind and my desire to fix it.

"That would be a task better suited to one such as myself. Why do you wish to heal this?"

The way her gaze drilled into me, I knew she already had her answer. But we were being honest. That was the price.

"I broke him. I should fix him."

She nodded. "That acknowledgment is progress from you, surely."

"This type of breaking is new. I'm still learning how to control it. I was very angry at the time."

She gazed into me again. "You blame him for losing Seeker Ikeri."

"I do, and yet, it was not entirely his fault."

"This new type of breaking, do you find it harder to resist?"

"I've always been heavy on the wrath, as Anastassia puts it. This new thing, it's easy to use, to let loose, it's with me all the time now, a part of me."

"I see."

"Do you wish to learn to control it?"

"Yes."

She nodded slowly. "Let me see it."

"How? I don't want to hurt you."

"Show me the memory of what you did that you now wish to fix."

"I'd rather not."

She smiled, an unsympathetic upturn of lips. "It makes you uncomfortable to acknowledge that you lost your temper."

This honesty thing wasn't at all comfortable. I nodded.

"Good. Then there is hope for you yet. Show me, or I will take the knowing for myself."

She could, as Ikeri did, just wisp in and peruse my memories at her leisure. At least she was offering me some semblance of control. I sighed and brought my tirade to the forefront.

"A weapon. You are a weapon," she mused, fingers folding together on her lap.

Hearing Etara's declaration brought Stassia's words on the same subject to the forefront, along with her concern and her rage. She'd done this to me, made me become this weapon, however inadvertently. Just as Jey had lost Ikeri. Neither of them were entirely to blame, but despite knowing this, anger was the one emotion underlying all else. My overwhelmed and exhausted mind held this understanding but couldn't seem to do anything productive with it.

"You were intended to be used against the Arpex, but you have also aimed your abilities at others."

"I have." I didn't appreciate the shaming and I made sure she felt that too.

"I can feel Ikeri in what you've done. She helped you, guided you."

"With the Arpex, yes, but not with the others." The terror on Ikeri's face when I'd come back to myself beside Ha'guris, was etched in my mind. "Seeing me use this ability for even its true purpose, scared her."

"You are a part of her and that scares her. She explored this with you, your weapon, and learned to use it with you. Finding that darkness in herself must have been terrifying."

"She doesn't have any darkness."

"Nonsense. We all do. It's just a matter of whether we channel it or not and the degree to which we allow ourselves."

"Do you think that's why she ran off? Not because she hates me but because she's scared of what she did with me?"

"It may play a part, but I am not the one to ease your conscience."

"No, that you're not." I found myself rubbing my face more often, trying to stay alert and awake.

Etara fell silent, closing her eyes again. Her hands fell still. With only the insects to keep me company, I was fast losing my battle to stay awake. The experiment with Jey and the crewman had left me tired in ways I was not used to combating. A stim may have helped, but that would mean being awake and likely working through the night that I hoped to spend in bed with Stassia.

Suddenly Etara was watching me again. "You have the rudimentary ability. Ikeri received her gift from you." She licked her lips and gazed up at the stars. "If you truly wish to learn how to heal, you will need to attend classes with the acolytes. Healing is not a skill I can just show you. It is a process we all come to know and practice in our own way."

I laughed. "I'm spending my days with the Jalvian fleet, hunting down the people who took Ikeri. My every other waking moment is taken with overseeing the Narvan and Rakon Nebula while hunting the Arpex before they come for us."

"You have made time to work with your mate. If you wish to heal your friend, you will find time for that too."

Stassia's arrival saved me from sharing the cutting remark on the tip of my tongue. She came over to sit beside me, armor fanning out on the ground.

"Before we get to business," Etara said, as though we'd not already been talking. "I did discuss your proposals for medical assistance and guards with Seeker Tomias. He is agreeable to both."

"He is?" I asked.

"You are surprised."

"Well, yes." My assistance with anything here had not been entertained before.

"Your offer does still stand?"

"I'll take care of everything in the morning."

"So you can find time for that," Etara said.

I let her barb hang for a moment, biting my tongue.

Stassia watched us both but remained silent. I was having a hard time gauging her mood even with our bonded connection. It was like she was scattered in a thousand places and there wasn't enough of her here to feel anything one way or the other.

"Those arrangements don't require me being here for more than a few moments to bring the doctors and guards to you, so yes. As to the other offer, I'll think on it," I said.

Etara inclined her bare head as though conceding me a battle point. She took a moment to give Stassia a long look-over. "It would seem that neither of you is in the mindset for the session you requested. Do you still wish to proceed?"

Stassia nodded, as did I.

"Very well. Anastassia, you will begin."

Our next two hours passed with a minimum of bickering as we exchanged memories with one another. She provided what she could of Gemmen and my time with Cragtek while I shared myself in her past. There were so many gaps to fill for both of us. By the time we bid a droopy-eyed Etara farewell, I felt as emotionally empty as Stassia had been when she'd arrived.

I took her home. We disarmed and undressed. All my plans of what I wanted to enjoy with her vacated my agenda in favor of sleeping. The bed in my Jalvian suite was comfortable but missing the warm body I now had next to me. We didn't talk, which also meant we didn't fight. She simply rested her back against my chest, intertwined her fingers with the hand I'd draped over her waist, bringing it up under her chin, and went to sleep. I followed her lead without protest.

The therapy session had held the promise of fixing our relationship, but now that it was over and we were just two empty people sharing a bed, I began to wonder if the lack of memories was the problem.

Maybe she was right. Maybe they all were. I was too much mutant and not enough man. A weapon, and nothing more.

NINETEEN

Weeks passed of traveling with the Jalvian fleet, slowly growing closer to the system that held the worlds I'd seen on the datapad. We had encountered three vessels along the way, but none of them held Ikeri or the Masters. I'd even brought in a few of Gamnock's smugglers to go over the ships to make sure we hadn't missed anything.

I'd met with Ha'guris twice, but while he'd been cooperative, I hadn't been able to recreate what we'd done with Ikeri. Hesitation may have been holding me back or perhaps I just wasn't strong enough on my own. While I pondered options for using him as a line of attack, I sent him back out to his assigned territory.

The jump point to the Arpex world that I'd thought I'd gathered gained me no more than a raging headache for trying to force it to work. I'd waited too long to try it, the details had gone hazy while I'd been unconscious for weeks. Thinking of Arpex brought on overwhelming bouts of frustration, both with the Arpex themselves and with myself for becoming so much one of them that I was losing even the rough semblance of a normal life I'd had.

If the boys hadn't been with me, I would have indulged my urge to lose myself in a couple drops from the hidden vials of endorphin booster, now profitably popular as Boost on the streets, but Daniel would have sensed my mood change right away, using our natural connection as much as he did. I wasn't prepared to explain my previous addiction or why I was inclined to give into it again.

Daniel spent time with the crew as long as he remained in my sight. Markus and Meera wandered the ship, exploring, and according to him, having grand adventures. I hadn't received any complaints yet, so I gathered he hadn't annoyed anyone too badly.

Both of them spent their evenings on the ship training with Meera.

Her cheery and youthful disposition belied the horrors of what she'd endured on Tacesh. Of the three women who lived with us, Meera was far ahead of the others in expressing her own personality. She'd started to ask questions, perhaps feeling more comfortable in doing so with Daniel than myself, but I overheard a good deal that assured me she would be fine in time. Witnessing her progress, how much she enjoyed playing with Markus, and even when she worked with both boys on their training, sharing the combat knowledge she'd been forced to learn, it absolved a little of my guilt for bringing the Masters into our lives.

Twice a week, Stassia and I met for our sessions, some with Tomias and others with Etara. Afterward, we fell into bed, sleeping side by side without talking. On one hand, we weren't arguing. On the other, beyond the couple hours a week that we were together in memory therapy, we were partners in advising our territories and little more.

I got daily updates from Neko, but I was beginning to miss being around him, his humor, and having someone at my back who effortlessly knew what I needed. We still talked, as did Stassia and I, but the distant, business-related conversation wasn't the same. And sharing a bed now and then with Stassia might have been keeping my bond under control, but it sure wasn't making me happy.

Even I was noticing my sour mood.

I'd managed to find time to attend Seeker classes a couple hours a week. It wasn't nearly enough, but all I had. Jey showed no sign of improvement. My initial victim of the three unfortunate Jalvian crewmembers had shown moderate results. The other two crewmen had fully recovered on their own and were back to work. I'd just confessed to Daniel that I'd been seeing Etara to learn healing and asked for his help in practicing, when nearly every alarm in my head went off.

The Narvan was under attack.

"Boss, if other boss hasn't yelled for you to get home yet, we could use your assistance," Neko said.

"Where are you? Who is it?"

"Arpex? Maybe investors? Not sure yet. They'll hit Syless first if they get that far. We're there now. Artorian fleet is already engaged. Jalvian is on the way."

The Jalvian communication pin on my coat pinged. "Advisor, we've overtaken another ship. Will you be joining the search?"

"Start without me. Wait."

I looked Daniel over. "I need your help with something more important than the Seeker business."

His eyes went wide. "Are you serious?"

"The Narvan is under attack. Your mother needs me. I need you to go with the soldiers just like we did before and sweep the ship. Listen for any hint of Ikeri. I'll bring in Gamnock's men again. They'll go with you."

"By myself?" His voice cracked.

"Meera, go with him. I'll bring Markus home where Hedvika can watch him." I grabbed Daniel by the shoulders. "And no, not by yourself. With the soldiers and Meera. Got it?"

He trembled under my hands but he nodded.

"Don't let the damned Jalvian's see that you're afraid. Pretend I'm right behind you and follow Meera's lead, all right?" I glared at Meera so she got the indirect order.

I leaned in close. "You're nervous? I have to go explain to your mother that I just sent you off to search an unknown ship without me."

He cracked a smile. "Good luck with that."

"You too." I gave him a little push toward the door and contacted the general to let him know Daniel would be taking my place. To his credit, Tellison didn't question my questionable choice.

I waved Markus over. "Come on. Let's get you home for now."

We Jumped to Artor where I left him with Hedvika, who seemed glad for the company since Saka was sleeping. Then I was off to Cragtek to double jump the two men I'd previously borrowed from Gamnock back to the Jalvian ship to go with Daniel. With everyone in place, I got Stassia's current location from Neko and met them on Syless. All the extra Jumping in quick succession left me lightheaded and more out of sorts than I already had been.

I was very much not anticipating Stassia barreling into me. Half hug, half tackle, I could do little more than catch her and try not to fall over.

"It's Arpex," she said, "I'm glad you're here."

While I was happy about that development, I did wonder why it was Neko that had informed me of what was going on rather than her.

She gave me a quick squeeze and detached herself, straightening her coat. "It's been a while since I've seen you standing and all ready to work."

Did she think I was just lounging around on the ship while she took care of the Narvan? "Happens every day, just not here lately."

Her welcoming demeanor vanished. "I've noticed."

In less than two minutes we were back to snide comments. I looked to Neko for any clues, but he was busy watching the sky.

"Neko, help me out here."

"Sorry, boss. You know the word mercurial?"

"What about it?"

"You're standing in close range of the definition."

That sounded like typical old Stassia to me. Maybe we were on the right track. She had been happy to see me. I just needed to give her a while longer to get her center back, and maybe figure out what my own was in the meantime.

"So, Arpex?" I prompted.

Stassia nodded. "Their presence on the incoming ships has been confirmed by one of the Arpex hunters. Gamnock also reported incoming ships from the direction of your new trade route."

"He didn't say anything about those. I was just there."

She shrugged. "He said he had it under control."

"Do we have the Arpex under control?"

"No," Neko said before Stassia could answer. "We do not. I've been delivering a few of your hunters to posts in the Artorian fleet so we can better gauge what is going on out there, but none of them are you, if you know what I mean."

Stassia shot Neko a shut-the-fuck-up glare. "He will not be going up there to employ whatever knocked him out for weeks last time. We're already barely treading water even with his help on advising everything as it is."

So it was not concern for my health, but for business. Old Stassia, indeed. At least that was familiar territory.

"What size invasion are we talking about here?"

"It's big, boss."

"Hey Neko," said Stassia. "Why don't you go somewhere else for a few minutes before I mistake you for an Arpex?"

He shot me his patented apologetic look and wandered off to stand with the milling crowd of citizens who were all raptly watching the sky. There was nothing to see as far as I could spot. I hoped there wouldn't be. If any of those ships were within the atmosphere, it would probably mean they were crashing, leading to mass destruction and casualties on the ground.

In the back of my mind, I started pouring through the reports while waiting for Stassia to continue.

"Where are the boys?"

I braced myself. "Markus is home. Daniel is with Meera."

"You left him with the Jalvian fleet?" She looked at me like I'd lost my mind. "Remember last time we left one of our children with Jalvians? She's gone."

"We're working on that. They'd just overtaken a ship. Ikeri and the Masters might be on it. They're searching it now."

Her eyes narrowed. "They who?"

"The people I picked to search it in my absence. Can we focus on the Arpex, please?"

She studied me, eyes narrowing further as she backed away. "You sent Daniel with them, onto a fucking unknown ship and into an entirely unknown situation." She shook her head. "I can't believe you."

"If she's going to reach out to anyone, it's him. If I can't be there to search, he's the next qualified to know exactly who to look for."

"Like anyone could adequately disguise a child whose head is covered in tattoos."

"There are plenty of ways to do that and you know it."

"I was quite serious when I said that if anything happened to Daniel, I won't forgive you."

"He's got a couple of Gamnock's men and Meera. He can Jump himself if it comes to that. He'll be fine."

"He better be."

Even I backed away from the tone in which she delivered those three words. I touched Daniel through our linked connection and found him to be nervous but otherwise well enough, reassuring me that I would at least live long enough to face the incoming Arpex.

I had little doubt Stassia was giving Daniel a mind full of safety instructions and threats. He needed to be able to pay attention to what he was doing . If something were to happen to him and he was unable to defend himself because of the distraction of her ranting in his head, I wouldn't forgive her either.

"Focus, for Geva's sake. Where do you need me?"

"I don't, according to you. But if you insist on helping, then I suppose I've done all I can here. We might as well go see what chaos you can cause up there."

"That wasn't what I meant about needing me, dammit, and you know it."

Her brows rose and she scowled. "Do I?"

"Yes." I took a chance and grabbed her so I could hold her

close. I needed a few seconds of calm before confronting the Arpex head-on again.

She stood stiff against my chest, even as I rested my forehead against hers, waiting for the peace to flow through our connection. It finally did.

"It would appear it's more that you need me," she said without quite as much venom.

"Always."

She eased against me. "Can you at least not get killed today?"

"No promises."

"If anyone gets to kill you, it's me."

"I wouldn't have it any other way."

She chuckled. I'd sorely missed the sound of her laughter. The bond between us flared.

"You're the only man I know who gets excited about me threatening to kill him."

"I like your threats."

Stassia pressed herself against me, arms wrapping around my waist. "Clearly."

"Uhh, boss? Glad to see you're getting along and all, but they need you up there," said Neko, who was again standing nearby.

"We're continuing this later," I informed Stassia.

"You bet we are." She didn't let go.

"Where are we going, Neko?"

He flashed me a jump point. Moments later, the three of us stepped out of the void and onto an Artorian ship that shuddered with the force of a blast.

I checked with all my contacts throughout the fleet. Small ships like we'd seen before, raced past us and into the Narvan, no doubt seeding my worlds with countless memory-eating creatures we'd have to deal with in short order. Or maybe this time, they'd go straight to reproducing and gorging themselves. I wasn't looking forward to learning what their second wave plan looked like.

"We need to stop those," I informed my contact on this ship.

"There are too many. If we don't concentrate our fire on the larger ships, they'll destroy us."

"Neko, I need all the hunters here. Now."

"But if they're here, they can't deal with those who have already made it past us."

"We'll deal with them later. You've delivered some to the fleet here already?"

"Three."

Surely the other hunters would equal Ikeri for amplification. I reviewed what we'd done with Ha'guris before and assured myself that I could do it again. I had to. No matter what the cost.

"I'll work with those. I need you to get Ha'guris here and then have Saka and Buria from Cragtek retrieve the rest. We will need you here."

"What are you going to do?" asked Stassia.

"Take out as many Arpex as I can. As we can," I amended quickly in light of her narrowed eyes.

The hunters began arriving within minutes. Once they were all there, Saka and Buria came to stand before me.

"Oh look, your harem is complete," Stassia said dryly.

While having more linked bodies nearby might be helpful, we had enough aggravating elements to contend with at the moment. I needed Stassia's ire down a degree or two. "Buria, I need you near Gamnock to keep me informed of the progress with the invading investors."

"He can keep you informed, can he not? I could be of use here."

"He's busy. I said, go."

She looked hurt, but I didn't have time for niceties or feelings, not while mentally preparing to do an up-close and internal war with the Arpex.

I addressed Saka, who appeared to be bracing for whatever I might throw at her. "Stay with Anastassia. I may need Neko. He's faster with Jumping me."

"Vayen," Stassia said as though my name were a curse. "There will be no later if you end up in a coma again or dead."

"Good thing we've had plenty of good times before this."

She strode forward to jab a finger into my chest. "I don't remember all of those yet so you better stay alive to share them. I meant what I said. They don't get to kill you."

"Well, if they don't finish the job, I'm all yours."

She glanced from me to the projected display of oncoming ships behind her. When she turned back, she pressed her eyes closed for a moment and nodded.

"Fine, but I need Neko." She backed off and addressed Saka. "If you adore him as much as you appear to, you better let Neko know the second he needs saving. Your life depends on it."

With our guard arrangements and threats taken care of, I

concentrated on getting my assembled hunters settled into an out-of-the-way corner at the back of the room. It took a few minutes to get us all attuned, but with all of our minds open to the Arpex frequency, it was easier to get a feel for how to place them in a way that best amplified the open channel Ha'guris possessed.

"Dad?" Daniel's voice penetrated everything.

My heart skipped a beat. *"Are you all right?"*

"Yes, but Meera isn't. She..."

The hysterical edge in his voice made me want to drop everything and Jump to his side.

"Can I bring her to the tank? Please? I know you said they had to earn it, but she's dying. I don't know what else to do."

"Jump her there now. She has a profile set up in the system. Get her in the tank and then tell me what happened. And for the love of Geva, don't say anything about this to your mother right now."

The circle of hunters had all turned to me. "I need a moment."

I needed a pause button. Time to plan more, make a practice run with all the hunters and the open channel. To only have the investors or Arpex to deal with. Every second I waited for Daniel to get back to me brought all of the other threats closer. But my son needed me.

Two breaths away from saying fuck it all and Jumping to the ship myself, Daniel's voice popped back into my head. *"I hope I did this right. She's going to be all right, isn't she?"*

"If the platform rose and she's in the tank, you did it right. Now tell me what happened."

"Gamnock's men found a hidden compartment on the ship we were searching. I thought we had something, that Ikeri might be on the other side of the door. But when they got it open, there were three armed mercenaries inside. They killed one of Gamnock's men. You should have seen Meera. She took two of them out real quick, but the third one went after me while she was busy."

I said a quick prayer. *"Are you injured?"*

"No. Gamnock's other man took out the mercenary, but he got one shot off at me. Meera leapt in front of me but it caught her in the neck. There was so much blood." His voice began to tremble.

"Sounds like she earned her right to use the tank. When she wakes up, show her how to use it and give her the jump point. And tell her thank you for me."

"Why can't you tell her?"

"I'm about to go up against an Arpex army. So you tell her for

me, and I mean it, don't tell your mother what happened until this is all over. There's a whole line of people waiting to kill me and I don't need her to be first in line."

"Dad?" He sounded so small. *"Please don't let anyone kill you."*

"I'll do my best. I've got to go."

"We did find a lead on Ikeri, so you can't die, all right?"

I glanced at the displays, the ships growing ever closer. The hunters mumbled around me. Stassia shouted orders. The crew relayed information between their stations. A fucking war was minutes away from exploding and now we get a lead on Ikeri?

"Tell me. Quickly."

"Right after I left with Meera, Nacen, that's Gamnock's surviving man, he let me know they found one of the Masters on the ship. He was dead. The crew thinks the other one ducked out with Ikeri at the last port where they docked a week ago, Brustus, he called it. It's one of the colony worlds that's thrived enough to grow a city around its supply port. Should I ask General Tellison to take us there?"

My mind spun, searching for a logical reason to ditch the ride they already had. Who had killed the one and why not the other? I rubbed my hands over my face. The frustration of not knowing was overwhelming.

"You've done well. I'll be back as soon as I can. Stick with Meera for now, and yes, tell the general to check out Brustus." I cut contact and returned my full attention to the people around me.

One of them was Stassia. She rested a hand on my shoulder. "What is it?"

I relayed what Daniel had told me about Ikeri.

"Then we're close. We'll find her," she said with a conviction I didn't share. "You deal with your hunters. I'll take care of the fleet."

The ship rocked again. The crew scrambled, shouting orders and reports. Stassia didn't wait for me to agree. She rushed over to Neko and dove into a serious conversation with the commander of the ship. Neko held the dazed look of relaying her orders to countless others through his link and the fleet network.

The fleet was in capable hands. Hands I loved quite thoroughly at that moment as I witnessed the Anastassia Kazan I knew had been lurking inside her all this time. All the weeks of lonely exhaustion had been worthwhile. I couldn't have been more proud of her in all her commanding glory.

She stopped mid-sentence and turned toward me with a smile

that melted my insides. The bond flared.

One of our forward ships burst into light that quickly became cold dead fragments drifting through space. I blinked the tragic image away. Stassia was back to work. I needed to do the same.

I'd just gathered myself to a point where I could focus on realigning with the hunters before me when Buria shouted in my head.

"We need backup. I don't know who these people are, but they keep coming, ship after ship through the jump gate."

"I'll send some of the Jalvian fleet your way." Not that we had ships to spare with the Arpex pounding on the Artorian fleet, but I couldn't go there myself to evaluate the situation. I had to trust that she and Gamnock knew how dire it was. I relayed my orders to the Jalvian Prime to send three of the large ships that had remained in the Narvan.

If Jey were conscious, I would have asked him to call in a favor with Fragia to get us some backup. But I didn't have Jey. I swore under my breath and gathered my nerve. Praying I wasn't opening the barely defended Narvan to a biding-their-time enemy force, I contacted the linked Fragian representative of their leadership with whom I'd had a brief introduction. Asking favors was not something I liked doing, and from questionable alliances even less, but I was out of options.

"We're in a bind. My forces are divided. Jump gates won't get you to me fast enough, but can I rely on you to assist with the conflict closer to you?" I relayed the coordinates and current situation.

Gamnock wouldn't be happy about the Fragian assistance, but if I could rely on them, we might be able to recall the Jalvian ships I'd sent to aid him. They were closer to us.

"I will bring your request to my people with urgency. You'll have your answer shortly," the representative said before cutting contact.

I eyed the display and the hunters waiting impatiently on the floor around me. Shortly would be too late.

If the Fragians took it upon themselves to earn my goodwill by assisting Gamnock, I'd thank them later. For now, I maintained the current orders to the Jalvian ships and offered up a quick prayer to Geva.

Knowing how well she listened, I then took matters into my own hands.

TWENTY

I shut out the noises of the busy command center, along with my concern for Daniel and spinning theories about Ikeri. Then I closed the connections with my contacts and muffled the bond with Stassia. As alone as I could be in my head, I slowly opened myself to the natural Artorian connections of the ten minds around me. We didn't have the luxury of time to train in the ways of wisping into minds or attacking the Arpex with outright anger, but they did offer amplification. I showed them what I intended to do and warned them of what it might cost. None of them stirred from their positions.

With nothing left to delay the inevitable, I directed all of our focus through Ha'guris. As a swirling dark mass of energy, we sought out Arpex minds, as many as we could reach. One by one, we gathered them into our net. We connected them with a fine thread disguised as purpose, a suggestion that one of their own was forming this connection to destroy the minds of those they wished to conquer.

There were so many Arpex.

Just when it felt as though we had them all, another crowd of minds came into focus. And then another. The task seemed endless. Every corner of my head ached from holding them all together.

Saka whispered in my ear, "Advisor, your hunters. They're falling. Should I take them to the University?"

"Not until we are finished."

Saka remained beside me but said no more.

I sensed no decrease in our energy level. If the hunters were leaving their physical selves behind to concentrate solely on our purpose, we didn't have much more time before they did begin to falter.

In a mad rush, we gathered Arpex connections in large numbers, perhaps entire ships of them at a time. When the connections began to reach back to those on the green tree world, my heart raced.

Our collective energy dipped, cutting lose the minds I'd just touched. I swore, seeking them out myself seconds before another hunter let go. We could wait no longer. I could hold no more.

We gathered the threads tightly together, pulling all the Arpex in close. Like children sitting at the feet of a storyteller, eagerly awaiting the next word, they clamored for the plan to begin. I could hear their claws clacking.

What they anticipated as our demise, would be their own. Greedy, blue-shelled bastards.

Our energy dipped again. Another hunter lost. The Arpex began to chatter, questioning. Doubts swirled, lessening their eagerness. Many of the threads began to strain against my hold.

I left my own body behind to funnel everything I had left into Ha'guris's open channel, wisping my way into the virtual armload of threads that led me into the minds of hundreds of thousands of Arpex at once. I couldn't breathe. I couldn't feel the link back to my own body. Ikeri wasn't there to hold onto me this time.

Drawing upon the terror rushing from the hunters who were encountering the same disembodied sensations, I unleashed the white-hot strike of anger I'd been building. It tore through the minds of the Arpex like fire through ancient paper. Their threads wilted with no minds to anchor them. They fell from my hands like ash, floating into the nothing that had swallowed me.

There was no sign of the other hunters, of the ship, of how the battle might be progressing. Of my body. Just the nothing. It wasn't the same as the peaceful nothing Ikeri had dragged me from. I wasn't dead then. That was good. I hoped.

There was no need for sleep in the nothing, which made time seem to go on forever. I spent a good deal of it practicing the healing lessons on myself Etara had taught me. Though I entertained little hope of them working while being both the practitioner and the patient, it felt good to be doing something. Eventually, I tired of that and wished I'd found more time to attend lessons on Prime with Etara, maybe I would have learned how Ikeri had pulled me back into my body last time. That would be really helpful about now.

I sunk deep into the nothing where I stumbled upon lessons I didn't remember learning. There was so much I didn't remember. Or maybe I'd never learned it at all. Maybe I was making it all up to occupy myself.

The more time I spent with the lessons, I began to wonder if I'd somehow rekindled my connection with Ikeri. Had she finally sought me out or was I the one doing the seeking? With no points of reference, I couldn't tell. I tried everything I could think of to speak to her, but there was no response.

Suddenly the nothing seemed not so entirely black. Darkness slowly faded to the point where I convinced myself it wasn't my imagination. There was definitely light, and I could see. Were my eyelids open? I couldn't feel them or anything else.

The face that slowly came into focus wasn't Stassia or Ikeri. Etara leaned over me, her face intent with her eyes closed. The ceiling of the common room in the Artor house registered. I tried to look around, but I couldn't move. I tried my bonded connection with Stassia, but there was nothing there, nor with anyone else. I tried to talk, but my mouth wouldn't open. Just as I was considering going into a full-blown panic, Etara opened her eyes. She smiled.

"There you are. You found your way back after all."

Her brows drew together. "Take your time, gather everything back into your body and let it settle. You've been gone a while." She turned to speak to someone else. "We'll leave the equipment hooked up for a bit, I think."

She stepped back, revealing Canelli who was busy tapping away on his datapad. He stood to adjust settings on the host of equipment I now realized surrounded me. I recognized the large clear tube snaking up my chest and into my mouth, along with the machines connected to me by tubes and wires. They were the same ones keeping Jey alive.

"He's improving fast," Canelli said. "Quite remarkable."

Etara tapped her chin. "That's one word for him."

Canelli came to stand beside me. "Do you think you're up for breathing on your own?"

I tried to nod, but couldn't. I tried Etara instead. Mind speech was second nature to me, nothing I'd had to strain over since learning how as a child. Now it made me tired just thinking about how to connect my mind with Etara's, even with her standing right there. I pushed through the fog and found her. *Tell him, yes.*

"He says, take it out," Etara relayed.

Once Canelli had freed me from the tube and a few other monitoring gadgets, he returned to consulting his datapad.

Etara took his place beside me. "Of all the people in the known universe you could go to for help, you had to pick me." She shook her head. "Anastassia says she hasn't heard from you. Why me?"

"I didn't know I did. I was practicing what you had shown me and then I found more."

She laughed softly. "Your subconscious has a strong sense of self-preservation."

"Kept me alive this long."

She nodded. "Once I figured out it was you buzzing around in my head, I contacted Neko and he brought me here. I'd like to say I helped guide you back to your own body, but I'm not sure that's entirely the case."

"I was nowhere and now I'm here."

"You should probably stick around here for a while. Anastassia would be quite thankful, I think."

"Where is she?"

"Let's get you fully back in your body before we update her on your condition, shall we?"

My mouth finally cooperated, forming raspy words. "See her now."

Etara shook her head. "You're not ready."

Footsteps rushed over the tile. Not Stassia, the strides were wrong. Saka rushed to my side. She grabbed my hand and held on tightly, though my own wasn't responding yet. Tears welled in her eyes as she gazed down on me. She cleared her throat and turned to Etara.

"He'll live?"

"That's up to him more than anyone else, it would seem."

The two of them talked, but I was busy doing as Etara had suggested, getting reconnected with my body. It was so much easier than ever before, clearer, how all the processes worked together, flowed one into another to make my body operate efficiently.

I sat up, focusing on the distress flowing from Saka and confusion from Etara. Both were clear and prominent, surrounding each of the women like a cloud of swirling nebulous gas. Quite mesmerizing, the longer I looked. They were both still speaking, their voices raised, but I realized I could make them feel better without having to answer. I didn't have answers anyway. Instead, I soothed their minds, calming them until their voices fell silent.

When I blinked away the clouds, I again saw their faces.

Saka stared at me like I was the mesmerizing cloud. Etara, on the other hand, looked horrified.

I cringed. I should have known better than to try to be nice. Doing so had rarely done me any favors. "Go away then. Leave me be." I yanked the wires and tubes out of my Arpex-thickened skin.

Etara shook her head, backing away and pulling Saka with her. "Get Anastassia here now. Right now."

Canelli tapped madly on his datapad, glancing up every few seconds as though gauging the point at which he should run.

Saka appeared dazed, or perhaps, the closer I looked, utterly relaxed, not at all sharing Etara's terror. The two of them could not have been more opposite at that moment.

As I got a tentative foot on the floor beside the bed, I reevaluated what I'd done to them. I'd given them both the same calm, the same reassurances. Why had they reacted so differently?

I tried my connection with Stassia again, finding it solidly in place this time, as were the rest of my usual connections. How long had I been gone? Was she in the middle of something? Was she pissed I'd ended up in this bed again? Probably. Not knowing what to say, I simply opened our connection to let her know I was awake.

The thundering of two pairs of boots on tile came from the foyer. Hedvika's footsteps pounded down the stairs, along with a shorter gait I discerned as Markus. They all converged around me.

Stassia took in Etara, Saka, and Canelli. She approached me cautiously, leaving Neko with Markus and the others. "You're awake."

"Maybe."

She studied me for a moment. "You are."

I expected her to come closer, to smile, to give some indication that she was pleased with this development. Uncertainty billowed off Neko, Hedvika, and Markus. Stassia stood locked in place, her tone that of delicate negotiation. She glanced over her shoulder to Neko. He nodded.

I glanced down at my hands. They hadn't turned to claws. My skin wasn't blue. I was pretty sure the rest of me was just as it had been too. The calming touch I'd tried with Etara and Saka hadn't gone as I'd expected so I sure as all hells wasn't going to try that again.

It had been a stupid thing to try. The few lessons I'd done had barely touched on doing anything of the sort. I'd just mimicked what I thought Ikeri did, what it felt like she did for me. But I'd gone too far with Saka and far awry with Etara.

The hesitation wafting at me from people I trusted rubbed me raw. I let go of the bed and took a step toward Stassia.

Canelli rushed at me with the resolve of someone facing certain death. "Advisor, please, I must ask you to return to the bed." He grimaced. "Or at least a chair. Someone get the man a chair."

Neko snapped into action. Grabbing a chair and sliding it next to me. He scurried back to his place beside Hedvika and Markus.

From the shaking in my legs, I decided the chair was a splendid idea. Though I preferred to be on my feet, my quaking grip on the arm of the chair wasn't going to keep me vertical much longer. I sat with as much grace as I could manage and tried not to look too grateful about it.

Canelli took a step back and ran his scanner over me from there. Etara stood behind him looking almost as horrified as Ikeri had the last time I'd seen her.

"I'm not going to bite anyone. What the hells is your problem?"

"It's not your teeth we're concerned about," Stassia said.

"Then I suggest you clarify what is."

Stassia looked to Neko again. He nodded. Again. If that wasn't aggravating enough, the subtle repositioning of his hand over his openly-worn stunner nearly pushed me over the edge. Even if we all knew the damned thing would do little more than slow me down for a few seconds, that he was ready to use it pissed me off. There wasn't even a snarky comment to offset his actions. I glared at him and his damned hand until he gulped. He then had the audacity to draw the stunner. Though not enough to aim it at me. At least not quite yet.

Hedvika took Markus by the shoulders and tried to maneuver him out of the room.

"Let go." Markus squirmed away. Before she could grab him again, he ran over and wrapped his arms around me.

"At least someone is happy to see me." I hugged him.

"Markus," Stassia hissed.

"Where's Daniel?" I asked.

"With the Jalvian fleet," said Markus. "She won't let me go anymore." His pouting lip indicated Stassia was the she in question. "Not since Meera got shot."

Stassia raised a brow. "You know what, Markus? How about you go there right now. Hedvika?"

"You said it wasn't safe," Hedvika said.

"It's safer than here at the moment. Go."

To her credit, Hedvika dodged forward, and seconds after laying a hand on Markus, they were gone.

"Was that necessary?"

"Was it?" Stassia asked, casting an uncertain glance at Etara.

"Yes," said Etara, who then turned to me, "Do you remember what you did?"

"I've done a lot. Could you be more specific?"

"With the Arpex. You were with the Artorian fleet," Etara said.

"I remember what I was trying to do. Did it work? Are they gone?"

"I'll show you what happened. You tell me if it worked," said Stassia.

I didn't particularly like the sound of that, but if she was willing to open her mind to me, she couldn't be that scared. That offset my trepidation enough that I lowered my defenses and let her in.

"Let me know if I need to stop at any point," she said to Etara.

Neko came closer, still holding the stunner. He took up a post just behind Stassia, close enough he could grab her just like Hedvika had done with Markus. I began to reconsider wanting to see what had them all so worried about me.

It was too late for second-guessing. Stassia's mind opened to mine, pulling us both to the command center on the Artorian ship. Through Stassia's eyes, I saw myself surrounded by the hunters, all of us sitting on the floor off in the corner, relatively out of the way of all the hustle of the crew.

She spoke with the commander, relaying orders, also passing them off through Neko. Her datapad flashed reports with such speed, I couldn't believe that she read through them, but her skimming method was clear enough in her mind, the information filtering through at a high rate. Just because she'd lost her access to linked networks, didn't mean she'd lost the ability to multitask on a manic level. Monitoring the destruction of our ships in the Arpex confrontation as well as Buria's reports on Gamnock's efforts against the investors on the other end of the Narvan, and the progress of the Jalvian fleet, kept her fully occupied.

Every few minutes, she'd slip out of her trance-like state to glance my way, and then speak to Neko or the commander. In those moments, I saw the eleven of us sitting there, eyes closed, looking as though we weren't doing a damned thing. Then one of the hunters swayed, falling onto his side, making no effort to catch himself. He went still.

Stassia's mind went empty, dropping the hundreds of tasks she'd been controlling. She watched beads of sweat run down my face. I didn't remember feeling heat or much of my body at all.

Another of the hunters collapsed.

She started toward me. Neko grabbed her.

"We need you here. Whatever he's doing, you can't help him."

"I can stop him."

"That won't help anyone, Ana. Let him be."

"Those two men are dead. I'm not letting him join them."

"That's his choice, not yours."

The ship rocked again. Another ship indicator on her datapad blinked out. Stassia swore, frustration and fear flooding her mind. All around her, the crew hustled and called out to one another, operating their defenses in a well-practiced manner despite the yelled report that more Arpex ships were still arriving through the jump gate. There were so many. Too many.

"Vayen never should have taken half the Jalvian fleet away. He knew the Arpex were coming," she said bitterly.

"He couldn't have foreseen the scope of this. None of us did." He stared at the screen in her hands, shaking his head. "They have to be sending everything. Please tell me this isn't just part of their fleet."

The Jalvian ships on her screen were too far away to be useful yet. A quarter of the Artorian ships were gone with more blinking out every minute.

Another hunter swayed. His head lolling before crumpling over.

The ship's commander leaned in close. "Have you considered offering terms?"

"Do you speak Arpex?" she snapped. "Our only translators are over there, killing themselves."

"Forgive me, Advisor," the commander said.

She rubbed her face and let out a deep sigh. "Some of them may speak through the boxes we've seen before, but they wouldn't accept our offer anyway. Vayen made it quite clear we're only food. They want the planets."

"At this rate, they're going to get them," Neko muttered.

"Fall back," Stassia ordered. "We'll see if we can bide some time until the Jalvian fleet catches up to us."

Even as the Artorian fleet fled before the Arpex, four more ships turned into debris fields.

"Ana!" Neko pointed at us.

My eyes moved wildly under my eyelids. Those of us who remained were swaying, rocking in a disconcerting discordant manner.

Stassia's vision blurred and her voice came out strangled, "Damn, you. We had an agreement, no one kills you but me."

Neko rested his hand on her arm. "He wouldn't break it lightly, Ana. We're desperate. Let him save us."

"You don't understand. His life is supposed to be in my hands because I'd never let him go."

For a split second in her memory, I caught flashes of all the times she'd laid down her threat. Now realizing it for the declaration that she'd intended, my own recollections altered, filling me with warmth.

Stassia threw her datapad aside and started for me. Neko caught her just as a horrifying cry flew from my mouth. We all toppled over.

Knowing what was going on inside in those moments, it was strange to see it from afar. We looked like some crazed cult in a drug-laden suicide ritual.

The crew spun around, staring. The commander gasped. Stassia escaped Neko's hold and rand to grab me, placing my head on her lap. I'd known nothing at that point and it was clear to her utter dismay, that my body was not responding either.

"Get someone in here and get him breathing," Stassia yelled.

"What about the tank?" Neko asked, desperation clear in his voice though his face was out of focus in Stassia's memory.

"If he's not breathing, the tank can't fix him."

Neko frantically waved help over to evaluate me and the rest of the fallen hunters.

Chaos erupted in the command center and her memory turned hazy, a flurry of medics rushing out with bodies.

"Advisor," the commander called out. "Look."

The Arpex ships had halted their pursuit. All weapons ceased firing.

"Do we attack?" asked the commander.

"Fall back. If they're still sitting there when the Jalvians meet us, we'll reevaluate."

"Advisor, we're receiving a transmission," announced a woman sitting at the communications terminal.

Stassia was half-listening while watching my body being carted out of the room.

"Bring it up," said the commander.

One of the blue bastards stood there, unadorned other than the box strapped around his top section. "We would speak to the death-bringer, the Taset."

Stassia's attention snapped to the projection. "He's too busy to speak to you."

"You speak for the Taset?"

"I do."

His claws clacked. "You are known. His mate? We have tasted you. Delicious."

She scowled. "Do we need to bring more death upon you?"

"No, mate of the Taset. We do not seek to anger the death-bringer further." Its wing-jaws snapped and fluttered. "Had he revealed his true form to us, we would have come to serve sooner."

Her voice rose, "You seek to serve?"

Neko rested a calming hand on her shoulder.

"Did Vayen mention anything about this to you?" she whispered.

"No, but run with it," he suggested.

"The death-bringer is very angry about the ships you destroyed," she declared.

The Arpex chittered. "Forgive us. We did not know."

"You were given warning. He revealed himself on your world."

The crew watched the exchange with incredulous faces. I had a feeling mine was no different now.

"You claim ignorance." She drew herself up, shaking off the despair over my condition. "You knew who he was, but you were greedy, wanting our worlds for your own. How many more does he need to kill before you understand you are not welcome here?"

Its wings popped open, but in a move I'd never seen before, they drooped low, the top barbs crossing out of sight behind its back. "We know. We do. No more."

"You want to serve? Prove it. The death-bringer demands you destroy the ships you will find here." She relayed the coordinates of the investor's invasion.

"Taset-mate, the death-bringer's wrath has destroyed our crews. Many of our ships are without life."

"Go. Or find all of your ships without life."

"Yes, Taset-mate. We would seek an audience with the death-bringer when we return."

"Return here. He will speak to you when he finds you worthy."

Stassia pulled out of the memory abruptly. Back in the common room with the others standing warily around me, I was again thankful for the chair Canelli had so thoughtfully suggested.

"Death-bringer? What in all the hells is that?" I asked.

"That would be you." She thrust her fists onto her hips. "Congratulations, your Arpex followers await your divine presence."

TWENTY-ONE

"Oh fuck no."

Of all the shit Geva had thrown at me, posing as a divine figure to the creatures that haunted my sleep was quite possibly the most fucked up.

Neko cracked a smile.

"Do you have your mutant Arpex-slaying mind shit under control?" Stassia asked.

"I think so? Not that any of you are Arpex, so you're safe regardless."

"Jey and Kess aren't Arpex either," Neko pointed out.

"That was different." I tried to get up, but the queasiness in my stomach convinced me that was a bad idea. "Is that what has you all so nervous? What we did there was damned hard and it took all of us. It doesn't just happen on a whim."

"Maybe before," said Etara. "What about now?"

"Why would now be any different?"

Canelli cleared his throat. "You've channeled a great deal of energy, a tremendous amount. You've paved the way, as it were. Just as it has been easier for you to use this ability with each successive use on the individual scale, you've now done this large scale, twice. We're concerned you may have opened yourself to this ability on too grand of a platform, that it might bleed over without your intent."

With an accusing tone that I didn't appreciate, Etara said, "And then there's the matter of what you did when you first came back to yourself, in addition to how you were able to figure out how to do that at all given the very few lessons we had."

"I was only trying to calm you."

"Exactly." She crossed her arms over her chest. "On a full Seeker scale. You didn't just locate me to help you, did you?"

"I told you, I didn't intentionally seek you out at all."

"And that, Advisor, is why we're being cautious," said Canelli.

"Go be cautious elsewhere. I'm hungry and I want to lie down."

Etara's facade of calm fractured into an angry young woman. I'd never seen an angry Seeker before. Disappointed or disapproving maybe, but not angry. It was like she shed all her training and came at me as the young woman she was under the robes and tattoos.

"You took the knowledge from me. All of it, didn't you? Everything I worked so hard for, you just wandered in without even thinking about it, with no effort at all, and copied it all into your own mind."

Her pale cheeks turned mottled pink. "That's how Ikeri learned so fast. She did it too, didn't she? Took what she wanted from all of us like it was her own. We celebrated her as though she was some sort of prodigy. She's only a thief, just like you."

My first reaction was to defend Ikeri, but Etara had a valid argument. I instead reached out with the calm and blanketed her with it so I could think on her accusations without her ire filling the room.

I considered, as Stassia slapped Etara across the face, that I should have encompassed her in my calming efforts as well.

Stassia turned to me. "You're just going to sit there?"

As if I had any choice about sitting. "Stassia, she might well be right. Ikeri was traipsing around in our heads from the day she was born. She's gifted in that regard for sure. But think about when she started to try to help you, where do you think she got the knowledge for the processes to do that?"

Stassia clasped the hand she'd used to strike Etara and scowled at me. "I liked it better when you got angry first and resorted to logic later."

Despite the red mark on her cheek, Etara gathered a semblance of her Seeker countenance around herself. "That's the second time you've reacted with peace rather than what comes naturally to you. Perhaps your theft was not all bad."

"Neither was Ikeri's," I said firmly.

She offered a conceding nod.

"Though, hers was far more intentional than mine. I'm sorry, Etara, I didn't realize I was absorbing knowledge from you without your consent."

Neko shared an incredulous look with Stassia.

Stassia said, "Who are you and what have you done with Vayen?"

Etara shook her head. "I think perhaps it would be wise to make some time to spend with me on Prime so we can explore this newly acquired knowledge together before you do anything else that you don't realize."

She turned to Canelli. "The overflow of his energy, do you think it manifested in the four days he was out?"

Canelli scuttled closer and did another scan. "His brain activity readings are dropping now. Perhaps, yes."

"Eat then," Etara said to me, "and rest. Come see me once you've dealt with your new followers." She held her hand out to Neko, who after a nod from Stassia, jumped her home.

Minutes later, Saka hurried over with a plate full of steaming noodles. When she'd left us to get it, I couldn't pinpoint. I managed a few bites before the urge to sleep took over.

"Help me get him to the bedroom," Stassia said to Saka.

"He should stay here," said Canelli, nodding to the bed I'd been in.

"If it would be safer for everyone, I can sleep here."

"Seriously, who the hell are you?" Stassia helped me up.

I wanted to hug her, but I was leaning on her too heavily for that. I let her and Saka help me back onto the bed and didn't argue when Canelli hesitantly suggested reapplying several of his monitoring patches.

Stassia and Saka stood aside until he was finished.

"Do you need anything else?" asked Saka, still wearing that beatific smile she'd taken on during my initial calming efforts.

Stassia elbowed Saka hard in the ribs. "Wipe that look off your face or you can find employment elsewhere."

"Stassia, come here. Leave her be."

After a quick bow, Saka made her escape.

"Don't you try any of that copied Seeker shit on me."

"Wouldn't think of it." I moved over as far as I could. "Do you have work to do?"

She glared at me. "Always, thanks to you."

"Would you mind doing it here?"

"Only if you could manage a more pathetic look." She sighed and held up a hand. "On second thought, I don't want to see that. Let me get my datapad. Mind if I finish your meal? It's been a while since I ate."

"Have at it." I sank back on the pillows. Being out in the open with Canelli observing me from a distance didn't irk me near as much as the voice in the back of my head told me it should have. Having the others around was calming. The sunlight through the windows reminded me of my time as an acolyte in the dorms.

I sat up with a deep gasp that seemed to suck all the air from the room. The edges of my vision turned black and hazy.

Canelli shouted. The plate smashed onto the floor and shattered. Stassia and Canelli were at my side an instant later, each holding me down onto the bed.

"Memories, I stole her memories too," I tried to explain. "She's in here. With me."

"Can we sedate him?" asked Stassia.

"With his readings spiking and diving, I'd rather not."

"Neko," Stassia yelled. "Get Etara back here."

Save Saka, everyone was back around me moments later. Etara appeared the most disconcerted. "What is it you think you took?"

"Look." Not that I needed to lower my defenses, as a Seeker she could plow through them as easily as Ikeri, but I wanted her to see everything, to help me sort it out, to make it stop.

She turned to Stassia. "He's offering me open access. Clearly, he's not in his right mind. Do I have your permission?"

"Stick to what you need." She nodded. "Do it."

Etara jumped back. "It's like staring into a mirror. I need a moment. And air. Outside."

Neko beckoned her down the hall. The foyer door opened and their voices faded.

"You've managed to unnerve a Seeker *and* make her lose her temper. You're checking off your list of dream accomplishments left and right today, aren't you?" Stassia yelled for Saka, directing her to clean up the broken plate and spilled food.

"I didn't want this. I didn't ask for it. Any of it."

Stassia nodded and slid onto the narrow spot I'd made for her earlier. She took my hand in hers and pulled it onto her lap. "We'll sort it out together, all right?"

I let my head rest on her shoulder and stopped trying to hold everything together. There was too much to hold. On top of everything else I'd had to take on, this was one change too many. I had to trust that Etara, Canelli, Neko, and Stassia would figure out a way to help me. In the distance, the faint voice screamed for me to fight this acquiescence, begging me to get my shit together and get out of the damned bed.

These people cared about me, or at least my wellbeing insofar as keeping me from going death-bringer angry. I told the voice to fuck off.

Arguing with myself was probably a sign that I needed to stay in bed for a while.

"Stassia"?

"What?"

"Thank you." I expanded our bonded connection and gave her access to the mass of emotions I normally kept locked down, to all the words I had a hard time saying.

She brushed the hair from my face and kissed my forehead. Moisture slipped from her cheek to my skin.

"I didn't mean to make you cry. I know how much you hate doing that."

Stassia let out a half-choked chuckle. She sniffed and wiped her face. Her hand squeezed mine.

We didn't talk about this shit, the emotional garbage that some people basked in and perpetuated as the ideal of a solid bond. We didn't have time for it. There was always some other crisis that needed our attention. We weren't talking now either, but everything felt right, at least in that one aspect of my life.

"For the record, I'm very impressed with how you handled that conversation with the Arpex," I said.

"Thank you. Now get some sleep while we figure out how to wash all this sweet, tractable goodness out of you so I can get my wrath-heavy, ill-tempered, death-bringer back."

TWENTY-TWO

I must have slept for a long time because when I woke, I was feeling much more myself. Etara's memories had faded, leaving me alone in my mind except for Stassia's bright presence through our bonded connection, which was, to my surprise, still wide open.

The monitoring patches were gone as was most of the equipment that had been around me when I'd first awoken. Saka sat nearby at the security station. She smiled when she saw me awake and came over. "Do you need anything?"

"A shower, my regular clothes, and a drink."

"I'd be happy to get the drink, but I think it would be wise to have Ana assist with the rest."

I brushed over our connection and found Stassia off working with Neko. "Is Etara still here?"

"Sleeping in Meera's bed. The boys are still with the fleet and Meera. Hedvika is sleeping. Canelli is also resting." She nodded toward the couch where the poor man was curled into a corner, one leg and a hand hanging off the front. He snored softly.

Sliding my legs off the bed, I gave standing another try. It was much more successful than before. I took a few steps and didn't get dizzy. "I'll give it a shot on my own."

My stomach growled as I started toward the bedroom. "Maybe it would be wise to eat something before that drink," I suggested.

"Of course." Saka bowed and headed for the kitchen.

The shower went well enough, but I ran out of energy once I'd gotten my pants on. I'd only pushed myself that far so that I could ask for help without feeling too guilty about it. And only after I'd dropped my shirt for the third time because my hands were shaking so badly. I was getting very sick of this whole recuperating routine.

"Saka," I said, trying to keep the annoyance out of my link summons.

Her discomfort was made quite clear by her stammering in the bedroom doorway. I finally convinced her to come in and help me get the shirt and boots on. The rest would have been a waste of time. I wasn't going anywhere today. Though, it did feel good to at least be at a reasonable degree of my normal self.

With her help, I made it out to the table where I managed to eat half a plate of food. Fortified with a light meal, I made it to a more comfortable chair in the common room with slightly less assistance. Saka delivered a well-deserved drink. After relaxing for a few minutes, which felt wrong in light of everything going on, I sunk into my link to catch up on all that had happened in the now five days since I'd been out of contact.

Daniel had left a message for me, saying that he'd returned to the ship they'd been searching once Meera was in the tank and promised he'd stuck with Nacen the whole time. He'd talked with some of the crew to find that Ikeri had done sessions for a few of them for payment, which he thought was odd. Seekers didn't typically charge cfor their services in a monetary sense.

I prayed it was only Seeker sessions those men were forcing her to do. The knowledge of what the two girls I'd rescued from the Masters on Tacesh had endured and knowing Ikeri might well be subjected to the same made my blood boil.

The crew had thought one of the men was her father as he seemed to be protecting her from the other one. They were known to argue loudly. Whether one killed the other, which man survived, or if someone else altogether had taken him out, no one knew.

If Ikeri was awake and alert, why hadn't she contacted any of us? Why was she still sealed off so securely? I wanted to punch something, throw something, beat the person nearest to my reach and pretend it was one of the Masters.

But none of that would help. I needed to recover so I could rejoin the ships that were on their way to Brustus. I was in the midst of replying to Daniel when Etara standing next to me caught my attention.

She spoke quietly to avoid waking Canelli, "Advisor?"

I let go of my reply to Daniel and returned my awareness to the room around me. "Yes?"

"My personal memories?"

"Gone for the most part. The rest are fading fast."

"So that's how Ikeri does the delayed memory transfers." Etara perched in the chair next to me and eyed my empty glass.

"You want one? I didn't know Seekers drank alcohol."

"We don't. You may be rubbing off on me."

I laughed and called for Saka to bring another glass and to fill them both. Etara sipped hers cautiously and frowned. It must not have tasted too bad, because she didn't set the glass down.

"Holding the memories, you mean?" I asked, returning to her original comment about Ikeri.

She nodded. "Our other memory menders, they can't do what the two of you did. Do you think other Artorians may be able to do this memory imprinting? That this ability is proprietary to your people, rather than a skill others can adopt?"

"I wasn't aware I was doing it so I couldn't tell you how it is done. Ikeri would know."

"Any word on her whereabouts?" Etara asked.

"Two ships have been dispatched to the port where she and the Master who remained with her were last seen. The rest of the fleet is continuing to our original destination."

"And the Seeker knowledge, has that faded as well?"

I turned inward, perusing until I located where my lessons were stored. This process had become almost natural after all the memory healing sessions.

"There, but not as clear."

"What of the calming balm?"

I delved deeper into the few lessons I'd attended, examining which were complete. There were those I'd practiced in what had seemed like an unending loop while I was unconscious. They were rudimentary lessons but polished to a habitual level. One other caught my attention, not quite as polished, but I could access it without much force of remembering.

"It's there as well. Whole, I think."

"You used that memory, made it your own." She set the glass down and clasped her hands together. The long sleeves of her robes hid all but her fingers from view. "If you wish to keep the rest, you will need to use those as well, and soon. Do you wish to retain this knowledge?"

Etara studied her half-empty glass. "I ask because it's not exactly beneficial to your line of work."

"It could be, some of it anyway. I spend a lot of time talking to people, negotiating, making deals. This calming, it could make a significant difference in avoiding unpleasant outcomes."

"You do understand that forcing calm could be seen as a form of manipulation. To force denotes removing a degree of free will. That's not what we do."

"I'm not part of your *we*."

"I'm infinitely aware of that fact and that's what concerns me. There is a reason why there are so few exceptions to giving full training to non-Verians."

"Like Anastassia."

Etara nodded. "I've seen into your mind several times, gotten a sense of what types of things are there. The flavor, if you will. When we first met, your mind was a terrifying place, filled with horrors I'd not even imagined. It hasn't improved, in that regard."

I drained my glass and set it down, debating on another in light of the conversation.

"The more I've seen of you, inside you, I've come to understand you are a complex man, Advisor Ta'set. Neither white nor black, but a grey that varies in shade by the hour. So tell me, other than manipulation of your people, what do you intend to do with the knowledge you have stolen from me?"

The skin on the back of my neck prickled and the room took on the sharpness I was accustomed to in combat situations. "Why do I get the feeling that you think you have the ability to contain this situation?"

She offered me a tight smile. "Answer the question."

"As I told you before when we started our lessons, I want to try to repair the damage I caused to my friend."

"And?"

"And I'm far less inclined to heal the others I've harmed."

"That's what sets us apart. Seekers are compelled to help everyone."

"Everyone didn't hand your daughter over to your enemies or set loose a few of those other terrifying things you mentioned seeing in my head."

Etara rubbed the center of her forehead with three fingers. "Do you intend to share what you have taken from me with other Artorians?"

"I hadn't given it any thought. Why would I do that?"

"Do you remember when we first met, when I wrongfully assumed that your people must live in peace like mine because we shared similar gifts?"

I nodded.

"Do you wish to maintain your grey status, Advisor Ta'set?"

"I don't think I have it in me to get much lighter than that."

Her lips quirked. "On that, we agree. But you can get much darker. The Arpex mutation has made you a powerful weapon, one you have employed with much destruction of life."

"They were Arpex lives."

"And one day, with the same off-handed callousness, you may tell me they were Jalvian lives or any other."

"If you're looking to wring a promise out of me that I won't use what I've gained, you're not going to get it."

"I know. We're linked now, you and I, having tasted each other's memories." She held up a hand. "Not in the sense you are familiar with, but as I am with Tomias. As Tomias is with Ikeri. My knowledge is yours now and I am responsible for what you do with it."

"Ikeri said something like that after she hauled me out of the nothing the first time, when she earned her Seeker status."

"Her imprint isn't on you. Mine is."

"What kind of imprint?"

"Like a key, if you will. The knowledge you have taken bears my stamp. If you misuse it, I am bound to turn that key and stop you."

"A kill switch?"

"Quite literally, yes."

It took me a second to process what she was saying. "Seekers can kill each other? A major misuse must have happened at some point to necessitate the need for this measure."

"Not in recent history, but there are reasons only Verians get full Seeker training."

Seeker Res's comments about Stassia not being good enough and his reluctance to fully train her made more sense now.

"Why train Ikeri then?"

Etara sighed. "She seemed so pure. What you and I have discovered, this will only reinforce the decree, and likely the reluctance to train non-Verians at all."

"I see." My mind was still spinning with the realization that little Etara had the power to drop me dead.

I craned around until I spotted Saka standing over by the kitchen. "I need a refill."

My shout woke Canelli. He sat up slowly, rubbing his face, which bore a deep red line from the seam of the couch cushion.

"Gather up what you need. I'll have Saka bring you back to the University," I told him.

"If you don't mind, Advisor, I'll take a transport. Jumping doesn't agree with my stomach."

"Suit yourself. I'll be by the University later. I have a feeling we'll be seeing a lot of one another until I get Jey back on his feet."

Canelli stumbled over to the remaining equipment and began packing it up. Saka refilled my glass and returned to her post. I picked it up and drained it. It occurred to me, as the effects of the first two drinks became more apparent, that my tolerance in that arena was likely quite low given my perpetual recuperating status of late. My judgment in slamming the third might have been a direct correlation to that issue. I glared at the empty glass.

"So what's your deal?" I asked Etara. "I'm grey. How do I keep you from turning the key?"

"Advisor, are you drunk?"

"I'm working on it. I'm told I'm more friendly when I'm drunk. Hey, what happens if you die? Would I be in the clear on the whole kill switch thing?"

She gasped. Her hand holding the glass shook. "What?"

"I'm not saying I would kill you, I'm just wondering."

Etara shook her head. "No, I'm pretty sure that's what you were getting at." She held up a finger and pointed it at me like a scolding mother. "And I'll have you know that's definitely not in the grey territory."

I pointed right back at her. "You didn't answer the question."

"I think it's safer not to," she said after taking a sip.

"Fine, be that way. You should probably get to your terms while I'm more agreeable."

Her eyes widened and she stammered a moment. "I haven't had a chance to come up with terms yet. We only just established our predicament."

"Got to think on your feet, Etara. No one is going to give you the luxury of time to ponder options in this universe. The situation could deteriorate at any second."

She looked to Saka. "What is he talking about? He might need to lie down."

Saka edged towards us. I waved her away.

"We're negotiating, Etara. Let's go. Terms. Now."

"I'm not seeing this friendly side you mentioned."

I shrugged. "Just wait until that third one kicks in."

"I'd rather not." She stood. "I'll get back to you on the terms. I think it's best I go now."

"I think you should sit back down and finish your drink. No one is leaving." I glanced at Canelli. "Except you. Why are you still here?"

"Sorry Advisor, I'm packing as fast as I can."

"Saka, help Canelli get out of here."

"Yes, Advisor." She cast me a worried glance before hurrying over to help Canelli push his equipment out to the foyer.

"There, you've had far more time than I usually get," I refocused on Etara. "Let's get on with it then."

"I—"

"And now your people are plotting to walk all over you. You've lost your upper hand. Someone in the room is probably wishing you were dead and formulating plans to make that happen."

Her gaze darted around the room while her hands gripped the arms of the chair. "I didn't plan this meeting. I didn't know I was expected to have terms ready. We didn't even know the situation."

"Stressful isn't it? And you can't panic. You've got to decide right now. What are you going to do? Negotiate? Storm out? Kill someone to make your point?"

"Maybe I'd ask for some time to consider the matter."

"Maybe there's a gun on you or the Arpex are taking out your fleet before your eyes, or someone is going to die if you don't figure it out this instant."

Etara threw her head back against the chair. "I'm beginning to see why you enjoy your alcohol."

"Speaking of which." I nodded to her glass.

"You're dead-set on me finishing that aren't you?"

"I'll be offended if you don't. We're having friendly negotiations, after all."

She picked up her glass and sipped at the brown liquid. "This is friendly?"

"I'm not even armed."

"You can kill without weapons."

"I'll tell you what. I'll teach the surviving hunters how to do a few of your Seeker skills, spread the light and all that, to offset me using the other thing I can do."

"That's a start."

"A start? Really?" I sighed. "All right then, what if I show you how to do what I do in return for what I took from you?"

"What need would I have of that?"

"Wouldn't it be handy if you're people were ever attacked? Seekers could help defend your world. You don't have the alteration, but I think you could use the ability on an individual level. Get close to the leader and take them out before military force is ever needed. Minimize losses on both sides." That sounded quite Seeker-like to me.

She nodded slowly. "But what you do, it could be misused so easily."

"You have your keys."

She stared at the remaining liquor in her glass.

"I can misuse your calming," I said. "I'm sure I could figure out how to twist most anything you've got to my advantage if I put my mind to it."

"You're not helping your case." She tossed back the remaining liquid and set the empty glass down with a victorious gleam in her eye.

"My point is, anything can be misused. It's the effectiveness and severity of the consequences that keeps us all in line," I said.

"So you're offering me a weapon in return for the tools for peace."

I nodded. "Thereby maintaining my grey range, yes?"

"The other Seekers aren't going to like this."

"They don't have to like it. The damage is already done. We're just making the best of it. Are we agreed then?"

"As long as you're not going to make me drink any more of that awful stuff to seal the deal."

"Now I am offended." I grabbed my empty glass, which I nearly knocked off the table before getting a solid hold on it. Having someone else around to find the bottle and pour without spilling was quite useful. "Saka, we need more."

"Not for me." Etara maneuvered to the edge of her chair. She sat there, blinking slowly.

There were voices in the foyer. I assumed Canelli's transport had arrived and someone was helping him load out the equipment. I pointed at Etara as though that would keep her in her chair. "Oh come on, have another. We should celebrate."

"Thank goodness," said Saka as Neko and Stassia left the tiled hallway and hurried over. "What took you so long?"

Stassia glared at her. "How many has he had?"

"Three. I delayed in pouring the fourth."

"Wise move."

"What did you bother them for?" I asked Saka as I got up.

Stassia knocked me back into the chair. "Etara, thank you for all your help, but…" She left my side to go to Etara. "Have you been drinking too?"

"It burned. It's still warm." She pondered Stassia's face. "I think I like it."

Stassia sighed long and loudly. "Saka, get Etara home before there's vomit on the rug."

"Might I have a little more?" asked Etara.

"See," I said, annoyed at how slurred the word came out. "It is good." I pointed at Stassia. "You ruined our celebration."

Neko started to pull me up and out of the chair. "Boss, I think you should lay down."

"Let go, dammit." I shoved him away.

"There's the ornery drunk we all know and love." He took a couple steps back. "Canelli and Etara were right. He just needed some time for all of it to wear off."

"And now he needs more time for *this* to wear off. I don't know how much longer I can keep the Arpex waiting."

"We'll get him there," Neko said. "Get some sleep, Ana."

"Help me get him to the bedroom." She maneuvered herself to one side of me and motioned for Neko to take the other.

"I can walk. I'm right here, dammit. I didn't drink that much."

She stood back, hands on her hips. "Have at it then."

I did manage to get to my feet and walk halfway to the bedroom on my own. It wasn't a straight line and the walls were closer than they should've been, but, given that Saka had helped me get to the chair to begin with, I considered my efforts progress. Stassia helped me the rest of the way.

"Has Daniel been home lately?" I asked as I not-so-gracefully sat on the edge of the bed.

"No. He managed to Jump a bag of clothes to the fleet the day after you left. He's feeling important now that you're not there."

"Good for him."

"I hope so." She took my shirt off and knocked me backward onto the bed. "Can you manage your own boots? I want to take a shower."

"Sure."

I stretched out, listening to her shed her clothes and the shower start. When I opened my eyes again, seven hours had passed and my boots were still on. Stassia lay curled against me in the quarter of the bed I wasn't sprawled over. I got up as quietly as I could, dressed on my own this time, and went out to the kitchen to get something to eat.

Neko was already there. "How are you feeling?"

"Better than yesterday. What's the situation with the Arpex?"

"If you want to keep control of this charade, you're going to have to make an appearance."

"I'm sensing a 'right now' at the end of that sentence."

"Only if you're up to it. They've been on hold for six days, but keeling over isn't going to make a good impression divine-being-wise."

"Right. Anything I need to know first?"

"If you could manage some Arpex-speak, I would recommend it. They scrambled their blue-shelled asses across the Narvan, beating the Jalvian fleet and the Fragian ships. The Fragians scared the shit out of us, by the way. You could have warned us that they were coming to help Gamnock."

"Sorry, I didn't get a solid answer from the Fragians, and then I was busy taking an unplanned vacation from living."

Neko shook his head, looking unamused. "The Arpex raced to the coordinates we gave them. The Jalvians weren't too happy about missing all the action or getting bested by Arpex and their tech."

"But the Arpex followed through?"

"Sure did. They managed to take out all the remaining ships the investors had left. However, they did blow two of Gamnock's in the process. He was even less happy than the Jalvians. You'll need to do some mollifying on both fronts there and thank the Fragians, even if they were late to the party. Neither Ana nor I have contacts for them. For the Arpex, I'd recommend going in as your usual pissed-off self and screw being thankful for the assist."

"I was planning on that regardless."

Neko grinned. He finished his meal and put his plate away. "Ana's still sleeping?"

I brushed over our connection. "Yes."

"Good. Think she'll hate us if you suited up and we got this Arpex thing taken care of without her? She could use a break."

"I guess we'll find out." I took care of my plate and snuck back down the hall to the closet to get my coat and weapons.

My hand slipped into the pants pocket where the two vials of boost were hidden. If ever there was a time would have a valid excuse to take a couple drops of conquer-it-all-with-a-smile, this was it.

I rolled the cold plaz vial in the palm of my hand, pondering the distortion of the lines on my palm through the golden liquid inside. Neko would notice, but he'd understand and I didn't think he'd say anything about it to Stassia. Maybe just this once.

My thumb rested on the cap, nail pressed under the lip. I licked my lips. Buria's face floated before me, *"Would you be satisfied with just this one time?"*

It seemed like everything I touched became an addiction, Stassia's peace, Ikeri's calm, Etara might have had a point about my drinking, the rush of a job, the fucking Narvan, and so much more. I'd managed to avoid adding Buria to that list, and if I could avoid that temptation, I could avoid this one. I was in control.

I slipped the vial back into the pocket and went to meet Neko in the foyer, he flashed me a jump point on one of the Arpex ships.

We stepped out of the void into a green corridor flooded with yellow light that immediately plunged me back to the Arpex room where I'd served in grey. My stomach heaved, but I kept everything inside.

"Boss?"

"I hate this."

"I can see that."

Oppressive heat baked the air around us. I squeezed my eyes shut and held onto the wall to get my bearings. "No, I really, really hate this."

"Do we need to leave before they see us"? he asked

"I'm not going to hate it any less tomorrow." I breathed in, my body remembering how to take shallow breaths of the hot air even though I wanted to gasp, feeling that I couldn't get enough into my lungs. I flexed my fingers, each of them slowly, counting my way out of the panic.

Neko rested a steady hand on my shoulder. I wasn't alone here, not stuck here. I had a job to do and then I could leave. I could leave.

I nodded to Neko. He let go but still watched me warily.

I shoved my memories back into the box I'd constructed to contain them. "Let's get this done."

Opening my mind to the Arpex now, since I'd flooded their collective minds with death, was far easier. I didn't have Ha'guris's open channel, but I only needed to reach the Arpex on this ship. That, I could manage on my own. I listened first, reacquainting myself with the language I still only understood fragments of.

The strange soft material of the floors swallowed sound and footsteps. Porous, like living tissue, cushioning each step, like walking on elastic. Maybe it was comfortable to the shelled feet of the Arpex. The yellow light emanated from semi-transparent walls rather than the ceiling, creating disconcerting shadows on Neko's face.

It didn't take me too long to locate a pocket of Arpex. Their clacking halted. I grabbed the internal thread of one of them and twisted.

A panicked cry spread through the ship. Arpex gathered all around us, clogging the corridor, spilling from doors and adjoining passageways. One voice, stronger than the others, ended the cry and sent an image of a large open space with something I could only describe as a push in a direction. Open sounded good, but I had to make my way past a couple hundred blue bastards to get there.

As we passed, I fought to keep my shuddering internal. Attuned to me as he was, Neko seemed to sense my anxiety and stuck even closer than usual. If he was uneasy about our surroundings, he hid it well.

The Arpex touched my mind with a sense of awe or maybe reverence. The images and thoughts they pushed at me were too foreign to fully understand. All I knew for sure was that what they felt for me now was something no other Arpex had ever conveyed in my presence. While I did appreciate the lack of pain or threats, having so many of them actively in my mind, in a manner I didn't have full control over, made me want to run, vanish, be anywhere else.

I kept pushing forward, one step at a time, each one taking a second longer than the last, each breath providing less air.

They reached out with closed claws, rubbing them against my sides and back as we passed. My skin crawled. The wrist now attached to my artificial hand ached. By the time we reached the opening, my mouth was so dry that my lips stuck to my teeth. I was so focused on keeping my second round of dry heaves under wraps that I walked right into Neko. Through some magic, he managed to make it look like I'd knocked him aside. He deserved a raise for that alone.

I found myself facing an Arpex with fine lines of yellow streaking its shell. I didn't recall ever meeting one with a shell that was anything other than solid blue.

It let loose a flurry of words in my head, about six percent of which I understood. I was quite familiar with servant and service. Flashes of images helped fill in some of the rest. Arpex falling dead, overwhelming pain in others, and a blurry, distorted version of my face, as if one Arpex had known my true form, but as the image was passed along through those that did not, it lost definition.

Arpex lined the room, flowing in from the corridors we'd walked through. Their feet made little sound on the soft floor. Once they'd gathered, they stood silently, but I could feel them in my head, waiting.

They all knew my true form now. All the moisture that had vacated my mouth seemed to be pooling in my palms.

Yellow Stripe conveyed that he was the leader, or was now that I had killed those above him. It seemed quite proud of its new stripes, showing me its surprise when they had appeared on its shell as Arpex lay dead on the floor all around it.

When it finally slowed down enough that I could better understand the individual words, I made out, *"You spared, chose me."*

"Yes. You serve me," I said.

I had no idea where this was going. If the damned thing were only wearing a translator box this would be so much easier, though, I supposed somewhat less divine if I couldn't speak their language. Besides, I had a feeling any vocalizing on my end would have been relegated to a fit of coughing followed by heaving. Thankfully, my internal voice was firm.

"You want?" it asked, among other words I didn't understand

I wanted them to leave. To die, to go outright extinct immediately.

"How many worlds do you have?"

It chittered, thoughts flashing to a room full of dead Arpex.

"You don't know?" I asked.

"Not my place then. Don't speak to those who have gone out. Many have gone out." It showed me ships traveling, leaving, not to be heard from again.

I showed it the green tree world I'd seen in their minds. *"Home?"*

A sense of reverence channeled through a single word, *"Home."*

The more I spoke, the words came easier. I'd hoped to never need to speak Arpex again, but Geva apparently had other plans for me.

I wormed my way into its mind, searching for any hints of what they thought me to be, of any sort of moral code or religion I might use. It had no images of those things, only words. I could speak their language, see into their minds, kill them without touching, without even tasting thoughts, and without warning. Death-bringer.

There had been others before me, performing cullings of Arpex, though this one thought of those events far in the past, much beyond its lifetime. I wondered if they'd been created like myself, food gone wrong, or if they were some other predatory race to which this ability came naturally. Yellow Stripe offered no clues on the previous death-bringers.

The Arpex seemed simple, or at least this one portrayed them to be. They had very little in the way of social hierarchy. Leaders were signaled with the markings this one wore. There was always one, sometimes more. This one didn't know if it was the only leader, but it basked in elation that the markings had come to it and not another. If there were others placed to steer the universe their way, as those with the High Council had been, this one did not know of them. It had heard of them, but again those things were beyond its lifetime.

They enjoyed eating, relished the tasty thoughts of their prey. Sentient beings were their desired food, though their young could feed on any living thing. Making more Arpex was its foremost directive. Attaining food and the prime environment for that purpose was a close second. They had no names as we did, no familial attachments. They only seemed to understand the power of those things as a seasoning on their meals. Only the threat of death with a thought without warning had them in my grasp.

It wasn't much to go on, but as long as I held the upper hand, I planned on using it.

"Others have left home. They will be punished." I backed out of its mind and sought out a handful of others who were close by, twisting until they cried loud enough in the minds of the rest to convey my displeasure.

"You will take what ships you can fill, leave the rest behind, and hunt these others. Then you will return home."

"Hungry," it whined. It couldn't eat other Arpex. It made that clear.

"I will provide food. You will not feed on other worlds. Eat lightly, make your food last. Breed more from this stock so you have no need to leave home."

It conveyed a burst of intense satisfaction, identical to the Arpex I'd served after it had feasted on a particularly tasty memory. The faces of the victims I'd supplied for it sped through my mind.

Now there would be so many more. A whole lot of my people, and they would be consigned to living as stock for future generations. I might be free, but I was still serving up lives for the damned Arpex.

The yellow light pulsed with every beat of my heart. I could feel them all, passing my proclamation through the ranks. They shared with me their exhilaration at having food provided with no effort on their part. Meals handed to them, served. The Arpex were very happy with the death-bringer.

I was working for...no, *with* the Arpex. I was making them happy. Revulsion filled my every thought.

Blackness edged my vision. I grabbed Neko's shoulder.

"I will be back with food." I forced myself to say though the words stuck even in my mind. *"Gather yourselves into only as many ships as you can fill."*

"Yes," it said.

I could take no more.

"Home," I whispered to Neko.

He Jumped the two of us without question. Out of the harsh light of the Arpex ship, away from the vacuum of minds sucking at me, the nausea began to ease. I made it to a chair in the common room and dropped into it.

I sat there with my head in my hands, massaging my temples and trying to figure out how I was going to fulfill my promise to the Arpex. Then I caught the tantalizing scent of liquor next to my face. Neko put the full glass in my hand and sat down beside me.

Stassia must have heard him in the kitchen because she appeared before I could get my lips on the glass. Hair down and rumpled from sleeping on it damp, and wearing the pale green shirt and pants she'd worn to bed, she got as far as, "What do you think, you're—"

"Ana," Neko snapped. His censure was so blatant that I had to glance over to verify that Fa'yet wasn't there. He was the only one I'd ever heard use that tone with her.

Neko shook his head.

She fell silent and sat across from us. "Visited the Arpex, I take it?" she asked quietly.

"We did," Neko answered before I could. He studied his fingertips before rubbing them together and facing her again. "Have you covered his previous Arpex encounters in your therapy sessions?"

"One, yes."

Given our separation, our therapy sessions were working double-time, not only to share memories to repair what we'd lost but also those that might keep us together. While I'd intended to mostly share the good memories, they felt empty without more context, like some of the darker moments of my life. My subconscious seemed to be taking Etara's pact of honesty quite seriously.

I sipped my drink, my internal regulator stuck on a sedate pace in Stassia's presence. What I really wanted to do was pour the entire bottle down my throat and forget about anything blue forever.

Neko and Stassia whispered back and forth, speculating if I was going to keel over again. I ignored them and tried to find something uplifting to focus on to cleanse the last couple hours from my system.

My efforts proved to be quite fruitless.

"I'm going to visit Etara," I announced to the table as I put my empty glass on it.

"You want company?" Neko asked.

"I've got it, thanks." I made myself face him and put on the semblance of a smile. "Remind me about that raise when I get back."

"Don't worry about it, boss. It's never been about the credits."

He deserved something meaningful. He didn't want credits. I didn't have words. Instead, I opened myself to him in the way I'd taken from Etara and showed him my gratitude. I might have gone rather heavy on sharing as raw as I was at the moment. He went still and his eyes took on a glassy cast. I Jumped to the point in the Seeker's yard on Veria Prime before I broke down any farther.

The grey sky emitted a drizzle but the thought of going inside any of the buildings, of facing anyone, was too much. The feeling of Arpex claws on my back, their voices in my head, paralyzed me. I dropped to the ground and sat, clutching the damp grass, trying to remind myself that I was in a safe place, outside, that there were others around me, even though they were sleeping and out of sight, and none of them were dressed in grey. Yet, flashes of yellow light, waves of heat, the hissing of the Arpex I'd first served, the throbbing pain at the end of my arm where I'd lost my hand, it all flooded back with such clarity that the muscles throughout my body clenched. Arin's voice whispered around me, alternately telling me to go to sleep, to do my job, that I wasn't important, and that he'd tend the Arpex for me while I slept.

It was the wet chill settling into my flesh that finally shattered the nightmare. It had never been outright cold in the cell where Arin and I had served the Council, and never anything below sweltering in the Arpex chamber. Rain masked the tears running down my face.

Slowly, the sensation of cool mud and shredded blades of wet grass registered on my hands. I'd dug holes on either side of me in my desperation to anchor myself to this place. Hoping to find a way to purge the terror of it all, I ransacked the remains of Etara's fading Seeker knowledge. One lesson called Singularity snagged my attention. Except for the fact that it was a self-soothing balm, the why of it was mostly gone, but that sounded like what I needed. I sorted through the instruction to find I needed a focus. A singular thing.

Rain. Drops. Wet on my face. My clothes clinging to my body under my armor. Drops running down the back of my neck, dripping down my back. Cold rain, the soft patter of it on the leaves overhead, the softer fizzle of water hitting the grass.

The deeper I sunk into the balm, the more the chill faded. I stood on the calm shore of the beach on Artor where I'd fished with my father when I was a child. The smell of home, of the water, the sun on the sand slowly permeated everything else until I could breathe easier and the shaking stopped.

Drops of water. Beads slipping down bare skin. I stood in the steaming shower with Stassia in the tiny house at Cragtek where Gemmen had offered to let us hide when we'd first come back to the Narvan. A fine collection of droplets gathered on her hair, sparkling under the bathroom lights. Steam filled the air. Wet bodies sliding against one another.

Thunder. Rain pelting through the heavy canopy of leaves that hid our house on Frique. Windows beaded with rain lit only by the glow of the security station where Fa'yet sat while my family slept. The pungent smell of wet soil. My boots shuffling through wet leaves as I made my way inside.

Water rising. Dark skies. Land disappearing beneath waves. I watched from a distorted distance as water drowned the Arpex world I'd seen in their minds. Lifeless blue-shelled bodies bobbed on the surface. The rain took back the world they'd claimed, washing away the Arpex, their young, and any sign that they'd ever been there. And then they were gone.

Another presence tickled my mind, slowly, not threatening. I opened my eyes to see Etara standing beside me under the tree where we often had our therapy sessions. She eyed the destroyed grass and my muddy hands.

Rain dripped down her face and onto her Seeker robes. "Would you like to come inside now?" she asked.

If I let the singularity go completely, would the terror rush back? Etara stood calmly, waiting, but I got the distinct feeling she didn't relish the thought of getting soaked. With her there beside me, I edged my way out of the balm, one tentative step at a time, until my focus was fully back in my drenched body sitting in the wet yard in the middle of the night. The only thing that flooded my awareness was that I was cold.

"I suppose." I got up and followed her inside.

"I gather we have much to discuss." Etara shut the back door to the entry room of the main house and shook off her robe.

I looked at the backside of the red door where I'd stood so many times before, knocking and waiting, thinking I didn't belong here. "Could we just sit for a while?"

Etara nodded. She went to a round wooden table in the next room and pulled out a chair. "Take off your coat and all the rest for that matter. I'll get you some dry clothes."

"I'm fine."

She gave me a mental nudge to do as she'd instructed. I took off my coat and put it on the back of the chair. Calling that good enough, I started to sit down but then considered that I'd come here for a reason, and part of that was because I'd known she'd take care of me as I was.

I made quick work of my weapons and tucked them under my coat, out of sight of the room, of the Seeker, of everything here that said they were wrong. Etara busied herself with boiling water in the little kitchen on the other side of the table. By the time I had taken off my shirt, she'd left the room and returned with a rust-colored tunic and towel. After drying myself, I pulled the tunic over my head. While it did manage to stretch over my shoulders, it was a tight fit and barely came to my knees rather than the floor as it should have.

She set two cups on the table and smiled. "We don't get many visitors in your size."

"I would imagine not."

My pants were soaked too, and now that I had dry cloth against my skin, sitting in wet clothes had lost its appeal. I pulled my pants and boots off and set them aside to dry. Etara poured the tea she'd made without any comment.

I dried my dripping hair and then draped the towel over one of the vacant chairs. Etara offered me a cup. I took it and sat carefully in the small chair, unsure if it would hold my weight. It creaked but otherwise seemed sturdy enough.

The warmth of the cup felt good in my hands. The tea didn't smell half bad either, not like the dried weed stink of the stuff Stassia often made.

Etara set the pot aside and lit a wide orange candle with two wicks, placing it in the middle of the table. Then she turned out the other lights and sat across from me. She sipped her tea, waiting.

The scent of the candle reminded me of the flowers that bloomed in the yard where I'd been sitting. I tried the tea, it wasn't half bad, sweet, and slightly fruity.

"I met with the Arpex today," I said eventually.

"It wasn't easy for you."

"No." I stared at my cup. "I'm sending them off to exterminate other Arpex."

She cocked her head and shrugged.

"In return, I need to send them off with provisions. As much as I'd prefer them all dead, mass starvation seems less than grey. I don't want them feeding off anyone else along the way. They need food."

Etara set her cup down. "Food, meaning people?"

"Yes. That's what they want." I swallowed hard, thinking of the power she now held over my life. "You're my conscience now, right? Who do I feed to the Arpex?"

She sat, watching me in silence, concern heavy on her flat face.

"I had to feed one of them before. A slave to it, bringing so many innocent people to be fed upon that I lost count." I kept my gaze on the cup in my hands, sensing the hounding spirits of those I'd served up as food. "Sometimes I see their faces. I hear them screaming. I can't add a thousand more faces to their ranks. My nightmares are already full." The warmth of the cup in my hands had dissipated, leaving only a cold glazed surface of hard clay.

"You're safe here." She took the cup from my hands. I didn't know when she'd stood. She took my hands in her own. "We'll find a solution. Together."

I nodded, asking her without words to unleash her peace upon me as she'd done before. She settled into the chair beside me and hummed softly while her fingers settled on pressure points in my hands. Her mind enveloped mine, offering me an escape from the obligation looming over me, a brief time to be without the weight of the full Narvan and the floundering Nebula, of the destructive power in my head, my tenuous relationship with Stassia, and Ikeri's absence.

For a few bright moments, I relaxed. Then the light dimmed, and reality, with all its spiked and poisoned weight, settled back in.

"Would you like to lie down?" She sent another nudge, compelling my compliance.

"No. There's too much to do."

Her voice lost its compelling force. "You are weary."

"Always, it seems."

She let go of my hands and settled back into her chair, arranging her robe in folds on her lap. "How are things with Anastassia? Have our sessions improved your relationship?"

"They have. She's much stronger now, like she used to be."

"And this makes you happy."

"It's what I always wanted."

"And Anastassia, she is also happy?"

I considered the smile she'd given me in the command center when we'd connected there during the chaos, the quick words, and touches we'd shared since. "I think so."

"Then I think we need to start working on making you less weary so you can do what must be done." She let the folds go. The fabric cascaded down, rippling and expanding, yet revealing no more or less.

"You were right," she said, "to practice singularity when you came here tonight. That will bring you more relief than the alcohol you rely heavily upon."

"I wouldn't say *heavily*."

She made a little clucking noise in the back of her throat. "I've been in your head. You've been in mine. We have no secrets, remember?"

Etara emptied the cold contents of my cup and refilled both of them. Steam rose from the brown shadowy surface. She returned the cup to my hand.

"Now then, this current weight upon you, what's to be done about that?" she asked.

I looked up at the young woman then, wise in some ways, inno-cent in so many others. "Perhaps you should just hit my switch now and save us all some aggravation. How am I supposed to maintain my middle ground while sending a thousand people off to die?"

"Must you send so many?" Her plaintive tone made it clear I wasn't the only one having a hard time with this decision.

"To build a sustainable breeding pool, while also feeding the Arpex a bare minimum of sustenance? Yes. It should be more, but that's all I'm willing to offer."

She stared into her cup and swirled the contents. "Could you have others choose the offerings? The guilt would rest on them instead."

"That's not how this position works, Etara. The choice and the guilt are mine."

She nodded, running her fingertip around the edge of her cup. "Then we should make the best of it, yes?"

"If there was a best in this, I'd have jumped on it already. What are you suggesting?"

"Who makes you weary?"

"Who? Are you suggesting I handpick them? That's not very

Seeker-like of you."

She offered the slightest shrug, unblinking. Maybe she hadn't been kidding when she'd said I'd rubbed off on her.

"That's a very long list," I admitted, thinking of Daniel and my explanation of who was in my favor and who wasn't.

How many people were on that list that might only be temporary, like Gamnock had been? Like Jey? How many would never get the chance to redeem themselves? And knowing this, could there ever be any redemption for me once this deed was done?

"Do you have more than a thousand names?" she asked.

I shook my head. "Will you judge me for who I send?"

"I have no desire to be your judge. I'll settle for your conscience, as you put it. If, together, we can live with your choices, then our agreed-upon middle ground is maintained."

This task didn't feel very grey, but I appreciated my living conscience trying to convince me that it was.

"I'll think on it."

We drank our tea in silence, watching the shadows cast by the candle flames dance on the table, walls, and ceiling.

"May I ask you about something I saw in your mind?" she said.

I braced myself for any of a hundred uncomfortable questions. "Sure."

"You recently tried a drug that lowered inhibitions," she said.

"Tried, implies I used it intentionally. I didn't."

"Not judging, remember?" She shook her head. "Did you enjoy this drug? Did you find that it brought you closer to Anastassia, helped you overlook the other problems in your relationship to simply enjoy yourselves together?"

I found myself smiling as I thought fondly on that night. "We did do a lot of enjoying."

Etara's lips curled. She averted her gaze. "Is this drug safe, tested? Can you get more of it?"

"Yes. I had it altered, broken down. It's selling well. Making quite a tidy profit, actually."

She shook her head. "I probably don't want to know what else you sell for profit."

"Probably not." While the profits of my many ventures did support the good we were doing in the Narvan, many of the products themselves weren't in Etara's grey zone.

She took a hurried sip of her tea. "I was thinking it could be useful, in a therapeutic sense, for those in our care. For those like you and Anastassia, struggling with their relationships."

"I can get you some. Free of charge. I owe you."

"That would be appreciated. I would like to use it to help people, to help them enjoy like you..." She cleared her throat, grasping her cup with both hands.

I chuckled to myself. "Does talking about sex make you uncomfortable? I would think, in your line of work, it would come up quite regularly."

"It does, but your thoughts are rather singular and graphic when you see Anastassia during our sessions. You and I," she said, "we're a little too familiar."

"Ah." I was glad my memories of Etara had faded. She led a very lonely life in that regard. Not that mine, for all my singular and graphic thoughts had been much more fulfilling of late. Our sessions left us emotionally exhausted. Work killed the rest of our enthusiasm.

"Perhaps you could skip a session or two with me and instead use that time to solidify your relationship with Anastassia in ways that involve making memories instead of sharing them? That may also make both of you less weary."

"You're really covering all areas, aren't you?"

Etara smiled. "It's what I do."

"I never thought you'd be doing it with me."

"That makes two of us." She stood, carrying the pot and her cup to the counter. "It's late. You have a list to make. I have acolytes to train in five hours."

I stood and handed her my cup. To my dismay, my pants were still wet as was everything else. "I'll get this back to you next time."

She nodded, yawning.

With my arms full of wet clothes, armor, and weapons, I Jumped to my bedroom on Artor. I pried off the tight tunic and put on proper-sized clothes, then hung up my coat and stored my weapons. Grabbing a spare datapad from Stassia's pile on the table on her side of the bed, I headed out to the comfortable chair in the common room I'd come to frequently occupy of late. I had a list to make and I already knew who would be number one.

TWENTY-THREE

Stassia had been standing over my shoulder for several minutes. I continued typing and waited for the question. She held out longer than I anticipated. I finally craned around to look up at her.

"Top one hundred people you'd like to have die a slow and painful death?"

"What makes you say that?"

"Kess is number one."

"Yes, but I need far more than a hundred. The Arpex are taking a thousand annoyances off our hands. Payment for leaving the Narvan alone for good. And everywhere else, we can hope." I held up the datapad. "Look at me, doing the known universe a favor."

She squeezed into the chair next to me. "Can I help? If we're shipping annoyances off, I have quite a long list myself."

"Are you sure you want to take part in this?"

"Quit being such a damn martyr and hand me the pad already."

We spent the next couple hours condemning people to slavery and death. For such an unpleasant task, I couldn't have asked for a better partner.

With Etara's talk of reestablishing pleasure in our relationship buzzing around in my head, and Stassia right next to me, the boys gone with Meera, Neko and Hedvika sleeping, and Saka minding her own business at the security station, it seemed the perfect time—if it weren't for the task at hand. I sighed, wishing my life was a whole lot simpler.

"Vayen?"

I stopped staring at the growing list of names to look at her. The green of her eyes had never changed, but there were more lines around them. They crinkled as she smiled.

"What do you have on your agenda for today?" she asked.

"Whatever you're about to tell me to do, I imagine. Why?"

Stassia laughed softly. She took the pad from my hands, turned it off, and set it aside. "I'd like to see Daniel. Markus too, for that matter. Would you take me to the fleet for a little while? Being there might help me feel closer to—" her voice faltered.

I knew exactly what she meant. Ikeri wasn't here. She was out there somewhere and being out there, floating in between here and there, it did somehow make her feel more in reach. Maybe it was seeing the ship and crew actively searching for her, seeing that something was happening, something other than the rush of daily life pulling us along as if our daughter had never existed.

"Yes, of course." I rested my forehead against hers. "I can work from there just as well."

She lifted her head. "I'm sure the boys would like to see you too."

"Right." I consulted my never-ending and utterly overwhelming list of tasks. One of them, I wasn't willing to put off now that I had Etara's knowledge to work from. "We need to stop and see Jey first."

"I would like that." She stood, pulling me out of the chair with her. "Give me a few minutes to get ready."

"Mind if we do this the official way?" I asked. "It's been a while since we've been in the public eye and the news feeds are full of speculation about my condition in light of the rumors lit by those returning from the war with the Arpex and your more accurate statement.

She nodded. "That will take longer, but I suppose that's a good idea. No armor then, or hell, anything else. Are you sure this is safe? Last time you went out in public you got pulsed."

"About time I fully recovered from that, I think. Now that I can either rip Arpex apart with my bare hands or command them to leave with just a few words,—I haven't decided which rumor I like best—are people really going to try to screw with me?"

"We're not taking any chances," she decreed.

I surveyed my casual clothes. "Doesn't make much an impression, does it?"

"On me or them? I rarely get to see you this way, when you're conscious, that is." She grinned. "I like it."

"Noted, but I was referring to the general populace."

She sighed dramatically. "It's never about what I want, is it?"

Her antics, despite everything weighing heavily on me, made me laugh. "It might be later."

"I'd like that too." Stassia turned serious. "We have a hard time finding later lately. Let's work on finding something suitable for now."

I nodded and followed her into the large closet. She reached for the pile of seldom worn pants. My heart raced as she worked her way down the stack. Thank Geva, she stopped one pair from where the vials were hidden. Vastly relieved to avoid that conversation, I didn't argue when she handed me a pair of black pants that, from the lack of wrinkles, stains, or tears, I gathered I'd never worn. They even had creases down the front after I'd put them on. They were too stiff and scratchy, which is probably why I'd never worn them. When she handed me a pressed white shirt, complete with a half collar like most of the governing class wore, I gave her a questioning look.

"I may have gotten you a few things since we stepped into the public eye. There just hasn't been much call for wearing them yet."

"You know I hate wearing white. It makes me feel like a giant, glowing target."

She gestured impatiently for me to put the shirt on. It fastened diagonally across the front under a wide band of soft, shiny fabric. It was a shame the whole shirt wasn't made of that because the rest didn't move with me like I was used to.

When I reached for my boots, she shook her head.

"Really? What else are you going to torture me with?"

Stassia shoved a pair of black slip-on half boots polished to a gleaming shine into my hands. Despite the weight being all wrong, they were quite comfortable.

"Here is where we compromise a little more." She pulled a long black coat off a hanger and held it out to me.

The fabric and general cut mimicked a high-end businessmen's coat, but the feel of it revealed its armored quality. I slid my arms in and settled onto my shoulders. It hung halfway down my thighs, shorter than my usual armor. The weight was only a quarter of what I was used to, but I rather liked the flow of it. With my skin altered, I didn't need the full armor anyway. She'd even had extra pockets installed inside with access slits hidden by accent trim on the outside.

"Do you like it?" she asked.

"I do."

She grinned. "Me too. One more thing though."

I braced myself for whatever else she might have in store but was caught unaware when she caught hold of my hair clasp and released it. My hair fell over my shoulders, damn near halfway down my back.

Longer than I'd realized. I hadn't paid much attention to it lately.

"You know that's going to be in the way if anything arises," I said.

"The other governing leaders don't wear their hair back. You should blend in more."

"They also don't wear it this long. I could cut it if you give me a few minutes."

She jumped in my path to the bathroom. "Don't you dare."

"Wow, all right then."

"Remember that thing you did with the braids? From when you showed me when you came to us on Pentares? I liked that. Will that work?"

"You liked that?"

"I never said I did?"

I shook my head.

"Yes, well, if our therapy sessions have revealed anything, it's that we don't talk enough." She guided me out of the closet and onto the edge of the bed. Her fingers made quick work of the braids. When she finished, she stood back and smiled.

I chuckled. "What was that look you claimed Saka gave me? Like she wanted to give me a tongue bath?

She snickered, shaking her head as she headed back to the closet. "I'll be right back."

When she returned a few minutes later, she was wearing her regular grey and black clothes along with her armor and scuffed boots.

"And what in all the hells is that about? I have to be uncomfortable and you get to be all business as usual?"

"You like me in business as usual."

"I do, but I thought we were making an impression."

"No, you were making an impression, Advisor. I'm just along as your bodyguard." She grinned and our bond flared. "You're going to need it."

"Stassia, you're just as much of an advisor as I am. You've proven that while I've been gone or next to dead the past few months."

"Shut up and let me stand next to you so I can enjoy the view."

I didn't know what happened to her bitter, jealous streak, but this was much better. Even if it meant dressing in this shit on occasion.

"Besides," she said, "The public has been clamoring to see you since that pulse attack. It's like I don't even exist."

"They know you exist. You deal with them as much as I do. More so, lately."

She shrugged. "I'm just the day-to-day asshole. You're the special asshole who plans the defeat of the Fragians, hunts the Arpex, almost joins the High fucking Council, though that only makes you special to me, and now the damned Arpex are bowing to you too."

"Arpex can't bow."

"Yes, well, you did manage to get the Arpex to help defend the Narvan in spite of their original intent. That's done wonders to repair your public image."

"You realize I ended up mostly dead after all those things you call special? I'd gladly settle for day-to-day asshole right beside you."

"You're not." She kissed me. "And today I get to enjoy this, so let's get moving. I ordered a transport while I was getting ready. It should be here by now."

We headed out of the bedroom. "Do we want Saka along too?" I asked.

She gave me her narrow-eyed laser look of doom. Apparently, she wasn't quite over that yet.

"No, then. Got it."

Saka, upon Stassia informing her we were leaving, had objections to that plan that I didn't entirely disagree with. Stassia did seem distracted, and I *had* been pulsed last time. What concerned me most was that Stassia didn't have the protection of Arpex altered skin. Having an extra person on alert wasn't a bad idea. However, having that person be Saka, who was looking at me much like Stassia in the bedroom, was definitely a bad idea.

"Neko?" I offered.

"He's sleeping. Sorry, you're all mine," Stassia called as she headed out the door and into the waiting transport.

I joined her in the transport after putting Saka on standby.

The drive to the University passed with me on my link, hurrying through as much as I could get done in an hour. Stassia was also engrossed in her datapad so I didn't feel too bad about the silence.

When the transport came to a halt and the door chimed, indicating we'd arrived, we both quit working and exited onto the front entrance. It took only seconds for the first vid bot to identify me. Three more hovered nearby before we got halfway up the bank of stairs.

I could just imagine what the news feeds were saying about my reappearance. Not only after the public release of my role in turning the tide on the Arpex but also in the wake of the earlier statement Stassia and I had released regarding our daughter's abduction and

Jey and Kess's role in it, speculation over the future of the Narvan was running rampant. Was there enough of the two of us to steer both the Narvan and Kess's Rakon worlds? Would the Fragians maintain their truce or take advantage of the change in leadership? Were we neglecting our duties to search for Ikeri? And now, showing up, dressed like this, they'd be wondering what the hells I was planning next. I could already hear the evening news feed claiming that I planned to oust the Premier and take on Artor myself. Like I had time for that.

Security waited at the entrance, waving us up the stairs. Le'rin seemed peeved I hadn't notified him of our arrival so that he could adequately do his job, or at least appear to be doing his job. Stassia could do it much better, but I had to remember that we cared about appearances now.

With the arrival of the vid bots, a crowd had begun to gather, no one wanting to miss out on what might be going on. The fact that people near me had died in a pulse blast last time didn't seem to keep them away. Maybe that's what Le'rin was annoyed about, me not giving him time to clear the entrance. I'd have to remember to attempt to follow proper procedure next time, not for my safety, but everyone else's.

We made it inside without incident, other than some shouting, which may have been positive or not. It was hard to tell from the distance and with all the traffic noise. It wouldn't have surprised me if it wasn't. Though Stassia seemed confident that we were back in public favor, I had a feeling it was more that they were hesitant to protest given that I could now apparently control Arpex. Fear didn't mean favor, but hopefully, that would come in time.

The security team brought us in. I made sure not to appear hurried and to turn to look into the cameras before the feeds were cut off at the doors.

We made our way into the University, being seen by those visiting for their own reasons. It wasn't until we got past the general public areas that we ditched the security detail and hurried deeper inward to the area where Canelli kept Jey and Kess.

Before we made it very far, a young man in a shirt denoting he worked in medical research approached us.

"Excuse me, Advisors." He gave us both a hesitant look before settling his attention on me. "I'm sure you're very busy, but we just got notice you were here and this will only take a moment. Would you please follow me?"

Stassia went on alert beside me, her work mask slipping into place as one hand rested near a slit in her armor. As it turned out, he led us most of the way we'd been heading anyway. He stopped at a block of offices just before the hallway that led to the room where my victims were kept. Opening the door for us, he stepped aside.

Stassia went in first. I followed right behind. A small woman sat at a desk, her back to us, a datapad in her trembling hand. With a disgusted grunt, she tossed it onto the desk beside her and spun around.

"What now?" she yelled. Upon seeing us, her eyes went wide. "Oh. He found you. And you actually came."

"Hello, Nan." I shook my head. "I'm glad to see you've recovered."

Stassia gave the square room a thorough look, but there was nothing there but a desk covered in whatever projects Nan was trying to work on, two chairs, in one of which she sat, and the three of us. Giving us a little room, Stassia excused herself to the doorway.

"Recovered." She snorted. "Damned nerve damage can't be fixed. Ruined my career."

"You're alive and conscious. That's a vast improvement from the last time I saw you."

The contentious woman's eyes drooped and she sat more slumped than I remembered.

"I suppose I have you to thank for this." Nan held up her left arm. It shook even as she made an obvious effort to hold the limb still. "Better than being dead, I guess."

"Looks like you're still working even with the ruined career."

"I can still oversee projects. I just can't take part in them. No more operating for me." She sat back and looked me over. "I hear you've been busy exploring your alterations. Is this a new one too?" She waved her less trembling hand at my clothing.

"Her idea." I nodded to Stassia. "Speaking of alterations, I might be able to help you with that nerve problem. Maybe. If you want me to take a look?"

"Canelli has been after me to ask you to do that. He's been gushing about your abilities." Nan rolled her eyes. "Oh, don't get that pinched and pissy look. He works for me. Why else do you think he was assigned to you?"

I hadn't given it much thought considering everything else that was going on. "Anastassia had that all set up when I was—"

"Unconscious, I heard about that too." She sighed again and held out her hand. "All right then. Do whatever it is you do, and we'll see if I turn out any better than your Advisor friends in the other room."

Her tone made me seriously consider walking out without another word, but then my conscience adopted Etara's voice to remind me about the grey zone I was supposed to be maintaining.

I pushed her hand down to rest on her lap and sat next to her. "Just relax for a few minutes."

I accessed the training I'd taken from Etara, searching for anything related to healing along the lines of what Ikeri had done for Stassia to regain the use of her mind speech. Like the singularity, these lessons were diffused. It took some effort to dig deep into them and bring them back into focus. Finding what I needed, I centered myself in the seat and wisped into Nan.

Her mind was full, working on a large number of projects at once, monitoring numerous teams, funding, results, and weighing the consequences of them all. She was a brilliant woman, even if I didn't like her very much. I got the sense that the feeling was mutual.

The state of concentration needed to see into the body rather than just the mind was much deeper than I'd gone before. Opening my internal eyes, as Etara thought of it, I saw three mounds of blue energy. Two were bright, one had flickers of grey running through it.

Was this how Seekers saw people when they worked on them? I'd never considered that they saw anything differently.

I followed the lines of energy within Nan's body, both big and small, seeking out the flickers. Even though I could see them clearly, nothing in my stolen knowledge was aimed at fixing them. I moved on to the broken connections, but had no luck connecting the ends of those either. Resolved to do something helpful, I made note of which connections controlled her arm and where the flickers were. Her spine had also fallen prey to the poison, whether Nan realized it or not. When I was sure I had all the damage assessed, I returned to my body.

"I wish I could be of more help, but I'm not familiar enough with all the intricate anatomy or how to fix it. I'm guessing you are though. Would you consent to me providing you with the memory of what I've found?"

"I'm not sure what you mean, but sure, I suppose so."

"Think of the last time you looked for a solution to your problem."

Nan regarded me now with a bemused smile. "What in Geva's name did we create when we altered you?"

It wasn't the alteration necessarily, but stealing Etara's training.

However, I didn't correct her, thinking that a little more positive spin on the Arpex alteration might not hurt.

"I'm sure you've heard a lot of words for it, though most of those are derogatory."

She nodded, not offering to add to the host of slurs people had been using for me and the other hunters.

I opened my mind to Nan, accessing the spot she held open in her memory and inserted all the information I'd gathered as gently as I could manage.

She leaned back in her chair, seemingly lost in thought for a moment. When she came back to herself, she grinned. "That is simply amazing. Thank you."

Damn, she truly sounded sincere. "You're welcome." I started for the doorway.

"Advisor?"

"Yes?" I turned back around.

"What the others are saying about you, they're wrong."

I wasn't at all sure about that, but it was nice to hear someone say so, especially coming from the normally intractable Nan. Stassia took my arm and extracted me from the office.

"I don't need you undoing the fear-the-Arpex-destroyer vibe we've got going on." She smiled. "It's keeping everyone in line so nicely and making my job easier."

"Speaking of keeping people in line..." I slowed our pace. "Etara kind of has a kill switch on me."

Stassia's head whipped toward me and she came to an instant stop. "What?"

"You know how this Seeker stuff works, keeping the balance and all that." I shrugged, trying to ease the sharp anxiety pounding through our bonded connection. "I stole her training, and as a trade-off, I'm supposed to maintain a neutral status, do good to balance out the bad. If she gets wind that I'm not, she can snap her fingers or some shit and I'm done."

"Absolutely not," she hissed through clenched teeth. "Your life is in my hands, no one else's."

"I love you too."

She smiled but gripped my arm tighter. "How much good do you plan on doing here because we have a thousand people to send to their deaths."

"As much as I can, I guess." I guided her to Canelli's lab.

Jey, the Jalvian crewman, and Kess lay on their beds, eyes closed, breathing thanks to the machines that lined the walls. Stassia went to Jey. I approached Kess.

"If I'm going to ship him off with the Arpex, I suppose I should fix him. They don't like spoiled food."

"He's spoiled all right," Stassia said.

"I'm sending most of his staff with him along with all the Masters that I've been able to locate."

"The Nebula is going to be deserted when you're done." She smoothed the lightweight blanket covering Jey and then sat on the stool beside him.

"Hardly, but his slaves will be free."

"Will any of them know how to be free? What will they do? How will they live?" She shook her head. "It would be kinder to bring in the families from Merchess and let them set up on Twelve and Thirteen. They treat their slaves well, give them a decent living. They're also profitable for us."

"How can you say that having seen Saka, Meera, and Hedvika make the progress they have? They're doing just fine being free."

"That's three women, in our care, not an entire populace."

"That entire populace is also in our care." I shook my head. "We're not going to argue about this right now."

Her brows rose. "I wasn't aware we were arguing."

"We're about to. Some of the Merchessian family members are on my list too."

Her lips drew tight, fingers curling at her sides. "We need to discuss this."

"Later. I need to concentrate."

I spotted a second stool in the corner. After retrieving it, I sat next to Kess. He'd be good practice for fixing the crewman before I hopefully worked my way up to fixing Jey. If I screwed Kess up permanently, that wasn't all bad.

"Can you locate Canelli? I'm sure he'll want to monitor this. It will take me a few minutes to prepare."

She was still far from smiling, but she did get Canelli, who took up a post near me with his monitoring equipment in hand and an eager expression. Stassia stood near him, giving me some space, at least physically. Her forceful waves of emotion over our connection clearly said I was making a big mistake about the slavery issue.

Feeling confident after helping Nan, I muffled our connection, and with the room gone dark and silent in my mind, wisped into Kess. It was easier now that I could see the clear path for myself, the channels, forks, branches, all working together to create a functional life form. Parts of the system were threaded with a mesmerizing pulse of midnight blue and silver.

Seeking out the lines where the blue light thinned and became gaps, I began to get an idea of what functions I'd broken. In the back of my mind, I began to note what the specific lines controlled so I'd know how to attack more effectively in the future. Etara probably would not have approved. Good thing she wasn't present

Once I'd isolated the area that controlled his breathing and organ functions, I concentrated my efforts there. The damage was different than it had been in Nan. The broken connections almost seemed to call to me. Fitting two ends together, I hesitantly let go. They stayed. Victorious, I continued weaving lines back together, pulling them tight. Healing took energy directly from me, but it was quite gratifying to see progress. I was doing this, fixing him, making him whole again. For once, I held the power to make something truly better, something I could apply to others that I hadn't had a hand in breaking. The elation was so intense that it knocked me out of the healing state.

Bright lights blinded me. I covered my eyes and tried to catch my breath. Stassia's hand was on my shoulder.

"Are you all right? You were way gone there for a bit."

"I think so, yes." I blinked until the room came back into focus. "How is he?"

"Much improved," said Canelli. "I'm assuming you want him to remain sedated?"

"Keep him restrained and sedated enough to prevent Jumping, but let's wake him," I said. "We need to make sure his mind is functional."

"If he's awake, he's going to be a problem," said Stassia. "You know he can work a deal with almost anyone."

"The only deal he's going to work with the Arpex is whether they eat him for lunch or dinner."

"You're really going to do this?" she asked.

"Is that a problem?" I unmuffled our connection, allowing me a better idea of what was going on behind her work face. I opened my thoughts to her too, wanting to make sure we were both in agreement on this.

She pondered his face, the man who had been her partner before me, whom she had entertained affection for at one time, who I knew still had some version of feelings for her. He'd asked about her, and it sure as all hells hadn't been for my benefit or to be polite.

Kess had always looked out for himself, but he had worked with us, sat at our table, and hashed out solutions long into the night for the betterment of the Narvan and the Nebula. He had his uses and moments of being a decent person.

He was also the reason our daughter was lost out there somewhere with a slaver as her only companion.

"No," she said. "Do it."

While we waited for Kess to come around, I moved the stool to the Jalvian crewman's side.

Sinking into the healing state, I was dismayed to find the connections were more disrupted than they'd been in Kess. rejoining his lines took twice as much energy and there were many levels of disconnection. I'd only made one swipe at Kess, just enough to take him down, but the crewman had suffered a more prolonged attack. I tried working on the fine lines more than the larger ones as that took less energy. Once I'd made some headway, I pulled back to my own body to find Canelli running a scanner over him.

"How is he?"

"Better, but he's got much further to go before he'll be ready to wake."

"I'll be back to make another pass."

Then I moved to Jey's bed.

"Don't wear yourself out," Stassia said, now standing behind me like a shadow.

"I won't."

Though I wanted to fix Jey right then and there, I first needed to know how much damage there was. Having done this a few times now, the deep state came upon me quickly, allowing me a clear image of Jey's internal workings. Devastation. So many torn connections, the dark blue and silver I'd seen in Kess and the crewman, vibrant and full of energy, were non-existent in Jey. I'd been angry, and perhaps rightfully so, but while I had no qualms about feeding Kess to an Arpex, seeing Jey like this left me hollow. I fell out of the healing state and couldn't get out of the room fast enough. Stassia was right on my heels.

"What is it? Are you all right"?

"I need a few minutes. Alone."

She nodded and backed away. I sensed she was right inside the doorway, but at least she was out of sight. She couldn't see what I'd done, not beyond the outward effects.

At the time, Stassia may have given her permission to terminate Jey, but from the way she'd looked at him on that bed, she regretted it.

Not as much as I did.

I hated to keep running to Etara, but I had so many questions. If Seekers could fix people, why had Tomias needed the doctors I'd sent? Why were there sick and injured people all over Prime despite having Seekers in almost every city? Why had no one been able to truly heal Stassia when we lived on Minor? It made no sense.

All the times I'd been hurt that Ikeri had been beside me, had she had a hand in holding me together, repairing what she could? I'd never quite gotten that sense from her. She'd helped Stassia regain her mind speech, but it had taken a long time and had seemed more of a therapy than any sort of major healing.

Maybe I was different. Maybe I hadn't lied to Nan, and the Arpex alteration allowed me to do this in combination with the stolen knowledge. Geva, truly being able to heal others would make what I'd endured worth it.

If I could heal the injuries the Council had inflicted, Stassia might be able to host a link again.

"Stassia, come here."

She was out in the hall in seconds, confirming my guess on her whereabouts.

"I need you to stand still. No talking. I want to look at something."

"For the record, you're acting all weird again, but why not." She stood against the wall and waited.

I slipped into the deep state and examined the pulsing blue of her. A fully functioning being was quite a glorious sight. The dark blues fully accented the silver highlights and the mid-tones efficiently worked to maintain the body.

There were a few spots where the lines didn't match up, where they'd rejoined off-center or at a new access point. I gathered these were injuries that had healed under poor or less than ideal circumstances. Unless I took it upon myself to sever the connections and try to reattach them as they should be, she would remain as she was. I didn't think she'd thank me for taking her apart to possibly put her back together just to alleviate a few aches.

As I followed a pale trail that ran upward along her spine, branching out in fine threads throughout her body, I came to a gap. Not even a gap, but an empty chasm—darkness that no lines, pale or otherwise touched. A pale network of threads bypassed this gap and connected with the swirl of silver that was her mind.

The hole had once held her link. The lines around it reconnected at odd angles, branching and re-branching at the edges of the chasm. There were no severed ends to bridge the gap, nothing to refill the place that the implant was built to access. Those lines had been repurposed, reworked. I got a sense of Ikeri in some of them, as though she'd left her imprint.

There was nothing I could do.

I backed out of the deep state and turned away. Even with everything I'd learned from Etara, I couldn't fix Stassia.

She rested her hand on my arm. "What's wrong?"

"Nothing. You're fine." I tried to hide my disappointment. "Quite beautiful inside actually."

She rolled her eyes but smiled. "You're not getting all soft on me again are you?"

"No."

"Good. I don't think I could take that on top of you all cleaned up nice like this."

I gave her a quick hug. If anyone was going soft, it was her.

She stepped out of my arms and glanced at the doorway. "So, Jey?"

"I need to talk to Etara."

"Now?"

"It won't take long."

"What's going on with you two? You've both been all peculiar with each other. I never thought I'd wish for the clarity of your mutual shunning, but I do."

I figured I might as well tell her the truth. Maybe honesty was becoming a new habit. "When I was gone, when I woke with her memories, it was more than that. I kind of inadvertently took all her Seeker training and copied it into my own memory."

"Kind of? Is that what you were doing in there with Kess? It wasn't just reversing what you learned from the Arpex? How did you..." She slapped me in the chest. "You're not a Seeker. You can't—"

I grabbed her, holding her close before she did more than slap me. "I don't know what I am anymore. That's why I need to see Etara. I need to fix Jey."

"I suppose healing is less...weapony. More Artorian and less Arpex?" she said against my chest. "I'm glad you didn't kill him."

"Me too, but this isn't any better. I need to fix him or we have to let him go."

"I won't pretend to understand what you mean by fixing or how you did what you did to him or those Arpex, but if Etara can help, go."

"Would you like to be with the boys or wait here?"

"With them. Meera and Hedvika are there," she said.

"Then let's take the transport back home first. I think I owe you a little more time to enjoy yourself."

She smiled. "Maintaining public appearances, you mean."

"Both?"

"I'll take it."

She ducked back into the room to speak to Canelli and then took hold of my arm, leading us back to the public areas of the University.

Those areas were now full, lined with Artorians and Jalvians alike, all watching our every move. It seemed we'd attracted a waiting crowd upon our arrival. The hum of the murmuring masses filled the air along with the smell of too many people crammed together. Le'rin got his team to work clearing a path to the doors for us.

"Do you have anything you'd like to say to them?" asked Stassia.

"Leave us the hells alone?"

"I was thinking something more like an official statement regarding the Arpex situation," she clarified.

"Pay no attention to the vast numbers of missing people in the upcoming days. We're simply shipping them off to feed the Arpex. Nothing to be alarmed about."

She gave me a look. "Maybe no statement then."

"You think?" I said under my breath as I smiled and waved at the crowd.

We slowly made our way out the door, down the steps, and into a waiting transport. Stassia stuck by my side with a forced smile and watched the crowd intently.

When the doors of the transport sealed around us, we both let out a sigh of relief. The ride back to the house passed in the same manner as the ride there. We got out and I went in to change.

She caught my hand. "Don't."

"I can't go to the fleet like this."

"Sure you can. You look like you're in charge. Officially, I mean. With Jey out of the picture, you are in charge. Enjoy it."

"I find very little enjoyable about any of this."

"You do though, even though you complain and stress about it."

She cocked a brow. "You wouldn't know what to do if we weren't advising the Narvan. Nothing else would make you happy."

"You make me happy."

"I will accept that answer." She kissed my cheek. "Now take me to the boys so you can go play Seeker with Etara. But don't you dare come back with tattoos all over your head."

TWENTY-FOUR

Given my attire, I opted for waiting for Etara on the bench in the garden rather than in the grass. Eight older acolytes sat in a circle around her near the main house. I couldn't hear them over the younger children who played nearby.

When her class finished, she approached me with open caution. Etara pointed at my clothes. "What's this all about?"

"Anastassia is attempting to improve my public image."

"She gets my vote." She sat down beside me. "Tomias is here, do you mind if he joins us? I've filled him in on our situation."

"Sure."

It must not have been a question, because Tomias was already on his way out of the back door of the main house. He walked stiffly, his arms unmoving at his sides and jaw held tight. He came to stand facing us and avoided looking at me.

"I have questions," I said.

"I'm sure," said Etara. "Can you be more specific?"

"Medical healing, why don't you do that here? Why did you need the doctors I sent if you could fix people on your own?"

That got Tomias's attention. "What do you mean fix people?"

"Heal them." The question seemed quite clear to me, but I attempted to remain patient.

"We help them as we can," said Etara.

"Yes, but the people who are sick and in pain, why don't you heal them?"

"We focus on the wellbeing of the mind. A healthy mind, helps maintain a healthy body," said Tomias.

"We can't just heal people, Advisor," said Etara. "We use the gifts we are given to do what good we can. My strength is in soothing minds, Tomias in offering comfort. Ikeri excels at helping to recover lost or fading abilities.”

“I saw that. She reworked the connections in Anastassia’s brain so that she could use mind-speech again.”

Tomias drew his arms up to his chest, the sleeves of his robe dangling in front of him. “What do you mean, saw?”

“After I fixed someone else, I went inside Anastassia to see if I could fix her so she could host a link again. The affected area had Ikeri’s imprint all over it.”

They glanced at one another. Etara sat up straight and said slowly, “How did you fix someone?”

“Two people, actually. The men I hurt with the Arpex ability, I went inside him and put the threads back together. I tried to do that with Anastassia, but Ikeri had rerouted the connections. There was nothing left to reattach. It was the same with her old injuries, though those weren’t as neatly done, they’d healed on their own. The only way to fix those seemed to be to take them apart and then try to put them back together correctly. Is that how it’s supposed to work?”

“No,” Tomias’s voice rose as he seared his displeasure into Etara. “What perverse thing have you created?”

“Wait.” Etara tapped Tomias’s arm and all but physically yanked his attention to me. “You put connections back together? You healed people?”

I nodded.

“There’s a prime example of balance maintaining itself,” she said to Tomias.

“Have you tried this with anyone else?” she asked me.

“Not fixing, but I did go inside Nan so I could see what was wrong with her. Parts of her body flickered inside, and there were also broken connections, but I couldn’t do anything about them. Her damage was different than the kind I caused, but I did gave her the memory of what I’d seen so maybe other doctors could help.”

Etara appeared both pleased and mystified. She called over one of the young boys who had been playing. “Can you stand still for a few minutes, Urial? The Advisor here is trying to practice his lesson.”

The boy grinned and did his best to stand still.

I slipped into the deep focus and went over his body, following the pulsing blue lines until I found a gap in his stomach. The lines faded to grey at the ends like they were withering. As I’d done before, I drew the end of one line toward the one it should connect with. They stretched well enough, but would not reconnect. I tried again with a different set. Again the two ends shrank back as if repelled from one another. It was like Nan all over again.

The process had been easy with Kess and the crewman, like the broken lines had been magnetized. Confused and frustrated, I returned to myself.

"I can see the problem, but I can't make the lines reconnect. What am I doing wrong?"

"What did you see?" Tomias asked.

I pointed to the exact spot on the boy's stomach and explained what I'd seen. Both of them seemed rather taken aback. Tomias dismissed the boy.

"But you couldn't repair him the way you did before?" Tomias asked.

"No."

Etara nodded. "You're not doing anything wrong. It's clear where Ikeri got her healing gifts. Her's are slightly different, I think, but our gifts all vary, so that is to be expected." She stood, tucking her hands into her sleeves like Tomias. "I do wonder if this is an ability your people all share or something partial to you. Gifts are not hereditary for us. The call to be a Seeker is rare."

She looked to Tomias. "Can you imagine a whole world full of untapped ability?"

"Or was this line chosen for a purpose?" he asked.

"Can we focus here? My immediate purpose is to fix Jey. I made a mess of him and I need to know the best route to go about undoing the damage. It feels like too much. I don't know where to start. Why can I fix some people, but not others?"

"It would seem you can only heal what you have broken," said Tomias. "Their severed connections bear your imprint. They are attuned to you. Nan and Anastassia do not, and Uriel was born this way. You do not have any imprint on them to work with." He turned to look at the boy who was again running around with the others and then spun back to me. "And before you ask, creating damage to make an imprint, will not allow you to fix damage that existed before yours."

Was he in my head? Having spent so much time with Etara lately, I'd forgotten how much Seekers used to unnerve me for exactly that reason.

"That's not to say that your skill for diagnosing others isn't also useful. The level of detail you relayed makes me think you see more clearly than any of us," he added.

"It's not much good to see the problem if I don't have the solution."

Etara smiled. "That's what doctors are for. You could be a very valuable asset to them. You said you did this with, Nan, was it?"

I nodded, seeing what she was getting at. Diagnosing others could be useful, but it didn't help me with Jey.

"I don't have time to be an asset to anyone else. My commitment schedule is already full into the next lifetime," I said.

Etara gave me a pointed look. "Making time would help you maintain the balance we agreed upon."

I sighed. "I'll think about it."

"As to fixing your friend, I'm afraid you're on your own. The gift you have is not one we share," she said.

That was less than helpful. "I'll let you go then. I have far too much work to do to ponder this further today."

I took my leave of them, but rather than going to the fleet to meet with Stassia and the boys, I found myself in the foyer of Jey's house.

Dallarayn yelped at my arrival and ran for her mother. Dayana rushed into the room, the former hospitality slave right beside her.

"Advisor, we weren't expecting you." Dayana's hands shook. She clasped them together and stepped closer to her companion before gesturing me toward the common room and a chair.

"It's been a long time. I'm sorry I haven't been here sooner, but I wanted to make sure you were all right in Jey's absence."

She crept closer. "So he's alive then?"

"Did the University not provide information on his condition? You haven't been to see him?"

"We've heard nothing beyond your statements and the news reports of his incarceration and guilt. Why is he at the University on Artor rather than a prison? What...condition?"

"I'm so sorry." Guilt hit me hard. I reached for the chair she'd offered and sat. Had I dropped this ball so badly that I'd forgotten it was even in play once Jey was not a threat? Was I so busy trying to keep the Narvan at peace and find Ikeri that I'd neglected Jey's family entirely? The confusion on Dayana's face said that I certainly had. "To prevent further upheaval between Artor and Jal, I haven't allowed the release of much information on your husband. He suffered grievous injuries."

Etara's imagined prickle of conscience became a jab. The truth then. Jey's family deserved that, and if Dayana felt the rest of her people needed to know what kind of monster I was, well, I supposed I'd held off the details long enough.

"The two of you fought. The way you do. Guns. Knives. Blood," she said, holding my gaze steadily. "He kept it out of the house, out of our lives, our conversations, but it was always there on the edges, part of him."

"We fought, but this was different. I took him apart from the inside."

"So those rumors are true."

Dayana slipped into a seat across from me. Her companion stood behind her, watching me, curious. I didn't remember her name.

"He claimed your mutation gave you abilities our people needed. I've heard other whispers since, they filter down from the men and women who faced the Arpex with you. My father keeps them quiet. At your request, I assume."

"Yes, the rumors are true, but the rest," I rubbed my face, wishing she'd yell at me, blame me, anything but offer this stoic acceptance. "The rest is unnecessary. The alteration, at this time, only works on Artorians because telepathy is a required element."

"He did mention something about that."

I was sure he did, probably loudly and punctuated with many expletives. "I was angry when we fought, lost my temper. I caused much more damage than I intended."

She just stared at me with her blue eyes, eyes like Jey's who couldn't open them thanks to what I'd done.

"That's not true," I admitted. "I wanted to kill him. I did catch myself. Not that it justifies the current state he's in, but I'm going to try to heal him."

"Why?"

Her question caught me off guard. "So he can come home? So you can have your husband back?"

Dayana sat up, her voice firm. "This is no longer his home."

"What do you mean?"

"After I learned of his part in abducting your daughter, I met with my father. The marriage contract has been voided. Whether he lives or not is no concern of mine."

"You can't mean that. You were happy together." At least I thought so, from what little I knew of her since the Arpex had erased her from my mind.

"I thought I knew him, understood him. But I could never trust him again, not after what he did." She shook her head. "My allegiance is to my father, and you, of course."

I had no idea what to say to that. For all the fights Stassia and I had, the lies, the countless manipulations we couldn't or didn't share, memory losses, and almost deaths, we were still together.

"What he did was what he thought was best for your people. From what I can tell, he was under a lot of pressure."

"Not from my father. He wouldn't go against you like that," she said quickly. "There is no need to defend him. What he did was wrong, children are not pawns. Not only your daughter but mine. He demanded that Dallarayn and I be present when he knew you were coming to confront him. He meant to use us as a shield. That, I cannot forgive."

Her inability to use Jey's name grated on me. And to not want to see him. At all. Maybe that was the difference between being bonded and only having a marriage contract. Had Jey never shared a degree of the connection Stassia and I did? Had it always been a balance of business and politics and nothing more? They'd seemed happy on the surface, but she'd made it clear he didn't talk to her about what he was doing, he didn't run plans past her, didn't have someone to help make major decisions.

I reached out to Stassia, brushing over our bonded connection, grateful that she was there, even after all we'd dragged each other through, even if we weren't always on speaking terms or I was getting boots thrown at my head.

The thought made me chuckle.

Dayana must have been used to Jey splitting his attention between her and his link because my random laugh didn't even make her blink.

"I appreciate your loyalty," I said finally.

"Have you had any luck finding your daughter?"

"No. We're still looking." I glanced around the house, noting small things missing, and realized they were all Jey's things.

She noticed my wandering gaze. "All his belongings are in storage. I didn't know what you'd want me to do with them. I've seen the news feeds. You've been busy. I didn't want to bother you."

"You can contact me anytime with your link."

"Oh, I had that removed. I never liked it. I only got it because he insisted."

"I see."

She'd had everything at her fingertips and she'd stripped it away. I thought of all the years on Minor where I'd regretted giving up my link in order to keep Stassia safe. I'd done it because I'd had to. She'd removed it because she simply didn't like it. I couldn't fathom her choice, but she'd been through enough and didn't need my ranting. She had never truly been part of our world.

Dayana turned to her companion. "Please provide the Advisor with the location of the items that were removed from the house."

"Do you wish to see him?" I asked. "He's unconscious, but if it would offer some sense of closure?"

"That isn't necessary." She unclasped her hands and placed her palms on her lap, reverting to the political front of her upbringing. "My father would like to meet with you at your earliest convenience."

"I'm sure he'd like his full fleet back," I muttered.

"Oh, no, not at all. They are at your disposal until your daughter is found."

Well, that was a pleasant surprise. "I'll contact him in a day or two when I get time."

"I hope you don't mind," Dayana said, "but I dismissed the other two women you provided. They were unnecessary once he was gone."

"That's fine. Have they been placed elsewhere?"

"They've gone to my father's household. Will there be anything else?"

"I suppose not." I got up and went to the foyer where I spent a few minutes scratching out the patterns Jey had made there to establish a jump point. "Goodbye, Dayana."

She and the former hospitality slave both bowed their heads. "Goodbye, Advisor."

I Jumped back to the University and found the three men unattended. Kess and the crewman had been detached from some of the equipment. Jey seemed to be attached to more. One of Canelli's assistants hurried in.

"Can I help you?" she asked.

"How is he?" I asked, nodding to Kess.

"Fully recovered. We can wake him at any time."

"How long will that take?"

"An hour or so."

"Do it. I'll work on this one while I wait." Somewhat rejuvenated by my trip to Veria Prime, I sunk into the crewman and got to work repairing connections. When I returned to myself, I found that only half an hour had passed.

The assistant ran a scanner over the crewman and smiled. "We'll keep him here a couple of days for observation, but he should wake on his own now. What would you have done with him when that happens?"

I pondered the Jalvian who had defied my orders. "He is free to return to Jal, but not to the fleet currently under my control."

"I'll let Canelli know." The assistant returned to monitoring Kess.

After taking a few minutes to access the crewman's record through my link to note his insubordination and his reassignment to a desk job on his homeworld, I settled onto the stool beside Jey. "And him?"

"Not good, sir. We're doing all we can, but..."

I'd seen the sheer number of broken connections. They were facing an impossible task. So was I.

"I'll try to help. Let me know when the former advisor is ready."

Former advisor. I enjoyed saying those words.

"Of course, sir."

I contacted Daniel and let him know I'd be a couple hours late. He seemed very distracted. Stassia had that effect. I let him be and returned to the task at hand.

Sinking into the deep focus, I went over Jey's broken connections one by one, reattaching the most vital. Each one pulled at me, some more than others, sucking energy from my body to put his back together. Balance, as Etara would say.

By the time the assistant tapped on my shoulder to let me know Kess was coming around, I was hungry and exhausted and regretting the choice to push through the last several reconnections I'd made.

"He'll be alert enough to Jump soon," the assistant said.

"We can't have that."

I left my stool to lay a hand on Kess. He wore nothing but the undignified medical gown. The Arpex wouldn't care. I Jumped him to the point on the Arpex ship Neko had given me.

Summoning Yellow Stripe took a few moments of concentration, but Kess was still pretty out of it. The muffled sound of a herd of Arpex feet coming at us made the muscles between my shoulder blades seize up. I breathed in through my mouth and out threw my nose in an attempt to keep my panic at bay. Neko wasn't here to help me stay calm this time.

Yellow Stripe emerged from the host of others. *"What is this?"* it asked.

"More will come soon. This one is a gift."

Its claws clacked as it reached out for Kess.

"Before you eat, ask him a question. Snack first to wake him up,

make him taste better.”

The Arpex fairly beamed with an internal appreciation for my suggestion. That should have made me feel ill. It sure did the last time I was there. But it didn't now. The man who delivered my daughter to slavers, who had been a major point of aggravation in my life since I'd met Stassia, was going to die. The satisfaction surrounding this task outweighed the panic at being surrounded by Arpex.

“Ask him how to jump.”

“This is a good ask?”

“A small ask so he can't escape.”

I gave Kess a hard shake. “Wake up.”

He became less of a dead weight, picking up his head and looking around. “Where?”

“Ask now,” I prompted the Arpex.

Kess stammered something unintelligible and clung to me. Yellow Stripe chittered, its claws clacking merrily.

“Too small of an ask. Want more,” it said.

“Ask his name.”

The Arpex did as I ordered.

“What are you doing? What's happening?” Kess looked around, lost and confused.

“Who are you?” I asked him.

“I'm...I...I don't know.”

“Do you know how to jump?”

Kess hopped up and down. I grinned.

“Ask him where he lives.”

“You are a good Arpex,” Yellow Stripe said.

Arpex didn't normally snack in such quick succession. I wondered how scrambled it was making Kess's brain. I slapped his face. “Do you know who I am?”

“I don't like you.” He shook his head and blinked several times. “Asshole, Advisor.”

“There we go. And do you know why I don't like you either?”

“A girl. I took a girl. She's gone.”

“Yes. My daughter. You took the brightest thing in my world and you lost her.” I turned to Yellow Stripe. “Ask him who Anastassia is.”

“You can't have her.” Kess fought harder to get away.

I kept him firmly in my grasp. He faltered in his struggling, going quiet for a moment.

“That was a good ask. More?”

What else did Kess care about? Nothing other than credits came to mind. "Ask him what he loves."

Kess leaned heavily on me. All the rapid memory sucking had to be entirely disorienting. I shook him again. "Do you still know who I am?"

He snarled. "The biggest fucking asshole."

"Correct. You should have remembered that before you chose to turn on us." I shoved him over to Yellow Stripe. *"Eat now."*

Excitement hummed through the attending Arpex. Yellow Stripe's wing jaws snapped open. Digestive fluids glistened on the semi-transparent membranes.

The wing jaws enveloped Kess, barbed ends driving him against the shell. He screamed. The membranes undulated as he struggled, the barbs digging deeper with every movement. His cries grew louder. Then the acid started to work. His feet, still bare from his stay at the University, pounded on the soft floor in a frantic dance.

I watched all this, considering the brutal effectiveness of the Arpex feeding process, detached from the terror that had accompanied this experience all the times before. The membranes massaged his body, slowing his struggles. His feet dangled limply, inches above the floor. Fluid dripped in wet splatters beneath him, tinged red with blood.

I'd never had the fortitude to observe how long it took to fully digest a body before. When Sonia had died, I'd been too distraught and under the influence of the Council's restrictive field. When I'd served the Council's Arpex, watching it eat was the last thing I wanted to do. I'd fed it and turned away, or covered my head with my hands to block out the sounds. But this time the meal was one I was happy to provide. If I had wing jaws of my own, I would have enjoyed eating him alive myself.

Stassia had often preached at me early on in my employment: to do the job right you didn't screw around, you just killed the target. I'd waited a very long time to kill this one.

As it turned out, I was much later than I'd anticipated when I finally Jumped to the Jalvian fleet.

Everyone had gathered in our suite. They were finishing a meal. Stassia caught sight of me and hurried over.

"Where have you been? Are you all right?"

I hugged her. The smell of the food made my stomach rumble and cramp with need. "You know what? I'm good. Hungry and tired, but good."

"Good, and you managed to keep your shirt clean? That's a first."

"Yes, well, I gave the Arpex plenty of space to eat."

She froze. "You didn't."

"Kess was number one," I shrugged. "A gesture of good faith, if you will."

"So he's gone?"

I thought about the gloppy mess the Arpex had left behind. "Yes."

"And you fed him to the Arpex." She said quietly, glancing at the boys who were watching us with interest.

Meera and Hedvika left their empty plates on the table and walked out. Glad to have a little time alone with my family, I didn't object.

"Yes, I did."

"And you're good," she said flatly.

"Let me rephrase that. I feel good as in lighter and satisfied. Having just fed our business partner to our enemy probably cancels out the other use of that word."

She detached herself from my side. "I need a minute. Go eat if you're hungry after that."

I was. Terribly so since working on Jey.

I left her to decide if she was relieved, pissed, mourning, or whichever of the mass of emotions she chose to settle on that were wafting my way. Markus ran over to hug me. Daniel did not.

After giving Markus a few minutes of my attention, I went to sit with Daniel. I foraged through what was left of the food and assembled a reasonable meal. That's when I noticed Stassia and Markus had also vacated the room.

I set my fork down before I'd even begun and gave Daniel my full attention. "I take it you have something you'd like to say?"

The muscles along his jaws twitched. He sat, glowering at me under dark and lowered brows. "You left me here alone. For a week."

"You could have Jumped home anytime." I realized I'd never finished my reply to him either. There was just too damned much going on.

"Could I? Who would be here to listen for Ikeri?" he said with a snarl.

"The length of my absence wasn't intentional."

He didn't blink. "It never is."

"No one killed me," I said, hoping to diffuse his ire by pointing out that I'd granted his request.

"Close enough, according to mom. Do you have any idea how worried Markus was? Any of us? Do you ever think of the consequences before charging headlong into whatever crazy thing you're doing?"

Good Geva, just who the hells was the parent here? I considered throwing some calm at him, but were I in his place, it would have only pissed me off further: manipulating, Etara's voice of conscience informed me.

"I don't always get time to consider the consequences beyond the bigger picture. In this case, it was do the crazy thing or surrender to the Arpex and watch you all get eaten. Isn't your freedom worth me dropping out of your life for a week?"

"A week?" He scoffed. "You've been absent more than you've ever been around."

"And yet, you've turned out just fine."

If I'd ever wondered what it was like to be on the receiving end of my not at all friendly smile, I now knew.

He sat there glaring until I wondered if he was thinking about taking a swing at me. Eventually, his ire dialed down to sharp disdain. "Nice suit."

"Your mother's doing." I hazarded taking a few bites before my stomach ripped its way out of my body to find its own sustenance. "We went to the University. Publicly. I'm trying to heal Jey."

When he still didn't say anything, I ate a little more. "How is the search for Ikeri going?"

"Do you see Ikeri? Brustus was a dead end."

I sat back and took a deep breath. "You're pissed. I get it. I promise I didn't intend to leave you here on your own. What do you want me to say?"

His gaze wavered. "I don't know."

"Me either." I resumed eating. "I did just feed Kess to an Arpex if that makes you feel any better."

"Very funny."

"I wasn't joking."

"So now you'll have to oversee the nebula too?" Daniel started to sound his age, his anger cracking to expose the emotions that lay beneath. "I can't do this by myself. You need to be here."

"I've been overseeing the nebula already. The investors have been dealt with. The Arpex will be leaving shortly. Other than working on Jey. I'll be focusing on finding Ikeri."

"Along with advising the Narvan."

"No. Your mother can handle the Narvan."

He let out a heavy sigh. "Why are you trying to help him anyway?

He's part of the reason Ikeri is missing."

"Part, yes. He made a bad choice in what he saw as a difficult position. I've made a few choices like that myself. He's suffered for it. If I can fix him, I will."

"Mom is right, you're different."

"What in all the hells does that mean?"

He studied me, openly judging, but remaining silent on his findings. "I'm glad you're here, but I have a shift with the maintenance crew in a few minutes." Daniel got up and walked out of the suite.

With my stomach full, I went to the room I'd used previously only to find Stassia on the bed with her datapad. As I turned to leave, she glanced up.

"How did that go?"

"I need to sleep."

She used her pad to close the door and then set it down beside her. "I thought we might finally get to that later we've been putting off."

"Did you." I pulled off the coat and threw it on the bed.

She grabbed the pad and slid over to give me plenty of room. "Or maybe not."

"What did you tell Daniel about me? Apparently, I'm different?" I yanked the clasps of my shirt open, whipped it down my arms, and threw it on the floor.

"Not at the moment, not one bit." She edged further away. "When you first woke this last time, you were not yourself. I only told him that. That's all. Really."

I halted halfway through pulling my boots off. Stassia had one foot on the floor. She licked her lips, gaze darting toward the door. The pad slid off the bed and fell onto the floor with a thump.

I sat down. "I might be annoyed and tired, but I'm not going to flip into berserker mode. Relax already."

"Could have fooled me." She let out a short burst of nervous laughter.

"Missing memories or not, you do know me better than that."

She managed a tremulous smile. "You know how you can emit calm now like a full Seeker?"

"Yes, so?"

"Do you realize that you just did quite the opposite?"

"I did?"

"Yes." She exhaled, shook out her arms, and rolled her neck. "You could never do that again and I'd be happy. At least not around me."

"I'm sorry." I got ahold of her arm and pulled her closer. "I'll talk to Etara about it tomorrow."

She gave me a long look and then nodded, easing against me. "Can you get the lights? I seem to have lost my pad for the moment."

In the darkness with her warm and against me, I wasn't quite as tired as I'd thought. I made my way under her shirt to the hard muscles on her back. She'd made a show of trying to shake off the strain, but everything was still tight. Using Etara's training I went to work on her shoulders.

Stassia sighed deeply. "Don't ever stop doing that."

"You're always trying to keep me in bed and out of trouble."

She laughed, further easing against me after pulling her shirt over her head. "Remind me to thank Etara for this."

"Speaking of Etara, she wants to use the new version of the sex drug I released in her therapy sessions. Bang, I think they're calling it on the steets."

"Oh my," She turned to half-look at me in the darkness, laughing. "I had no idea Seekers would offer such a thing."

"Full-service couples therapy, I guess."

"You didn't tell her we'd use it, did you? I don't think I could take being tormented with that again."

"I did not, but don't recall you being tormented last time I was on it."

"Depends on your definition."

I fully opened our bonded connection. "I'm sure I can think of a few ways to torment you without it."

TWENTY-FIVE

With the more enjoyable part of our relationship rekindled, I returned Stassia to the house on Artor. Neko stepped back into doing everything he could to assist her. Now that I had time to observe them, albeit through my link rather than in person, I was impressed by how much he'd taken on to help ease the load. He might not have wanted a reward, but I sent a ship stocked with building materials, food, and medical supplies to Risa, the colony where his family lived. He was well worth it.

While Stassia was distracted with advising the Narvan and the public was riveted to the feeds the University was releasing of their investigations onboard the deserted host of Arpex ships, I directed a large number of my contacts to deliver certain members of society to drop points. Gamnock's few linked employees, along with Buria, then delivered those on my list to the much reduced number of Arpex-populated ships waiting on the edge of Narvan space.

When the news feeds began reporting about the rash of missing persons, they also started bringing up the threat of the Arpex still looming on the outskirts of Narvan space. Some speculated that I was keeping them here to use against anyone that opposed my rule. Others said I didn't have them under control as much as was reported and that the Arpex were just biding their time, planning a second attack. The speculation that got on my nerves most, emanated from Jal. They claimed I'd staged Ikeri's disappearance to frame Jey and Kess so I could take their territories for myself. As if I would have asked for this level of stress for Stassia and I, or Neko or Markus and Daniel for that matter. Even Saka, Meera, and Hedvika were looking more drained with each passing day.

Hedvika took on the sleep shift at our Artorian estate so Neko and

Stassia could rest. Meera had been on permanent Daniel duty since we'd joined the fleet, and was now also balancing Markus and all his energy because I needed Saka with me.

Since I'd administered the calming balm on her, Saka had been extra attentive, but I'd been making every effort to stick to business no matter how she might smile at me or subtly offer herself. After all, she wasn't Buria, who was my first and far more conveniently located choice if I was going to give in to any whims.

Any time a Buria thought crossed my mind, I considered the vials of boost that I'd hidden in the closet on Artor. Knowing that I could get a single drop at any time, but making the conscious choice not to, helped to keep my mind and body under control. My choice on both fronts, no one else's.

After a couple weeks, Saka seemed to finally get the hint. She turned her amorous efforts toward one of the Jalvian officers during the little free time she had while we were with the fleet.

We weren't with the fleet today. I'd left Daniel there with Markus and Meera to have a meeting with the Merchessian families. With my positive press wavering, I needed to get the Arpex out of Narvan space as soon as possible. That meant wrapping up my obligation of finding a thousand bodies to ship out of my system and reorganizing the ones who were to remain.

I met with all three Merchessian families at once, not wanting any of them to have time to warn the others. Saka stood beside me in the Nikera stronghold. The weakest of the families, their staff and security were the most suited to my purpose.

The heads of the Ka'opul, Nikera, and Keefe families stood on opposite sides of the room. When I entered, I went straight into their minds. I didn't do anything yet, only waited, present and ready to strike if needed.

"Where is Kess Atta?" demanded the Keefe head in his shimmering, silver-grey suit. Gawdy jeweled rings adorned each of his fingers. He even had tiny blue jewels implanted alongside his left eye like teardrops. The current level of taxation wasn't hurting him too badly.

"In the belly of an Arpex. Would you like to join him?"

The Keefe head scowled. "You have no hold over us. If Advisor Atta is no longer, we are free."

"As to freedom, I have a proposal for you," I announced

That got their attention. Or maybe it was Saka's presence at my side rather than Stassia or Neko. The Ka'opul head watched her with great interest. I didn't blame him.

"We will be changing the way things are done on Merchess. There will be no more slaves," I said.

Siro Ka'opul, his hair gone white, but looking sturdy and refined as ever, let out an incredulous huff. "You can't do that. That's our livelihood. Your income, if you're intent on retaking Advisor Atta's position."

"I didn't say I was taking away your livelihood. However, we will be changing the way you operate. You will not own people. You will employ them."

The Keefe head's face went red. "That's not how we do things."

"It is now. I will assist with this transition in practices. Now, I would have your agreement before we move on to incentives."

"What incentive could you possibly offer that would make up for this upheaval. This is absurd," sputtered Siro Ka'opul.

Eta Nikera, the girl, who, years ago, I'd carried to safety after she'd been shot by a Kryon agent who'd been after me, was now a young woman. She'd traded the glow of youth for hard edges and a shrewd eye for business. She watched the other two leaders as they muttered blistering comments about the change I was thrusting upon them. Turning to me, she said, "I agree."

With sneers and obscene gestures, the protests of the other two heads grew louder. They threw in jabs regarding Eta selling out to me in graphic detail.

Saka seemed to take great offense to their verbal attack, taking up a clear defensive stance between me and the other two family heads. She didn't often utilize link speech, but she did a fine job watching me for cues. My subtle head shake kept her hands at her sides but empty.

"Eta, Control of Merchess is yours," I said, ignoring the others for a moment. "You will have full access to the current Nikera populace to occupy all Merchessian cities. However, you will employ them to do the work they currently do as slaves. You have three months to complete the transition. The rest of your business, including all substance manufacturing and distribution, can continue without interference or any additional taxes."

Eta nodded. Her hands also seemed to be twitching to make the other heads shut up. I gave her a less subtle head shake.

"You will need to adjust your pricing and perhaps downgrade your massive estate and staff to account for the wages you will now pay your employees. I would suggest spreading your family into the other cities and splitting your businesses between them. That should offer you plenty of upgrade incentives for your hierarchy of employees."

"But the other cities are occupied, Advisor."

"They won't be within two weeks," I said, turning my attention to the less lucky family heads.

"You can't do this! Without us, you'll go broke in days," snarled Siro.

"You can't think to spread yourself over the Narvan and the Rakon. There isn't enough of even you to go around," said the Keefe head.

I applied enough pressure to knock both of the offending heads to their knees. "Keep it up and I'll give your people to the Nikeras too."

Siro held up his hand, waving it. "We're in agreement."

"Good. You get control of Twelve. Same agreement. Three months for the full transition from slavery."

"Twelve is a cesspool of thieves and mercenaries," he grumbled.

"Then you have a lot of work to do. Of course, that also means you have an existing population to work with and employ as needed as well as local customers who are already familiar with your other products beyond slaves."

I eased the pressure on the bejeweled Keefe head. "Do we need to continue?"

He shook his head while rubbing his temples and grimacing. "No."

"Good. You will be running Thirteen. I would like those clubs gone, or toned down, or leveled, whatever you can make work most profitably. The majority of the existing populace are also slaves. They will need reconditioning along with those you will take with you."

I gave them all a long hard look. "You're creative business people. I understand this is a major change, but I'm confident you'll make it work. Instead of cities, your families now each have an entire world. You will work together to make the Rakon Nebula a profitable place. No slaves, no infighting. Leave your Merchessian cities here as they are, take only your belongings and your employees. Any deviation from this order will have deadly consequences. Am I clear?"

"Advisor." Saka's sharp warning and the sound of her firing a single shot were all I needed to brace myself. A heavy pulse blast hit me a second later.

The blast knocked me back. I landed on my hip and elbow, both now throbbing as I got back on my feet. My skin hurt. Everything under my skin hurt. Fucking pulse blasts. At least this one wasn't captured on live news feed.

Saka dropped to the floor, unmoving and bleeding from her ears, nose, and mouth. I'd have to wrap this up fast so I could get her to the tank.

Hot warmth trickled down my lips and chin. My hand came away drizzled in blood as I wiped at my nose.

The Keefe head held a pistol in his hand, gaping at me, not seeming to notice his own injury. Blood seeped through his shirt, just above his heart. Not a bad shot for as little warning as she'd had.

Before he could form a Jump, if he could in his stunned state, or summon help, I forced my way into his head, bypassing the wisp in favor of ripping my way through every nerve I could get my mental hands on.

He fell near Saka, screaming and clutching at his head until he seized once and then went still. I hoped his heir was more agreeable.

The blood flowing down my throat made me cough. I spat it onto the floor. "Yes, the rumors are all true. Keep that in mind in the coming weeks."

Eta and Siro nodded, looking from me to the dead man on the floor.

"I'm confident that you both can handle this adjustment. If you have a problem, contact me. If you become a problem, I will be contacting you."

Doing my best to hide my wince as I bent down, I got ahold of Saka and Jumped us to the tank room. My mind was too focused on my own pain to pay much attention to my hands as I undressed Saka on the tank platform and then got her profile loaded up. As soon as I heard the platform lifting, I headed for the bathroom to get cleaned up and pop a stim.

While I waited for the effects to offset some of the pain from the pulse, I dispatched my contacts to deliver the last of the chosen victims on the Arpex list to the drop spots. Then I left a message with my contact within the Keefe family household to notify the Keefe heir that she was up for duty and to get in touch with me directly for further instruction. Next on my list was contacting Gamnock to pick up the people who were being delivered, but I didn't particularly feel like talking to Gamnock in my wounded state. I contacted Buria instead, and after getting her location at Cragtek, Jumped there and made my way to her.

Buria her hair again done up in knots, opened the door to her apartment. She was also still barefoot but looking much more relaxed about it in her rumpled shirt and loose pants. She gasped. "Come in. Sit down. Why are you out and about wounded like this?"

While I'd cleaned up my bloody face and wiped down my armor, the stim hadn't toned down the pained grimace caused by any amount of movement.

"I'll be fine. Just waiting for the stim to kick in."

With my hip still pounding from my off-kilter landing, I gingerly made my way over and took the seat she offered, one of three mismatched chairs in the mostly empty one bedroom unit Cragtek supplied to its single full-time employees. It made me happy to see she'd started collecting a few things of her own, even if they were simple things like the candle on the kitchen table or the bright yellow pillow on the unoccupied chair.

She gave me a dubious look. "How long ago did you take this stim you're waiting on?"

Long enough that I knew it wasn't going to do more than take the edge off until I could get in the tank myself, but I waved her concern aside. "I'm not out and about, I'm in here. Unless you plan on attacking me?"

Buria grinned. "Not unless you're inviting me to do so."

"That's one of the reasons I'm here." I held up my hand, then realized that it was shaking and quickly put it back down. Damned pulse. I didn't have time for a dip in the tank. There was far too much to do and Ikeri to find. "Not an invitation, but I wanted to talk to you."

She pulled her feet up under her in the chair and rested her hands on her lap. "What about?"

"Let's get business out of the way first." I gave her the information to pass along to Gamnock.

"He's going to think you're here for other reasons. You should tell him yourself."

"I really don't care what he thinks. You, on the other hand..." I shook my head, then winced, belatedly remembering how much my muscles ached despite the lackluster effects of the stim. "I wanted to apologize for snapping at you the last time we spoke."

"Thank you for that, but really, you were in the middle of a battle. I did not take offense."

I'd seen the hurt on her face and it had been eating at me since. "You did, and rightly so. I'm not a very nice person most of the time. Nearly all of the time actually, as anyone close to me can attest to. But I'm trying to be with Anastassia, and having both you and Saka there on top of the battle was inviting disaster."

"I understand," she said softly.

My thoughts went to the vials of golden liquid hidden in my closet. If I could get through the next few minutes, maybe I could let those go too. I took a deep breath. And winced.

Buria was at my side in an instant. "What's wrong? What can I do?" Her hands hovered over me.

"Remind me not to do anything but sit here and breathe normally. I got pulsed just before I came here."

"You should be at the clinic. I could bring you. Gamnock made me learn the direct jump point there."

"I have a fix, I'm just waiting my turn."

"If you say so." She backed away to her chair and settled into it.

"Are you happy here?" I asked.

She nodded.

"Would you be happy here knowing that you will ever only be my contact and nothing more? If remaining my contact is a problem, I will release you from that obligation too."

Buria studied me and then dropped her gaze to her hands for a moment before nodding again. "I am happy here. There are many opportunities and I've only begun to explore them, but I would also like to remain in your service. If that would be all right?"

Relief relaxed my neck muscles a fraction. "I would like that."

She slid out of her chair and again came to my side. "As a concerned contact, I would like you to take better care of yourself."

"I'll try."

"Good, now before you get into any more trouble, go somewhere safe until your fix becomes available." She took two steps back, allowing me room to stand.

Not knowing how to politely end this sort of conversation, I opted to simply take her advice. I Jumped back to the ship. Saka was still in the tank so I went to the little room we used as an office and lowered myself carefully into the chair there to contact Stassia. I filled her in on the last deliveries to the Arpex and my announcement to the Merchessian families. I left out the part about getting pulsed.

"I can't believe you did that. If this blows up on us, it's on you," she said tightly.

"I'm well aware of that. It won't."

"You're awfully optimistic for a man who just handed two worlds already overflowing with slaves to slaver families who go back many generations."

"You'll just have to trust me on this one."

"I don't have any choice, do I?" She cut contact.

I'd expected more venom, but perhaps she was only waiting for the first issue to arise to throw the decision in my face. The more I thought about it, I knew that was exactly what she was going to do. I shrugged it off. We'd dive into that fight another day.

Since Meera now had tank access, I decided to bring Saka in on it too. I left a message for Neko to fill Hedvika in on the tank when time allowed. While I waited for Saka's tank cycle to finish and then for her to wake, I made a suitable dent in my workload. After giving Saka the ship tour and tank instructions, I sent her back to the house and then took a dip of my own. When I woke, I Jumped back to the bedroom on Artor to shower and then took a few minutes in the closet to cut myself off of one last thing. I poured the contents of the vials down the sink. No more fallback plans. I would move forward with only Stassia, whatever that might bring.

Feeling like I was on a roll with checking off important tasks, I went to the University to see Jey. His condition had improved minimally. Canelli kept a close watch on my progress and on me in general, scanning while I wisped inside and sorted through more shredded lines to make reconnections. I'd grown so used to him waving his equipment over me that I didn't pay attention to it anymore.

After the first time straining myself, I'd figured out when to call it quits for the day. Once I was done there, I went to the Jalvian fleet to spend time with Daniel and Markus and oversee the search for Ikeri.

Thus became my pattern throughout the next weeks, and eventually, months. Working on Jey became a break from the frustrating lack of progress in finding Ikeri, as well as solidifying my place with the Fragians and overseeing the Merchessian families who were now running the free worlds of the nebula. Stassia and Neko pointed me toward numerous time-consuming opportunities to repair my public image within the Narvan. The Arpex may have left the system, but the missing person reports, especially those who had been in direct opposition of me, kept trickling into the news feeds.

Speculation regarding what I might do with the mutated ability I'd used on the Arpex was also running rampant. No matter how much time I devoted to diagnosing people, the only ones that thanked me were those directly involved. The newsfeeds focused on how many diagnosing requests I'd declined and for who, and what that must mean. Etara, during our twice-a-week memory sharing sessions with Stassia, assured me that my efforts to do good would be recognized. I wasn't so optimistic.

The awe of turning away the Arpex had worn off. Whispers of Tyrant Ta'set again followed me almost everywhere.

Only traveling with the Jalvian fleet offered some respite. Much of that reception I owed to Markus and Daniel who stayed pretty much full-time with the crew, working alongside them and making friends. Daniel, with Meera at his side, and alternating Jalvian teams, assisted me in searching space ports, ships, and stations as we traveled on shipping routes toward our destination. After having seen how hard the disappointment of finding nothing on Brustus had hit Daniel, I'd made every effort to make sure he didn't have to face that alone again. We suffered the disappointments together.

In the eight months of our search, we'd traveled beyond the network of jump gates, slowing our speed considerably and reminding me of my travel to Pentares to reunite with my family. Like then, I spent many an hour when I should have been sleeping, wondering what I would do when I found Ikeri, and in what condition I might find her. All of it left me filled with an equal mix of dread and anticipation.

We conducted trades and made contacts along the way, expanding our routes as we traveled. Most of our stops were to small colonies which had no interest in objecting to the arrival of a fleet of well-armed ships. Some of the space ports and stations were more hesitant to be friendly, but to the annoyance of much of the Jalvian crew, very few had put up a large-scale resistance. I heard the griping but ignored it. Searching for Ikeri was my priority.

General Tellison asked me to meet him in his briefing room. We'd reached and then spent weeks searching the three worlds I'd set as our destination. I hoped he had news for me, any hint at all, but my optimism was running dry and my gut told me I wasn't going to like what he had to say.

He fussed with the fringe on one of the medals on his uniform, and then polished it with his thumb before meeting my waiting gaze. "I understand that it must be difficult to lose your daughter, Advisor. Truly, I do. However, the trail has long gone cold. We've had nothing to go on since the Brustus lead. My crew is growing restless and would like to see their families."

When we'd set off, I'd envisioned far more resistance, but after our initial military presence had been established with a few shows of force, that hadn't been the case. Most of those we came across had heard of our reputation from traders. Others just weren't in a position to put up a fight against a force as large as we were.

Having spent nearly all of my life in the bountiful Narvan, I was surprised to see that most colonies out here were barely scraping by. It seemed some knew the Jalvian fleet from Jey's previous forays, which had been on less friendly terms. Now the worlds I'd set as our destination had come and gone without results. As much as it pained me to admit it, Tellison was right, the trail was cold and his time and people were, on the whole, being wasted.

We'd made many trade arrangements and established amicable contacts with countless colonies, stations, and several fully-populated worlds. I couldn't call the mission a loss, but Ikeri was still missing. Months of holding out hope, of shouldering the disappointment for the boys and Stassia, caught up to me. I may have already been sitting, but it felt like I was sinking into the chair now, like it was sitting on me. The meeting room where Tellison and I had shared updates and plans over these past months lost its solidness. The edges of my vision wavered. I rubbed my eyes, willing all moisture to stay contained, and cleared my throat to kill the waver hiding there.

"Take your people home. Leave this ship and a crew to operate it. I'll keep searching."

The pity on his face almost undid my efforts to keep it together.

"We could leave two ships if you'd like. There are plenty who would follow you and Daniel. He's made a lot of friends."

"Thank you for your help with that. He's had a hard time finding his place."

"He found it. Be just like you in a few years."

"Good Geva, I hope not."

The general chuckled. "It was a good call throwing him into this. He wasn't ready, but he figured it out quickly. I'm guessing your goal was to get him some Jalvian support. It worked."

Had that been my goal? Not foremost, for sure. I hadn't committed to grooming Daniel for any particular role yet.

"I also wanted to formally thank you for healing the last crewman who was, well, obstinate in following your orders. News of your abilities has gained you favor on the Jalvian worlds."

I hadn't noticed any particular favor, but it was nice to hear that perhaps Etara had been right.

"I'm considering asking the University to test a wide selection of

Artorians to see if others may also possess a latent healing ability. What if we've been sitting on this gift for generations? I would have never stumbled upon it had it not been for Ikeri."

He nodded. "I hope you succeed. Training a host of Artorian healers would be a fitting way to honor the loss of your daughter."

The loss of my daughter.

His words buffeted against my brain. The general might be leaving me a couple ships, but it was only a show of mercy for a truth I didn't want to accept. I couldn't.

Finding one person in all of the known universe might be an impossible task, but I had no other choice. I'd promised Stassia that I would bring Ikeri home. I would spend every day until my last breath trying.

Resolved to continuing the search and with our meeting concluded, I walked to our quarters to tell Daniel about the change in the fleet, hoping he would hear it from me first.

Hedvika, who was playing a game with Markus at the table, informed me that Daniel was off shadowing someone in engineering. The kid had been making his rounds of the entire ship, following anyone who would take him on for a few shifts. He spent days with some and weeks with others. In all my skimming of records, I couldn't find much negativity about him. Most of what I did encounter was rooted in a general dislike for Artorians or directly related to him being associated with me, the Tyrant. If I ever did manage to wake Jey, I'd have to thank him for condoning all the shitty propaganda against me.

While I waited for Daniel's shift to end, I gave Hedvika a break and spent some time at the table helping Markus with his lessons. Stassia had enrolled him in remote education months ago when it was clear we were going to be searching long-term. Answering his questions reminded me of when I'd homeschooled Daniel during our time on Pentares. Thankfully Markus was far more focused than Daniel had ever been, which allowed me to also get some work done through my link.

Meera entered first, alerting me to Daniel's return.

Daniel halted just inside the room. "I didn't know you were here. You weren't in the command center."

"I talked with the General today."

"About?" He made his way over to me but remained standing.

"First, why were you in the command center? I thought you were working in engineering today?"

"I try to stop there after each shift to keep an eye on what's going on. Usually, the general is there and we talk. He wasn't today."

"He's preparing the fleet to return to the Narvan."

Daniel's head and shoulders sagged. "You're giving up?"

"No. We're continuing, but the majority of the fleet is going home."

"But what if we need them?" he asked.

"There are other methods of defense beyond this show of force."

I stood and went over to him. "General Tellison tells me you've done well here with the fleet."

"He did?"

I nodded. He went stiff when I pulled him into a hug.

"What are you doing?" he asked, his question muffled against my coat.

"Shut up and let me be proud of you for five minutes."

"As long as you don't hug me for five minutes. Your armor is scratchy."

"Sorry."

Daniel wrapped his arms around me. "It's all right."

"Are we done with this then?"

He laughed, stepping away and shoving his hair out of his face. "Yes. Definitely. Never happened."

"Good." I straightened my coat. "It's my night on Artor. Are you staying here or coming home?"

"I'll stay." Daniel turned to the ball of energy now play-sparring with Hedvika. "Markus, staying or going tonight?"

"Here, with Daniel," Markus managed between squeals as Hedvika chased him around the couch.

"Don't forget to bring mom a flower," Daniel said, nodding to the glass on the table that held several options from the last world we'd visited. "She'll probably never tell you that she likes them, but she does."

Markus nodded. "They make her smile when you're not there."

I wished she smiled more when I was there, but we were often both exhausted on the two nights a week we made time to spend with each other. I'd been keeping something in the vase since she'd put it on the table when I'd brought her the Verian candy. This visit was likely to be no different, but I chose a delicate red flower from the glass and Jumped home.

TWENTY-SIX

On Stassia's suggestion, I had Etara help me evaluate the surviving eight Arpex hunters for healing abilities before we launched a full-scale study at the University. With the Arpex banished to their homeworld, the hunters no longer needed to be on constant patrol. Stassia had suggested that having them be seen in a role that had nothing to do with defense, might also ease the tension with non-Artorian races that were not able to undergo the alteration procedure.

Etara evaluated them all. According to our agreement, if she found any of them able to destroy minds and bodies as I could, she would take that knowledge from them. The men had all given their consent, and so they went one by one into the meeting room in the hotel on Artor where I'd first housed the women from Tacesh. Those that came out with no healing ability, were posted on the outlying Narvan worlds in case the Arpex got any inclination to return. The four who did, stayed at the hotel. None of them had my destructive ability on their own.

In the hopes of further dissuading the Arpex from any future attacks, I pulled Ha'guris aside while Etara talked with the others about training opportunities.

"Do you still hear them? Is the channel still open?"

His forehead furrowed and he closed his eyes. "Only faintly. Like they are all far away."

"Far away is good. I'd like to try something, if you wouldn't mind?"

Ha'guris shrugged. Seeing Etara was finished, I waved the other three hunters over.

"I'd like to send the Arpex a message. To let them know we can still reach them, that we're watching. If you'll help me?"

Grins and enthusiastic nods were all the answers I needed. I wisped into the open channel, using the other three men to amplify my efforts, and reached out to the green world.

"What do you think you're doing?" asked Etara as if she were scolding children. "Whatever it is, it had better at least be grey."

Grey. Right. Revising my plan, I touched as many Arpex minds as I could reach, and instead of smiting a few as I'd originally intended, spoke to them, reminding them that the death-bringer was pleased they were home and staying there.

It occurred to me that if we could form this channel of communication with five of us, as long as we had Ha'guris, we could utilize the Arpex if needed, reward them for behaving by giving them our enemies should we encounter any that we could not subdue alone. Was this similar to how the High Council had used them? Yes. And was that especially grey? Probably not, but knowing we had the option made me feel a little lighter. I considered it grey enough.

Our warning given, I released the four men to Etara's care for intensive training in the hopes that if we did find other Artorians with healing abilities, the hunters could train them.

Stassia and I surrendered our memory-mending therapy time so that Etara could focus on training the new healers. I also spent several hours each day with them, learning from Etara and helping to teach them. Each of their abilities was a little different, requiring one on one time with either Etara or myself. Through this process, I came to better understand what Etara called a key. She allowed me to form the dominant imprint on them so I could hold control of their switches in case any of them should misuse her teachings. After much debate, I also convinced her to teach them the calming balm as a means for putting patients at ease.

"Are they ready?" Stassia asked one night after dinner at our Artorian estate.

I poured her a glass of her favorite Friquen red and sat at the table across from her with my third drink in hand. "Ready enough. Release whatever statement you've undoubtedly got prepared."

"Neko wrote it. He's getting quite good at them."

I raised my glass. "He's learning from the best."

She grinned. "We can hope this takes a little of the focus off of you for diagnosis requests."

"One can hope." Though I didn't mind appeasing Etara by using my diagnosing abilities, I longed to be devoting my time to searching for Ikeri and enjoying my couple nights a week at home with Stassia, preferably uninterrupted by kids, guards, or business.

"The field offices for the healer discovery program are in place and the University has confirmed that they have the staffing sorted out. Etara has been integral in getting the program set up," Stassia said.

"She's been getting a lot of grief from the other Seekers on Prime for spending so much time here. I'd like to send her home before her reputation suffers permanent damage."

The boys raced into the kitchen and began raiding the cold storage. Stassia grabbed her glass and nodded for me to follow her to our bedroom sanctuary.

"We need Seekers here to train any healers we do find," Stassia said, settling onto the short couch she'd had moved into our room. "Maybe she can recommend some others to take over for her?"

I squeezed in next to her, glad to be in quieter and closer confines. The peace of our bond washed over me, providing as much of a relaxing effect as the liquor. "A sort of Seeker immersion program? Where they can get a taste for what the rest of the Universe has to offer? I like it."

She eyed my half-empty third glass. I could almost hear her asking if that was a good idea, but she didn't. The only thing that would drag me away from our nights together was news of Ikeri and we both knew that was unlikely. That was also unspoken.

"Maybe mingling with you deviant Artorians will loosen them up a little," she said.

"We're deviants now?" I laughed and tossed back the remaining contents of my glass.

She drained hers and set it on the floor, snuggling closer. Our bond flared. "Only in the best ways."

I'd been working on healing Jey on and off for nearly ten months. My progress had been slow both because of my limited free time and because I was learning as I went, but also because I wasn't sure what to do with him when I finished.

The day I was ready to try to wake him, I asked Stassia to be there with me.

"It would be best if he saw your face instead of mine," I said.

"Agreed." She smoothed the blanket over Jey's chest and waited patiently.

"You're sure his system is ready?" I asked Canelli for the third time.

He checked his readings again and nodded. Urging me to get on with it with an impatient wave.

Standing behind the head of the bed, out of immediate view, I wisped into Jey's body. The last couple of connections were simple enough to make but made me anxious nevertheless. When I'd woken Kess, it had been with the intent to bring him to his death. The Jalvian crewman had returned to Jal within days of waking. Jey had been down for a long time. His body would need to regain strength before he was going anywhere, no matter what decisions we made about his future.

Jey's eyelids fluttered, then opened, blinking slowly.

Canelli met my gaze and nodded, then returned his attention to the scanners linked to the bed.

"Jey?" Stassia said.

He stared vacantly at the ceiling, silent and unmoving.

I double-checked my work, tracing the hundreds of lines that ran from Jey's brain to the rest of his body. I sunk deeper, racing over thousands of finer lines. I was sure I had them all spliced back together. I'd double and triple checked before we'd taken him off the last of the life support.

"Is there still something wrong?" Stassia asked.

A very welcome voice rasped, "Anastassia?"

She grabbed my hand and gripped it hard as she nodded to Jey. "Welcome back."

"Everything seems to be in order, Advisor," Canelli said. "Impressive work."

At the mention of advisor, Jey tore his gaze from Stassia and craned awkwardly around to spot me. He clumsily clawed at the bed. "Get away."

Several machines began to ping rapidly. Alarms rang. Jey shrank away from Stassia's attempts to calm him. "You told him to kill me," he rasped.

"Be thankful he didn't listen," she said.

Canelli cast a concerned glance at the equipment. "Perhaps, Advisor, for the benefit of the patient, you might step outside?"

"I'm done here for now. I should get back to Daniel. There are still a few missing connections with his link. He shouldn't be able to utilize it until I finish them."

"Can you send Neko?" asked Stassia. "I'd like to stay with Jey for a while."

"Sure."

She hugged me before I could leave. "Thank you for healing him. And for not listening to me."

"You're welcome." Before the alarms got any louder or Jey managed to squirm his way out of the bed, I gave her a quick kiss and left.

How Stassia had convinced Jey to see me, I wasn't sure. The two of them had always been close in their own way.

I'd been bringing her to the University to sit with him for a couple hours each day for the past week. My usual spot was in the hallway where I got some work done, yet could remain close enough to take him back apart if she gave me the slightest indication that needed to happen.

We'd been coming here publicly after releasing a statement that I was personally attending to former Advisor Te, who had suffered grievous injuries when his guilt in the abduction of our daughter had come to light. It was well known that I had caused those injuries, though the specifics of how they'd been inflicted were not.

Stassia nudged my shoulder. "Are you going in?"

"Are you sure this is a good idea?" I'd spent an awful lot of time repairing the damage I'd caused. Putting myself in the position to get angry and go all Arpex on him again didn't seem the wisest course of action.

"You two can't avoid each other forever." She shrugged. "Besides, I need your opinion on what we should do with him. He can't stay here indefinitely. Put some of that stolen Seeker training to good use."

I willed myself to stay calm and keep my temper under control. "Are you waiting out here then?"

"Like I'd leave the two of you alone? Canelli has fled the room, by the way."

"Good call, for both of you."

She pushed me toward the door. "Go."

Jey sat in his bed, resting against several pillows, most of which were propping him up. A host of therapists had been working with him on strength and mobility. We'd chased them off when we'd arrived an hour ago. If they'd made any progress, it was hard to tell.

His large frame had grown thin. His eyes were sunken, his wan face missing its usual tenacity and vigor. While his voice had the same tone, it lacked resolve and volume.

"Why am I here?" he asked.

To be seen as less of a threat, I sat on the stool where I'd spent so many hours healing him. "I don't know yet."

"I never should have let you walk back into advising the Narvan. Should have kept you back on Pentares, offering advice from afar," he said quietly.

"What you should have never done was coerce my daughter to go along with your plan. You almost succeeded in plunging the Narvan back into war! Was that what you wanted? After everything we'd done to maintain peace?"

He merely shook his head.

The anger I'd felt when I'd ripped him apart threatened to rise. Instead of giving in to it, I sat there clinging to Etara's calming lessons like a life raft.

I'd been doing good at keeping my wrath at bay, but it was quickly becoming apparent that it wasn't so much a newfound control as I'd just not encountered anything to push me over the edge in a while. Stassia, seeming to sense my struggle from her post in the hallway, sent a wave of peace through our bonded connection.

Jey's gaze dropped to his hands, gaunt atop the blanket. He blinked, his chest rose and fell, but for all else, he could have still been unconscious.

The machines that had sustained him were gone, leaving only a large rectangular room with walls the color of dried seaweed and bright lights glaring off the shiny, white tiled floor.

I settled my lightweight armor around me. "Anastassia said you asked to see me?"

"And now I have."

His eyelids slid closed, masking the emptiness in his blue eyes. I'd seen a lot of Jalvian blue eyes lately, far more than enough to notice the fierceness had fled from Jey's.

"Do you want me to go?" I asked.

"Do you want to go? It would seem that I'm at your mercy."

That was true, but I didn't enjoy him saying so. Not like this. "I'll stay."

"Anastassia tells me Ikeri is still missing," he said.

I nodded, then realized his eyes were still closed. "We're still searching."

"Vayen, I'm sorry. You know I never intended for this to happen."

"I know. That's why you're still here and Kess isn't."

"Fed him to an Arpex, I hear."

"Anastassia has been filling you in?"

His eyes opened slowly as if giving up on the idea of me leaving him alone. "Somewhat. She spends a lot of time sitting where you are, thinking at me but not sharing. I'd guess whatever is going on in there is unpleasant, the kinds of things that lose their power when you turn them into words. You know what I mean?"

He shook his head the slightest bit and settled his gaze on the blank wall next to me. "Of course you do. I'm just glad Anastassia doesn't have your abilities. I couldn't go through that again."

"I'm sorry you went through it the first time. I was angry."

"I noticed."

University staff walked down the hallway, their voices and footsteps muffled by the door. The stool creaked as I shifted, trying to find relief for my back.

"Do you need anything?" I asked.

He turned to look at me. A momentary flash of fire lit his gaze but then it fizzled out. "No."

"Have you spoken to anyone else?"

"Who would I speak to? You've disconnected my link and I'm stuck in this room under observation every minute of the day and night. Anastassia tells me I've lost Dayana, my position, everything. Who would talk to me?"

"I tried to get Dayana to come to see you. I'm sorry, she'd made up her mind long before I got a chance to bring her here."

"Why do you keep saying that? That you're sorry? I screwed you over. For fuck's sake, I talked your kid into screwing you over. You were on the right track with flaying me alive from the inside."

"Because I am sorry. Yes, you did do those things, but I didn't mean for you to end up like this, to lose everything, not your family at the very least."

He rubbed a fold of the blanket between two fingers, his gaze now fixated on the beige expanse that covered his body. His hair hung in his face, brushing against the bridge of his nose, but he made no move to push it back.

"That wasn't your fault. We'd always had more of an business contract than a proper marriage. An arrangement." He sighed. "We tried to make it real, but we'd been arguing long before you showed up with those women. She didn't forgive me for that. Ikeri was the last straw, I guess."

"No, she made it very clear that the last straw was making them be present when you knew I was showing up to take you down. I'd ask how you could do that to your family, but hells, look what you did to mine."

He flinched as if I'd raised a hand to strike him. When I didn't, he glanced up as if he was begging me to follow through.

"Tell me something," he said after a moment. "Why am I still here? Alive, here I mean. Anastassia said you merged with a Seeker? That was how you figured out how to heal me? She said it changed you."

"That's what I've been told."

He let out a broken laugh. "We both know you've changed so many times that there's no telling what's different from what should have been. Do your people even consider you one of them anymore?"

He might have been trying to prod me into anger, but it was a valid question that I'd asked myself many times. "Probably not. Thanks for igniting the whole mutant tyrant movement." I glared at him. "Yes, that's still floating around, but in general, the Narvan populace has been cooperative since I sent the Arpex off."

Before he did hit on a comment that truely did aggravate me, I said, "To answer your first question, you and I have been through a lot of shit. I've hated you. You've hated me. But we had a good middle ground going before you went off the traitorous deep end."

His gaze dropped back to the blanket. "I never meant for Ikeri to go missing for real. You believe me, don't you? It was just..." He pressed his fingertips to his forehead. "There were so many demands for me to stand my ground, to put us back on top. I needed a big win. Just one. One that would prove to my people that I could bring us securely into the future."

When I'd been on my mental rampage I'd seen enough hints and flashes to know what he was saying was true. "I believe you. That's why I'm willing to let you try to make up for the mess you had a hand in creating."

He lifted his head. "Seriously?"

I nodded.

"I expected you to tear into me a few more times until you grew tired of it and killed me for good. Anastassia wasn't kidding. You have changed."

"Dammit. Everyone can stop fucking saying that. Do I need to kill a few people a day to be considered normal again?"

Jey smiled. It wasn't the grin I'd been hoping to get out of him, but it was a start.

"I seem to have acquired the Rakon Nebula and traded for a majority share in several other colonies during our search for Ikeri. The Fragians also like you better. A little help with any or all of those would be appreciated. If you know anyone who is qualified?"

"So you're doing exactly what the Council always wanted us to do."

"On my own terms. And I'll have you know force wasn't necessary most of the time."

His mouth opened and closed before he committed to words. "You do realize that you are the damned force, right? I'm sure word of what you did with the Arpex has spread everywhere. And you know how shit gets exaggerated. You're a fucking one-man High Council. Congratulations."

That sounded more like the Jey I knew. "Not really what I was going for, but thank you."

"What about helping with the Narvan?" he asked.

"Definitely not." I held up three fingers. "First and foremost, the Narvan is in Anastassia's capable hands. Second, you may not have caught wind of it yet, but the Jalvian Prime has revoked your citizenship and banned you from all Jalvian territories. You put him in a precarious place and he's now covering his ass on all fronts."

"I hadn't heard," he said quietly. "And third?"

Unable to keep my calm any longer, I burst from the stool to shove a finger into his chest. "Dammit, you betrayed not only me but my family."

"I did." He met my gaze but there was no defiance in it. "I'm sorry."

"If you want to get out of this room and off my shit list, you're going to work for it. You won't set a foot in the Narvan. You will take up residence in the Nebula, return to your position as liaison with the Fragians, and oversee the three former Merchessian families who now control the now slave-free, non-Fragian worlds. They need constant oversight and you will be under mine. You'll report directly to me."

Jey stared at the ceiling. As one, his fingers tapped out a slow ponderous beat on the bed. "I'm not much good for anything without the use of my link."

"Tell that to Anastassia."

His fingers stilled. "Will I ever be able to access it again?"

"Prove to me that you can be trusted, and then we'll talk." I started for the door. "Are you in?"

"Fuck you."

"Is that a yes or no?"

Jey let out a low growl. "Yes."

I wanted to turn and appreciate the fire encompassed in that single word, but he'd see me grinning. That would ruin everything.

"Good. I'll have Neko deliver a suitable datapad in a few hours. Get some rest. You'll need it."

I went out into the hallway and closed the door behind me. My momentary good spirit fled with the click of the lock. One big task done meant I could devote myself to the next one: Finding Ikeri.

If I had to fly over every damned world in the known universe and listen for her as I'd done with the Arpex, I would. I needed her back. Even if we never spoke another word or touched one another again, I needed to see her and know she was safe.

My gut turned cold as the truth of it all stared me in the face, the one everyone else kept trying to tell me. The truth I didn't want to even consider.

I needed to know she was alive. Because if she was gone...

Etara's voice of reason tried to calm me, to explain the natural order of things, rationalize that the loss of one life, no matter how precious it might be to me, didn't warrant the darkness building in my head.

Screw her grey balance. If Ikeri was gone, the whole fucking universe would burn.

TWENTY-SEVEN

Two years later

Daniel put his weights down. I realized the rhythmic sound beside me had halted minutes ago. He stared at the floor of the gym we had to ourselves. The Jalvian crew tended to avoid it when I was there.

"Can I ask you something?" he said hesitantly.

"Sure."

I let go of the report I'd been skimming over through my link and returned the heavily weighted bar onto the rack next to my head. In truth, I hadn't been paying much attention to either activity. As with every other day we'd been searching for Ikeri, I was going through the motions of daily life, attempting to set a good example for my sons, and maintaining muscle mass for the sake of appearances. With the Arpex mind-shredding ability dialed in tightly now, I didn't often need to employ my other skills.

Daniel sat on the next weight bench, working over his bottom lip. "We've been searching for years. Do you think we'll ever find her?" He looked up at me then, his younger version of my face full of desperation for an answer I didn't have.

"Yes."

The answer had to be yes.

Visions of her sobbing in a dark room, of Masters touching my daughter, of what they might be forcing her to do haunted every moment of my days and nights. I'd brought this on her.

I had to find her. Alive.

Should the alternative prove true, I didn't think I could continue to face Stassia or the haunted man who already avoided my gaze in the mirror.

Daniel had put his future on hold to stay on the Jalvian ship with me. Though I'd asked him repeatedly to consider taking up training somewhere back home with his mother, he just shook his head and went to join another crewmember for their shift. He knew all of them now, their names, details of their lives, their jobs. At only fifteen he probably understood Jalvians far better than I did. Maybe that wasn't all bad.

He still dressed like me, not directly affiliating himself with one race or another. Markus, on the other hand, had been wearing a Jalvian cadet uniform since shortly after we'd sent the rest of the fleet home. When I'd questioned Markus about his wardrobe, he'd divulged, only after wringing a promise from me not to be mad at Daniel for circumventing me, that it had been Daniel who had reached out to General Tellison to sponsor him to attend the very same Jalvian academy that Daniel had dropped out of. They were allowing him to take his classes on board with the help of several crewmembers. I was far more astonished than mad.

The whole Jalvian academy experience had been a sore spot for Daniel. I didn't question him, instead chalking it up to unexpected maturity. He often surprised me in that regard.

There were moments Daniel still sounded like Fa'yet, but lately, I'd noticed he mostly sounded like me. We hadn't spent this much time together since his early years on Veria Minor, but now he knew the real me, not the quiet businessman who was struggling to keep his head down. Daniel had started to fill out, losing the awkwardness of his early teen years, and was now putting on muscle.

According to the one still frame I had of my family and my father's records, I'd looked just like him. To look at Daniel, no one would ever suspect his mother wasn't Artorian. Or that I wasn't his biological father. Our family genetics were strong and had run true for generations.

Except for Ikeri.

I realized Daniel was watching me. Grabbing a towel, I wiped the already chilled sweat from my face and stood.

I cleared the thickness from my throat with a cough. "We should get to work."

The one thing he hadn't lost of his earlier youth was that damned Seeker look and tone. "Dad, it's all right. Either we'll find her or we won't, but I'll keep looking with you as long as you need to."

Damned perceptive kid. I cursed Jey and Merkief, the Council, the fucking Arpex, and everything that had necessitated us placing our kids in that damned Seeker school.

I would have never talked to my father that way, or Chesser, or hells, Stassia and I rarely did the feelings thing either. Daniel did. He also talked to Jalvians, had made Jalvian friends here in the crew, had impressed a damned Jalvian general even. At his age, I'd hated Jalvians. I'd dreamed of killing them. Until I'd had to work with Jey, and even then only after a good long while, the thought of having a friendly conversation with one had never crossed my mind.

Maybe the Seeker training wasn't all bad either.

Except it had made Ikeri a glaring target and now my daughter was gone. The paralyzing blackness that seemed to linger at the edge of every thought of her flowed over me, dragging me down into depths I couldn't escape.

Daniel's arms were suddenly around me. He held me up while I broke down.

The sensation of a Jump brought a glimmer of light for me to hold onto. Something other than the soul-sucking grief to focus on.

"Sit." Daniel gently pushed me away and onto the couch in our Jalvian suite. "I figured you wouldn't want anyone to see you."

"Thanks."

Geva, the poor kid was probably having flashbacks to when I'd lost my shit after my Arpex-induced memory loss had come to light years ago.

He nodded, stepping back to ponder me for a moment. "Do you want Mom?"

"No. I just need a minute."

After Jey had rejoined our team on probationary terms and certainly not in any official advisory manner, Stassia and I had come to the agreement of spending three nights a week together. Not that she wanted me gone, but I needed to be. I couldn't stand to be home, pretending all was well while Ikeri was still missing.

Our relationship was relegated to discussing business over dinner and then enjoying one another in bed if we had the energy for it or just being near one another while we slept. While I searched for Ikeri, the Narvan was in Stassia's hands and it took most of her time and energy. I made appearances only as she felt warranted my attention.

I'd passed many of my contacts onto Neko so he could better support Stassia, and I couldn't even pinpoint the last time I'd talked with Fa'yet that hadn't had to do with business. He'd been short with me since I'd thrust the Narvan into Stassia's hands and pulled Daniel into our behind-the-scenes world.

Though Stassia and I didn't outrightly fight about it and she'd only screamed it in my face the one time, I knew she still blamed me for Ikeri's kidnapping. And for occupying Daniel so far from home. And Geva, probably for so many other things.

Stassia had plenty on her hands, she didn't need to deal with me breaking down for something that we both knew was my fault.

Daniel shook his head slowly. "You need more than a minute," he muttered. "Maybe talk to Neko then."

"He's busy helping your mother and he's got his own mate to eat up his free time."

Neko had asked for my approval for a marriage contract with Hedvika almost two years ago. The man deserved a woman to enjoy the company of on more than a one-night basis, and after what Hedvika been through, she deserved someone who would treat her right. They now shared his room at the Artorian estate and otherwise operated as usual.

The two of them seemed happy according to the brief moments I hazarded to ask. It's not like I had any wise advice to offer if he'd said they weren't.

"Etara?" Daniel offered.

"Hells no."

Despite our agreement to maintain a balance between black and white, the frustration of our long search had led me into the darker side of grey. She'd sent me numerous messages voicing her suspicions that I'd deviated from our agreement.

I'd avoided going anywhere near Veria Prime since I'd brought Jey back among the living. And just to be safe, I didn't publicly stay anywhere in the Narvan longer than it would take her to travel there. I couldn't very well find Ikeri if Etara caught wind of the colonies I'd lost patience with or the uncooperative people I'd interrogated. If I didn't see her in person, she couldn't look into my mind and see the smoldering remains or the writhing bodies on the floor going still.

I couldn't chance her flipping my kill switch, leaving Daniel to search alone.

Daniel nodded. "Right. Bad idea."

"I'll be fine," I assured him. "I'll get some rest and then we can look at the next options to search."

"Sure." He looked relieved. "Just stay off your link for a while, all right? Actually sleep."

I nodded and pushed myself off the couch.

The door to the main suite opened. I recognized Meera's foot-steps behind me.

Daniel glanced toward the door with a smile.

He'd been doing that a lot around her lately. And she'd been exclusively on Daniel duty since Neko's marriage contract had readjusted everyone's schedule. I grimaced. We were going to have to have a talk about bonds and bodyguards and being only fifteen. Thank Geva she wasn't Artorian and didn't have any hint of telepathy.

A wave of cold hit me. We'd never looked into whether Daniel had inherited the natural Artorian impotency or if he'd skirted around that with Stassia's genes.

"Dad?"

"What?"

"Is something wrong? More wrong, I mean?"

"We'll talk about it later, but for the love of Geva, remember that she's your bodyguard and she works for me. Got it?"

He looked startled and confused. Maybe I'd misread the situation.

"Sure. Whatever. Get some rest all right? I'm going to go work in the med lab for a shift. Meera will be with me so you can relax."

Not likely, but I nodded.

Once the two of them were out the door, I headed for my bed. There was plenty of room to stretch out on the comfortable mattress. I'd been short on sleep going on most of my adult life, but sleep, as usual, refused to come. Or maybe it was more that I subconsciously clung to a very firm resolve not to let my mind relax. When it did, it tended to wander into nightmare territory, and since Ikeri's kidnapping, nightmare was a term I wasn't going to deny.

To put Daniel at ease, I got up and took a shower, changed into the clothes I wore when attempting to sleep, and tried the bed again. I had to be exhausted enough by now to drop into a dreamless state. I'd broken down in front of my kid for Geva's sake. If that wasn't the definition of exhausted beyond reason, I didn't know what was.

My mind refused to be quiet. I eyed the sleeping pills Daniel had procured for me on his last med clinic foray. But what if someone needed me while I was out? What if there was news about Ikeri? And like I had eight consecutive hours to devote to sleep?

In the hopes I'd eventually drift off, I sunk into my link. Reports waited from Jey and others I'd elevated to advising the colonies we'd encountered during our search. Once I'd worked through those, my usual host of tasks awaited, some of which I'd begun to further delegate to other contacts.

Trade flourished along the new routes we created, bringing wealth to the Narvan that rivaled the credits we used to provide from Kryon contracts. While that should have provided some level of satisfaction, I only seemed capable of feeling hollow and worn.

Saka checked in, letting me know she and Markus were on their way to the gym. According to Stassia, Saka was supposed to be watching over me and Markus. She did when we happened to be in the same room. Markus often spent time in the command center with me combing the projection maps, but I'd deferred her services in favor of keeping Markus safe. I had armor and Arpex enhancements for that.

"After his training here, would you like me to bring you something to eat?" Saka asked.

"No, I should be sleeping by then."

"Good luck with that," she said softly before leaving me to my thoughts."

She may have firmly attached her affections to one of the Jalvian soldiers in the crew that had stayed with us, but she didn't hide that she still cared for me in a Stassia-approved way. If it weren't for the uncertainty of our future here with the Jalvian crew, I had little doubt she'd have requested leave for a marriage contract by now. I hoped there would be a time when that did happen. Saka deserved to be happy too.

My weary mind refused to hold onto any further tasks, instead intent on dwelling on my children. As much as Daniel and Markus had grown over the last three years since Ikeri had gone missing, I couldn't help but wonder what changes had befallen my daughter. Did she resemble Stassia even more now? At thirteen, she'd have lost the semblance of being a child. Not that she'd ever been much of one. Had she let her curls return or did she still keep her brightly colored head bare?

In my dreams, I saw her both ways. I wasn't sure which I wanted, not even when asleep. It only mattered that she wrapped her arms around me, sometimes my waist, other times my shoulders. When I could hold her there, smell her, hear her voice, I was whole again. But when I woke, I only tasted the salt of tears.

"Isnar tells me you're obsessed," Stassia said one night over dinner.

"Isnar should mind his own fucking business."

Stassia tapped her fork on the edge of her plate. The constant clinking made my neck tense. It had already been a long day with a less than cooperative population that wanted no part of our trade proposals. Things had taken a turn for the worse when someone had the audacity to take a shot not at me, but at Daniel, who, as he often did now, had come with me to the planet's surface.

Thank Geva he'd seen the shooter and had fulfilled his goal of being faster at a Jump than Neko. I got hit instead. Between my armor and my enhanced skin, I only suffered a little bruising. Those within my sight suffered far worse. I didn't want to think about all the bodies or the fact that I was sitting in the Narvan, only a system away from Etara.

"Vayen," she said in a sharp tone that indicated she'd been trying to get my attention.

"What?"

"We agreed on no work at the table on our nights."

"I wasn't. Just thinking."

"Me too." She sucked on her bottom lip and sighed. "You've been looking for three years. I'd like you to come home. All the way home. For good."

What had been a tasty dinner turned to stone in my stomach. "I can't."

She set the fork down, her meal only half-eaten. "So is this what our future looks like? You do your job. I do mine. We communicate through traded messages except for three nights a week?

"I hadn't thought that far ahead."

"Clearly." Stassia got up and took care of her plate. "You know I want Ikeri back just as much as you do, but the trail is so cold it's in deep freeze. With everywhere you've been, there would have been some hint if she was still out there. There aren't that many tattooed kids in Seeker robes."

"We don't know if she's maintaining her Seeker apperance."

"Still, you know she wouldn't stop practicing. People would talk about that." She came to stand next to me, placing her hands on my shoulders. "We have to accept that she might be..."

"Don't."

She sighed heavily. "Vayen."

"I'd know if that was the truth."

She guided my head until I had to look up at her. "Would you? Truthfully?"

I would. I would feel something. Reaching out as far as I could, I sought Ikeri out, some inkling of her, the barest of hints. Anything.

But there was only silence.

Was I roaming the trade routes for nothing? Was I continually placing Daniel in danger and keeping Markus from a full education on a three-year-long belligerent quest because I couldn't accept reality?

I hated Stassia a little for planting that doubt. Sure, I'd heard the same hedged argument from Jey, Fa'yet, Gamnock, and even Buria for Geva's sake. But to hear it from Stassia made it real, words I couldn't just brush off.

Noticing the tears glistening in her eyes, I got up and held her. Without the watchful eyes of Neko and Hedvika who were off enjoying a night of their own in the city, we were free to be distraught parents, sharing tears with no fear of judgment. When we did eventually get to bed, we were both weary. Spirits demolished, we fell asleep side by side.

When I woke, she was sitting on the edge of the bed, her back to me. "Half a year more. Can we agree on that?"

I hadn't expected an offer. She'd not indicated that she'd had any doubt that the truth hadn't been settled between us. I hadn't argued or pleaded for more time. Yet, there it was. She'd taken my hope away and then dangled it back in front of me.

"Yes."

"If she's out there." Her voice broke. "You'll find her. You'll bring her home."

Stassia went into the bathroom and didn't come out. The time for sharing tears was over. She made no move to expand our connection to clarify the cause of her distress. I didn't push for an answer. Instead, I let her be, got dressed, and returned to my suite on the ship. If I had six months, I was damn well going to use every second of it.

TWENTY-EIGHT

I sat alone in our suite aboard the Jalvian ship, Daniel and Markus and their guards off on their duties. Where had we gone wrong in our search? We'd followed the path on which the Masters had set out. We'd been all around that damned path, up and down it, searching systems with nearby jump gates and those far beyond without. We'd missed something. Somewhere. I got up and went to hunt for my Jalvian son.

Markus often spent his free time in the command center shadowing everyone there, but mostly he could be found glued to the projection map while the crew worked around him, as he was now. It appeared that the crew was so used to him being in the way, they'd adjusted their positions and relayed conversations around Markus and Saka, who did her best to be unobtrusive nearby.

"Markus, I need your help with something."

He tore his gaze away from the map, blue eyes locking onto me instead. It was hard to believe he was the same boy who'd spent so many nights curled up beside me to keep the nightmares away. He had enough new memories now, a new life and friends, to form a solid foundation of sanity. Not to say that I didn't catch him crying out at night, but the occasions were few and far between.

"Sure, what?"

"Can you show me the chart that includes the port where Ikeri was last seen?"

He toggled the controls to bring up a new chart and then illuminated it. "Here." He pointed to a dot.

"And all the places we checked on that chart?"

His face scrunched up and he pursed his thin lips, as he often did when concentrating. He pulled out a datapad from the pouch he carried with him and consulted it.

"Sir," said a quiet voice to my left. "I can pull those points from the system for you."

"Thank you," I whispered. "Perhaps later. Markus has it under control for now."

Markus typed at a manic pace on the map terminal, creating a firework effect as all the ports, stations, and colonies we'd combed through lit up on the chart. "I've been keeping a record since we started," he said proudly.

Out of the corner of my eye, I spotted the helpful crewmember ready to speak. I shook my head. If keeping his own records kept Markus busy and feeling useful, I wasn't going to ruin it for him. At this rate, he had a promising future in navigation should he choose to pursue it.

The points on the chart seemed awfully damn complete to me. What had we missed? "Can you bring up the adjoining charts and do the same thing?"

He nodded and got to work, reducing the size of the first chart and seaming the others onto it, turning the places we'd stopped into tiny particles in the grand scope of things. While we had ventured into a few points in all directions on the adjoining charts, there were so many more possibilities. She could be anywhere. I had nothing to go on. My gut didn't tug me one way or the other. Geva offered no inspiration.

All my efforts to reach out to Ikeri had yielded nothing more than raging headaches. I couldn't search all of that vastness in six months. The thought of going home empty-handed, of giving up, made me ill.

Markus studied the chart, contracting the view to only the combined sections where points were lit. His gaze was so intense it was like I could see his mind working behind them.

"We should go back to that port, Brustus," he announced, pointing to where Ikeri and the single Master had changed flights years before.

"Why do you say that?"

"If they departed from there to somewhere else, they had to book passage. There must be records, vid feeds, something that got missed the first time we looked. The crew talked to a lot of people, but maybe people will say more to you. You know, since word has spread about what you did."

I'd done a lot of things, but I gathered he meant now that word had spread far and wide of my role in the departure of the Arpex. "Maybe." Hells, I had nothing better to suggest.

I contacted Daniel, filling him in. He joined us, looking over the chart.

"What do you think of Markus's idea?" I asked.

"We should Jump, you and me. It will take weeks to get there by ship. We can work on finding someone who will talk while they travel."

"You know I don't like you around when I make people talk."

He gave me a droll stare. "I've seen it enough times."

"Enough, is exactly my point."

"Meera can cover my eyes. Are we going or not?"

I couldn't help but enjoy Daniel's version of Fa'yet's dry humor.

"Yes, I suppose we are."

We used the jump point Daniel had set when the crew had done their first extended search of the bustling port city. I hoped this time our efforts had a better payoff.

When Daniel, Meera, and I arrived, the city was quiet. My nerves went on high alert.

The air was still, no rushing wind of shuttles landing or departing with their loads. The few shuttles on the landing pads sat empty, devoid of pilots or cargo. The mover units sat in standby stance. I checked their cycle to find they'd all lost their charge. They had to have been sitting unused for months on standby for that to happen.

A quick check of the port channel confirmed that the port was closed, but the standard repeated message stated no reason. The message had been activated almost two years ago.

"Advisor." Meera pointed to a shuffling form on the street nearby.

"Keep Daniel back and safe," I said, already heading for the only person in view in the otherwise deserted city.

The woman wore a port uniform, so dirty that it was impossible to ascertain her duty or name on the patch on her chest. She stopped still, staring at my face.

"What happened here?" I asked.

She made a few quiet garbled noises, but I couldn't make out any words.

"Where is everyone?"

Again she seemed to be making an effort to speak but provided nothing that sounded like a coherent answer in any language. At least she didn't appear to be a danger. I waved Meera and Daniel over. "I'm going in for a moment. Keep a lookout."

Both of them nodded.

The inside of the head of the woman that thought of herself as Anesse was just as garbled as the words she'd tried to form. It was almost as if an Arpex had been snacking and been interrupted, repeatedly. I sat down in the street, sinking deep into Anesse to observe the lackluster blue lines of her inner system. I couldn't find any broken connections, but it was as though all the lines were withering. Searching deeper into the minute layers I began to find connections rerouted, intersecting one another in a tangled maze of angles rather than naturally curved lines. The angles caused energy to flow unevenly, rushing in some areas, but trickling in most.

It was the imprint on those changes that knocked me out of Anesse and flat onto my back on the street. My head hit the plascrete with a crack that made lights dance in my vision.

"Ikeri was here," I managed to choke out while trying to regain my bearings.

"We know that," said Daniel.

"No, she worked on this woman."

"You can tell that?" asked Meera.

I nodded. "When we heal someone, it leaves an imprint behind. Whatever happened to Anesse, Ikeri tried to fix it."

Recovering my wits, I wisped into her mind again, digging for memories of Ikeri. Everything was scattered and fragmented, as if no timeline existed in her memories and her life had been sliced into two-minute fragments. Seeking out meaning in the mind of an Arpex was easier than this. Frustrated, I released Anesse.

The woman meandered away after I'd vacated her head. Maybe whatever had happened to her was the reason everyone else had evacuated the area. None of the buildings appeared damaged. A shipment sat unmolested out in the open on one of the landing pads by a shuttle. The streets were empty of bodies. The air was clean and breathable. With no obvious answers, we needed to venture further into the city.

We'd gotten no further than a minute down the street when Daniel reached out to one of the posts by the street side and hit the button to call a public transport. "I don't even hear people around here. They must have fallen back. This will be faster."

A transport showed up moments later. Either we were very lucky or Daniel was right about no one else being in the vicinity. He consulted the map inside the transport. The port where we were sat on the edge of the city. He pointed to the middle and glanced at me. I nodded.

He entered the destination and we were off. The streets were empty but for an occasional shuffling form like Anesse. With no hum of factories or traffic or even a single conversation, the city lay under an eerie silence.

The city and port had been full of activity when Daniel had been here years before. If Ikeri had tried to fix Anesse, she would have had to have been here during or after what had befallen these people.

She hadn't just passed from one ship to another here. She'd stayed, practiced her healing. Someone had to know where she went. My heart raced.

All that time looking, and we'd missed her right from the start. I wanted to punch something, but the close confines of the transport offered nowhere to vent out of Daniel's sight.

When we came upon the next shuffler, I stopped the transport. Grabbing the hapless man, I dove into him, examining the damage and finding him similar to Anesse. Ikeri's imprint was also there.

I tried multiple times to connect with him, to get him to form whole words, but like Anesse, that seemed difficult. There was one word he managed.

"Worship?" I repeated.

The man's head bobbed as his body rocked awkwardly. One arm rose and he pointed off to the right, along a major traffic vein that led to the other side of the city. I let the man's mind go and consulted the local network. A map showed that direction belonged to the affluent.

Far from the noise and transient nature of the port, sat a smattering of large estates, each taking up as much land as several blocks of the city. I could appreciate the desire for space and privacy.

Thanks to the empty streets, we made excellent time. Other transports sat by the street side, some of the public ones in their docking stations, private models parked as if their owners had traveled there and walked away, never to return.

The lack of traffic in the sky seemed very strange, far too quiet for any city. No lights lit the windows in the buildings we passed. We spotted a few animals roaming the streets, perhaps pets that had escaped.

Not trusting myself to keep my exhilaration over even a stale lead under control, I contacted Neko. *"Let Anastassia know we may have a new lead on Ikeri. I've found some people she healed. But don't get her hopes up too high, I'm not sure what we're dealing with here yet."*

"Will do, boss."

The industrial section of the city gave way to a commercial spread interspersed with residential. The greener spaces offered a measure of calm. At least those were alive and thriving.

"What's that?" asked Daniel, pointing out the window to a dark swath in what might have been a park. As we came closer, the answer became clear. Bodies. A vast rectangle of them.

"Stay in the transport," I said to both of them.

"Advisor, we don't know what killed them," said Meera. "You may be exposed if you get close."

"We could already be exposed." I shook my head. "I need answers. Stay here."

Daniel didn't say anything, but his concern hit me through our natural connection.

"I'll be fine. Nothing's killed me yet."

His concern skyrocketed.

"Relax, dammit. I said, I'll be fine."

I left them there and went to examine the bodies. Four large birds loudly protested my arrival and then conceded their meals to me, flying off to perch in a nearby tree.

The smell was horrendous. The more recently dead were stacked atop the old in layers. The elements and animals were doing their work to assist in the clean-up, but the newer bodies, discolored and bloated, some more decomposed than others, made for a gruesome sight. Exposure or not, I was glad Daniel was only seeing them at a distance.

Their clothes were dirty like Anesse. Thin bodies, some entirely emaciated, made me think they'd starved to death. Yet, we'd seen no signs of looting, panic, or violence. A port city like this had to have plenty of supplies. Even if, for some reason they didn't, they were on the trade route for Geva's sake. They wouldn't close the port if they needed food.

All the bodies faced the same direction. I followed a pair of empty eye sockets to a mammoth home set on a green hill. A tall, solid wall lined the estate.

"Follow in the transport," I said to Daniel.

Just as I set off toward the hill, a man opened a door in the wall and shambled toward me. I hurried to meet him.

"What's in there?" I asked.

He smiled blissfully and walked by as if I didn't exist. He narrowly missed being run down by the transport, saved only by the auto-sensing feature which must have severely jostled Daniel and Meera inside. The man didn't seem to notice. He continued across the street and into the grassy area around the pile of bodies. Stunned, I watched as he climbed onto the top layer and walked across to the most recent body. He lay down next to it, looking for all the universe that he was settling in for a comfortable nap. He gazed at the house beyond the fence for a few minutes and then closed his eyes.

Had they all done that? Hundreds of them, voluntarily coming out here to die in the open, one by one? What in all the nine hells was wrong with these people?

I sprinted to the gate. Finding it unlocked, I went inside. Like most everywhere else, the greenery was overgrown, verging on going wild. The distant sound of voices reached my ears. I climbed the hill. The house did not sit atop it, as I'd thought, but was built into it. What we had seen from the street were only the two upper floors. The other three faced outward from the hillside into a low-lying garden. Or what had been a garden. Every inch seemed to be covered in people. Sitting, standing, even perched in the branches of trees, all of them muttering together as one.

Standing on the hillside along the edge of the house, I first thought they were all looking at me, but just to my left and a floor down, was a long balcony. A man stood behind the wire railing, his boney arms raised. Shaggy hair hung to his shoulders. He faced the gathered masses, speaking to them. The billowing black and violet clothing he wore reminded me of a poor imitation of Seeker robes. They were missing the distinctive patterns and orderly form, but they had a similar cut.

"It's some sort of cult," I said to Daniel.

"Are they dangerous?"

"To themselves, it would seem so, but to us? I'm not sure yet."

I didn't relish the thought of the thousand-some bodies down there deciding I was a threat. There didn't appear to be guards set anywhere. I got no sense of being watched or even noticed by anyone below. A quick scan of the crowd didn't reveal any weapons.

Daniel's curiosity was palpable.

"Stay down, but yes, you can come look."

The voice of the man on the balcony rose, his open hands shaking toward the sky.

"Bring her back. Back to us. Let her rise and walk among us again."

A hush fell over the crowd. They all raised their hands as he did.

He left the railing, went into the house, and returned, pushing a long metal cylinder. I immediately recognized what it was. It was a different model, newer than the one I'd encountered before. This one had a clearplaz top. A body lay inside.

Daniel peeked around me. "What is that?"

"A stasis tube. Like the one you were in when you were an infant."

I lost my voice when the man flipped a switch, illuminating the girl inside. Soft brown curls again adorned her head, though only a couple inches long. Her face appeared sunken, ashen. The Seeker robes had grown short, her wrists and ankles protruding from the voluminous folds of fabric draped over her still form.

Daniel's voice cracked. "Ikeri."

I could only nod.

"Look at all those credit chips," said Meera, peering down.

My eyes refused to focus. I stepped away from the edge before I fell over. Daniel stayed with Meera.

"Why would they leave all that sitting there? It's a miracle no one has stolen it. Are they insane?" asked Daniel

I hazarded a glance down to the patio on the ground level. Peeking out from the shadow of the balcony was a mound of credit chips and jewelry

+ along with a host of trade currency in the abundant variety common to a port city.

Somewhere below us, a door opened, the vibration carrying up through the soil. Children poured out from the house, bearing baskets of bread and fruit. They wove among the crowd, offering sustenance to the worshippers. The children, at least, appeared healthy. Most of those in the crowd were too busy gazing up to the lit stasis tube to pay any attention to the food.

Three children came out onto the balcony with three adults. The man in the robe gestured for the adults to approach the tube. One by one, they put their hands onto the plaz window, each emitting an almost orgasmic gasp before letting go and falling to their knees. The children went back inside.

"We have to get Ikeri out of there," said Daniel.

"We do," I affirmed. "Keep watch."

I was farther away than I'd ever tried diagnosing before, but I reached out into the man in the robes. Ikeri's imprint was everywhere, but it was too hard to focus, to sink into the multiple layers without touching him.

Leaving the plane used for healing, I went into his mind as I did when attacking. That was easier. I was used to working at a distance there. Wisping into his mind, I saw him with Ikeri before she'd been put into stasis.

They sat in a dark building, a deserted house, the memory clarified. Men and women stood in a line, each bearing a form of payment, which they dropped at the man's feet before kneeling in front of Ikeri. She touched their heads, closed her eyes, and went limp in her chair for a few moments. Then she was back and the person smiled, moving aside for the next in line. What was she doing?

"Healing," said the mind of the man as though he were breathing the word.

"Who are you?" I asked, drilling deeper into his memories.

He fumbled, memories darting to and fro. Flashes of the complex on Tacesh where I'd freed the slaves and the flashing lights and pounding music that I recognized as one of Kess's clubs confirmed my guess. He might not remember his name or what he was, but I knew. I also knew Ikeri wouldn't be healing for payment. That went against everything the Seekers had taught her. She may have scrambled his mind enough to make him less of a threat, but he hadn't changed, still using others for profit.

But he had a pile of profit on the ground. Why was he still here?

"What happened to her?" I asked, guiding his mind to Ikeri's face.

Confusion swirled, making the process heavier and harder. Memories jumped to endless lines, of Ikeri not waking from her healing state, of panic, and credit chips gleaming in the sunlight. Faces flashed by, men and women trying to wake Ikeri, the stark cleanliness of a clinic or lab, and finally the tube.

He'd used her, even after he'd forgotten who he was, he'd used her until there was nothing left. They all had. All those rerouted connections, the healing they'd asked for, that they'd paid for. She'd tried to help, but they kept coming, all of them.

Whatever had gone wrong after that, they deserved. They weren't worshipping her, they were draining her dry.

Distantly, I heard Daniel calling to me. He grabbed at my hand. I shook him off. "Get away, down the hill."

"What are you going to do?" he asked.

"Shut up and run," said Meera.

Staggering footsteps told me she was dragging him with her.

In all the obstinate colonies, ports, and stations we'd encountered, I'd restrained myself to only the number necessary to make a statement. Those deaths were offset as best I could with offers of trade, assistance, and the occasional diagnosis in keeping with Etara's deal. Here, however, I hoped to never cross paths with Etara again, because there could be no offset for what I was about to do.

As with the Arpex, I sought out each life thread before me and gathered it into my hand. I had no hunters to help me this time, but I'd had a lot of practice on my own. It wasn't until I was gasping for breath and faltering on my hold, that I released my fury for what they'd done to my daughter.

There were no screams, no pleas for mercy. I required no show of force. I had no forgiveness to offer.

I gripped the threads of life tightly until they melded into one thick, brittle strand. Hollow at its core, the strand snapped.

When I came back to myself, bodies lay strewn across the ground, toppled and crumpled, fallen where they'd been. There was no sign of struggle or pain. Most still wore the beatific smiles they'd had while gazing at the balcony. There would be no more shuffling out to die in a neat stack beyond the wall, no more starvation.

A wail went up, breaking the silent peace in the field of death. Another joined it. The children that had served the food, ran from one body to the next, crying and shrieking. More poured from the house, frantically trying to wake the fallen.

The three children who had been on the balcony returned, shaking the three adults who lay around the tube. One noticed the still form of the Master. The wailing grew to a desperate keening.

Now that the crowd was no longer a threat, I climbed down the hillside far enough to jump the gap between the ground and the balcony. I landed with a heavy thud. The children scattered.

Through the tall windows that lined the side of the house, I could see children running around inside, sharing the news of what had happened. They pointed and gaped, tear-filled faces pressed against the clearplaz.

The room on the other side of the door from which Ikeri had come was full of flowers. Where they had found room for the tube to rest in all that, I couldn't guess. She might have appreciated the view and scent if she'd been awake.

But she wasn't.

I started to lash out at everyone left still alive in the house and around it, but caught myself. They were only children.

"I have her," I said to Stassia, but blocked out the myriad of questions she threw my way. Instead, I flashed Neko a jump point so they could see for themselves.

After I gave Daniel and Meera the all-clear, they made quick time onto the balcony from below.

"The children have been living in the house. All of them. Everywhere," said Daniel. "It's a mess in there."

He approached the stasis tube. "Was I really in one of those?"

"Yes. Your mother kept you hidden for a long time, even from me."

Inspiration hit me on multiple fronts.

Jey had slowly integrated himself into the Nebula, and while he was still unwelcome in the Narvan, I was anxious to end the tension Ikeri's abduction had caused not only with Jal and Artor but also with him. Bringing Ikeri home would give me a good reason to return Jey's link privileges. He'd been beyond accommodating to my every request since I'd healed him.

"Daniel, I need you to do something for me." And only because I couldn't bear the thought of leaving her side now that we'd found her.

He tore his attention away from his sister. "Will she be all right? I can't talk to her. I can't even feel her."

That had to be intentional. If she could connect, even unconsciously with her followers while in stasis, we should be able to feel her too.

"If I have anything to say about it, she will be."

That brought a smile to his lips.

"Your mother had a doctor friend who watched over you when you were in stasis. He was also the one to revive you. I need you to find him and bring him here to do the same for Ikeri."

"Can't we just bring her to the University?" asked Meera.

"The Narvan doesn't need that spectacle. Not to mention, I'm not comfortable with Jumping an entire stasis tank with Ikeri in a questionable condition inside. Transporting her by ship will take longer than I'm willing to wait. Strauss can wake her here, quietly."

I flashed Daniel the image of Strauss's clinic for lack of a solid jump point. "If it doesn't work, I'll find another way to contact him. I've checked the records, he's still employed there. Explain who you are. That will get his attention. Tell him to bring what he needs to wake Ikeri and then Jump him back here."

"Shouldn't you go? He knows you. He'll listen to you."

I chuckled. "He doesn't need me for motivation. Just mention your mother's name and he'll jump backward through flaming hoops with his eyes closed."

Daniel must have shared the jump point with Meera because the two of them vanished a minute later.

Stassia arrived with Neko and rushed over to the tube, pressing herself onto it much like the children against the windows.

I let her have a moment. "Neko, we're going to need to do some clean up here. There are a large number of orphans that will need wrangling onto a ship for relocation. They can't stay here alone."

He cringed. "I don't know as I'm the best choice for that particular task, boss."

"Then get someone here who is."

"Got it." He turned to regard the large number of bodies below. "And the clean-up?"

"Burn the damned city for all I care."

He shook his head. "That seems rather wasteful. How about we revisit that topic when your wrath meter has gone down."

"You did this?" asked Stassia taking in the death toll.

"They did that." I pointed to Ikeri.

She nodded, but still looked uncertainly between me and the field of bodies. After a moment, she turned back to the tube. "She looks awful."

Neko glanced at Ikeri. "Should I get Etara? Maybe she could—"

"No," we both said in unison.

"She'd off you in a second," Stassia said.

"I'm well aware of that."

She wrapped her hand around the sleeve of my armor. "What if we do need her?"

"We'll deal with that then."

She bit her lip and nodded. "And now? Do we know if it's safe to wake her?"

Daniel returned with Meera and an overwhelmed-looking Strauss, whose eyes lit up the moment he spotted Stassia.

"Peter?" She peeled herself off of me and embraced the doctor.

He held her for a long minute and then stepped back, glancing from her to me and then back again. "We were told you were dead years ago. I'm so glad to see that wasn't true."

Strauss took the bag that Daniel offered him and gathered himself up to stand before me. "It would appear that a lot has changed since we last met. The time I remember, anyway."

"I'm sure Anastassia will fill you in later. Right now, I need you to work your magic on our daughter."

"Yes, I heard there was a situation?"

I nodded toward the stasis tube. Daniel followed Strauss over to the control panel at the foot end, where he stood back, as I'd seen him do with the Jalvian crew, quiet and observing, logging everything away in his mind.

We also stayed back, giving Strauss space to work. I figured it would be in our best interest to not make him more nervous. The plethora of dead bodies around us set a dark ambiance of their own.

Buria, Hedvika, and Saka with Markus in tow, arrived. The three women went with Neko into the house. Meera gave Daniel a questioning look. He nodded and she went in with the others. Children ran in all directions except out onto the balcony. Markus went to Daniel's side, peering at Ikeri through the clearplaz.

"This will take a few hours," announced Strauss. "I will warn you, her condition is not good. It has deteriorated since she entered stasis." His brow furrowed. "I'm not sure how that is possible."

"I've seen how that happened," I said. "Do what you can and leave the rest to me."

Stassia spun to face me. "Vayen, what are you going to do?"

"Get Ikeri back." And if I had to bargain with Geva herself in person to make that happen, I would.

TWENTY-NINE

From the frenzy of Strauss's fingers on the controls of the tube and the monitoring equipment that he'd brought, I gathered we were getting close.

"How's the kid gathering going?" I asked Neko.

"Evasive little bastards."

"Spread the word that she's waking. If they want to see her, they better cooperate."

Daniel stood close by with Markus beside him. Stassia stood closer, her back pressed against my chest. A crowd of children began to gather by the windows. Neko stood in front of them, keeping the door firmly closed.

I glanced around and realized the former Master's body still adorned the balcony. Ikeri didn't need to see that. I pried myself away from Stassia to toss him over the railing.

When I turned back to the tube, Strauss had the top open. Ikeri didn't move.

Stassia crept closer. "How is she?"

"She's not responding," said Strauss. "She should be awake. I don't understand." He ran his scanner over her again.

"Can she be moved?" I asked.

"There's nothing broken, no obvious injury preventing her from fully waking." He shook his head. "I don't know what more to do."

"Let me look." I picked her up. So light. Even at thirteen now she was small. Sitting down on the balcony, I settled her onto my lap, her head resting on my shoulder. For a moment I savored having her in my arms again, her soft curls against my cheek. I'd missed this so much.

The balcony vibrated as Strauss pushed the stasis tube back toward the house and out of the way. I felt Stassia and Daniel close by, but I didn't dare look away from Ikeri for fear she might vanish from my arms. We'd searched so long, but now that we'd found her, she was still so far away.

I sunk deep into her, searching for broken connections. Finding none on the larger scale, I went deeper into the fine lines. That's where I found them, so many connections grown thin, barely holding together. Nothing was more frustrating at that moment than knowing I could see the problem but do nothing to fix it. I pulled back.

"She's worn out, overworked her abilities," I announced. "You did nothing wrong," I assured Strauss. "I may be gone a while. Don't be alarmed."

Without further warning, I sunk back into Ikeri, pulling in with me every method of calming that I'd copied from Etara. Ikeri needed to rest peacefully, to regenerate. It would take time, but she would recover.

I expected to feel some sort of response, a relaxing of muscles, a sigh, a flutter of eyelids, something. But she remained as lifeless as before. It was as though she were impervious to my efforts.

Not to be deterred, I wisped into her mind. Rather than the vivid landscape of images, feelings, and sensations I encountered with everyone else, Ikeri's mind was cold and dark. Almost as if she'd packed everything up and left.

"Ikeri." Her name echoed in the empty space. I shouted for her again and again, growing angrier by the second. I hadn't found her only to have her slip away in my arms.

As the last of the echoes faded, I ranted to Geva. My ranting quickly turned to bargaining. But my offers were swallowed by the darkness and the body in my arms remained unresponsive.

Leaving all awareness of my own body behind, I crawled inside hers, knocking on every surface I could find in my bumbling about in the dark. I called for her until even my mental voice lost its strength.

A flicker of light caught my eye. A flash of memory so quick that I was sure I'd imagined it. Then there came another, Ikeri laughing, the crinkling of pages of a storybook Stassia had brought to Pentares, my voice, raspy as it had been when I had returned from destroying the Council, reading to her.

"Ikeri?"

She cried as a tower of blocks tumbled to the floor and Daniel laughed, running in circles around their room on Minor.

Then she was in Stassia's mind, trying to calm her mother, trying to see what was wrong, why Stassia didn't know who anyone was. Ikeri tried to heal her, to make her remember.

Memories flickered to life all around me, flashing brightly like lightning strikes, the voices rising to a deafening din. I tried to press my hands over my ears but I had no body.

The cacophony fell suddenly silent and darkness descended.

A frail voice whispered, *"Daddy?"*

Overwhelmed by the single word, I fought to keep my hold on our connection. I poured my energy into calming her. *"I'm here."*

"How are you doing that?" she asked.

"Etara taught me."

"You're lying."

"Etara did teach me, but I copied the rest. It wasn't on purpose. I think you did the same thing with the other acolytes and Seekers."

Her presence shrank away.

"It's all right. Come back."

She didn't. The darkness grew more solid, the silence crushing.

"Ikeri," I shouted with all the voice I had left.

When she spoke again, her voice was tired. *"Do you know you stopped breathing five minutes ago?"*

"I'm sure Strauss is doing something about that."

"What if he's not?"

"Your mother will make him." I gathered every speck of her I could sense and pulled them close. *"Don't worry about me. I'm here to bring you home."*

I could almost feel her warmth, more of her gathering near me, slowly building into a semi-solid form.

"I can't go home," she whispered.

"You can. Whatever happened to these people, it wasn't your fault."

"It was."

Her form had weight now, the face I'd seen in the stasis tube, gaining definition. I almost had her.

"Tell me then and we'll figure it out together."

The form in the nothing where we were solidified. Ikeri opened her eyes. The fact that they weren't filled with disdain, that she was still resting in my arms rather than scrambling away, filled me with hope.

"The Masters, when they took me, they touched me." She shuddered.

The only thing that kept me calm at that moment was that I knew they were already dead.

"I went into their minds like we did with Ha'guris. And then, like you did, with the Arpex, I hurt them, not killed, not like you, but enough that they didn't do that again."

I didn't think I could take her giving words to what that might have been. Instead, I hugged her, wishing I could do more, erase everything the Masters had done and all the darkness I'd shown her. If only I could return her to the innocent girl she'd been before we'd returned to the Narvan. She burrowed in closer as if she wished for that too.

At the edges of my awareness, far from the quiet place where Ikeri and I sat, I was distantly aware of shouting and chaos, of Markus holding my hand, of Stassia's arms around me, Strauss busy with some equipment in front of me, of Ikeri's dead weight in my arms. If I didn't get back there soon, I'd lose them all.

"Ikeri, we need to—"

She ignored me *"Ector was easier to work on, to get him to leave me alone, but the other one confronted him about how he was acting."* Her voice shook as did the rest of her. *"I convinced Ector to kill his partner for our protection."*

"It's all right. You wouldn't have done that if it hadn't been necessary to survive."

"It's not all right," she said bitterly. *"I didn't want to be like you."*

"You're not," I assured her, kissing the top of her head. *"Come back to your body before your Mother has a fit. She's been through a lot. Let's not give her any more grief."*

"I don't think I can. I'm so tired."

"There's a doctor here to help you. And me, your mother, Daniel and Markus, even Neko."

She turned to face me. *"You all came?"*

"Of course. We all love you."

Ikeri smiled. *"I'll try."*

"Go on then," I said, giving her a mental push with what little energy I had left. Holding us both here was draining me fast.

Ikeri hugged me and then her image vanished as did the sensation of her in the nothing with me. Alone, I recalled the quiet peace of a place like this that I'd once inhabited, that Ikeri had pulled me from. If I stayed a few moments longer, I'd find myself there again. At one time, I was angry to have left that serenity, but now, with Ikeri back, with my family around me, I no longer wanted to rush off to that place again.

Releasing my hold on the nothing, I drifted to the body that called to me. It was easier to see how to do it this time, to pull myself back and settle in. I didn't rush as I had before, taking the time to reacquaint myself with the processes of living that were so natural they were not otherwise given any thought. It was only in the absence of doing those things, breathing, the pumping of blood, the operation of organs, that each of them became clear. With my body firmly back in my grasp, I opened my eyes.

My family knelt around me, Ikeri on one side, her hand weakly grasping mine, and Stassia, Daniel, and Markus on the other. Neko and the others stood behind them with a host of wide-eyed children gathered tightly around. Strauss pulled a clear breather mask from my face and stood aside.

After a moment of coughing, I cleared my throat enough to say, "I told you I'd bring her back."

Stassia leaned in and hugged me tightly. "Thank you."

"We need to get them both to my clinic," Strauss announced.

Neko looked to Stassia who was too busy stroking Ikeri's arm and clutching my hand to notice.

"Hey," said Daniel, clapping his hands. "Listen to the doctor. We have to go. Now."

I nodded my approval to Daniel for taking command of the situation. That seemed to be all the encouragement he needed.

"Here's the jump point," Daniel said, giving Neko, Saka and Meera an intense look in turn. "Meera, take my mother. Neko, my father and the doctor. I'll get Ikeri. Saka, get Markus. Buria, contact Gamnock to arrange transport for the kids. They can't be left alone here. Hedvika, secure that horde of credit chips and the rest of it before Gamnock gets here and then help Buria." He glanced around and seemed satisfied that he'd not left anyone unassigned.

Neko gently untangled Stassia from us and nodded Meera over. The two of them vanished. Strauss packed his supplies in a mad rush while Saka left with Markus. Daniel knelt next to Ikeri and hugged her. The two of them were gone a second later.

"You ready, boss?"

"For answers as to what happened here? Yes."

"I'll look into it. Maybe give Ikeri a day or two before the interrogation?" he suggested.

"You know patience isn't my thing."

He chuckled. "Even so. Maybe just this one time?"

I nodded and beckoned Neko closer. "I'm going to need a little help getting up."

Strauss shook his head. "Not recommended."

Neko knelt beside me and performed a quick once over of the doctor and his jumble of hastily packed supplies. He gestured for Strauss to stand beside him, then knelt and put a hand on each of us.

A moment later, we were in the middle of the clinic on the station over Veria Prime with a frantic and panicked staff darting around us.

THIRTY

"Ikeri?" Despite Neko holding me down, I struggled to find my daughter from my vantage point on the floor.

"She's fine, boss. They're not used to people Jumping into the clinic here. We caused a bit of a scene." He nodded toward a hulking, scarred security guard with one bare mechanical arm and two tiny Verian guards beside him.

Strauss hurried over to them. "Officer Barnes, thank you for your swift arrival. I'll vouch for them. They're not a threat."

Barnes gave the doctor a dubious look but left with the Verian guards in his wake. With their exodus, Strauss quickly got his staff and the situation under control.

It took Neko and five Verians to hoist me onto a bed. Ikeri was already in the one next to me. Stassia hovered between the two of us with Daniel and Markus posting themselves at whichever bed she wasn't currently at. Neko and Saka headed back to the port we'd vacated to begin clean up while Meera took up her post at the end of my bed, watching over us all. The number of times I caught her and Daniel locking gazes prompted me to harass my son through our natural connection.

"I thought we talked about this, you and your guard, all the moony eye-making."

For a split second, he looked terrified but his calm demeanor slid back into place just like my work face used to, back before it had become permanent. *"You did. Nothing is going on."*

"Should I ask her what's going on?" I asked, half-joking.

"Don't." He rammed the word into my head as if I'd just threatened to kill the woman.

Fucking hells. Nothing, my ass. Had the boy learned nothing from seeing how hard it was for Stassia and I with the mixed-race relationship? Couldn't he find some nice Artorian girl?

"Isn't she like ten years older than you?"

"Nine. Mom is eight years older than you."

"You're fifteen!"

He shrugged. *"Rest. You can yell at me later."*

Annoyed, I glared at Meera instead. She noticed immediately. Her worried look stayed in place as I drifted off.

When I woke a day and a half later, Canelli was tapping away at a datapad while conferring with Strauss, the two of them in an animated conversation. Stassia's hand squeezing my shoulder pulled my attention away from them.

"Neko brought him. I thought it would be a good idea to make sure you hadn't strained anything. The two of them have been babbling like giddy teenage girls since Canelli arrived."

I noted her lack of armor and visible weapons. It reminded me of the first time I saw her here, being her true self on the station.

"And am I all good?" I asked.

She gave me a dry stare. "You do remember snuffing the life out of the remaining population of Brustus, don't you?"

"I meant in the health sort of way."

"Yes." She brushed a hand over my cheek. "Exhausted, but otherwise all clear."

"And Ikeri"? I glanced over to her bed but found it empty.

"Doing a session with a physical therapist. She should be back soon. I warned her that we have questions. Go easy on her?"

I had no intention of pushing my daughter away again. She knew full well what was out in the universe now. No more darkness on my part was needed.

"I will. Before I see her again, there's something I need to do."

Stassia crossed her arms over her chest. "I don't like the sound of that. Don't leave this bed. You're still recovering."

"I'll stay right here, I promise, but I do need to see Etara."

"Absolutely not. She'll show up, take one look at you and end your life. I won't allow that to happen, now that we're all finally back together."

"I can't avoid her forever."

"Sure you can. Just don't go to Veria Prime."

"Ikeri's return will flood the news feeds. We're going to have to make scheduled public appearances if we hope to unify the Narvan in the wake of all this. I'm sure you've already released a statement?"

Her determined gaze fizzled. "I did. I thought we could all use some positive press and that it would ease some of the tension between Artor and Jal."

"All true. Now, I need to face her before she flips my switch in front of the kids or in public."

"Maybe we could have Ikeri talk to her first?"

"I'm not going to hide behind Ikeri, Stassia." Before I could talk myself out of it, I contacted Saka to have her Jump Etara to the station. "You've got about five minutes to berate me for setting up this meeting before she shows up."

"Only five minutes?" She sat on the bed and clutched my hand.

I fully expected her to launch into some level of tirade but she just sat there with tears welling in her eyes. "Thank you for finding her." She sniffed and wiped at the tears. "I don't know what all you did while you were out there searching for her, but Daniel told me enough to know that you lost touch with grey a long time ago."

"We did do some good along the way. It wasn't all death and destruction."

"I hope you have a better argument for your life ready for Etara," she said brokenly.

"I wasn't planning on arguing. You know Seekers don't work that way. They see and make their judgment."

Saka appeared in the middle of the clinic with Etara at her side. Their sudden arrival caused a few gasps and one patient to shriek, but our initial group arrival must have desensitized most of the occupants.

I dismissed Saka and prepared to face Etara. Stassia didn't move from my side. That was all I knew before everything turned black.

A squeezing pain that verged on the Arpex torture took hold of my brain. Had I not been subjected to it countless times before, I'd have been going out of my mind. Not that I was far from it.

"Am I doing it wrong?" Etara hissed in my mind.

"No." I managed to say. I didn't push back, letting her fully exercise the power she'd copied from my mind in return for what I'd taken from hers.

The squeeze eased to a heavy pressure that still felt like it might crack my skull wide open. Then that too eased, leaving me with a throbbing migraine. I opened my eyes to confirm that I was still among the living only to get hit with a light so bright that it seemed to sear my eyes. I squeezed them shut again. My stomach flipped. I reached out, seeking something other than Stassia's lap to vomit into.

Someone shoved a plas pan into my hand that I utilized a second later.

Stassia's hands registered on my back. She rubbed frantically while whispering, "I told you this was a bad idea," over and over.

When I dared to open my eyes again, I made out Etara standing at the end of the bed with a grimace etched on her paler than usual face.

"First time?" I asked through clenched teeth.

"Not much evil to fend off on Prime. I haven't needed to use that until now," she said flatly.

"Stassia, get her a chair. Her head has to be hurting at least half as bad as mine."

"Are you kidding? She just tried to rip you apart and you want her to sit down?"

"She didn't kill me. The least we can do is be polite."

Stassia let out a disgusted growl but left my side to locate a stool for Etara, which she gratefully took and then proceeded to rub her temples.

"I'll give you two a minute. I'm not feeling all that polite." Stassia stalked off to talk to Canelli.

"You want some help with that?" I pointed at Etara's head.

"We both know exactly why it hurts, no diagnosis needed."

"I don't think I could muster anything in that realm at the moment, but I do have fingers and a lot of practice. Come sit over here and let me help you."

If anything, her scowl deepened, but in the end, she sighed and came to sit on the edge of my bed. I closed my eyes against the still too bright light and let habit take over as my fingers took the first position on her scalp.

She sighed again, but much more peacefully this time.

"Tomias was very adamant that I put an end to your misuse of our gifts."

"Thank you for not listening to him." I shifted to the next position.

"He hasn't seen into your mind to know the evils outside of the common threats on our homeworld. But still, I didn't know what I would do until I saw you, until I examined everything you've done since we last met."

"And?"

"You've shown me that there is a lot of good you could do. If you choose not to, we can return to giving you a more permanent dose of what you have done to others. Simply flipping your switch would be too kind."

"Got it."

She was quiet for the next two positions before she said, "You've avoided me and moved too quickly for me to have time to travel to you on the rare occasions you publicly returned to worlds I could reach."

"I couldn't let you stop me before I found Ikeri."

She uttered an assenting noise. "Do you think Anastassia will forgive me?"

"It will take a while, but yes. As to Tomias, we'll stay away from the Verian Cluster. I don't put it past him to try culling me on his own."

"Wise choice. However, I'm afraid you're stuck with me. I'm not welcome to return if I don't put an end to the problem I created."

"Don't your people need every Seeker they can get?"

"It would seem they are willing to do without this one. But, as I've said, I consider everyone my people, not just those on Veria Prime."

I took in the wise young woman in front of me. We'd come a long way from our first terrifying meeting in the Seeker's courtyard so long ago. "Thank you, Etara."

She nodded, "You should rest now."

Grateful to be alive, I settled my aching head onto the pillow and closed my eyes.

A tug on my sleeve woke me. Markus stood next to me, beaming.

"What's got you in such a good mood?"

He held up a datapad with shaking hands, making it impossible for me to focus on the wavering text. "It's from the academy."

I noted the familiar insignia at the top and nodded.

Stassia noticed Markus and left Canelli's side, who appeared to be wrapping up an exam on Etara. I hoped she enjoyed his monitoring as much as I did. Served her right for using the Arpex shit on me.

"What's going on?" Stassia asked, taking up her post beside my bed.

"They want me at the academy tomorrow for a celebration ceremony, for finding Ikeri, for the crew," said Markus, clutching the datapad to his chest. "General Tellison is a guest of honor at the celebration. Dad, he sent me a private message asking if you would also attend?"

"Am I cleared for that?" I asked Stassia.

"Celebrating? Yes. In moderation. But don't you dare consider slipping off on another slave-freeing expedition."

"I'm sure Markus will keep me in line."

Markus laughed, the joy on his young Jalvian face plain for all to see.

"How about we assign Saka to you permanently so you can officially attend classes in person? Now that the search is over, we could even get that Jalvian she likes assigned to the academy or at least to Jal so they can stay together," I suggested.

"Wouldn't you miss having Saka around?" Stassia asked in a not very veiled manner that even Markus caught.

"No. You're all I need."

"You mean, all you can handle." She laughed.

Our bonded connection flared to a degree that I wished we were alone, preferably somewhere else.

"I have to go show Daniel." Markus darted away, all gawky arms and legs and bursting with energy.

Even in his sudden absence, we were sadly, still very much in the open in the middle of a damned clinic.

"Where is Daniel?" I asked, looking for a distraction.

"Exploring the station with Meera. While you and Ikeri were sleeping, I told him that I used to live here and gave him a quick tour, including where I met his father. I hope you don't mind?"

"Why would I? He knows the truth. It's good for him."

She nodded. "Peter said most of the crew I knew has retired or been posted elsewhere, but it was fun to walk these halls again."

The light in her eyes and the blissful smile on her lips ignited an thought I never expected I'd have the chance to give voice to.

"Stassia?"

She cocked her head. "You're not going to get all mushy on me again, are you? You have that look." She leaned in close and whispered, "Not that I'd mind once we get home."

"Right, keeping the mushy behind closed doors." I tugged her onto the bed with me.

"Hey!"

Her startled shout brought the attention of everyone in the clinic our way. Her face turned red.

"I suppose you'd rather I keep this behind closed doors too," I said, kissing her neck.

"Yes, but I'll let it go this one time."

Strauss loudly cleared his throat. "It looks like you're feeling better. Ahem, Anastassia? I do hate to be a pain, but those beds are barely rated for his weight, let alone..."

"Sorry." She slid off the bed and straightened her clothes.

"Perhaps, it wouldn't hurt for Vayen to get some moderate exercise.

A walk maybe? I'd like to check him once more this evening and then he should be cleared for discharge."

"And Ikeri?" I asked, already making my way out of the bed.

"The stasis tube did slow the decline of her health, but she's weak, in many ways," he said carefully. "I've done a thorough examination, and while I see no permanent physical damage, she has endured trauma that she may not feel comfortable discussing with you, as her parents, and you," he gestured vaguely at me, "being her father and with what she says you can do."

Stassia nodded while my heart sunk into the cold hollow of my stomach. Knowing what I'd seen in Buria's mind and what the other women who had suffered the attentions of the Masters had been put though, I didn't think I could take hearing a similar recounting from my own daughter.

The wrath Ikeri feared would gain me nothing. The men who had done those things were already dead. Devastation over all Ikeri had lost hit me hard. Stassia reached out and took my hand.

"You'll want to get her into physical therapy and into the care of whatever you call a therapist, counselor, or psychologist on Artor."

"We will. Thank you." Stassia's voice was as thick as my throat felt.

Strauss offered me a pained smile. "From your eagerness to leave the bed, I'm assuming you'll all be wanting to return to your home-world as soon as possible?"

"Yes, thank you for your help." I started for the door with Stassia beside me, needing to leave his words behind, to escape the room where my fears about Ikeri's well-being had been confirmed.

Stassia walked in silence with me as we left the clinic, each of us lost in our thoughts. We'd get Ikeri all the help she needed or wanted. She'd be all right. I'd do everything I could to make sure of that.

Once we reached the main corridor and fell into the light foot traffic at a sedate pace, I attempted to steer Stassia back to the topic I'd tried to broach before her shout had derailed us.

"I was thinking it would be nice—"

"Oh, look, there's Ikeri." Stassia tugged me toward the aide who was guiding Ikeri back to clinic at a painfully slow pace.

Ikeri grimaced with each step. As we approached, I caught the aide's patient tone, encouraging her to keep going, that she needed to rebuild her muscles.

There would be time enough for that later. I scooped her up in my arms. The aide did not appear pleased.

"We'll bring her back shortly," Stassia assured the aide while shaking her head at me.

Deciding I shouldn't physically push my luck if I wanted my quick discharge, I carried Ikeri to a public lounge set against the wall where the corridor widened. Stassia slipped onto the bench seat beside me. I settled Ikeri onto my lap. That she didn't scramble to get away reassured me that what we'd shared in the nothing hadn't only been my imagination.

"Thanks," she said, resting her head against my chest. "I didn't think walking could be so hard."

"It will take time." Stassia took one of Ikeri's hands in her own.

Ikeri sighed. "That's what everyone keeps telling me."

"Can I look? Inside? Just to make sure the doctor didn't miss anything?" I asked.

"You can do that?"

"Diagnosing is my thing, according to Etara. I'm supposed to be doing it to stay grey."

"You're going to need to do a hell of a lot more than that if you want to get back to grey," Stassia muttered.

"No fighting," Ikeri said firmly.

"We're not. She's right." I thought about what Etara had said. "Maybe you and I could get some doctors from the University and go do a healing tour? I can think of a few of the colonies we set up agreements with on our search that could use help."

Ikeri's brows rose. "You'd take the time to go heal people?"

"He kind of has to." Stassia squeezed Ikeri's hand. "Etara controls his kill switch since he copied her Seeker knowledge."

Ikeri sat up, her back against my chest, her head just below my chin. A rightness filled me, a piece that I'd been missing, sliding back into place. Her mind opened to mine, initiating the natural connection we'd once shared.

"Yes, you may look," she said.

I closed my eyes and wisped into Ikeri, examining the blue lines of energy and life flowing through her body. They were stronger than before, but still extremely thin and sluggish. Sinking deeper, I checked her brain, heart, and every organ. Everything appeared whole and functional. Assured nothing had been overlooked by Strauss and his team, my awareness flowed back into my own body.

"All clear." At least physically. The rest would take time.

"You're much better at that than the time you tried with Ha'guris."

"I've had a lot of practice, but not with everything. I was only able to keep the lessons from Etara that I practiced after I copied them. It didn't occur to me at the time to use the memory transfer one. I'd like to copy from you how to do it. The correct way. I tried it once on my own, but it was messy."

Ikeri slid off my lap to sit between us. She gave me a long look before turning to Stassia. "He wants to transfer memories directly to you himself. Do you want that?"

"Could you?" Stassia asked me.

I deferred to Ikeri.

"He could. If you want him to."

The way Ikeri kept hammering the desire for consent served as a warning that she wasn't going to put up with lies or any manipulation on my part. I supposed her lack of consent in what had happened to her played into it too. I wanted to keep her next to me permanently, where I could prevent anything bad from happening to her ever again.

Ikeri smiled and rested her head against my shoulder. *"Maybe not forever, but I'd like that for a little while,"* she whispered in my head.

"As long as you'd like."

I'd forgotten how easily she could read my thoughts, especially now that we had a connection between us again. Not that it mattered anymore. As with Daniel, I no longer had to hide who I was from Ikeri.

I tore my gaze from Ikeri to look at Stassia, "I would feel much more comfortable sharing everything you're still missing if it didn't have to go through a filter first. Some things are private. Closed doors?"

Stassia grinned. "Yes, I'd like that very much."

I took a deep breath and let it out. Nothing was going to get easier until we knew what had happened. I'd leave the hardest topics to the professionals, but there were things I needed to know.

"Before we get to that, Ikeri, I have some questions about the people who were, well, worshipping you. Neko has been examining security footage on-site and reporting to me, but we're still not able to pinpoint what turned a city full of people into scrambled zombies."

"I did," she said quietly. "It wasn't on purpose. Not at first, anyway. "When I convinced Ector to kill his partner, I suggested that we should switch ships, to avoid being caught. But once we got to the port to look for outgoing passage, I decided that I wanted to stay there. I thought that being not so terribly far from home, that someday, I might be able to go back. So I convinced Ector that if we stayed, I could make him rich. That's all he really wanted."

I noticed Stassia's hand on Ikeri's had taken on a white-knuckled appearance. *"You're hurting her."*

"Sorry." Stassia let Ikeri go.

"Neko said that people started showing up in droves at the estate where we found you. That, within five months, the entire city had shut down and the port had ceased operation."

"Seeker Tomias holds my switch," Ikeri whispered.

Fear flowed through our newly formed connection. I shook my head at Stassia who had her mouth open to prod for an explanation. Though I wanted answers just as badly, I opted to use the calming balm and give her a few minutes to start talking on her own.

It was odd to sit on the edge of the conversations passing us by in the corridor. Without armor, with our daughter between us. We were just a family, no one of notice amid the varied visitors of the station. For the first time, it felt normal to be there, perhaps not that I belonged but was acceptable.

"You're very good at that one," Ikeri said.

"It feels easy."

"You," Ikeri giggled, "Calming people."

"Ironic. I know."

Stassia smiled, watching the two of us.

I cleared my throat. "All right, according to Etara, neither of us should go near Veria Prime for a while. But she is here and not angry with you." I thought back to the whisper she'd used to ease the trauma of my first Arpex larva hatching experience. "She can help you, maybe?"

Ikeri nodded thoughtfully. "Maybe."

"Go ahead and tell us what you did," I urged.

"I wanted to perfect what I started with Ector, the fixing, removing the bad parts of his personality."

Ector had been a test subject for me. Hearing her baldly stating that she felt I had bad parts of my personality and that I needed to be fixed, made me bristle both inside and out.

She avoided my gaze, staring at her lap instead. "I'd already ruined Ector, broken too many connections to make him a guardian for much longer. I needed a new one. We made a deal to visit the Admiral, the man they'd elected to run the colony. Ector bragged about my abilities over a fancy dinner and we were instantly permanent houseguests. I started with simple healings, that went well enough to have the Admiral invite every person in the city that he wanted to have owe him a favor. I started fixing whenever I found a good candidate. But I needed them to keep coming back because I couldn't do a whole fix in one session, you know?"

I nodded, enjoying the sound of her voice in a civil tone, the one I remembered fondly.

"I'm guessing the coming back part spiraled out of control quickly?" Stassia said.

"Very. I'd implanted the suggestion to return and they did. By force. Hordes of them, not just the ones I'd started fixing, but everyone, they all wanted to meet the healer and not be left out. Someone killed the Admiral when he tried to defend me from the initial rush of supplicants. Shot him," she said despondently. "I eventually found the man who killed him as I worked through the long line and tried to fix him too.

"Ector charged for each session and he was overjoyed with my success. But the people didn't stop coming. It was like they finished a session and instead of going home, they just went to the end of the line."

"You took breaks? Ate? Slept?" Stassia asked. "Ector took care of you? His investment?" She spit out the last word.

Ikeri shook her head. "When we were first traveling together on the ship, they made me work on the crew to buy them favors and earn my meals. If I refused, they'd hit me or not feed me, or both. I only used the Arpex mind twist the one time. It hurt bad."

I could only imagine her young mind, never having dealt with anything like that, would be in great pain. And she'd not even pushed enough to kill either of them, just enough to drive them back. I didn't want to think about what they'd tried to do that time compared to the others that drove her to use the attack that had scared her so badly before.

"Ector lorded over his growing pile of credit chips and queued the line. The only breaks I got were when he halted to eat or sleep. Days into the mess, I couldn't keep my eyes open and I felt sick all the time."

"Did the people leave then? Let you recover?" Stassia asked.

Having seen the mass of bodies and how fragile our daughter had become, I had to restrain myself from snapping at Stassia's optimism.

"No. They just waited in longer lines. I started to implant the idea that they should lay down when they were tired, that I would remain here. They all had to be tired. I thought they would leave me alone for a while."

"But they only went to the park beyond the estate. And only when they were so tired that they never got back up," I said, putting the situation together.

Tears trickled down her cheeks. "I didn't mean for any of them to die. I only wanted to help them."

Stassia hugged her. "I know you didn't intend to hurt anyone but you can't help people by forcing them to change."

"And I don't need to be fixed," I said, unable to keep my mouth shut any longer.

Ikeri's tear-filled eyes looked up at me. "Not anymore."

Maybe that's what made Etara spare me.

She sniffed and wiped her eyes. "I started fainting and it took longer and longer for me to wake up. Ector found a doctor to bring a stasis chamber so that he could continue to charge people to see me even if I couldn't do anything for them. But even with my body asleep, I could feel them near me. My mind was still working, just slowly."

Stassia glared at the floor, the walls, and everyone passing by. "So they were still putting a drain on you even when you were in stasis."

Ikeri nodded and glanced at me. "You ended them?"

"I did. They were a mess inside, scattered, so many connections broken." I said it as if I'd acted out of mercy, but that hadn't been the case at all and she probably knew it.

"Why didn't you contact us?" Stassia finally gave voice to the question we'd both wondered about. "You had to know we were looking for you. That we'd do anything to get you back from those men."

Ikeri seemed to shrink into herself. "They didn't take me, Mother, not at the beginning. I agreed to Uncle Jey's plan. Helped him with it even. I knew you'd be mad. The rest was my fault for trusting Kess and Uncle Jey."

"What happened after you left Kess was none of your fault. None of it." Stassia said firmly. "And you can drop the Uncle, Jey is no longer welcome in our home."

"Or the Narvan," I added.

Ikeri stilled. "He's alive? You didn't kill him?"

"Should I have?"

"No." She peeked up at me. "Maybe Kess though, he wasn't nice at all and he allowed those men to take me."

"He's been disposed of," Stassia assured her.

I couldn't believe what I'd just heard. "Wait, you're telling me I should have killed Kess? That's not very Seeker-like."

"Neither was he. He was beyond fixing." She clasped her arms together as if she were still wearing her Seeker robes and taking the position of passing judgment.

"That he was," Stassia decreed. "Are you ready to go back to the clinic? Doctor Strauss wants to keep you here until tonight. He's formulating a care plan for you for when we get home."

"About home, I was thinking—"

"Hey, boss." Neko hurried over. "I'm glad I found you. I wanted to ask about Brustus. Not trying to overstep here, but..."

He was rarely so flustered so it had to be good. "Spit it out already."

"I was thinking about how to further improve Artor's public relations."

He had my full attention and Stassia's too.

"Yes?" she prompted.

"Those kids, the ones we can't find relatives for, do you think we could adopt them out to Artorian families? Wouldn't hurt to get some future goodwill ambassadors in the works? Some non-Artorian faces to promote what you can do for others, maybe a better version of what you had going on during your search for Ikeri?"

"Good plan. Do it," I said.

He nodded but didn't move.

"What else?"

"Wouldn't Brustus be a great new location for Cragtek? Move them out of Jalvian territory so they don't have to hide anymore. The location puts them near several trade routes too. It's all set up, plenty of room for expansion, their families, and legal employment for all the business fronts."

"That's a great idea," Stassia said. "Impressive even."

"Yes, it is. Set it up with Gamnock, and use a good portion of those credit chips for the Brustus orphans."

"Will do."

I stood, as did Stassia and Ikeri. Then I spotted Daniel in the oncoming traffic about the same moment he spotted me. I knew that because his hand instantly disengaged from Meera's and I could almost hear the prayer to Geva that I'd not seen him doing so. Meera took two steps aside, revealing Markus, whose gaze locked with mine. He said something that made Daniel grimace.

"Did I just see, what I thought I saw?" Stassia asked.

"You did. We'll deal with it later." I wrapped one arm around her and started back to the clinic. Ikeri walked in front of us, setting a sedate pace. Neko, Daniel, Markus, and Meera fell in behind.

"As I've been trying to suggest, if everyone would stop interrupting me," I glared over my shoulder. "I'd like to return to Artor, but only long enough to get Ikeri back in good health."

"Oh?" Stassia's attention locked onto me as we meandered back to the clinic.

"I was serious about the tour with Ikeri. But more than that, I was thinking that perhaps we could step back a little? Slow down?"

"It almost sounds like your dancing around the word *retire*."

"Almost. I never intended to be, as Jey put it, a one-man High Council. The organization they offered wasn't all bad, I saw that in the time I observed for them. What if we appointed advisors as we traveled and joined them together into a collaborative network? Something that once it got established, wouldn't need our oversight?"

"Ours?"

"I did say not one-man, didn't I?"

She grinned. "I would love to be the other half of your temporary council."

"That's settled then. Markus can join us when he's able. Geva, we're way overdue for a dinner with Fa'yet. It would seem that he's talking to me again because he's demanding we bring Ikeri by so he can verify that she's all right."

"Not that he's attached to her or anything." Stassia snickered.

"Just a little. He said he'd like to see you too, outside of you making demands on Karin."

"I'd like that."

"We can take the kids to see Fragia and your old house on Merchess. I can show you all the worlds we made contact with these past few years. We'll take the Jalvian ship we've been using and send the second one home. The crew is used to us. There's plenty of room to carry the resources I'd like to take with us to offer the worlds where we stop to appoint advisors."

"I can see only one problem with your plan," she said.

"What's that?"

"If we're busy regaining your grey status all around the known universe, who's going to advise the Narvan?" She cast a questioning glance over her shoulder, confirming that she'd had the same thought I did.

I turned around to face our family with Stassia beside me. "Hey Neko, it's time we talked about a promotion."

Anastassia

When your mate holds the power to kill with roughly twenty seconds of thought, people get twitchy if he falls into a sour funk. Despite the general continuing success of Vayen's mission to bring healing and unification to worlds and colonies surrounding the Narvan and beyond, his mood had gradually been growing darker. He'd been downright angry at everyone and everything for the past few months. I'd held out hope that he'd get over whatever was pissing him off, that maybe it was being away from his homeworld for too long. But a week-long visit with Neko, who'd taken over the Narvan Advisory position, and even some quiet time at our Artorian estate, away from the Iber's crew and demands of our mission hadn't helped. If anything, the one night he'd stayed up late talking and drinking with Neko had worsened his mood. I'd asked Neko for some insight, but he'd kept his mouth shut. That could mean only one thing, whatever Vayen was angry about, it had to do with me.

I'd spent six days away to give him some space. Maybe I'd been hovering, or nagging, or we'd just been spending too damned much time together. To feel useful, I checked in with several of the planetary advisors that we'd set up on our travels along the universal trade routes and did a few Seeker sessions with clients I'd reconnected with on Veria Minor. I'd planned to be gone longer, but Ikeri sent me a message, begging me to return. If our daughter couldn't calm the savage beast, trouble was only a breath away.

Trouble, in Vayen's case, could mean nearly instantaneous death for thousands or himself. With Seeker Etara traveling with us, directly monitoring Vayen's quest to not go off the evil deep end, I couldn't chance him doing something that would drive her to flip his kill switch.

I'd never minded his darker side, with the exception of it being aimed at me on rare occasions. Honestly, I was drawn to it. We were alike in that, as with many other traits that would scare away any other sane person; our maladjusted moods and habits drew us together, made us perfect for one another even though we fought and often spent days not speaking. We understood each other. I loved him dearly and didn't want to see him die. Ever.

I contacted Daniel, who took care of Jumping me whenever his father wasn't the one to do it, to bring me back to the Iber, the massive Jalvian cruiser that we'd commandeered when we'd set out to sow our vast advisory union.

Daniel arrived in our mostly unused house on Veria Minor where he'd spent the first few years of his life as a carefree child. He wasn't at all care-free now. His glower near rivaled his father's.

"What's got you in a mood? Trouble with the wives?"

A grin flashed over his face, proving my guess was far off the mark. "Meera and Arden are fine, Mom. Quite fine. They both had scans at the clinic yesterday. I got to see the babies."

Babies. I was going to be a fucking grandmother. Maybe that's what had Vayen in a mood. But he'd been pissy far longer than that. Daniel had only announced that both of his wives were pregnant a few weeks ago.

"That's wonderful." Barely nineteen and already married. Twice. Now with kids on the way. I shuddered. "So why the scrunchy face?"

Rather than take my offered hand and Jump me to the Iber, he took a seat, filling the chair that had been his father's. He nodded me toward the my-sized chair. Curious, I sat.

"He doesn't think it's wonderful. Any of it." Daniel ran his hands through his long, dark hair, pulling the thick mass behind his broad shoulders. The armor he wore looked just like his father's, well-used, comfortable, and hiding a small arsenal.

"What do you mean?" I tried not to slip into my Seeker tone, but I'd been doing it for days. It was a hard habit to break.

"What do you think I mean?" He glared at me. "I don't need a damned counseling session, Mother. He does."

"Your father?"

"Yes, the walking bomb that is my father. Is it too much to ask that he be happy for me? I've always done everything he's asked."

Whatever tension had been brewing between father and son since Daniel had taken on non-official command of the Iber when we'd set out nearly four years ago had remained strictly between them. The rift seemed to deepen with each passing year. Neither side was forthcoming. I'd chalked it up to two strong personalities in tight confines—if an entire cruiser could be considered tight.

The crew loved and respected Daniel, even beyond his fame as the son of the Advisors of All. He had a solid understanding of the ship's systems and everyone's position in it that impressed even me. Our son had put the years he and his father spent searching for Ikeri to good use. That a Jalvian crew would choose to follow an Artorian signified great strides toward the unity Vayen and I had sought to establish when we'd held the Narvan. One would have thought this would have greatly pleased his father, but the man who had been Daniel's partner in mischief earlier in his life was a far cry from the tight-lipped, time-bomb we lived with now.

"You have," I put on my best reassuring smile. "I'll talk to him."

"Mom, it isn't talking he wants." He let out a disgusted growl. "Ikeri said she'd talk to you about it."

Unease formed a cool puddle in my stomach. Did everyone know what had Vayen on edge but me? He'd been cordial enough toward me, considering his mood.

"Dammit, I shouldn't have said anything." He stood, offering me a sympathetic smile.

The chill in my gut amplified. I stood and held out my hand. This time, he took it without hesitation.

About the Author

Jean Davis writes an array of speculative fiction and plays with chickens. When not ruining fictional lives from the comfort of her writing chair, she can be found devouring books and sushi, weeding her flower garden, or picking up hundreds of sticks while attempting to avoid the abundant snake population that also shares her yard. She lives in West Michigan with her musical husband, an attention-craving terrier, and a small flock of chickens and ducks.

Read her blog, and sign up for her mailing list at www.jeandavisauthor.com. You'll also find her on Facebook and Instagram at JeanDavisAuthor, and on Goodreads and Amazon.

If you enjoyed this book, please consider leaving a review. They are much appreciated. Thank you!

www.ingramcontent.com/pod-product-compliance
Lightning Source LLC
Chambersburg PA
CBHW070307310726
48976CB00005B/1613